CatStronauts

MISSION MOON

CatStronauts
MISSION MOON

BY DREW BROCKINGTON

Ⓛ Ⓑ

Little, Brown and Company
New York Boston

Little, Brown and Company

Hachette Book Group
1290 Avenue of the Americas, New York, NY 10104
Visit us at lb-kids.com

Little, Brown and Company is a division of Hachette Book Group, Inc.
The Little, Brown name and logo are trademarks of Hachette Book Group, Inc.

First Edition: April 2017

Library of Congress Cataloging-in-Publication Data
Names: Brockington, Drew.
Title: Cat-stronauts : Mission Moon / by Drew Brockington.
Description: First edition. | New York ; Boston : Little, Brown and Company, 2017. |
Summary: Alerted to a global energy crisis, the President consults with the World's Best Scientist, who suggests sending a special group of astronauts to turn the Moon into a solar power plant.
Identifiers: LCCN 2015039108| ISBN 9780316307475 (hardcover) | ISBN 9780316307451 (trade pbk.) | ISBN 9780316307468 (ebook)
Subjects: LCSH: Graphic novels. | CYAC: Graphic novels. | Astronauts—Fiction. | Space Flight to the moon—Fiction. | Presidents—Fiction. | Cats—Fiction.
Classification: LCC PZ7.7.B76 Cat 2017 | DDC 741.5/973—dc23
LC record available at http://lccn.loc.gov/2015039108

20 19 18 17 16 15 14

1010

Printed in China

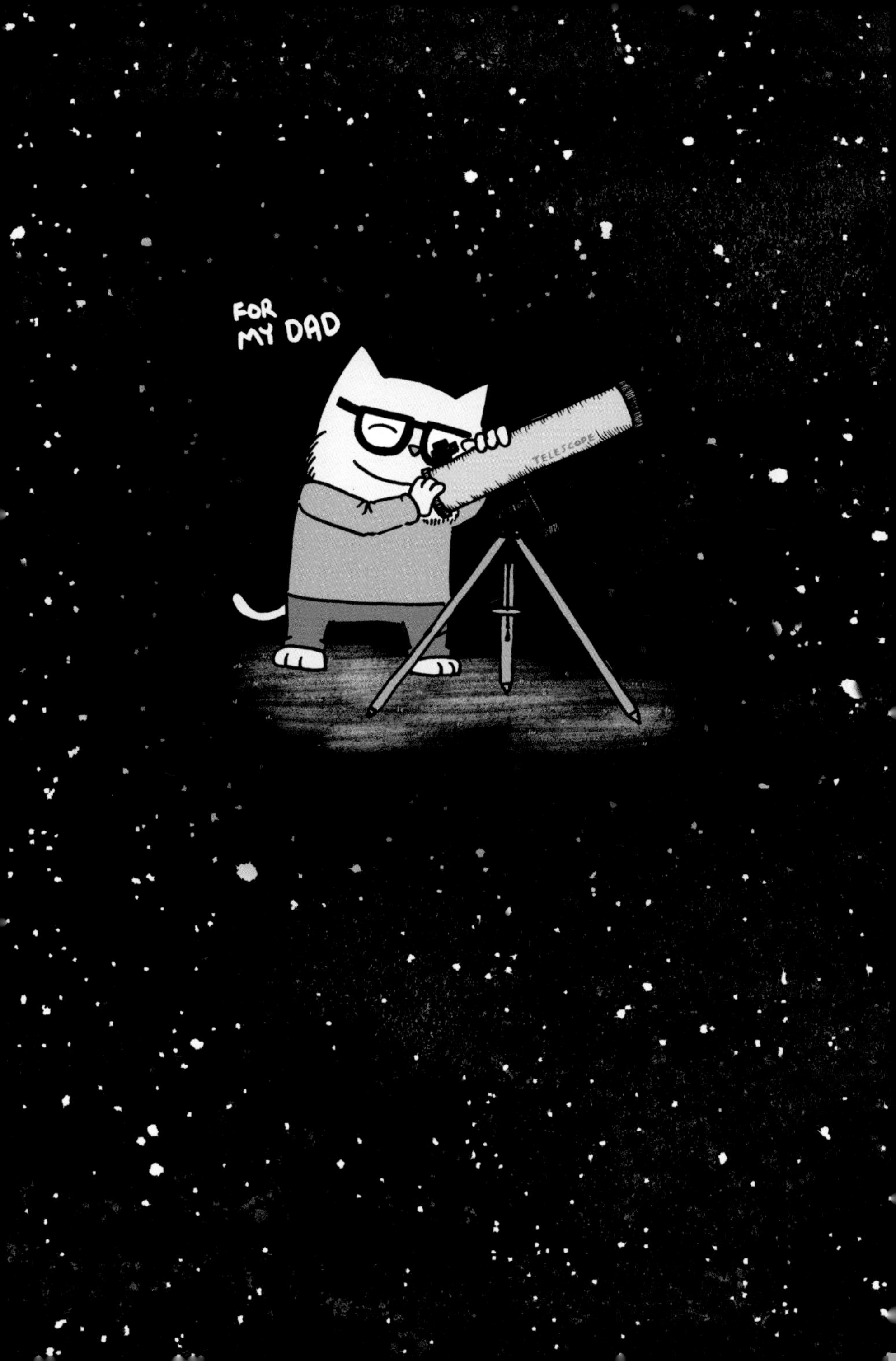
FOR MY DAD
TELESCOPE

CatStronauts

MISSION MOON

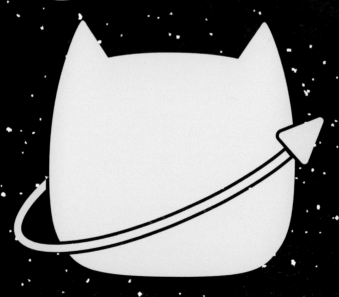

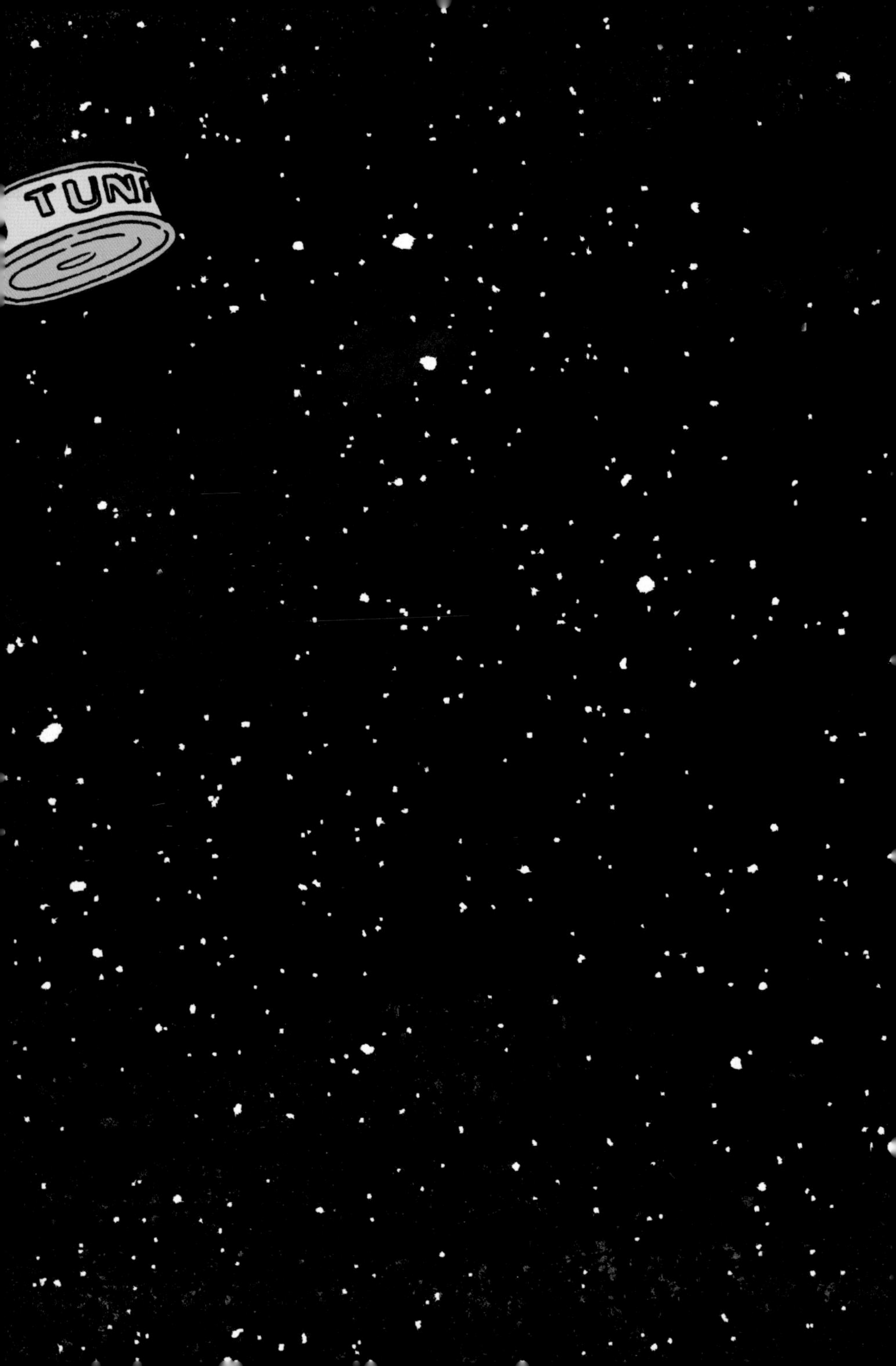

CHAPTER 1

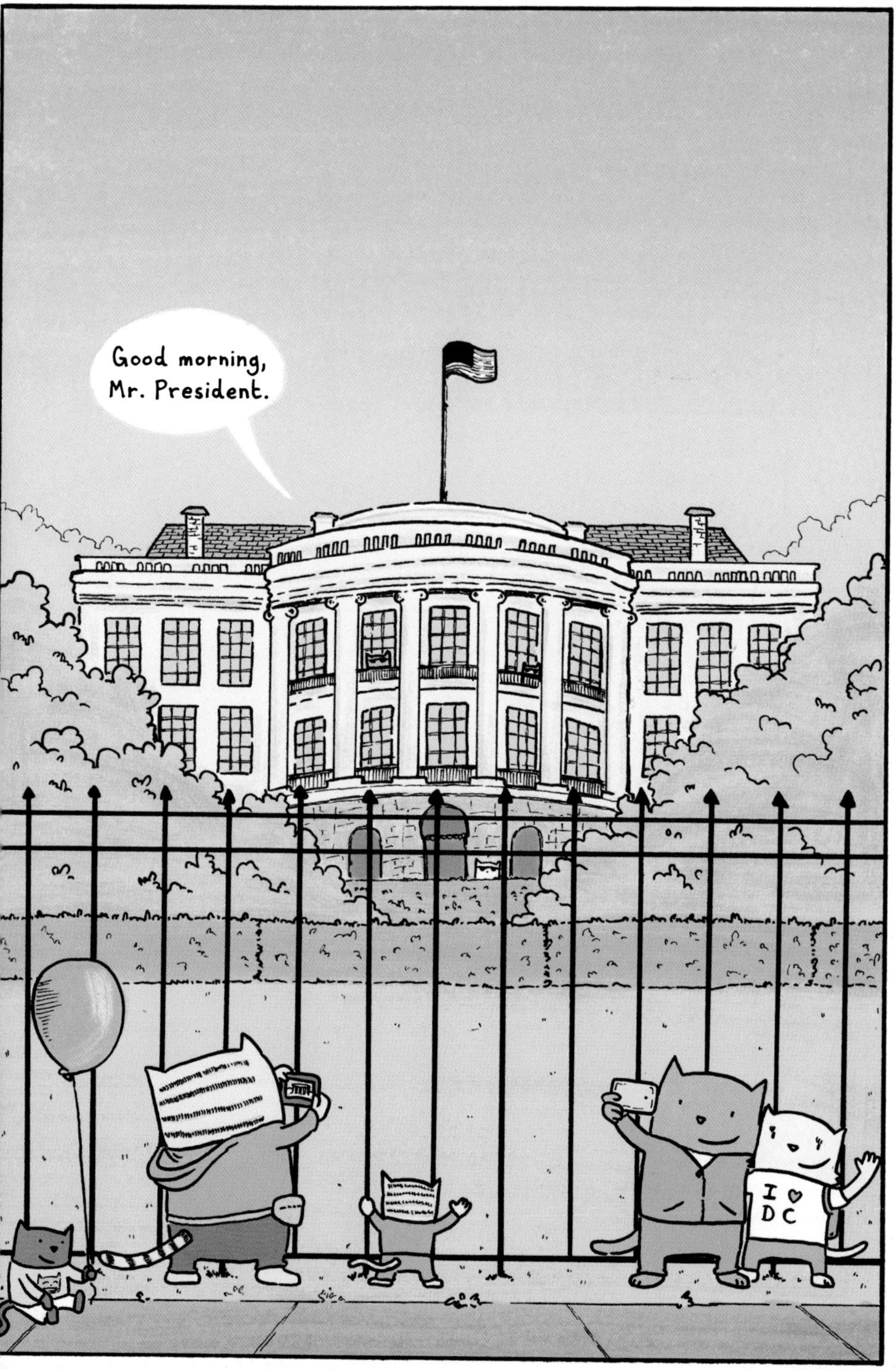
Good morning, Mr. President.
I ♥ DC

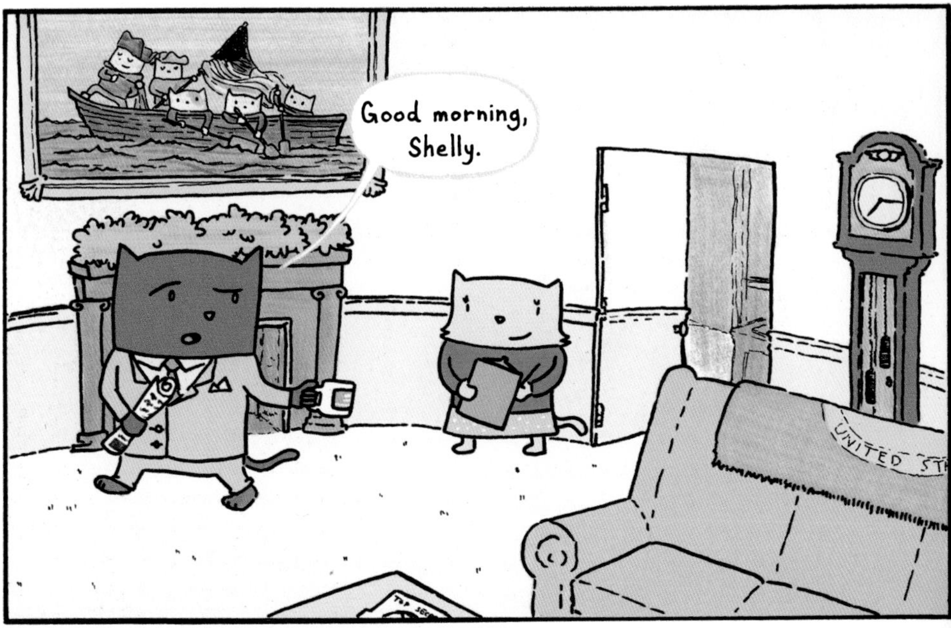
Good morning, Shelly.

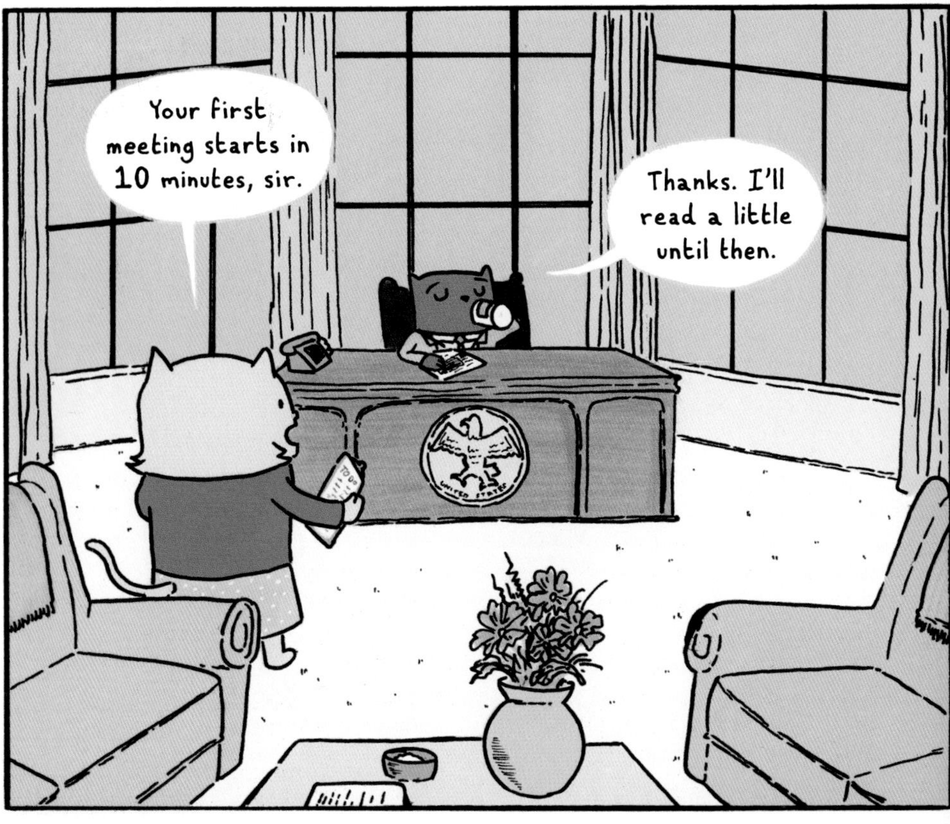
Your first meeting starts in 10 minutes, sir.
Thanks. I'll read a little until then.

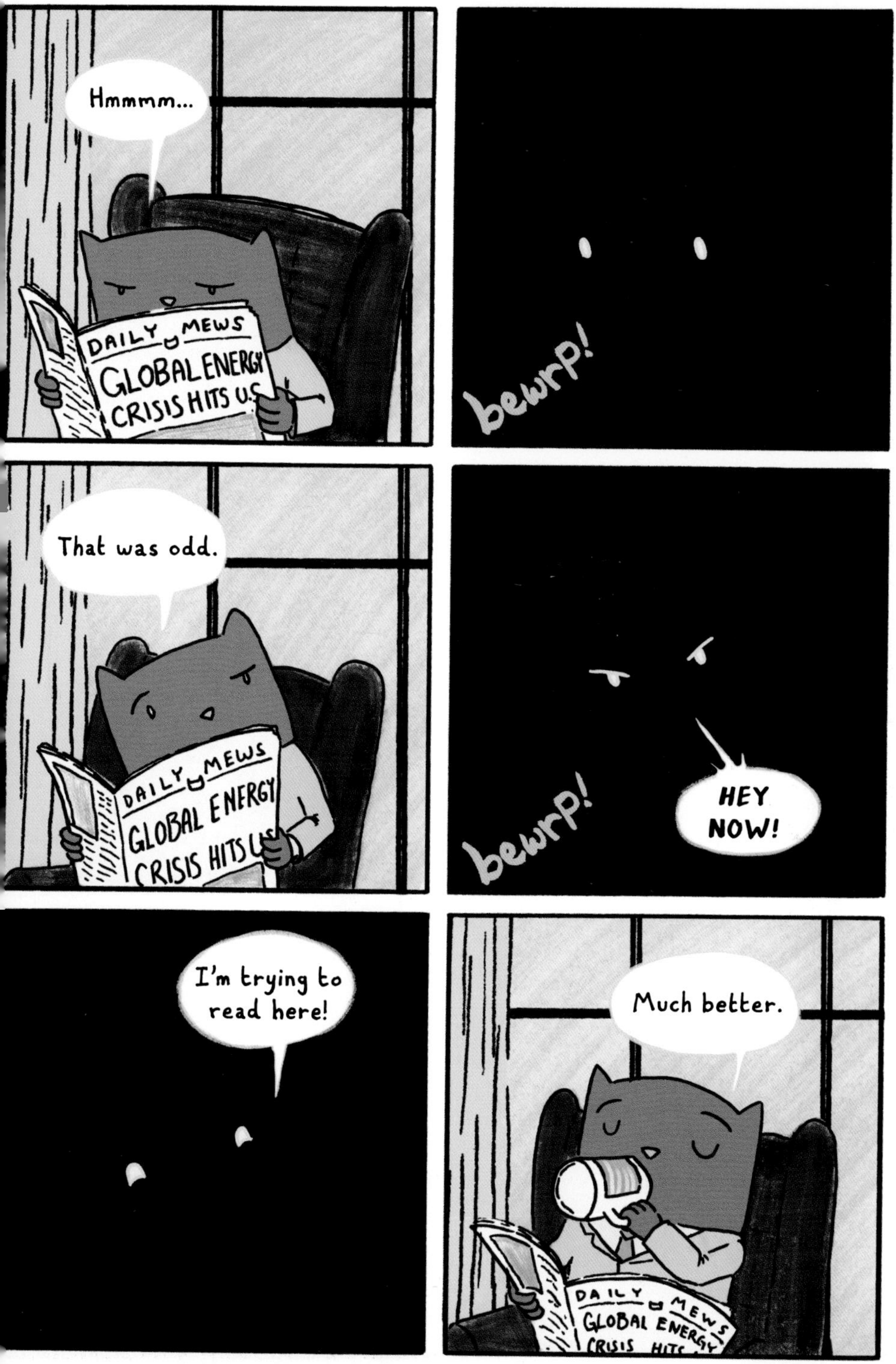
Hmmmm...
DAILY MEWS
GLOBAL ENERGY CRISIS HITS U.S.
bewrp!
That was odd.
DAILY MEWS
GLOBAL ENERGY CRISIS HITS U.S.
bewrp!
HEY NOW!
I'm trying to read here!
Much better.
DAILY MEWS
GLOBAL ENERGY CRISIS HITS

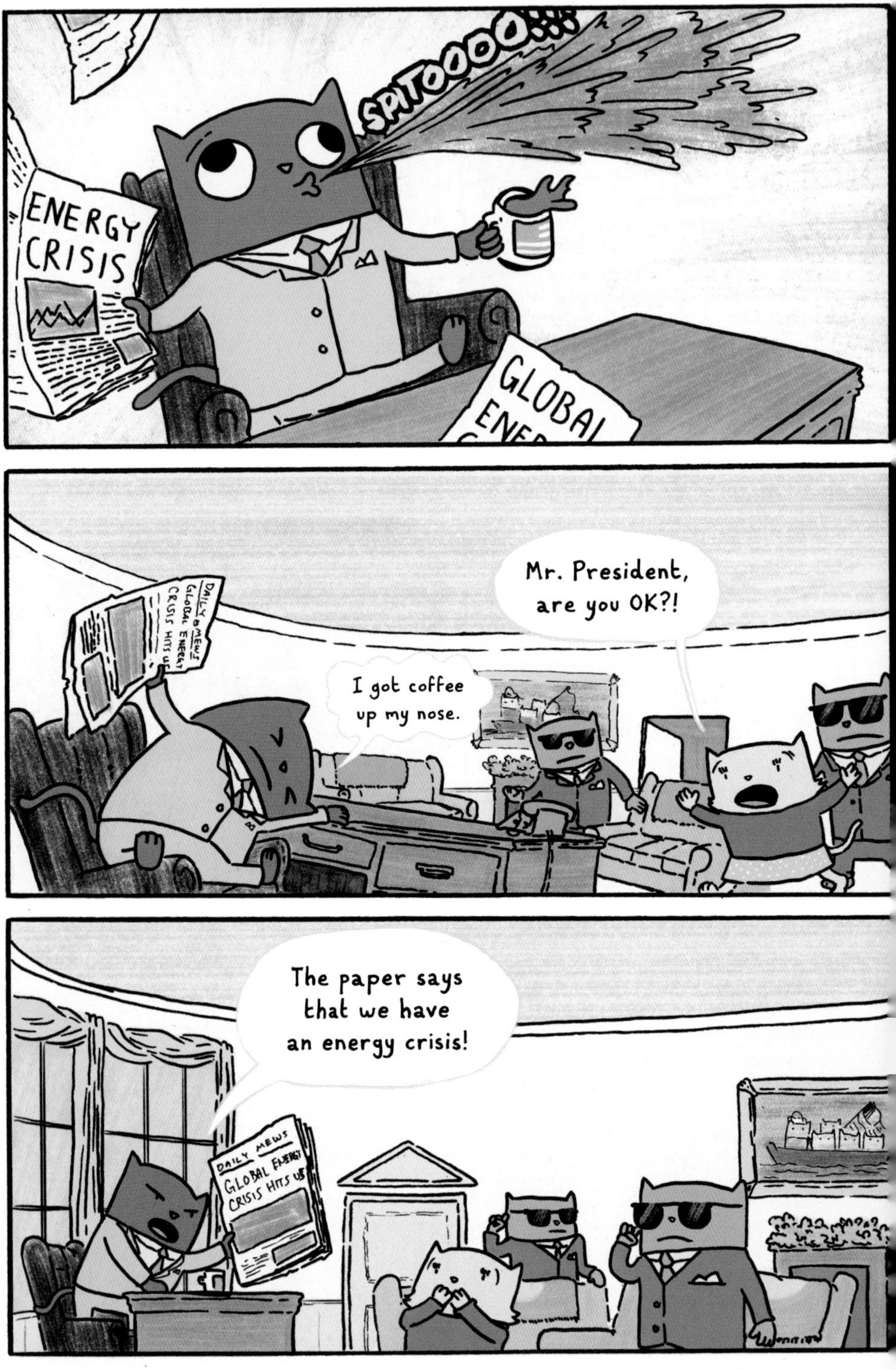
ENERGY CRISIS
SPITOOOO!!!
GLOBAL
DAILY MEWS GLOBAL ENERGY CRISIS HITS US
Mr. President, are you OK?!
I got coffee up my nose.
The paper says that we have an energy crisis!
DAILY MEWS GLOBAL ENERGY CRISIS HITS US

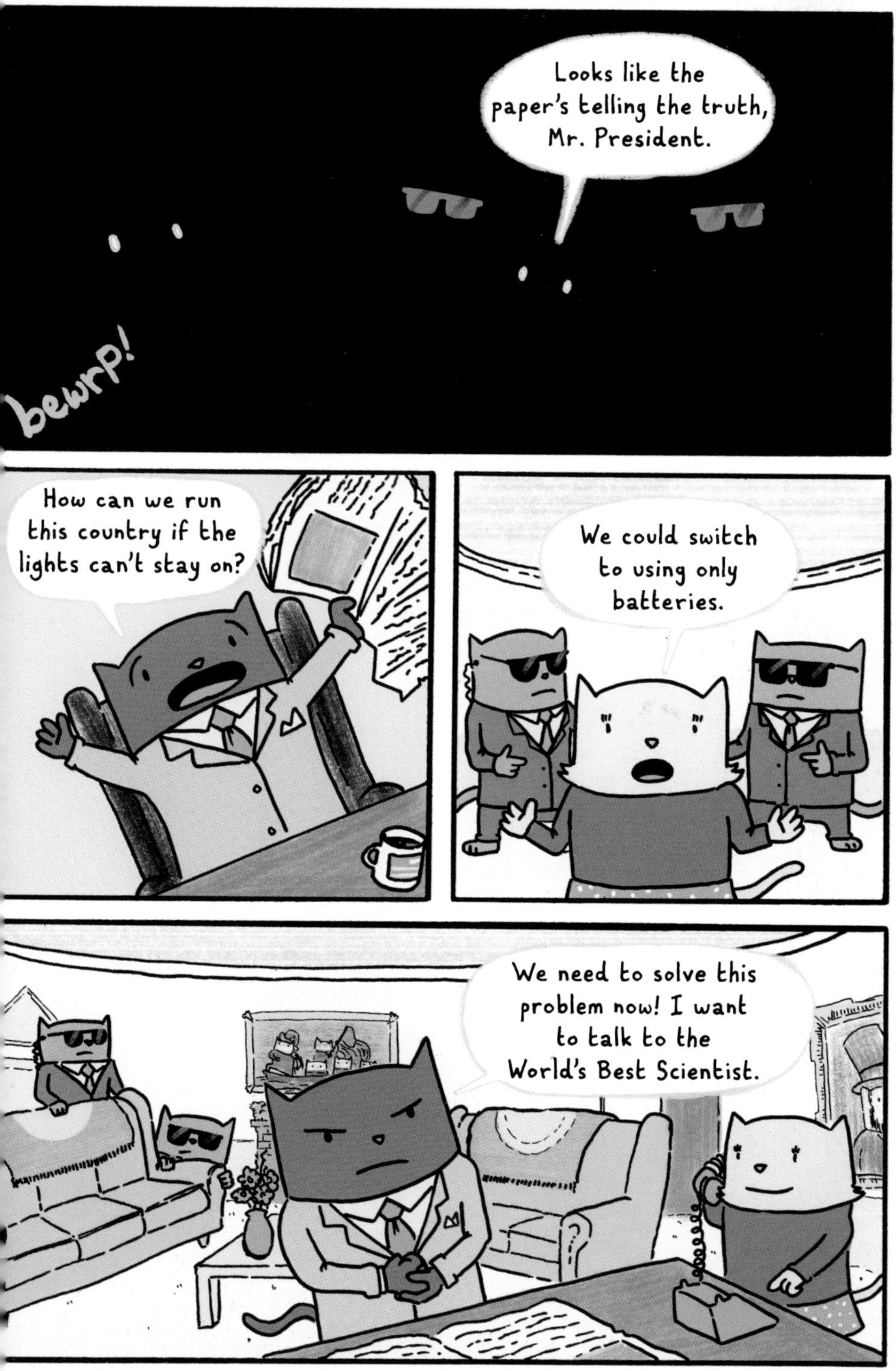
bewrp!
Looks like the paper's telling the truth, Mr. President.
How can we run this country if the lights can't stay on?
We could switch to using only batteries.
We need to solve this problem now! I want to talk to the World's Best Scientist.

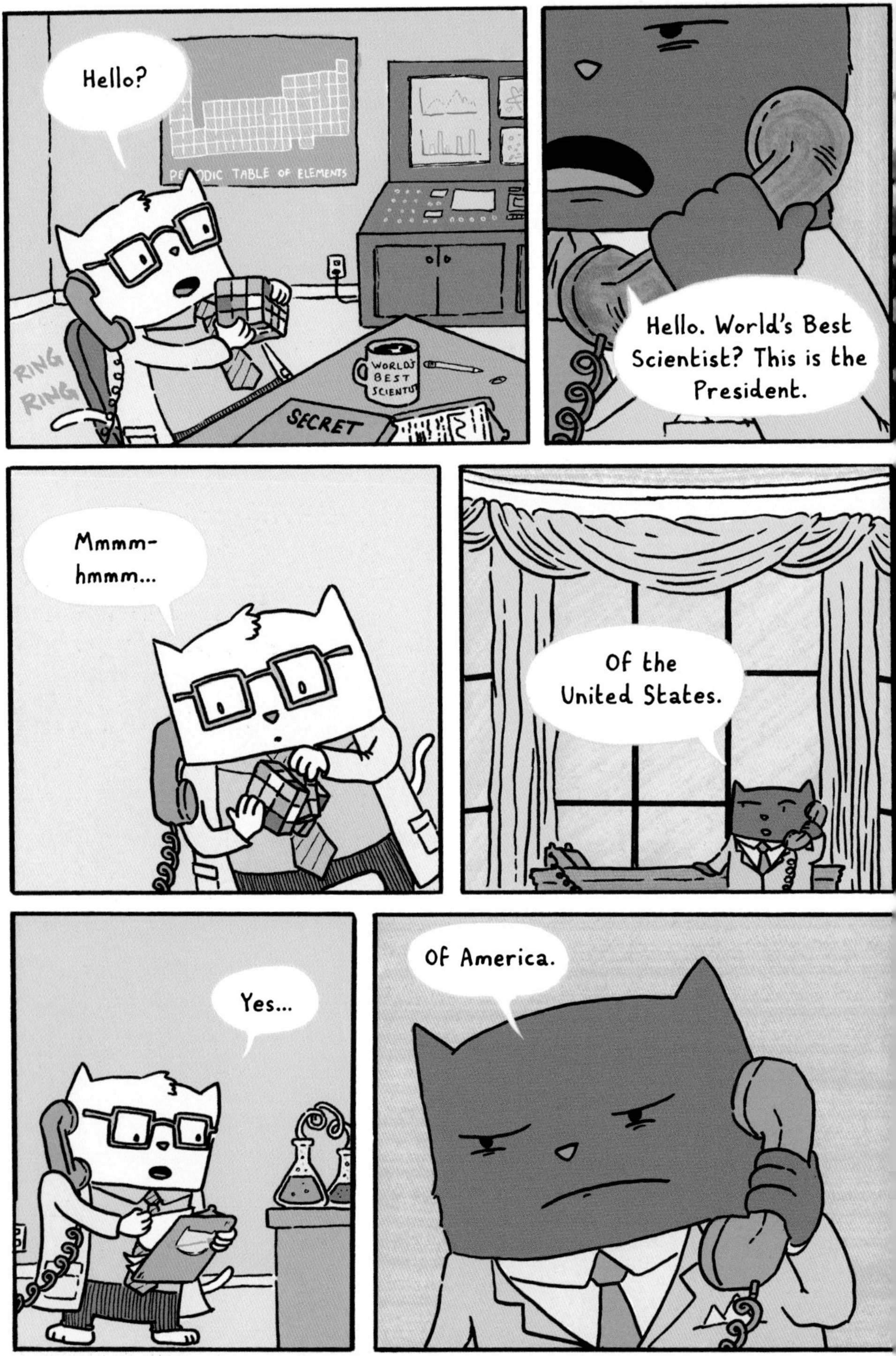
Hello?
RING
RING
SECRET
Hello. World's Best Scientist? This is the President.
Mmmm-hmmm...
Of the United States.
Yes...
Of America.

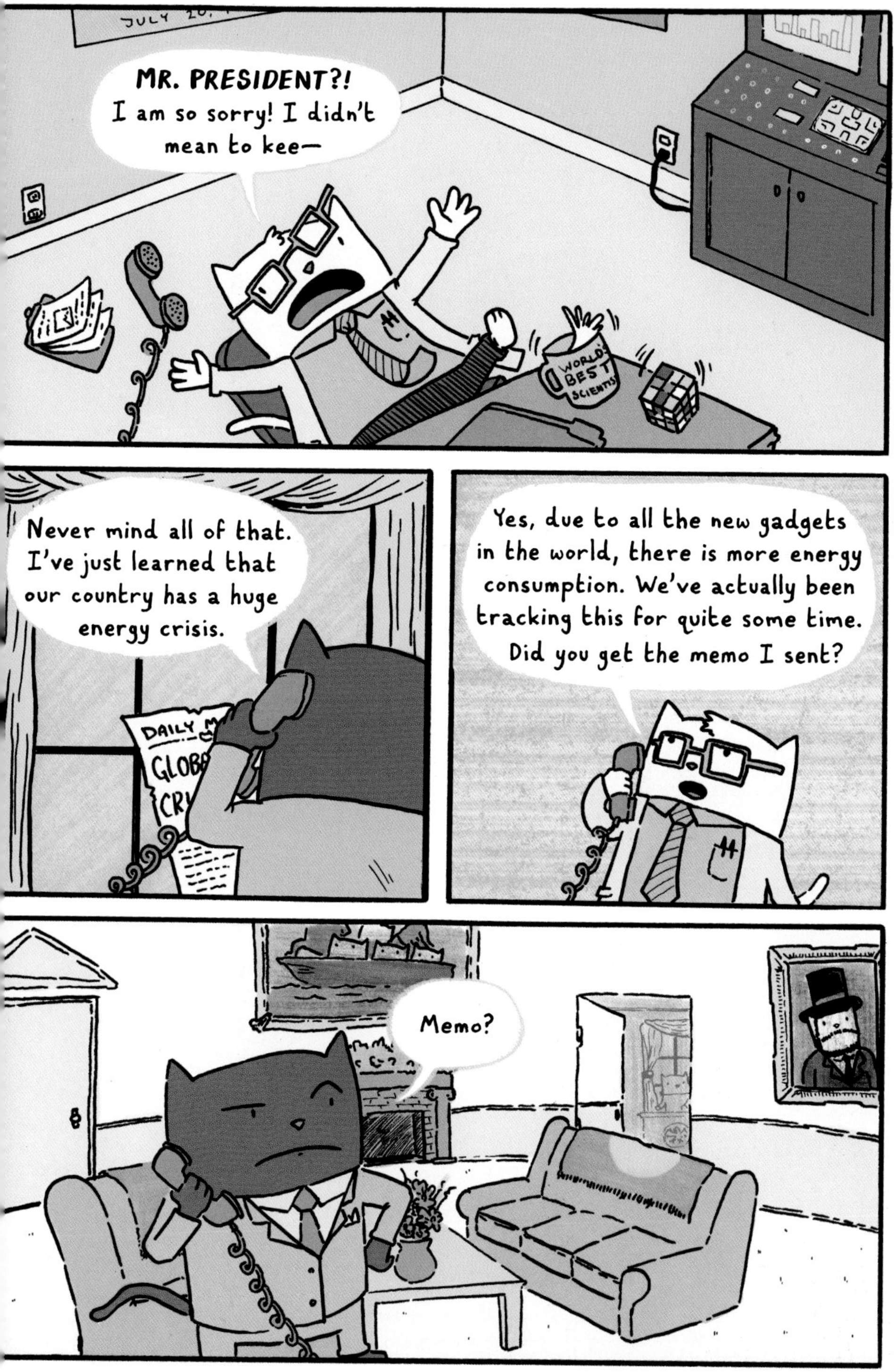
MR. PRESIDENT?! I am so sorry! I didn't mean to kee—
WORLD'S BEST
Never mind all of that. I've just learned that our country has a huge energy crisis.
Yes, due to all the new gadgets in the world, there is more energy consumption. We've actually been tracking this for quite some time. Did you get the memo I sent?
Memo?

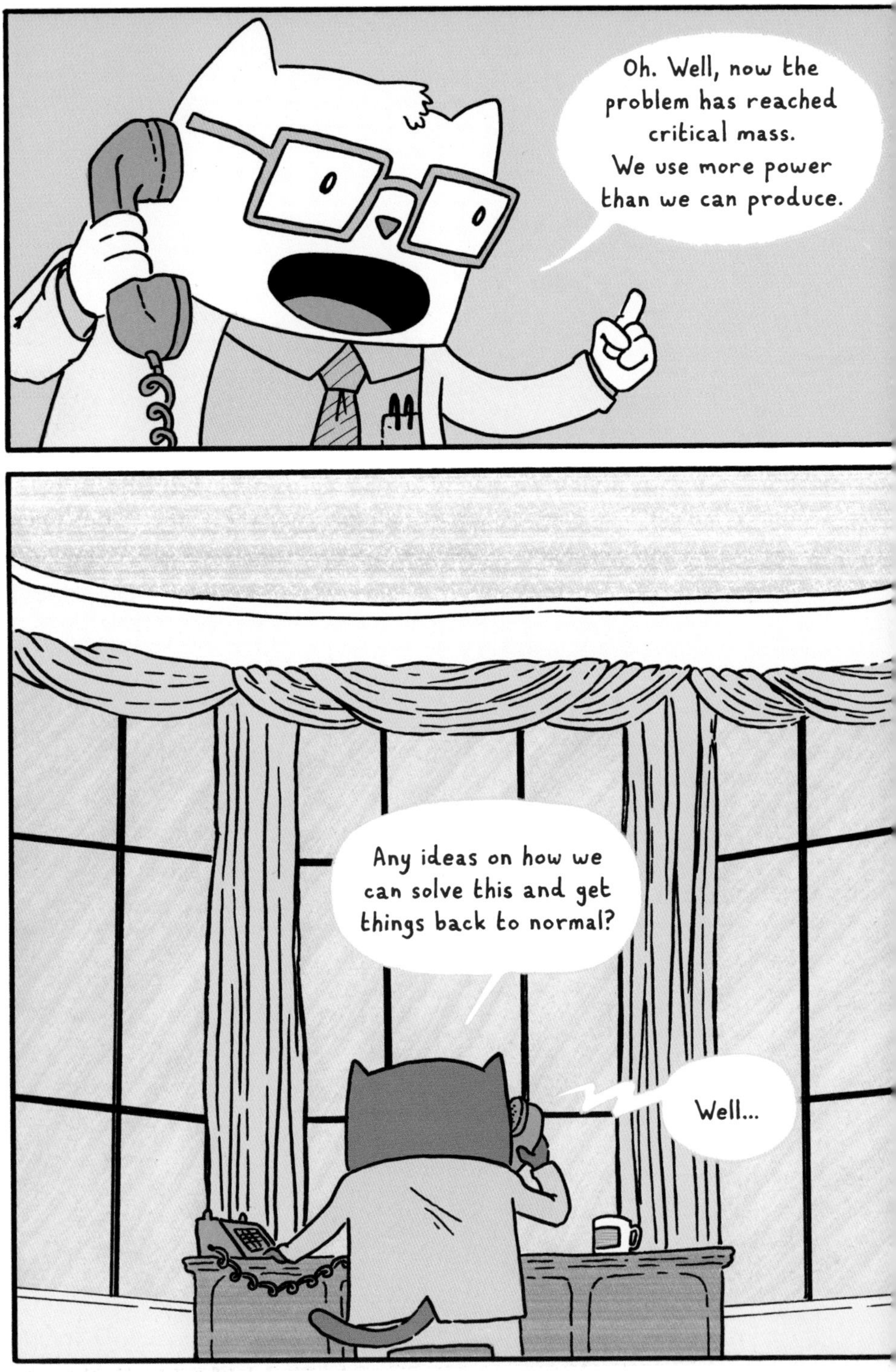
Oh. Well, now the problem has reached critical mass. We use more power than we can produce.
Any ideas on how we can solve this and get things back to normal?
Well...

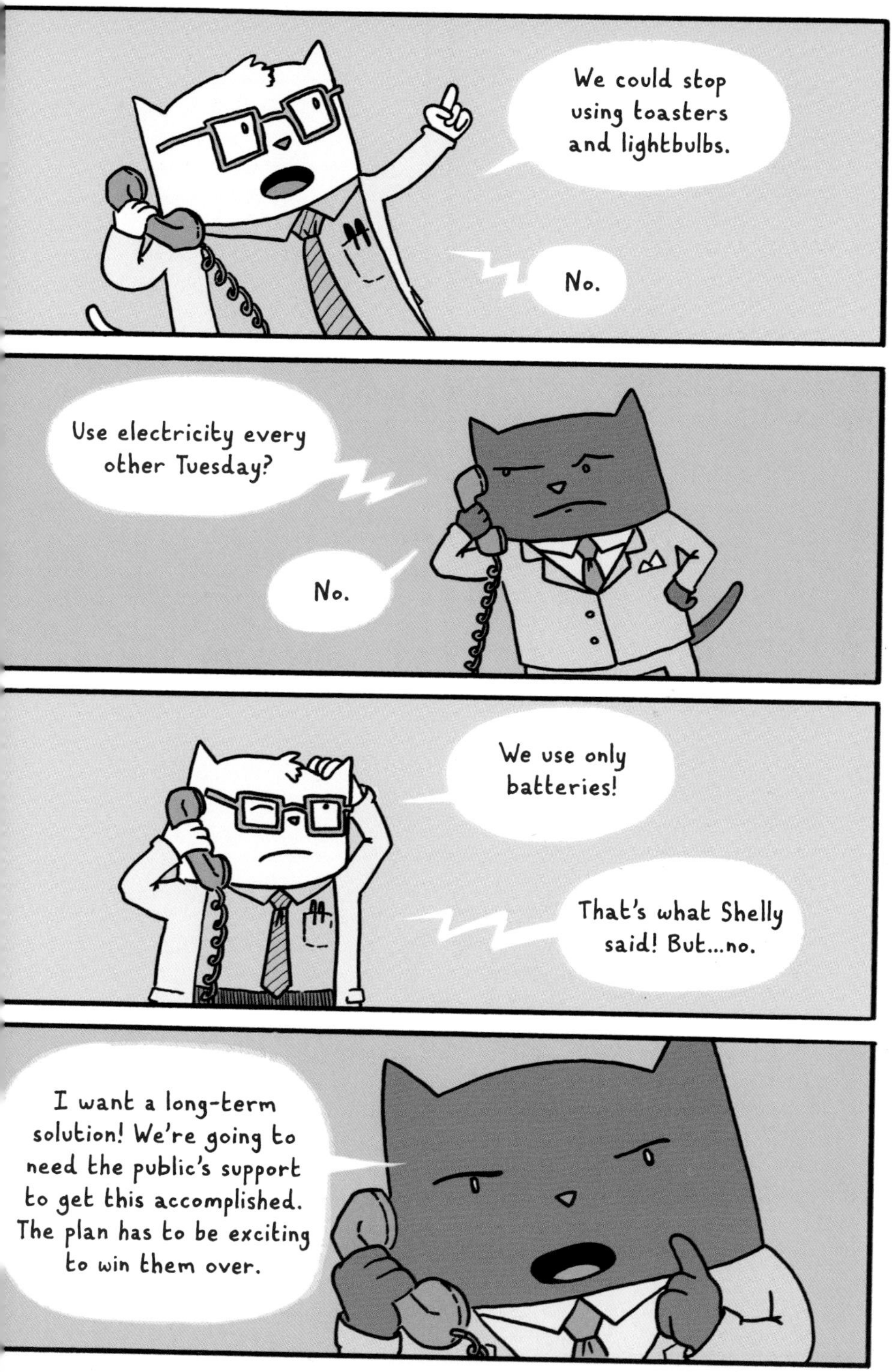
We could stop using toasters and lightbulbs.
No.
Use electricity every other Tuesday?
No.
We use only batteries!
That's what Shelly said! But...no.
I want a long-term solution! We're going to need the public's support to get this accomplished. The plan has to be exciting to win them over.

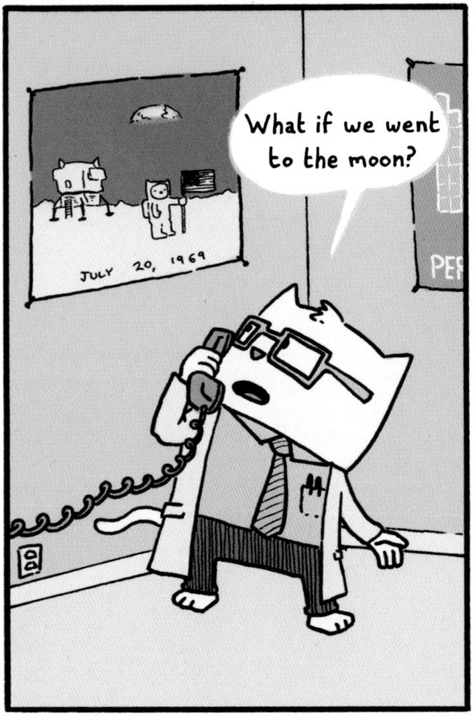
JULY 20, 1969
What if we went to the moon?

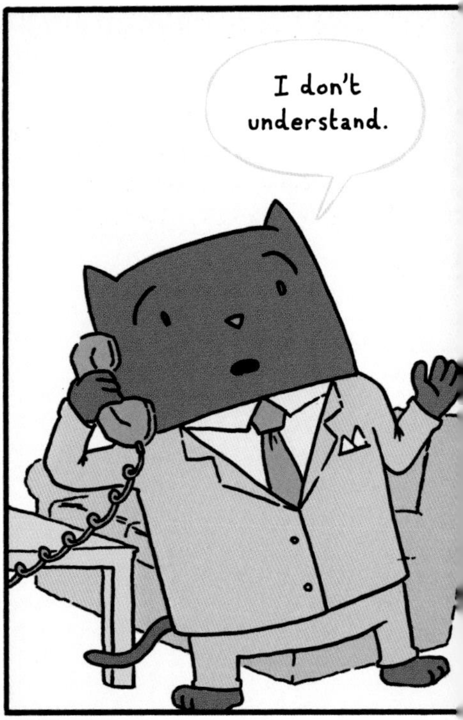
I don't understand.

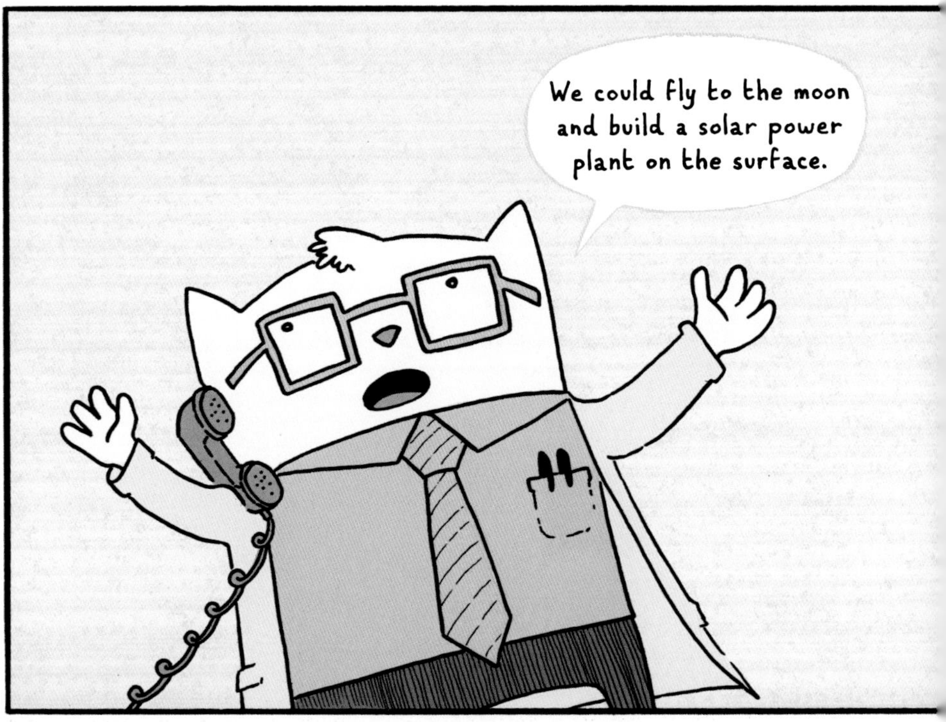
We could fly to the moon and build a solar power plant on the surface.

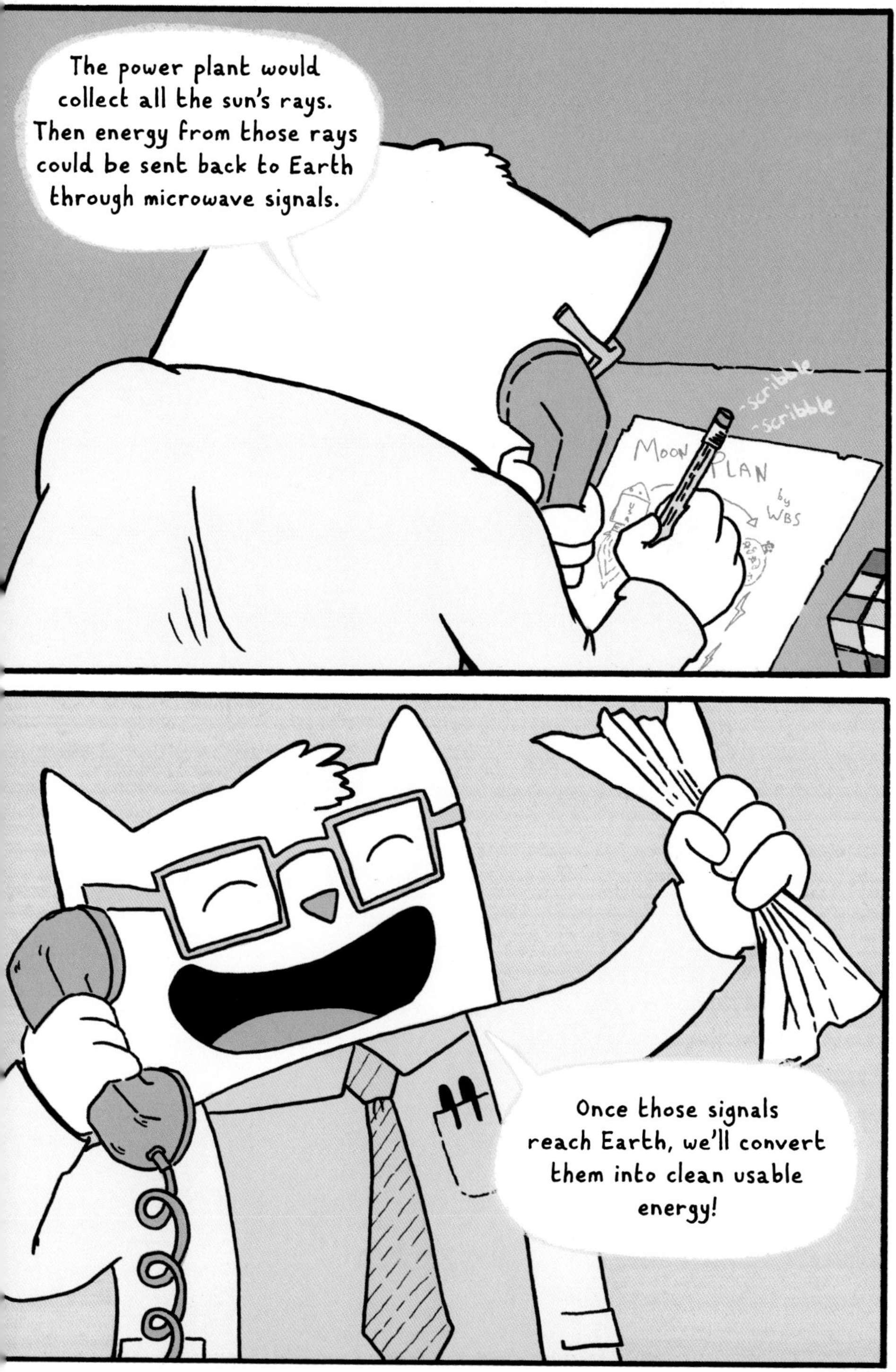
The power plant would collect all the sun's rays. Then energy from those rays could be sent back to Earth through microwave signals.
-scribble
-scribble
MOON PLAN
by WBS
Once those signals reach Earth, we'll convert them into clean usable energy!

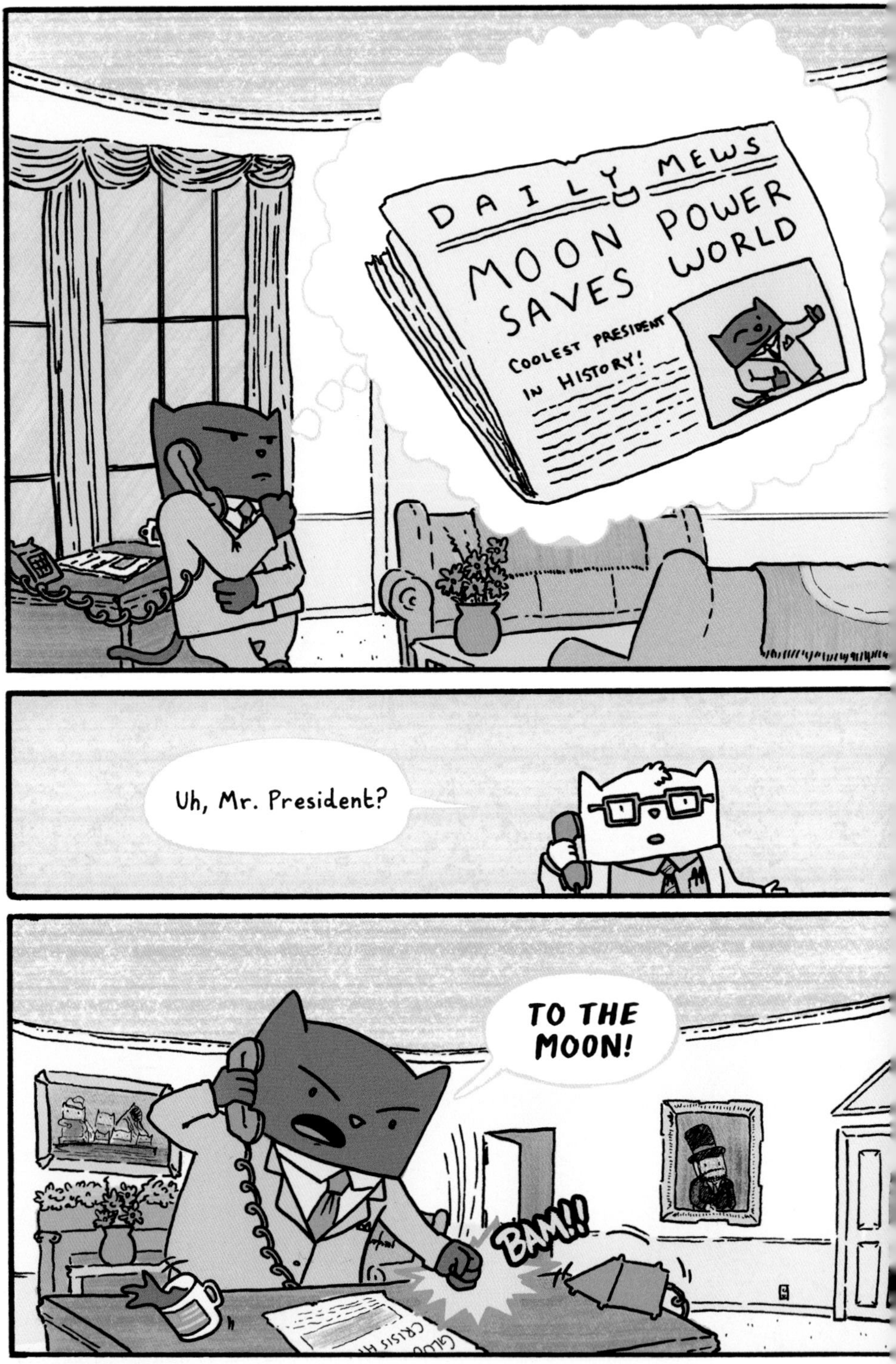
DAILY MEWS
MOON POWER SAVES WORLD
COOLEST PRESIDENT IN HISTORY!
Uh, Mr. President?
TO THE MOON!
BAM!!

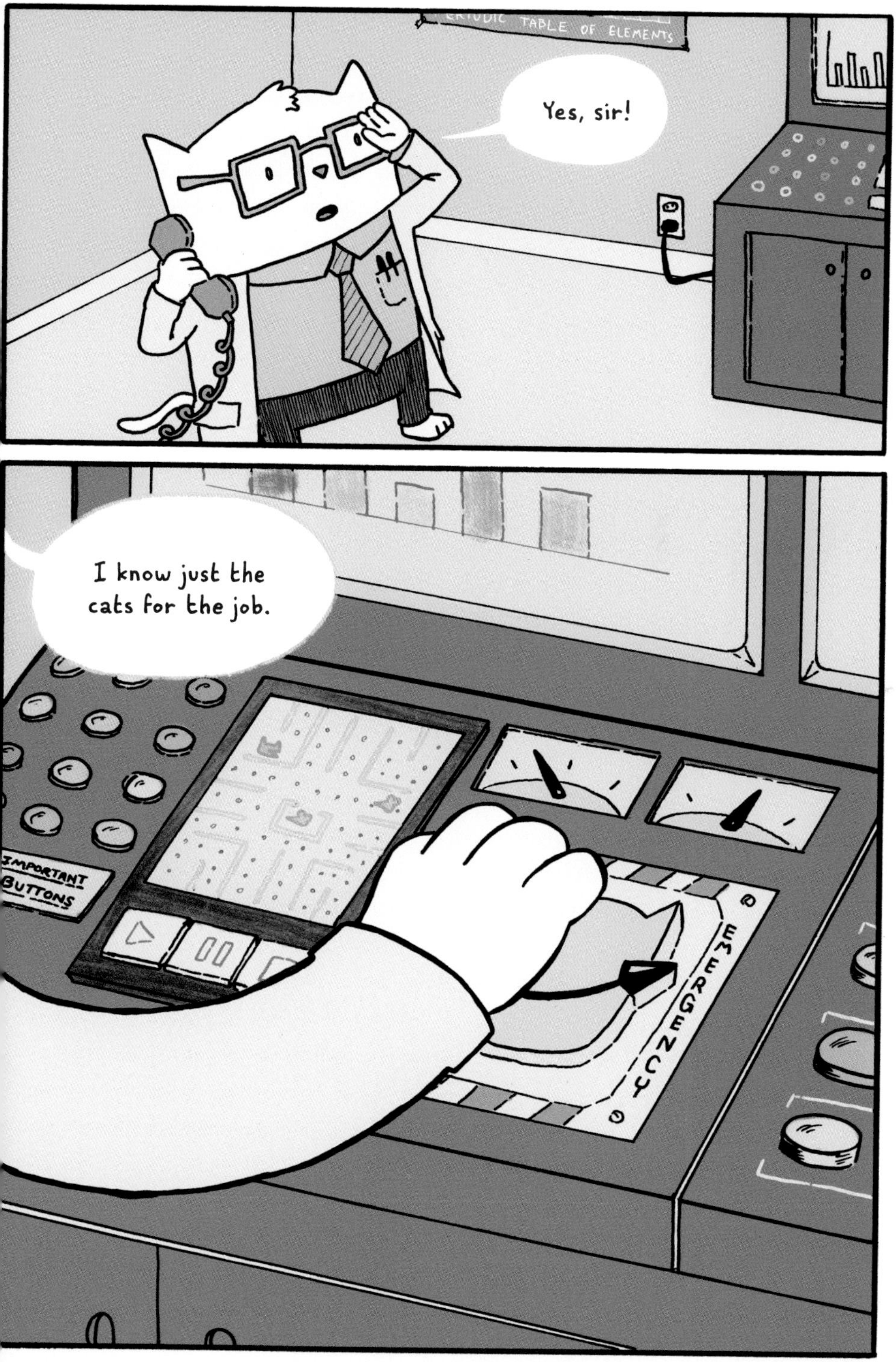
TABLE OF ELEMENTS
Yes, sir!
I know just the cats for the job.
IMPORTANT BUTTONS
EMERGENCY

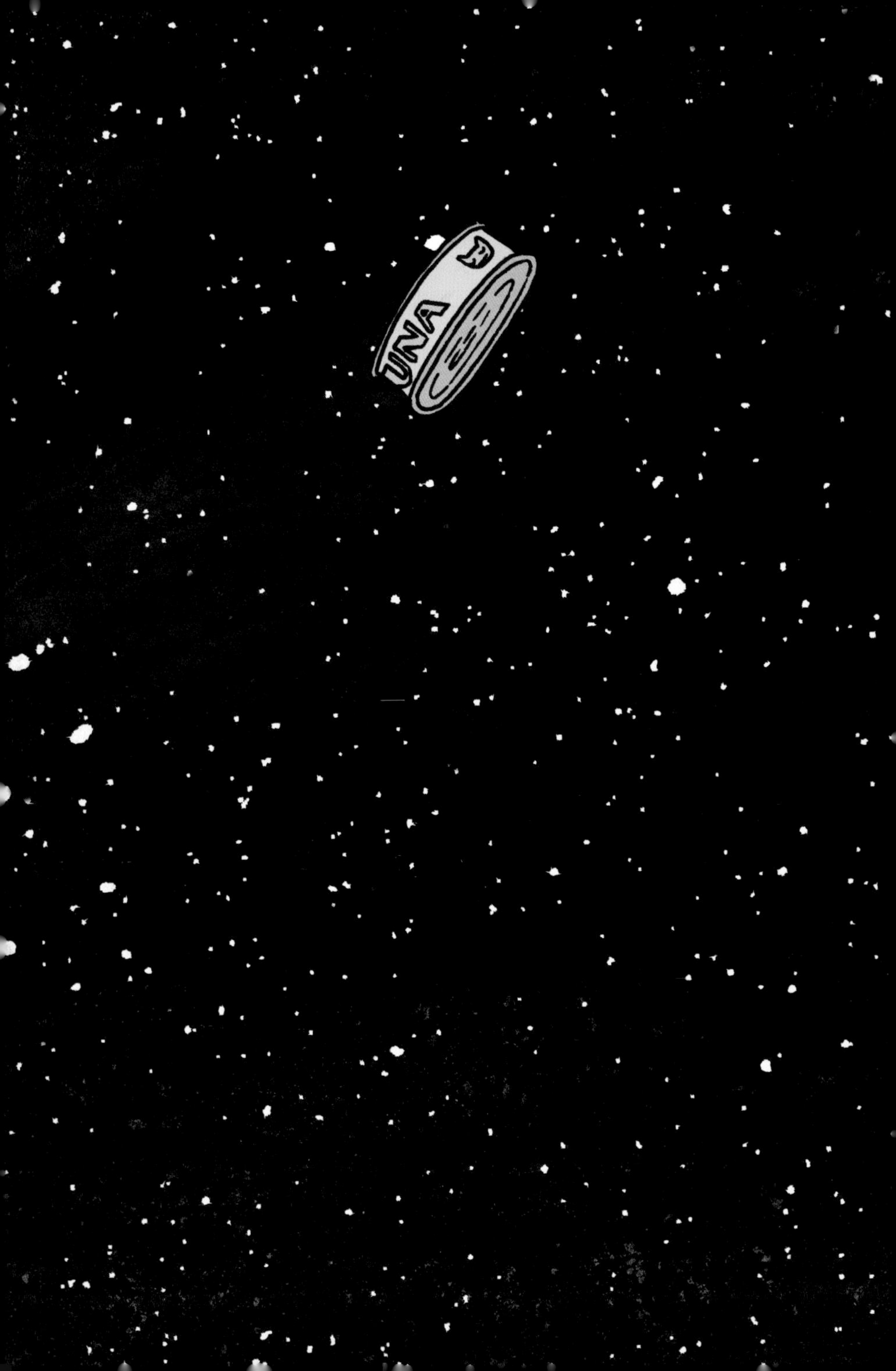

UNA

CHAPTER 2

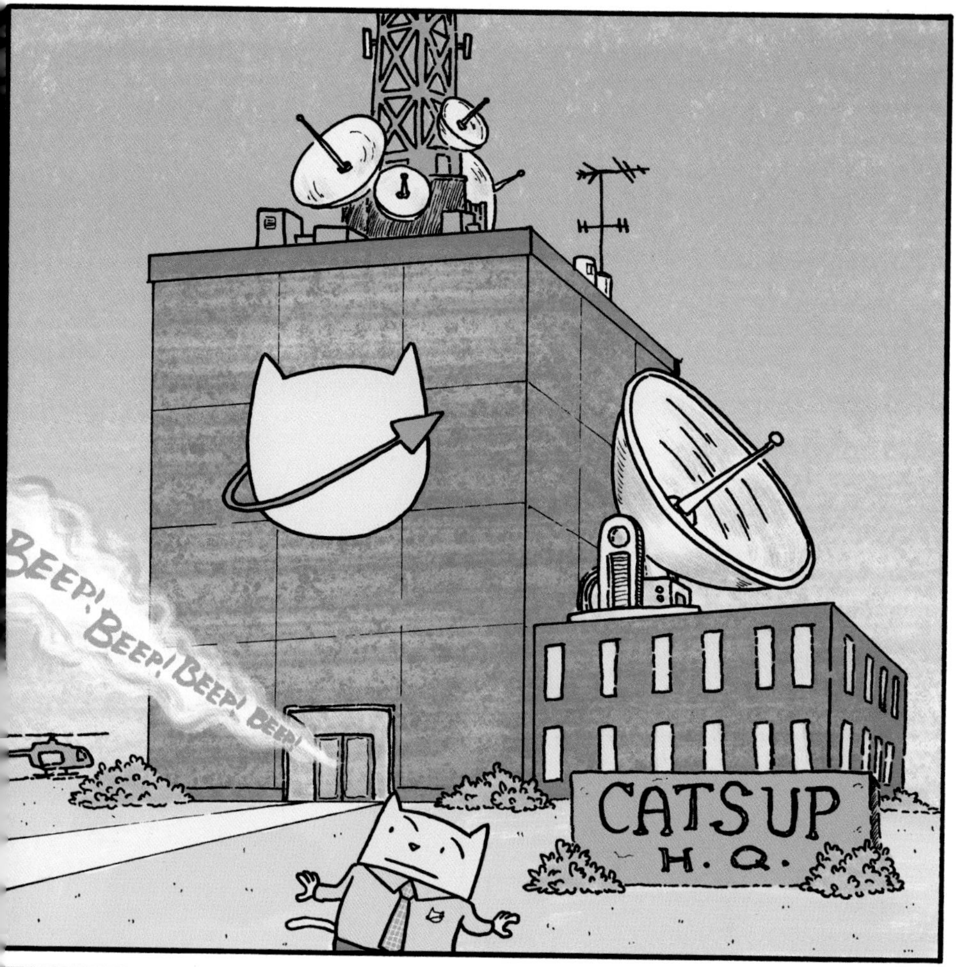
BEEP! BEEP! BEEP! BEEP! BEEP!
CATSUP H.Q.
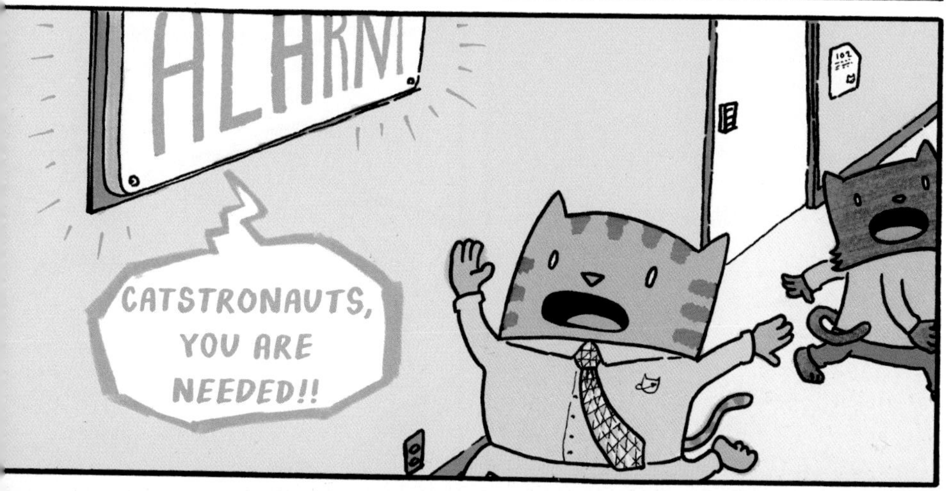
ALARM
CATSTRONAUTS, YOU ARE NEEDED!!

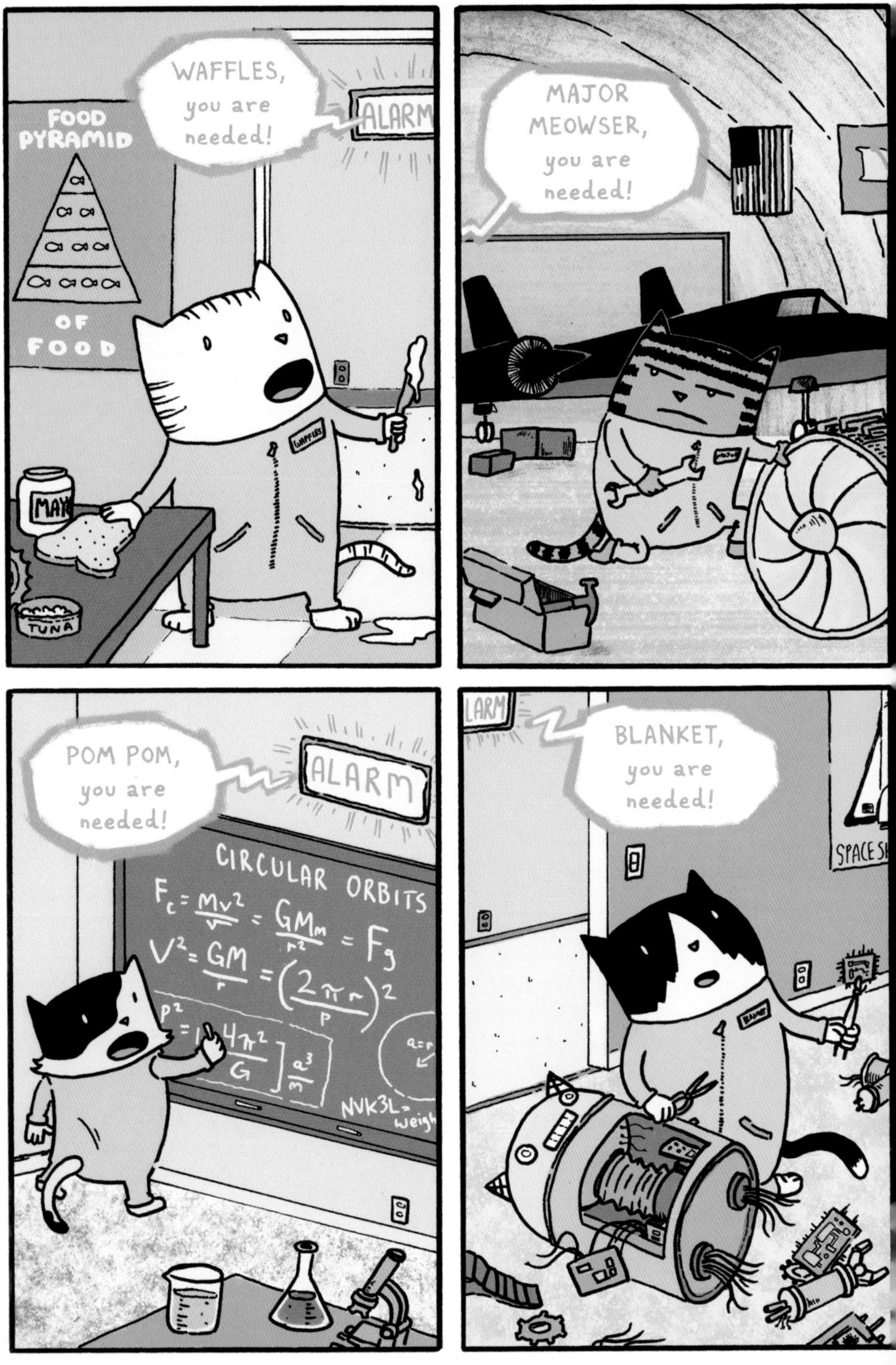

FOOD PYRAMID OF FOOD
ALARM
WAFFLES, you are needed!
MAYO
TUNA
WAFFLES
MAJOR MEOWSER, you are needed!
POM POM, you are needed!
ALARM
CIRCULAR ORBITS
ALARM
BLANKET, you are needed!

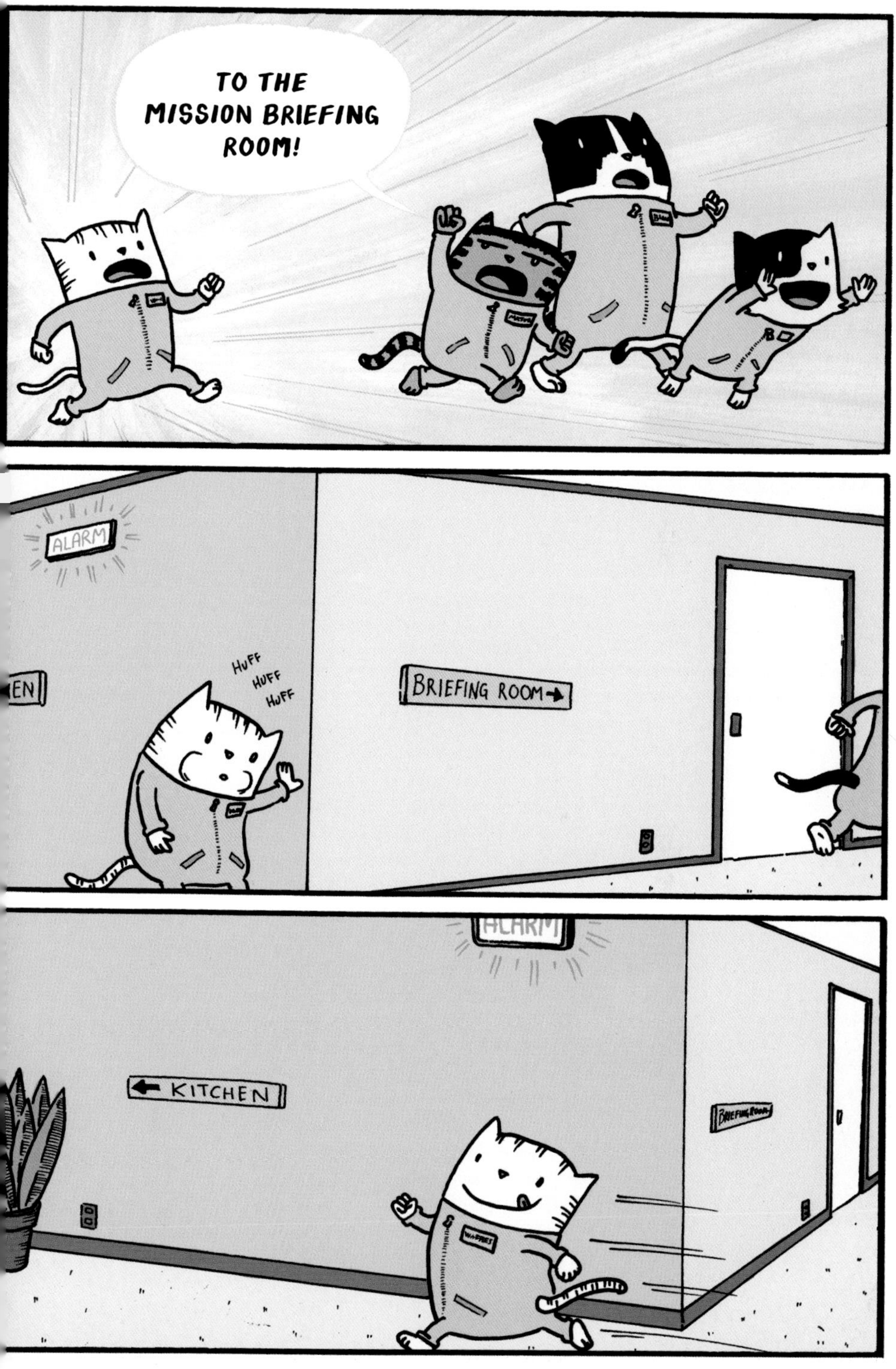
TO THE MISSION BRIEFING ROOM!
ALARM
EN
HUFF HUFF HUFF
BRIEFING ROOM →
ALARM
← KITCHEN
BRIEFING ROOM

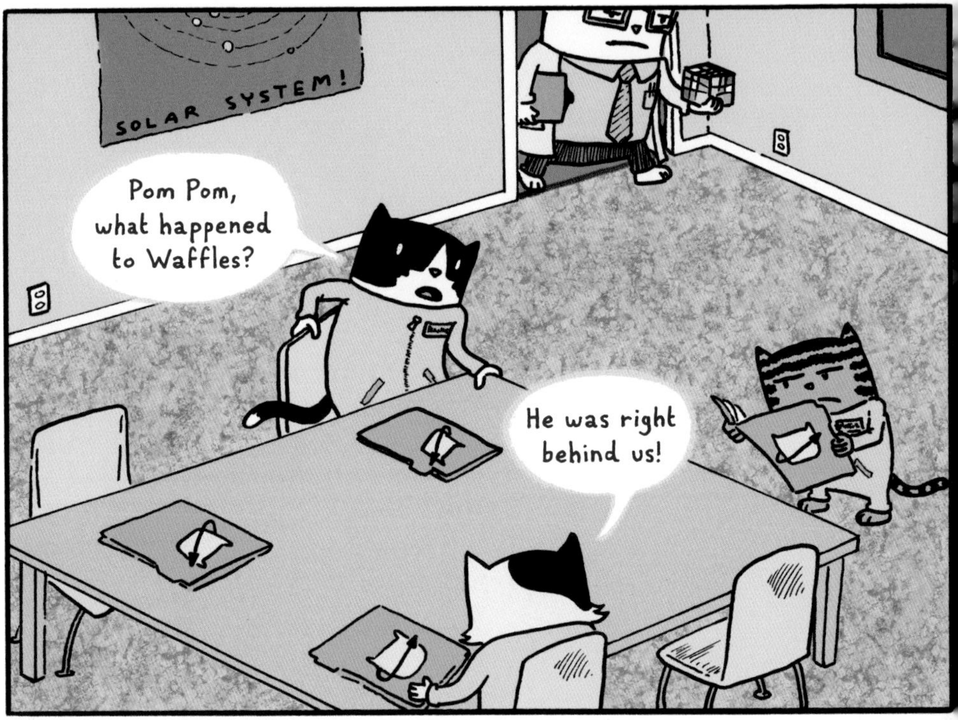
SOLAR SYSTEM!
Pom Pom, what happened to Waffles?
He was right behind us!

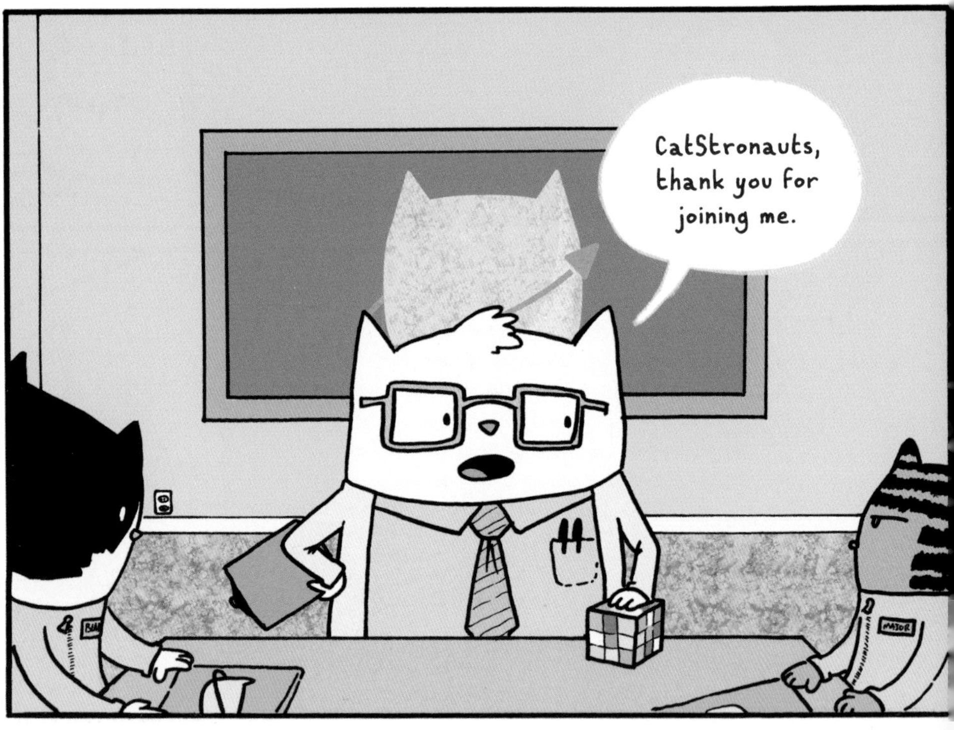
CatStronauts, thank you for joining me.
MAJOR

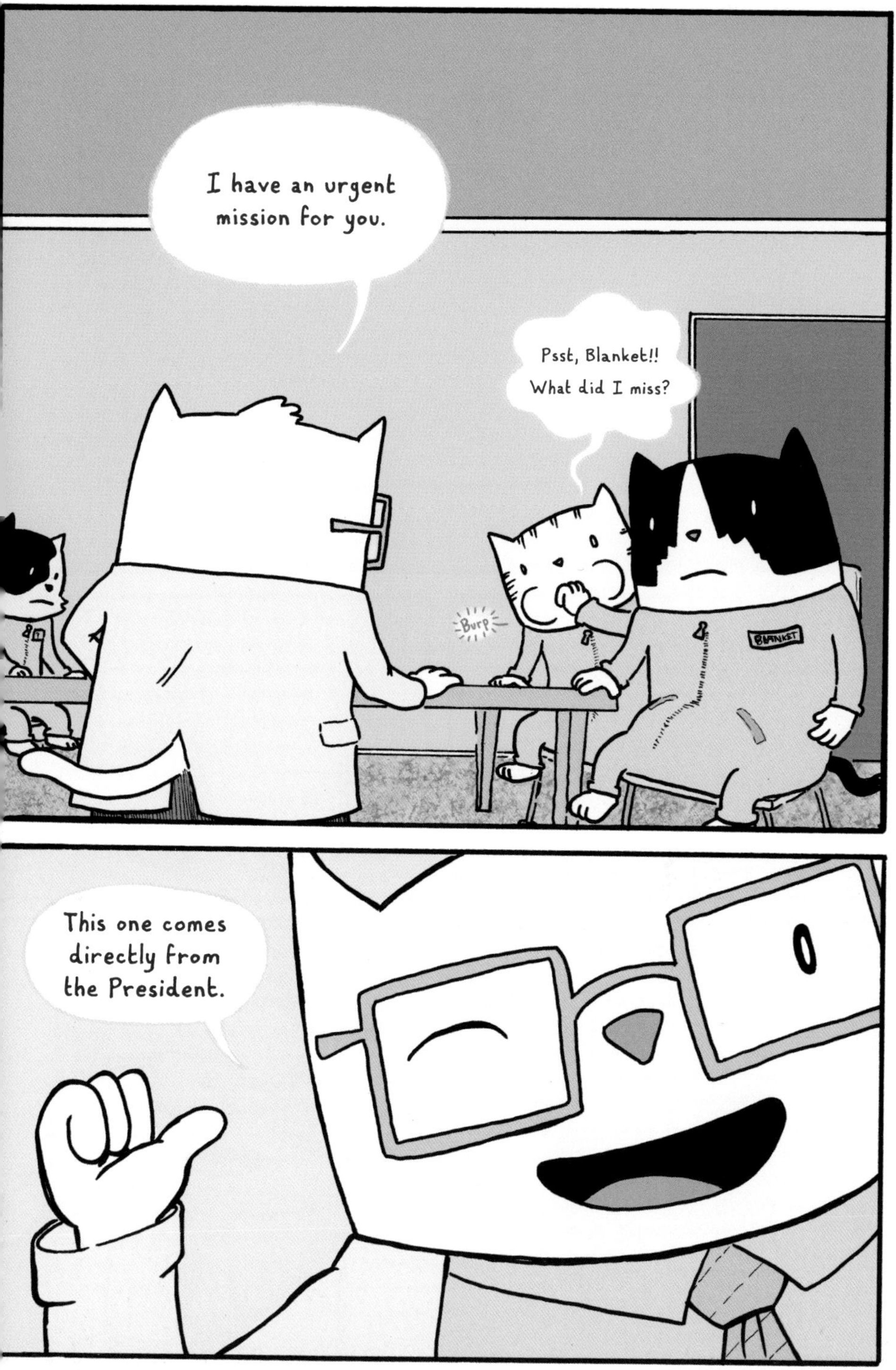
I have an urgent mission for you.
Psst, Blanket!! What did I miss?
Burp
BLANKET
This one comes directly from the President.

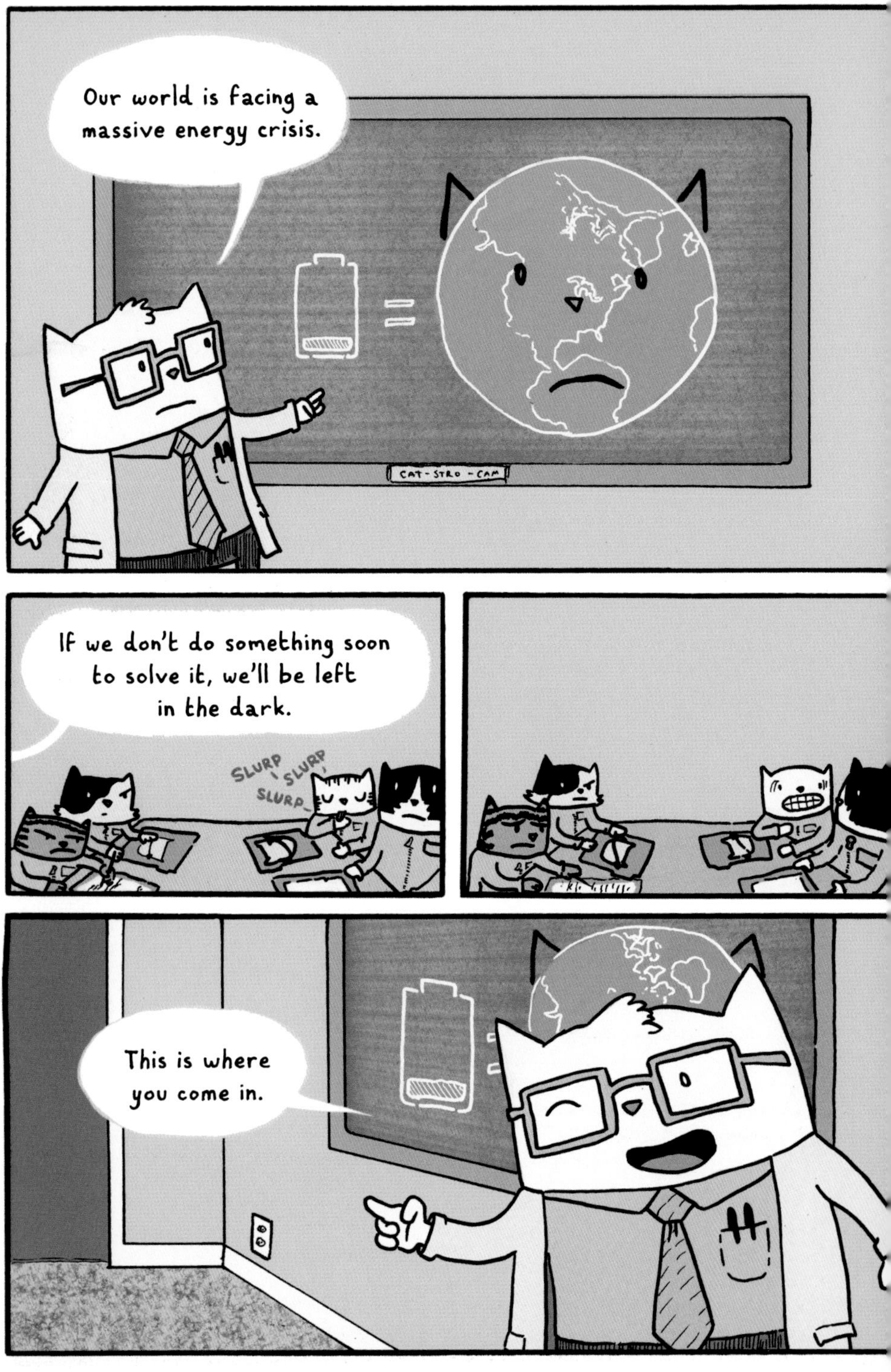
Our world is facing a massive energy crisis.
CAT-STRO-CAM
If we don't do something soon to solve it, we'll be left in the dark.
SLURP SLURP SLURP
This is where you come in.

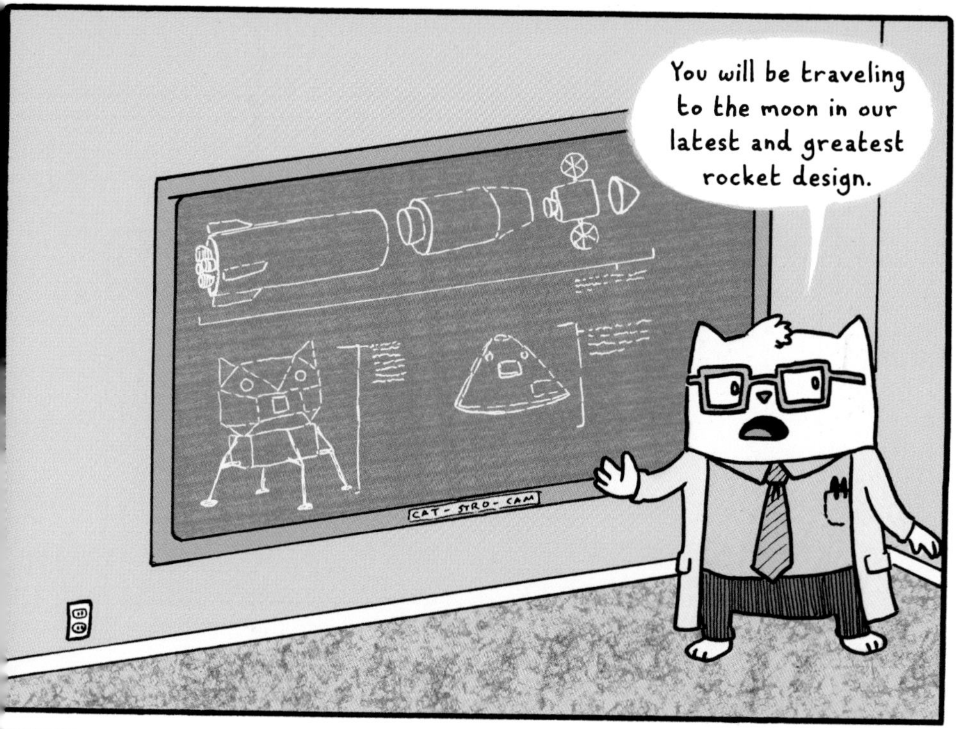
You will be traveling to the moon in our latest and greatest rocket design.
CAT-STRO-CAM

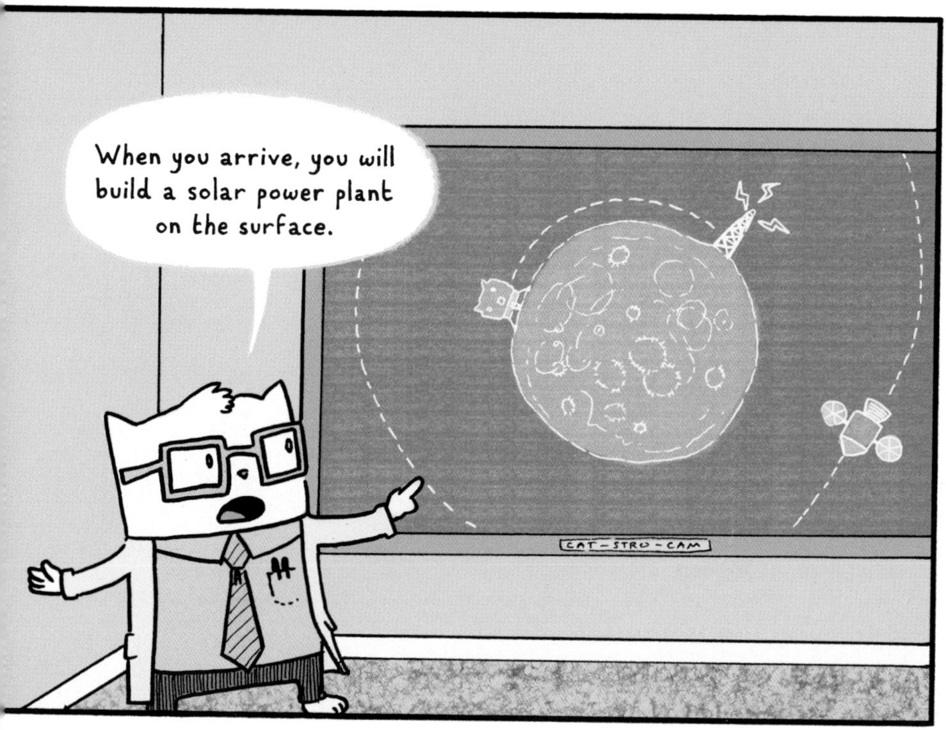
When you arrive, you will build a solar power plant on the surface.
CAT-STRO-CAM

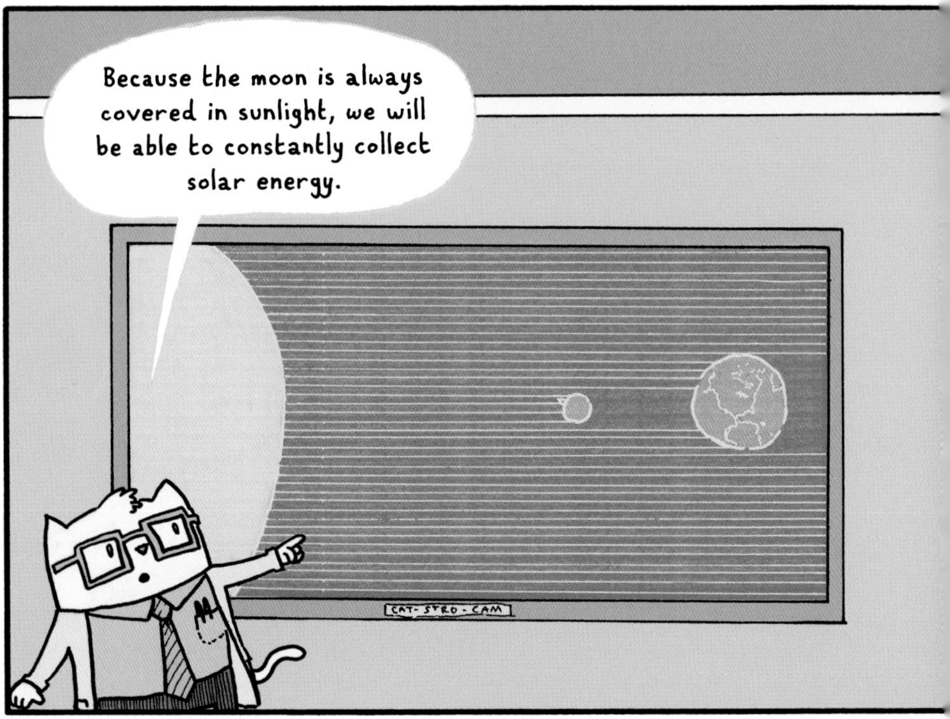
Because the moon is always covered in sunlight, we will be able to constantly collect solar energy.
CAT-STRO-CAM

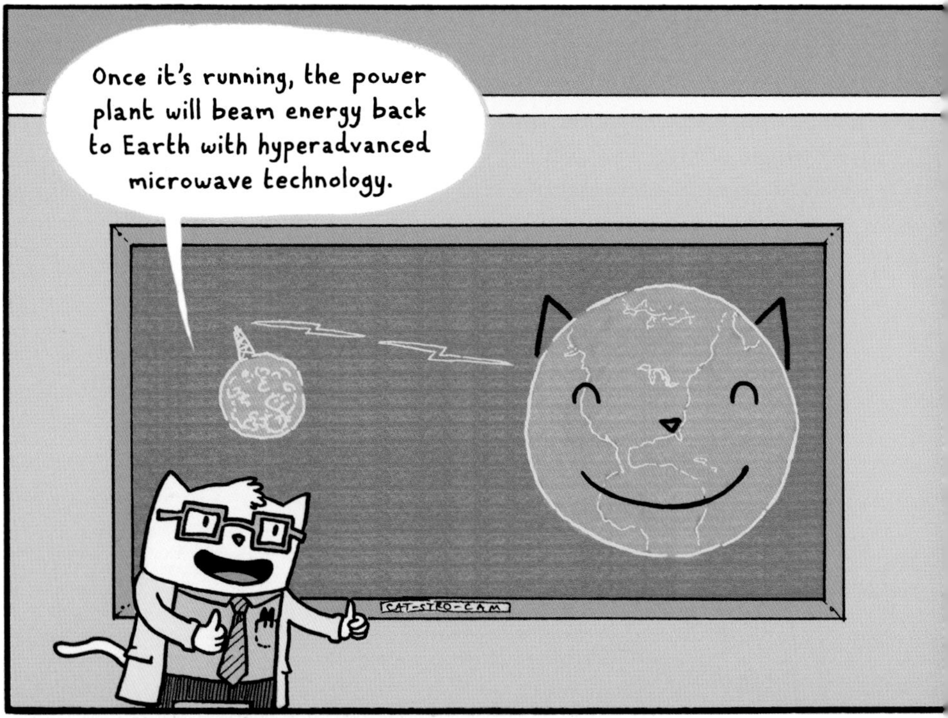
Once it's running, the power plant will beam energy back to Earth with hyperadvanced microwave technology.
CAT-STRO-CAM

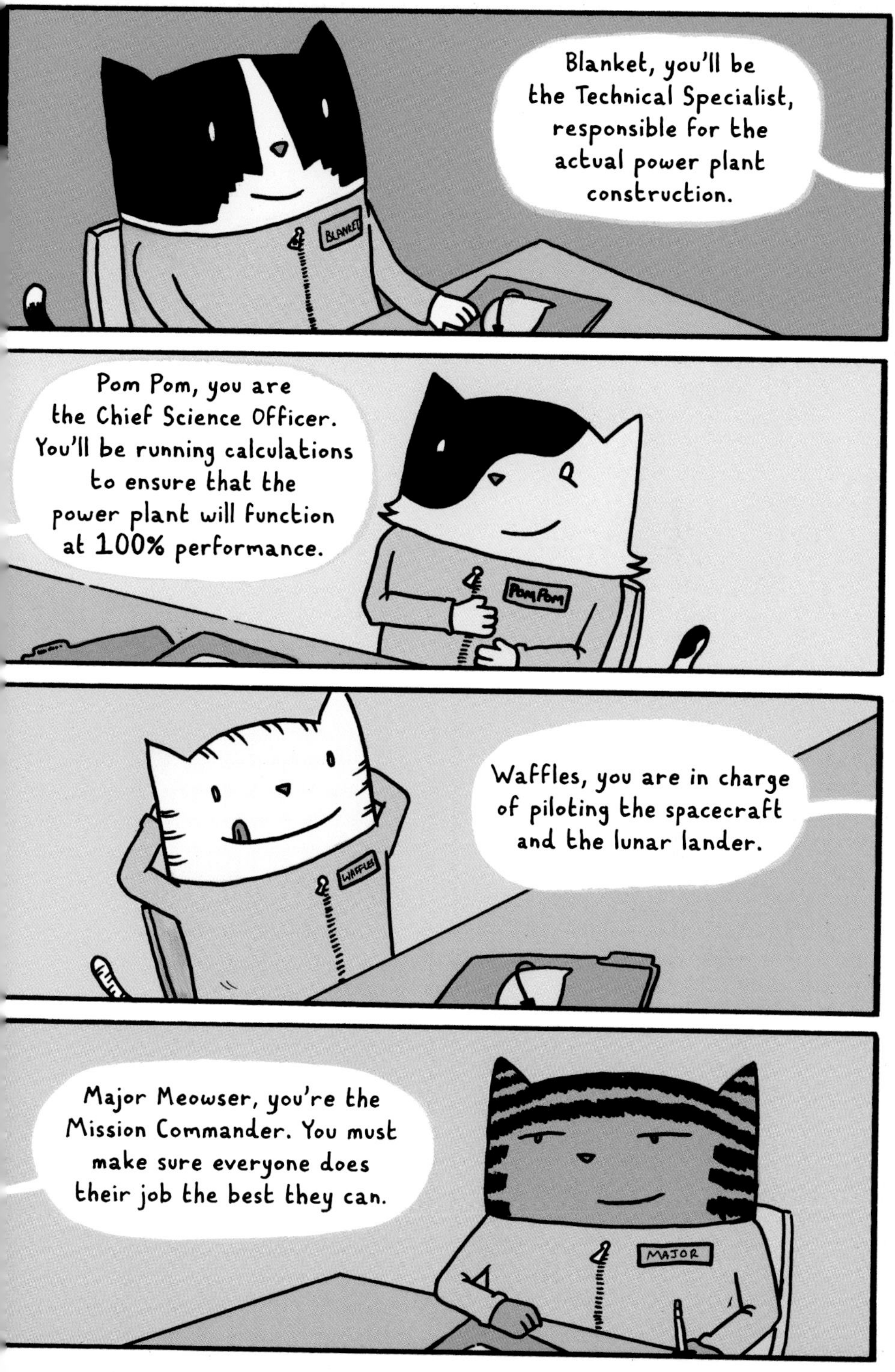

Blanket, you'll be the Technical Specialist, responsible for the actual power plant construction.
BLANKET
Pom Pom, you are the Chief Science Officer. You'll be running calculations to ensure that the power plant will function at 100% performance.
Pom Pom
Waffles, you are in charge of piloting the spacecraft and the lunar lander.
WAFFLES
Major Meowser, you're the Mission Commander. You must make sure everyone does their job the best they can.
MAJOR

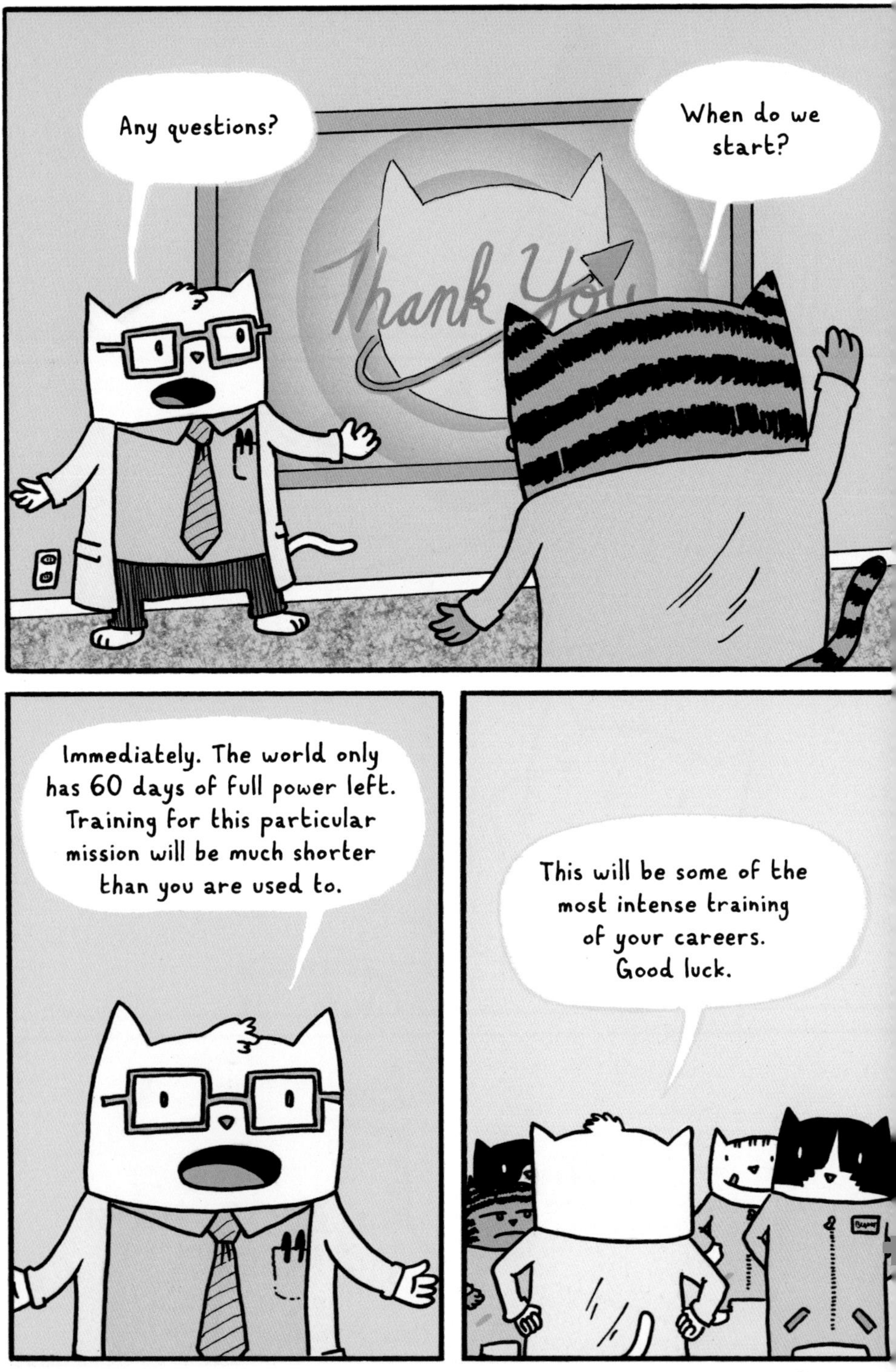
Any questions?
Thank You
When do we start?
Immediately. The world only has 60 days of full power left. Training for this particular mission will be much shorter than you are used to.
This will be some of the most intense training of your careers. Good luck.

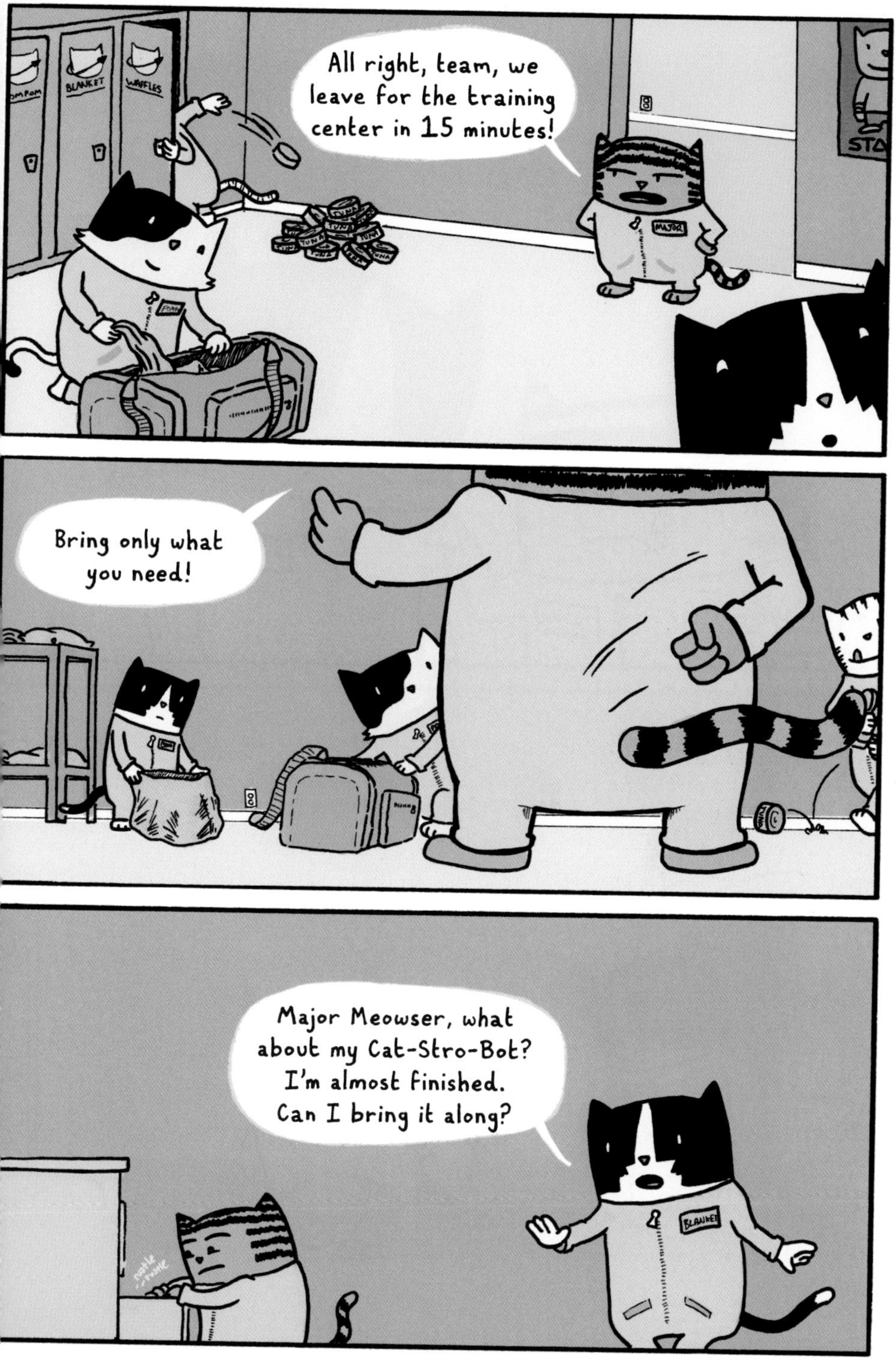
All right, team, we leave for the training center in 15 minutes!
Bring only what you need!
Major Meowser, what about my Cat-Stro-Bot? I'm almost finished. Can I bring it along?

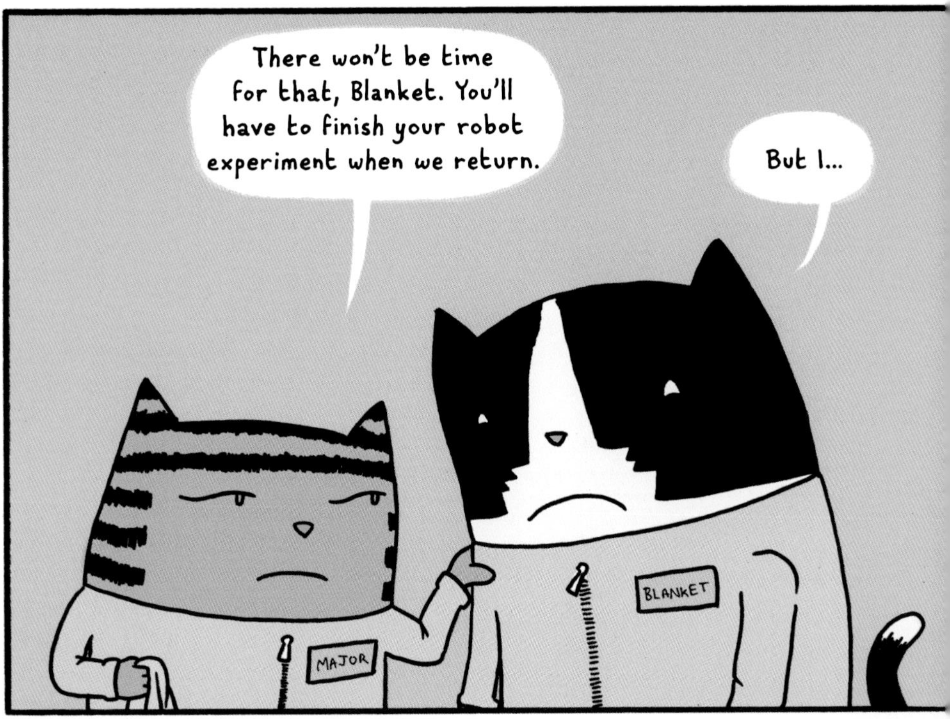
There won't be time for that, Blanket. You'll have to finish your robot experiment when we return.
But I...
BLANKET
MAJOR

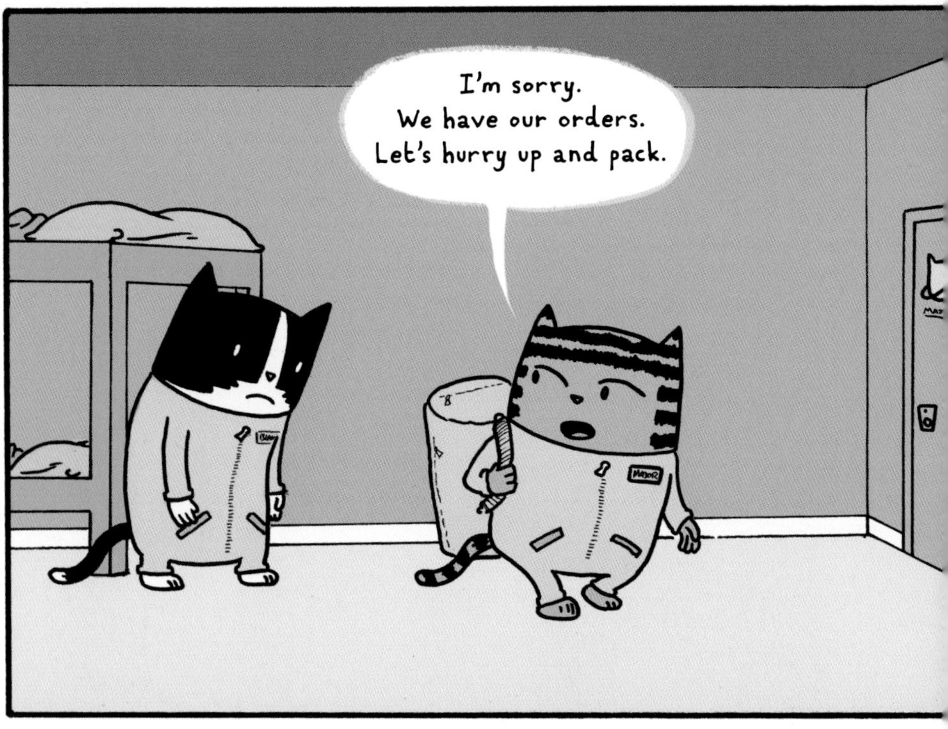
I'm sorry. We have our orders. Let's hurry up and pack.

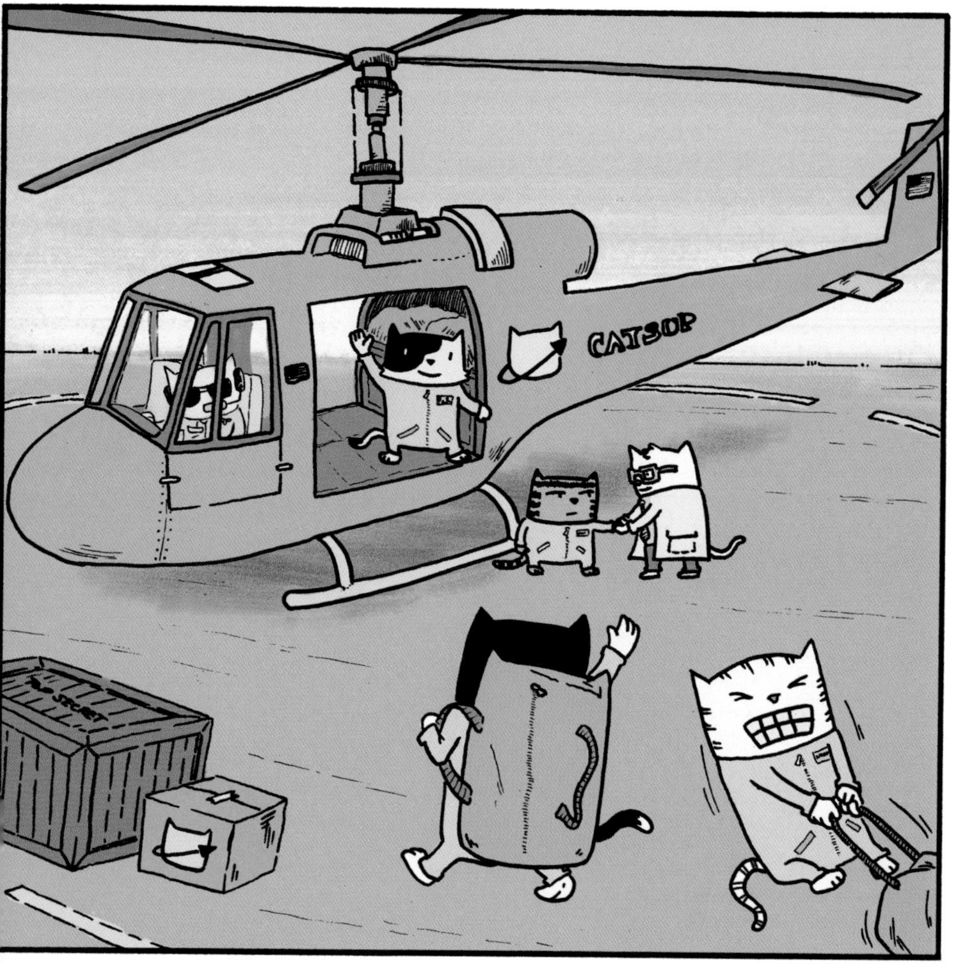
CATSOP

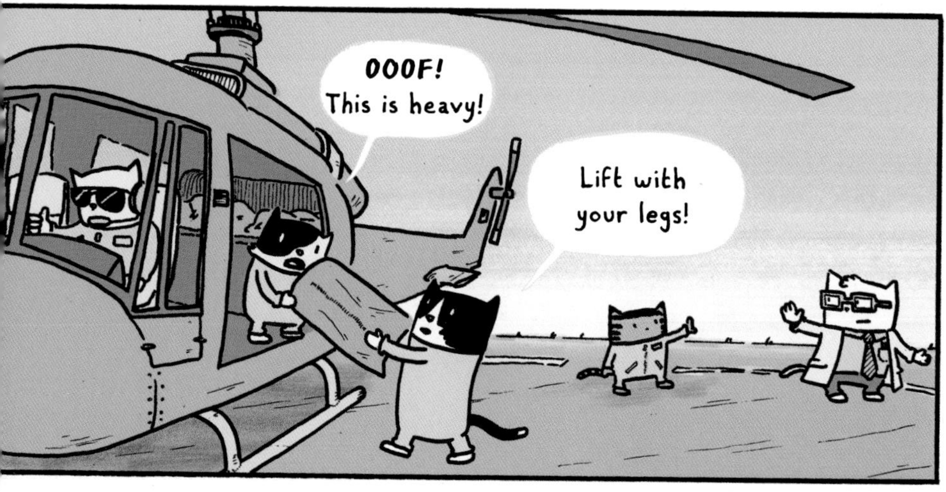
OOOF!
This is heavy!
Lift with your legs!

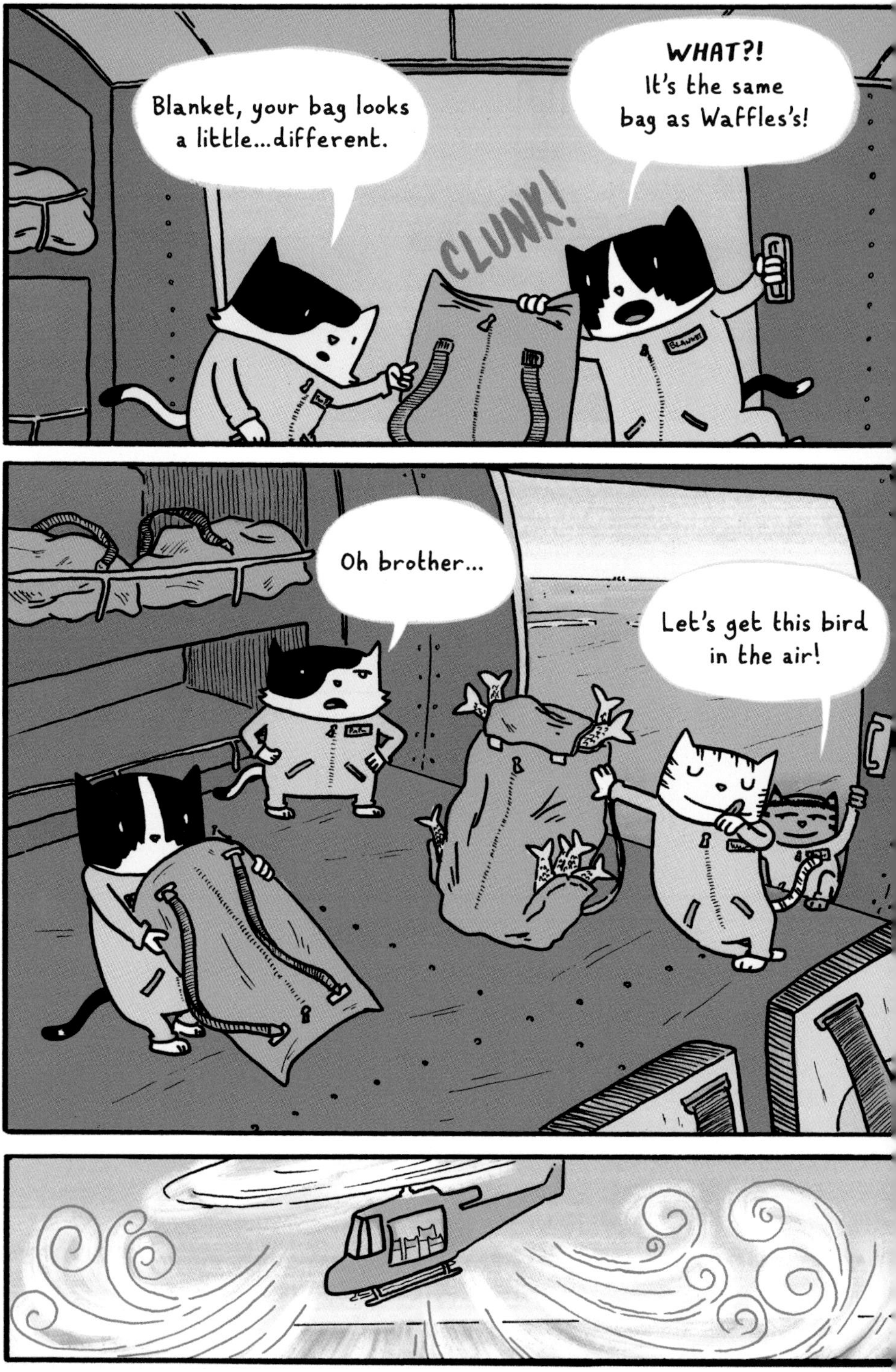
Blanket, your bag looks a little...different.
WHAT?! It's the same bag as Waffles's!
CLUNK!
Oh brother...
Let's get this bird in the air!

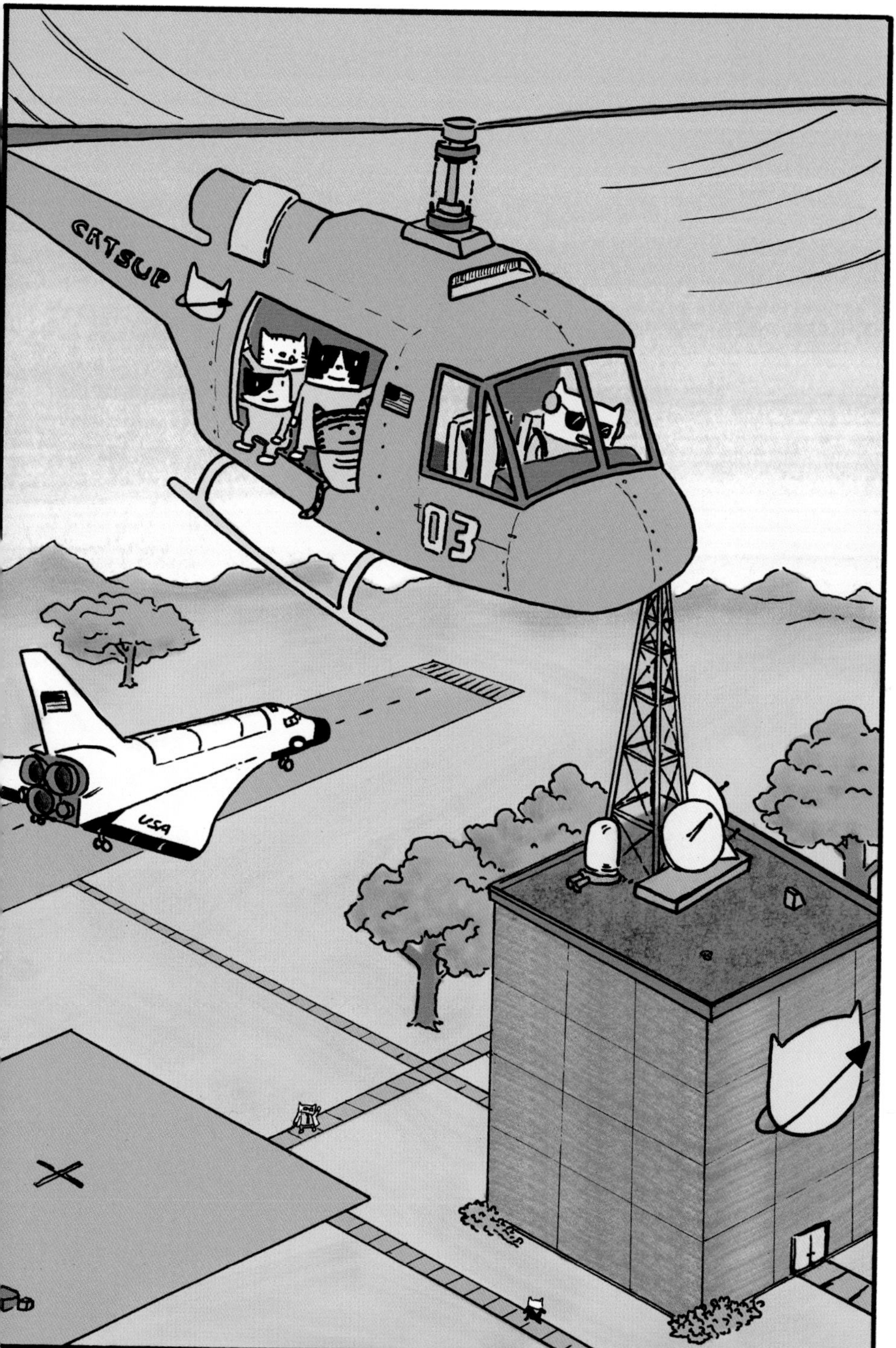
CATSUP
03
USA

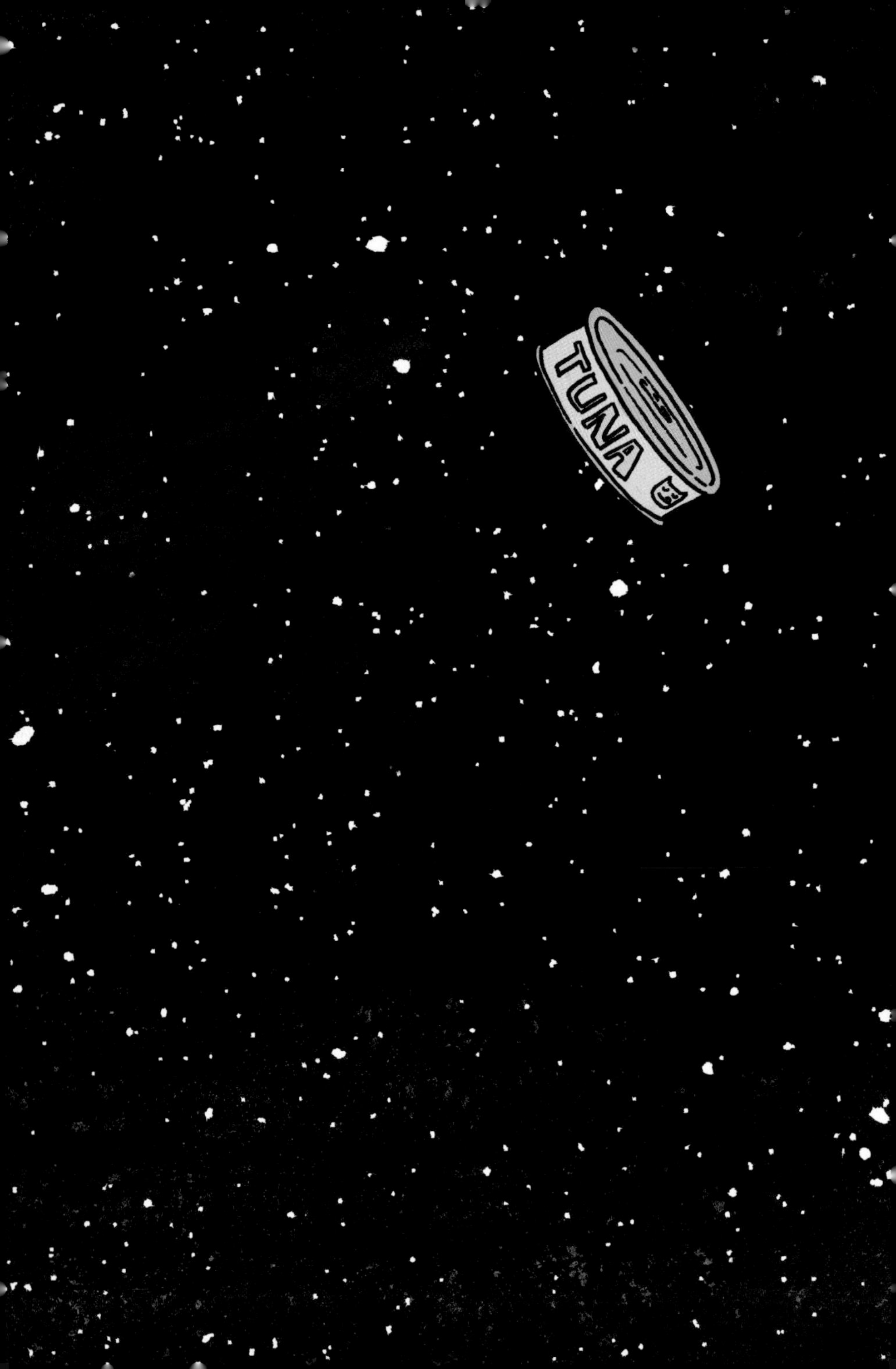
TUNA

CHAPTER 3

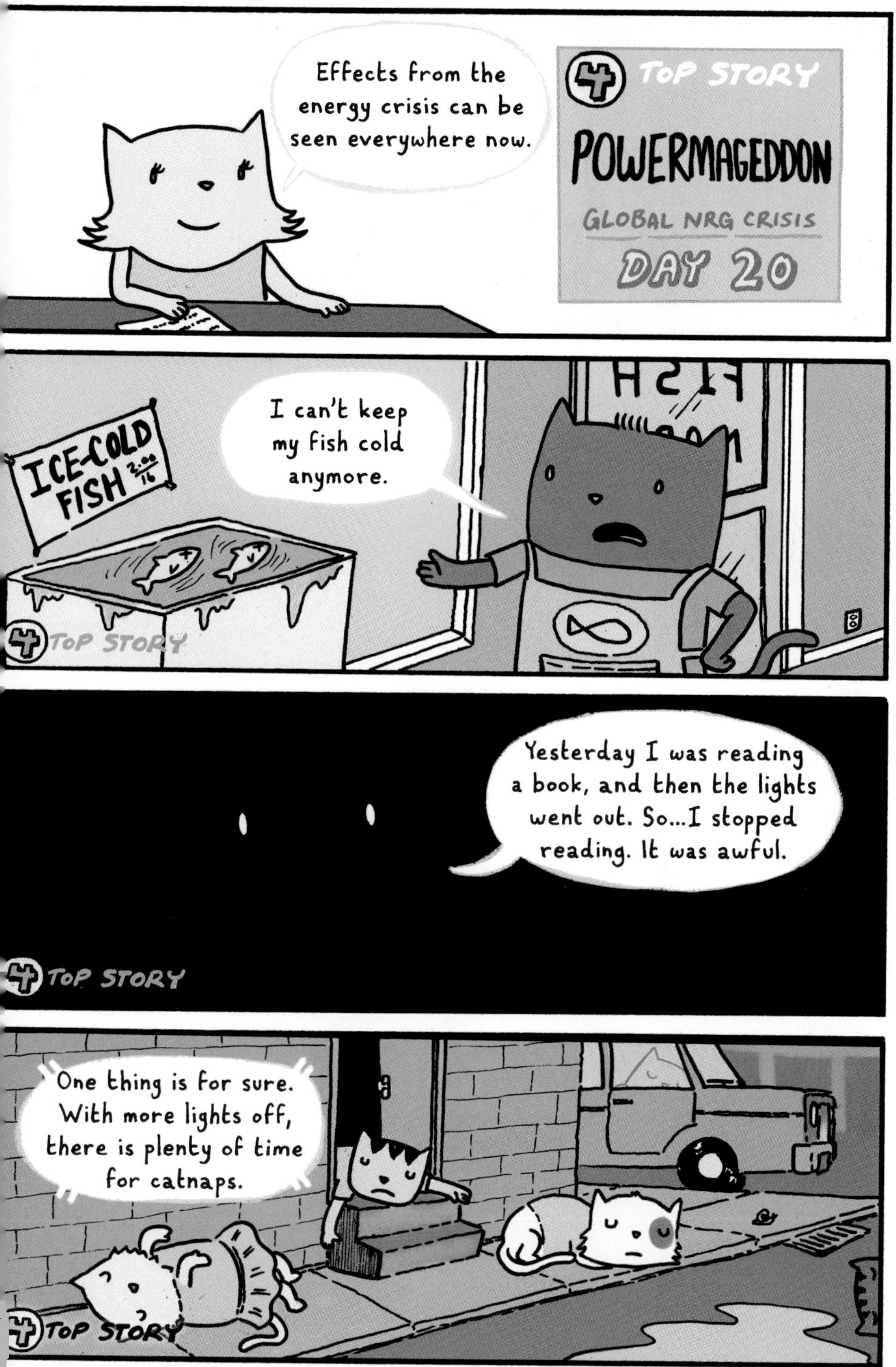
Effects from the energy crisis can be seen everywhere now.
TOP STORY
POWERMAGEDDON
GLOBAL NRG CRISIS
DAY 20
ICE-COLD FISH
I can't keep my fish cold anymore.
TOP STORY
Yesterday I was reading a book, and then the lights went out. So...I stopped reading. It was awful.
TOP STORY
One thing is for sure. With more lights off, there is plenty of time for catnaps.
TOP STORY

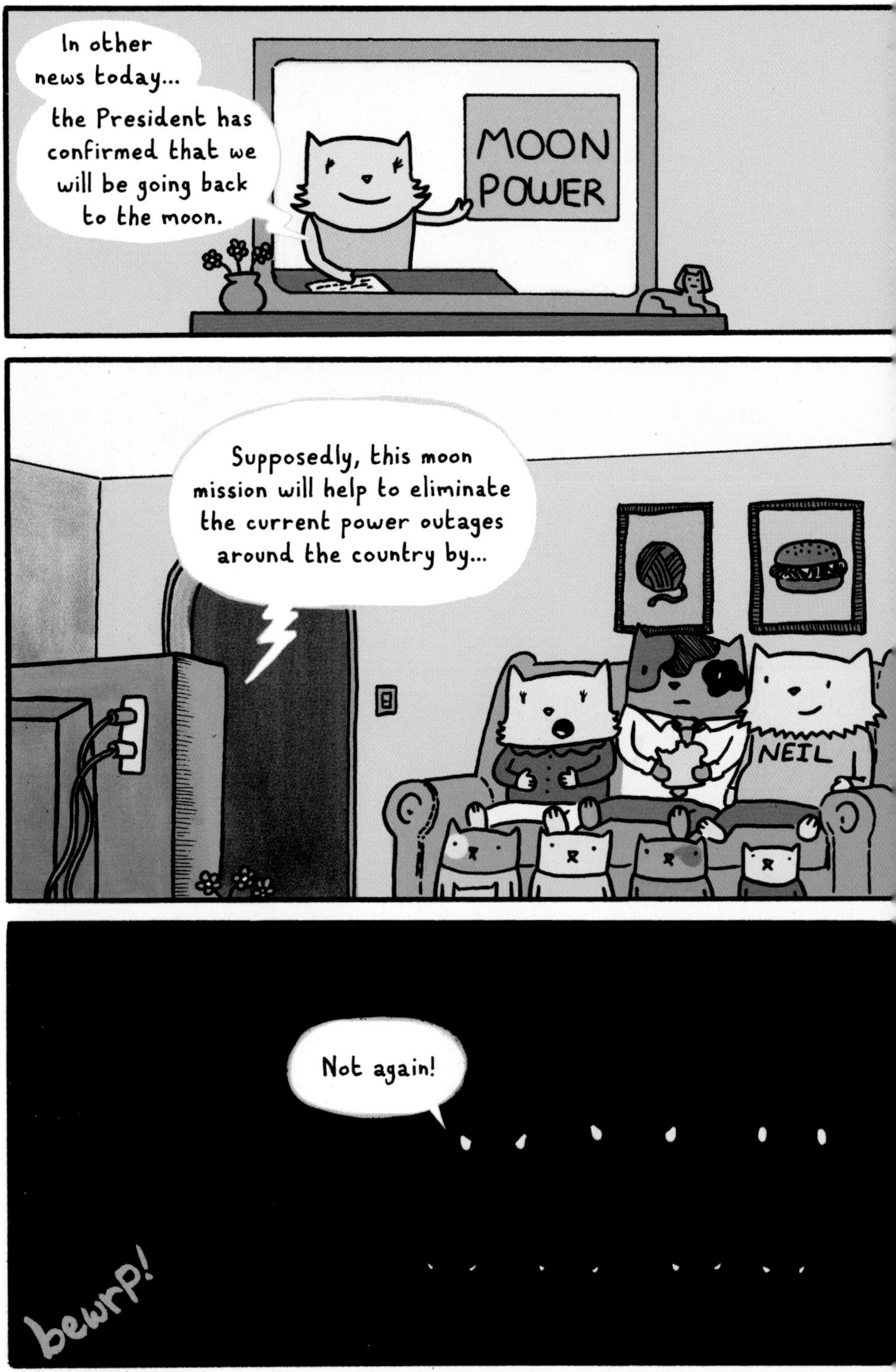
In other news today...
the President has confirmed that we will be going back to the moon.
MOON POWER
Supposedly, this moon mission will help to eliminate the current power outages around the country by...
NEIL
Not again!
bewrp!

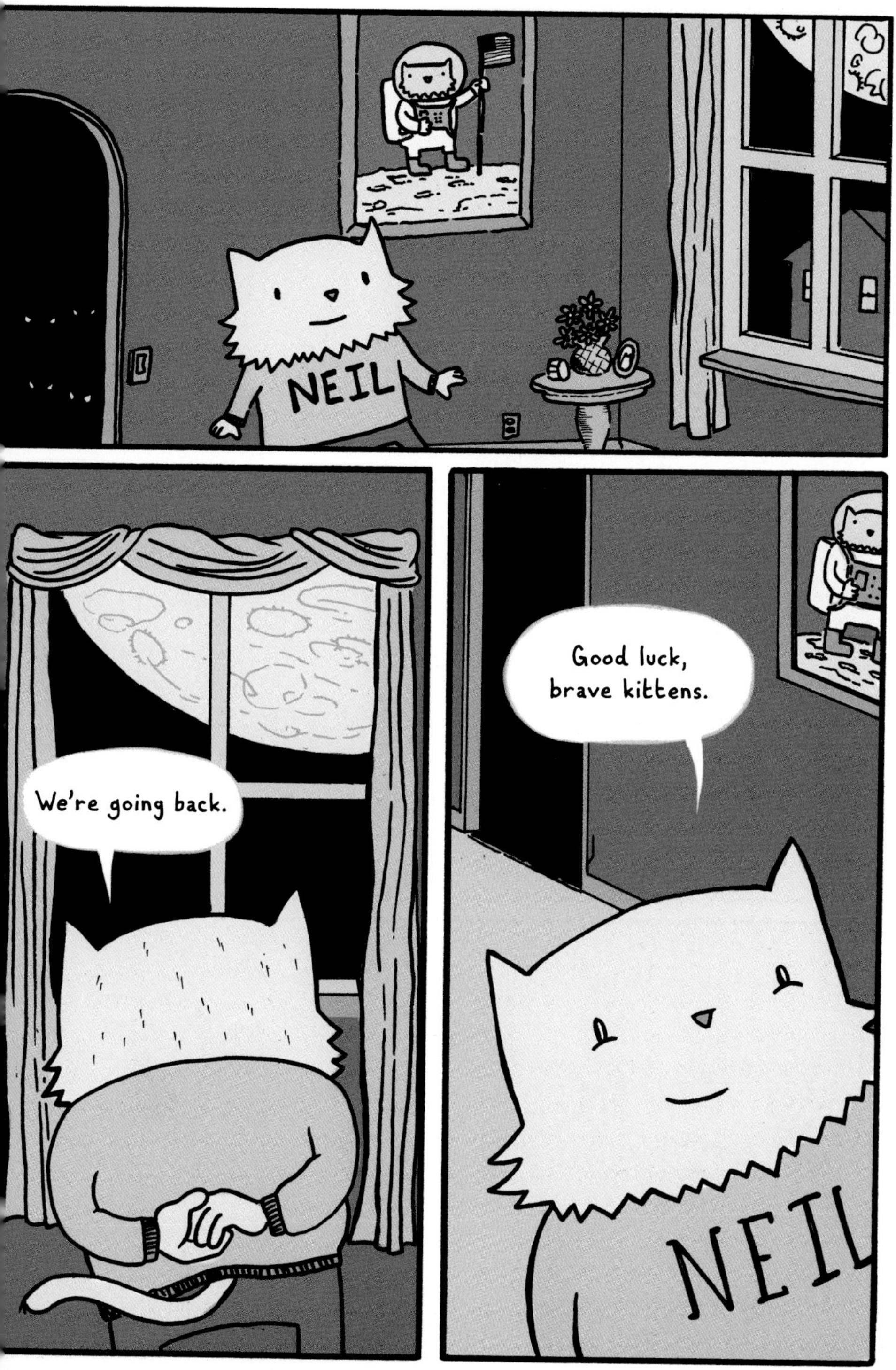
NEIL
We're going back.
Good luck, brave kittens.
NEIL

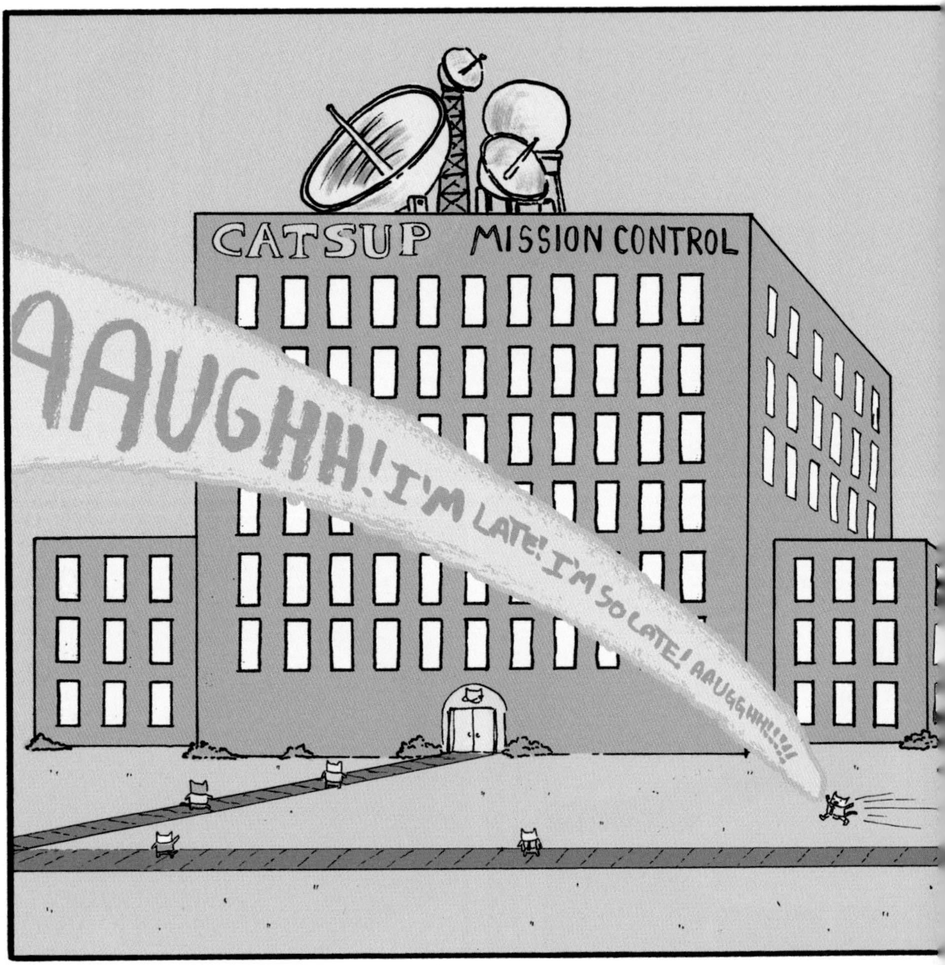
CATSUP MISSION CONTROL
AAUGHH! I'M LATE! I'M SO LATE! AAUGGHH!!!!!

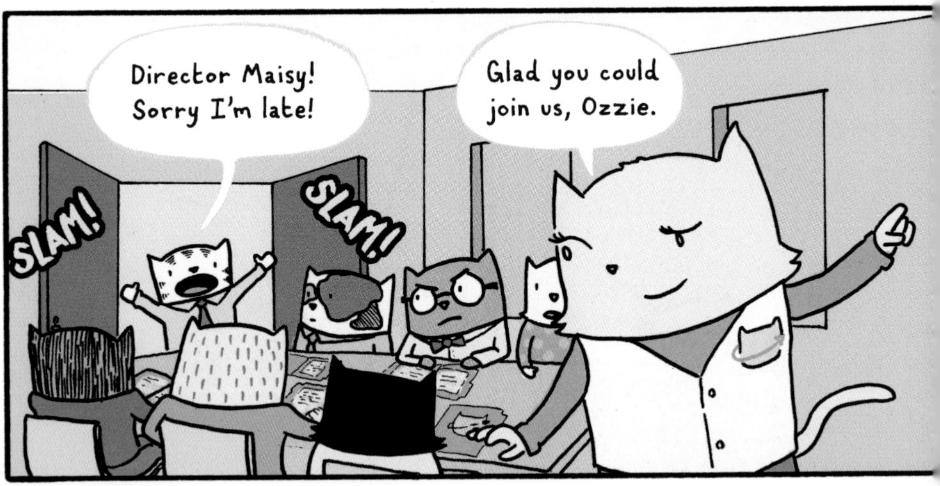
SLAM!
SLAM!
Director Maisy! Sorry I'm late!
Glad you could join us, Ozzie.

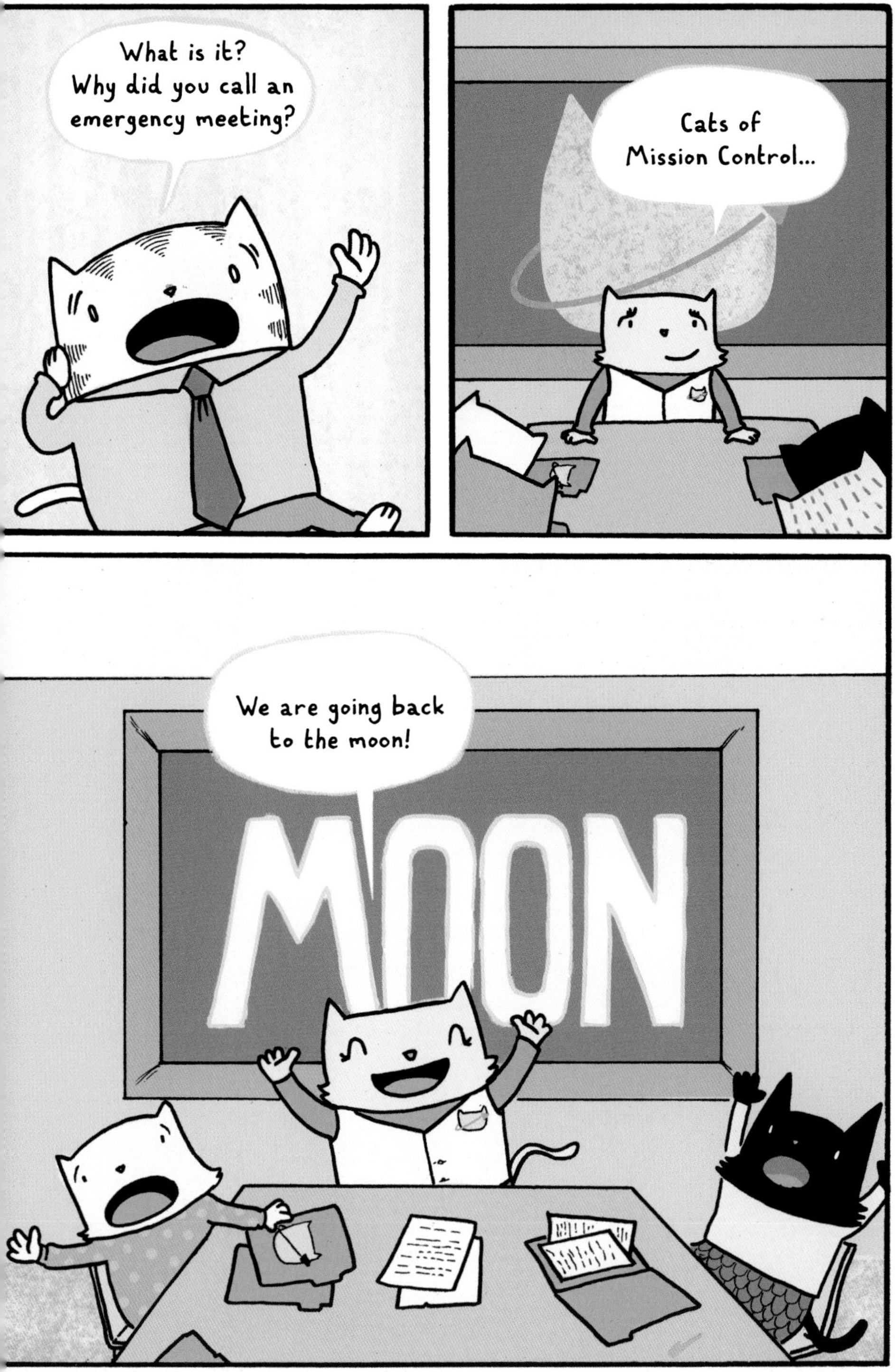
What is it?
Why did you call an
emergency meeting?
Cats of
Mission Control...
We are going back
to the moon!
MOON

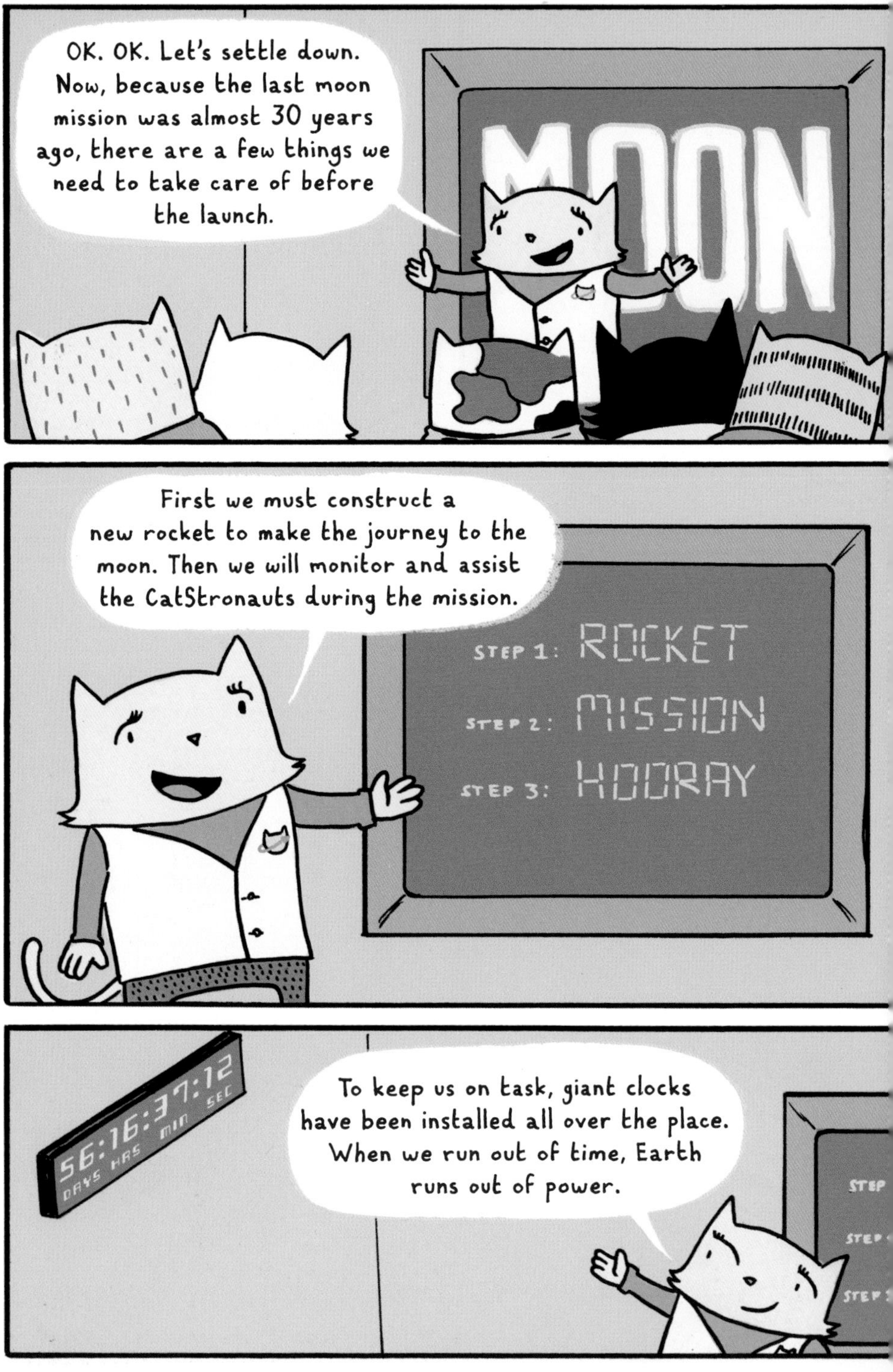
OK. OK. Let's settle down. Now, because the last moon mission was almost 30 years ago, there are a few things we need to take care of before the launch.
MOON
First we must construct a new rocket to make the journey to the moon. Then we will monitor and assist the CatStronauts during the mission.
STEP 1: ROCKET
STEP 2: MISSION
STEP 3: HOORAY
56:16:37:12
DAYS HRS MIN SEC
To keep us on task, giant clocks have been installed all over the place. When we run out of time, Earth runs out of power.

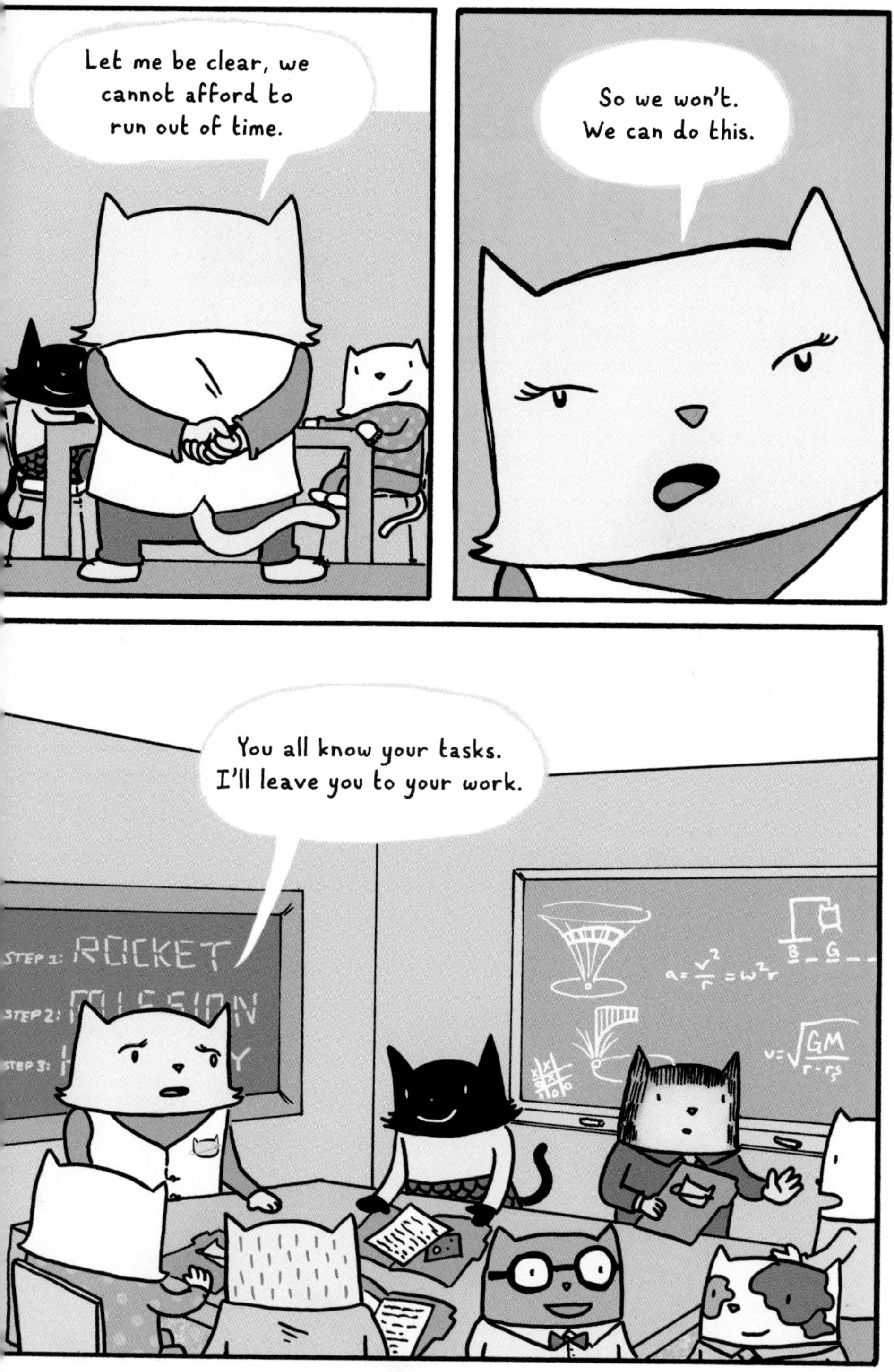
Let me be clear, we cannot afford to run out of time.
So we won't. We can do this.
You all know your tasks. I'll leave you to your work.
STEP 1: ROCKET
STEP 2:
STEP 3:
a = v²/r = ω²r
v = √(GM/(r − rs))
B _ G _ _

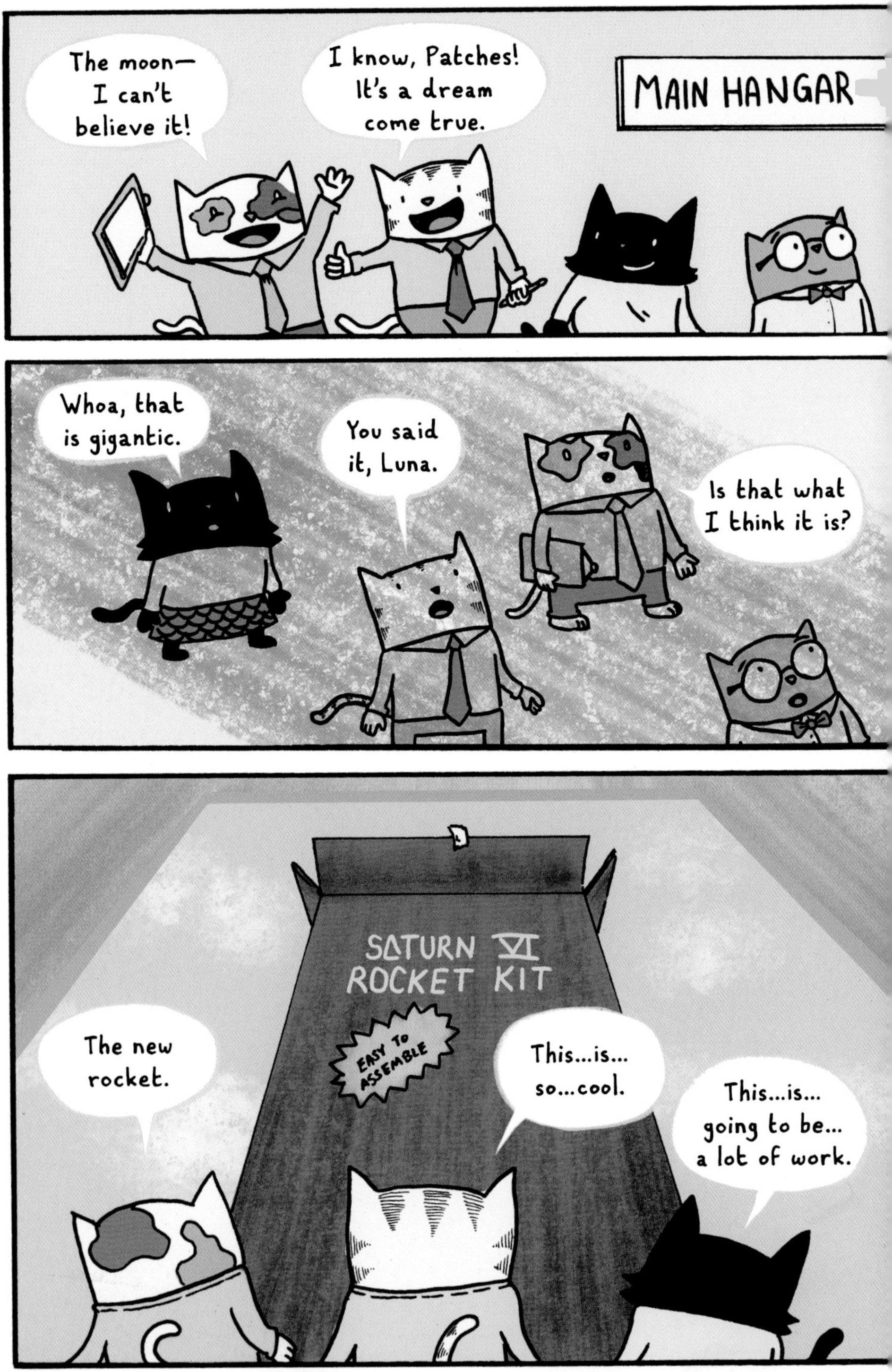
The moon— I can't believe it!
I know, Patches! It's a dream come true.
MAIN HANGAR
Whoa, that is gigantic.
You said it, Luna.
Is that what I think it is?
SATURN VI ROCKET KIT
EASY TO ASSEMBLE
The new rocket.
This...is... so...cool.
This...is... going to be... a lot of work.

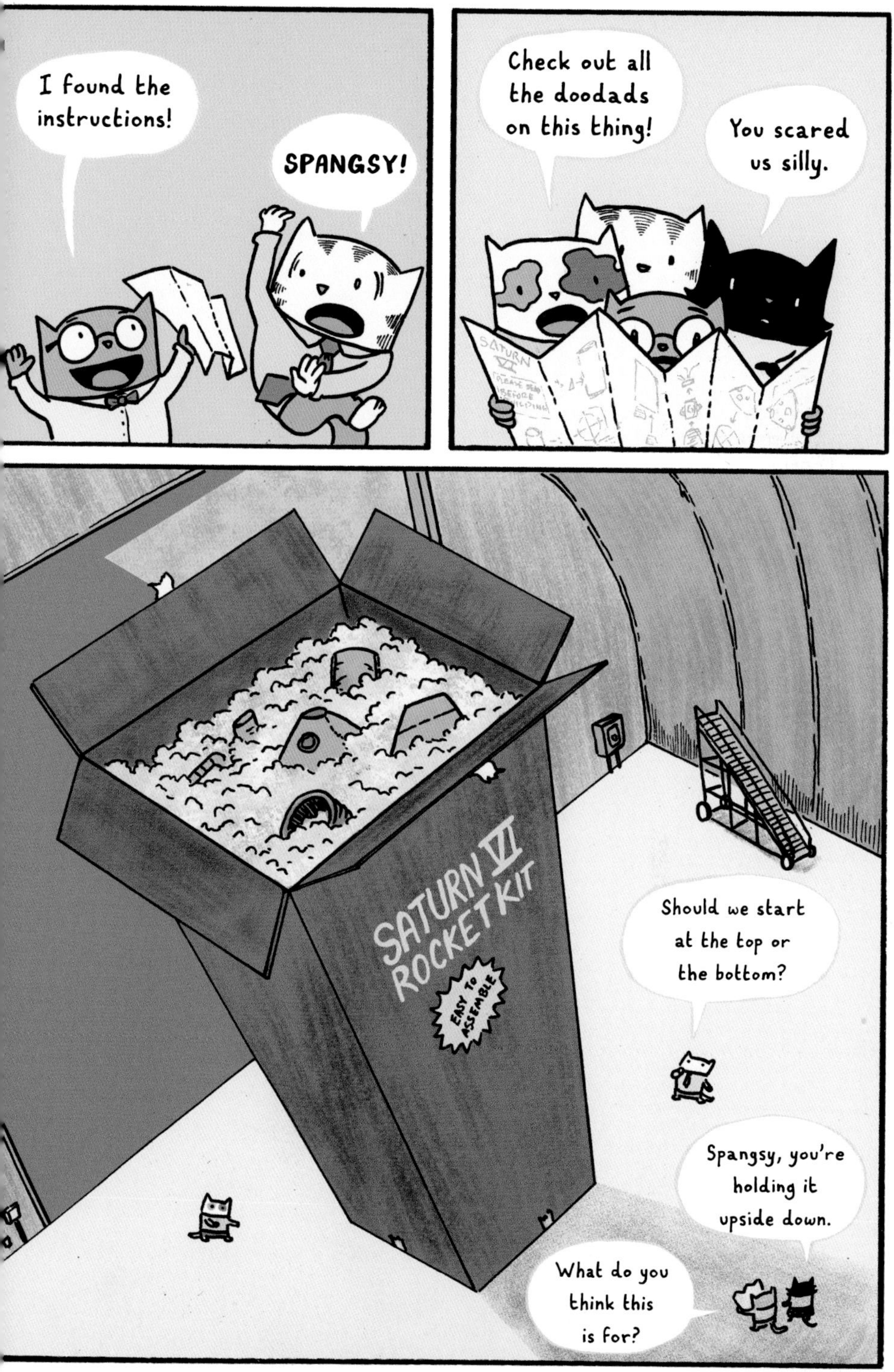
I found the instructions!
SPANGSY!
Check out all the doodads on this thing!
You scared us silly.
SATURN VI ROCKET KIT
EASY TO ASSEMBLE
Should we start at the top or the bottom?
Spangsy, you're holding it upside down.
What do you think this is for?

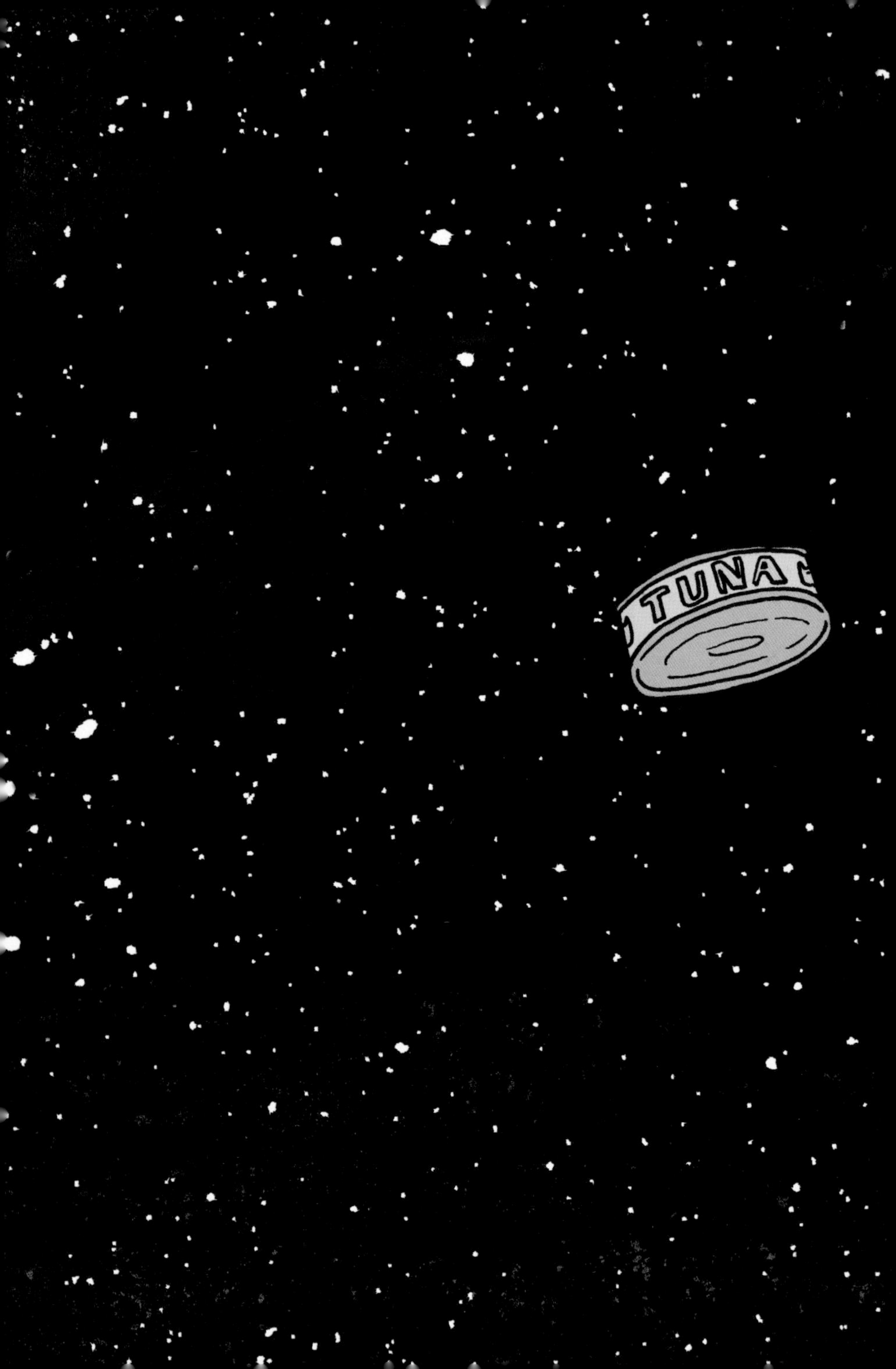
TUNA

CHAPTER 4

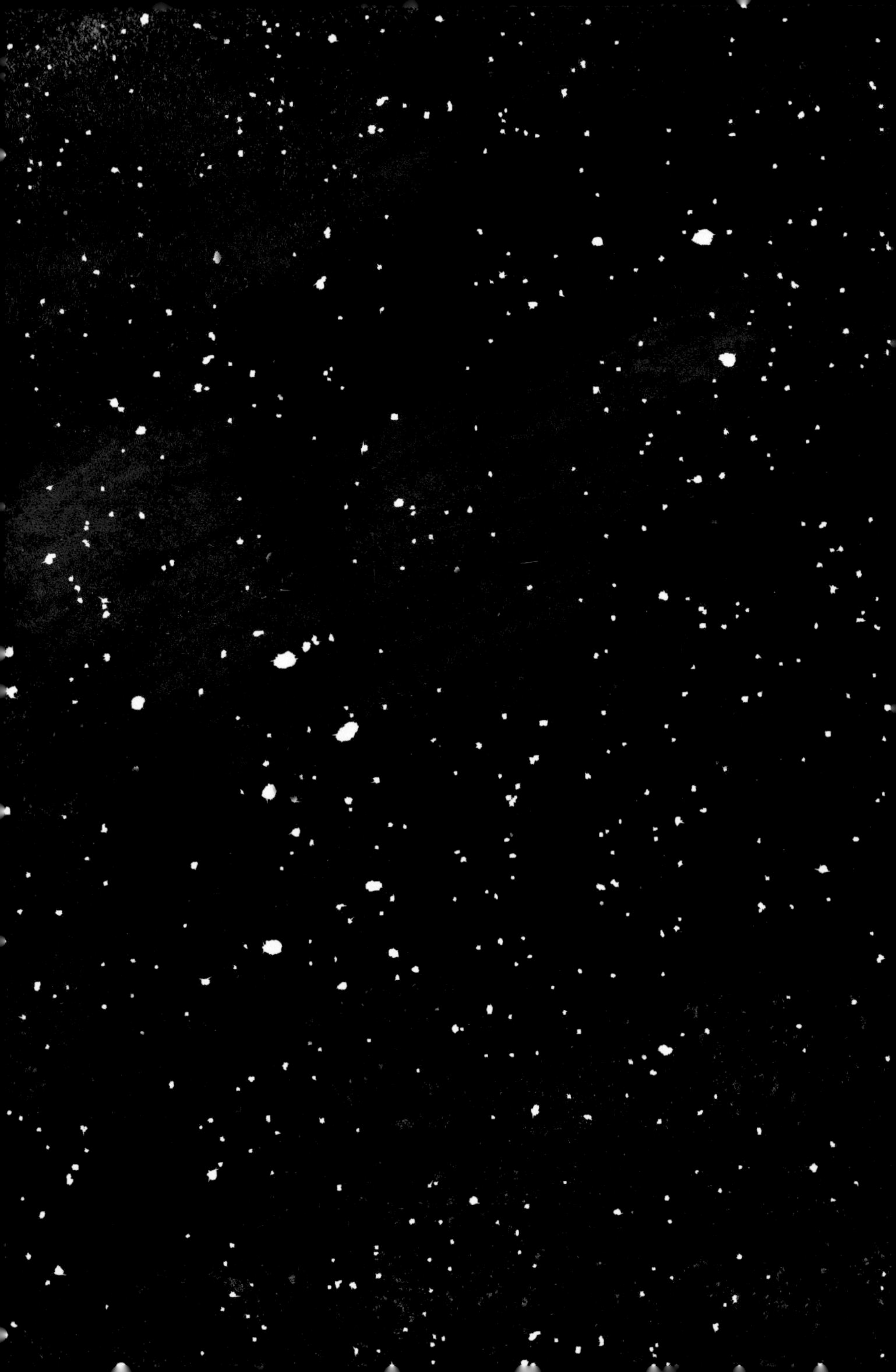

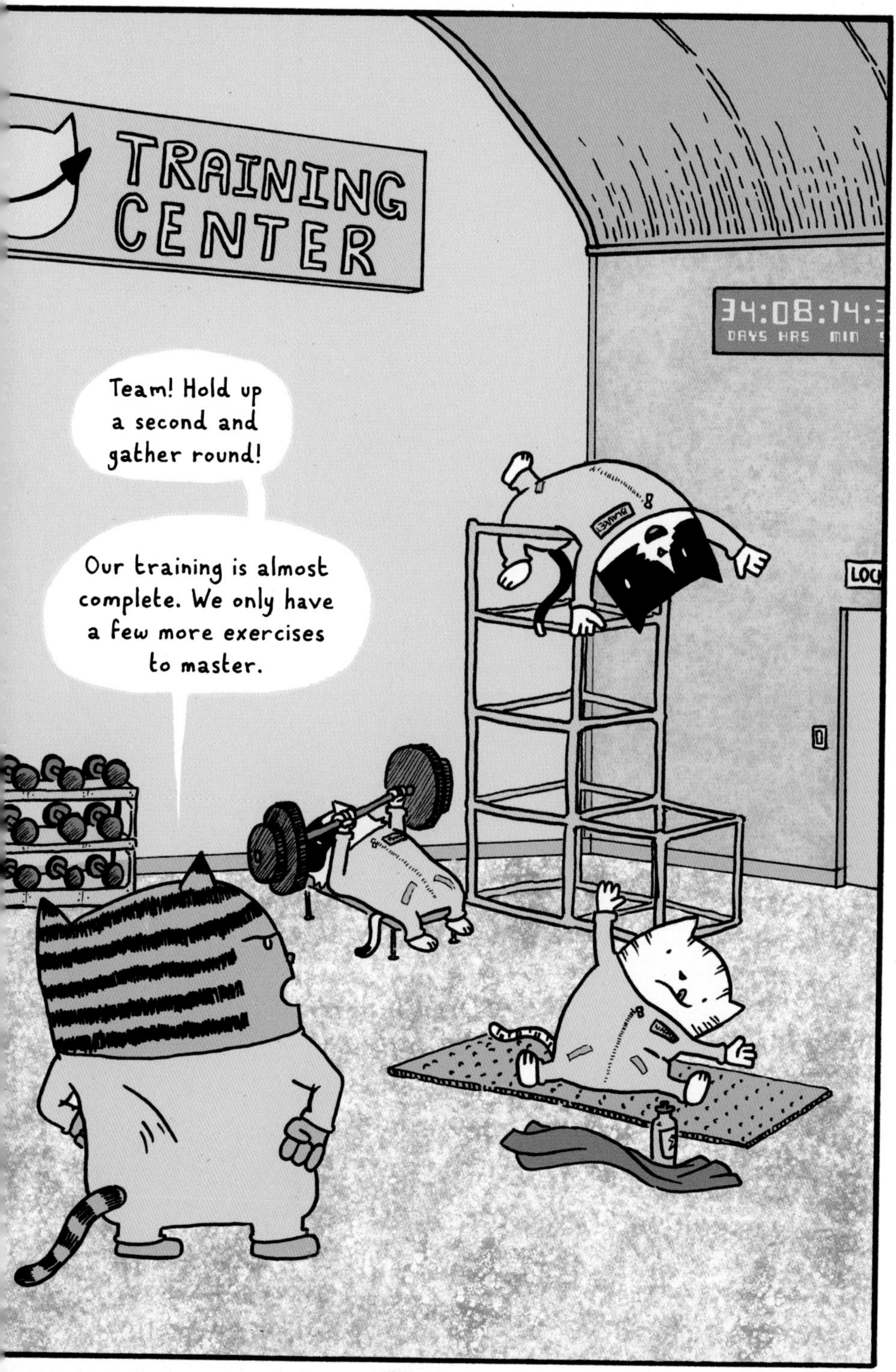
TRAINING CENTER
34:08:14:3
DAYS HRS MIN
Team! Hold up a second and gather round!
Our training is almost complete. We only have a few more exercises to master.

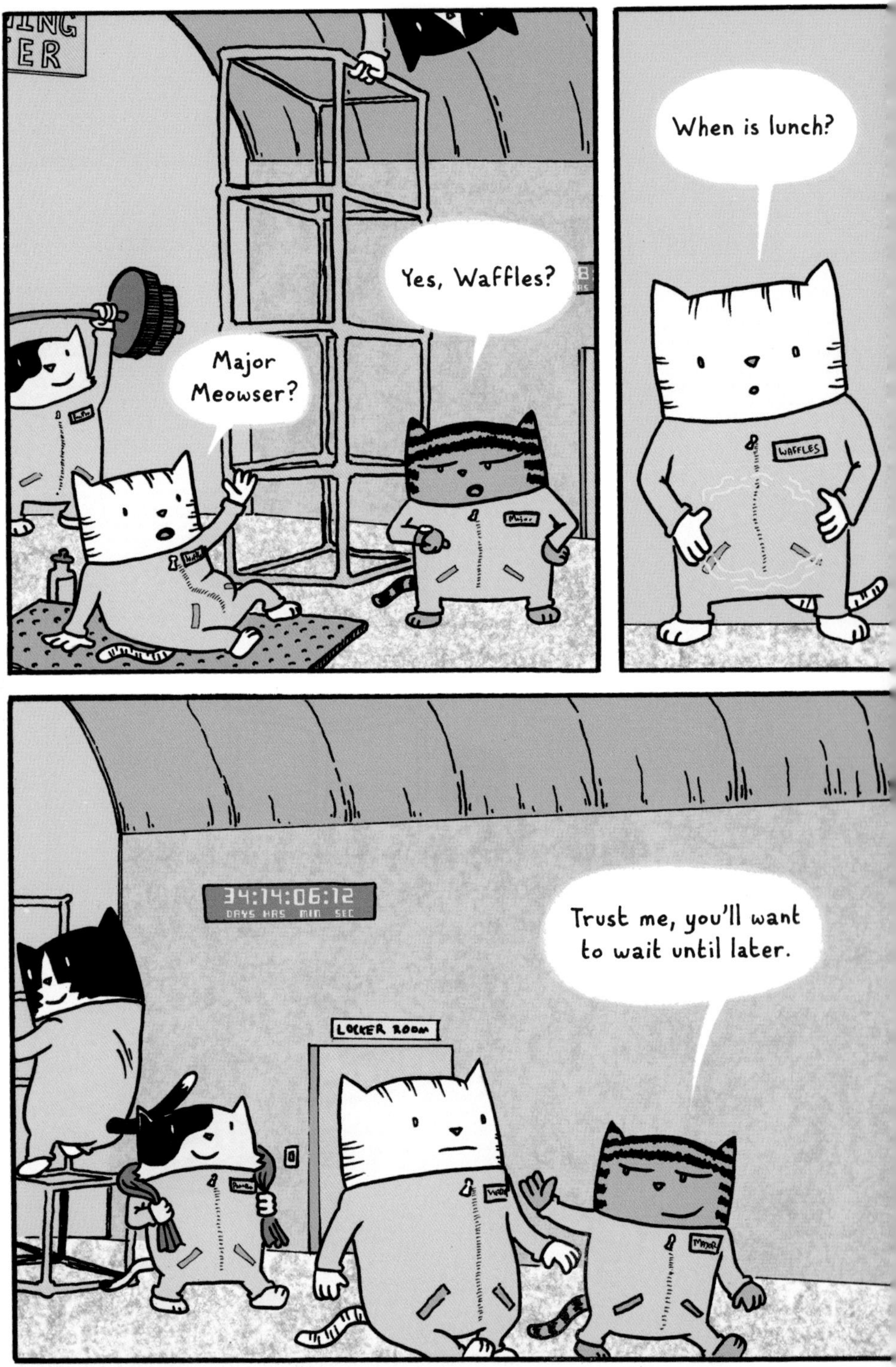
Major Meowser?
Yes, Waffles?
When is lunch?
WAFFLES
34:14:06:12
DAYS HRS MIN SEC
LOCKER ROOM
Trust me, you'll want to wait until later.

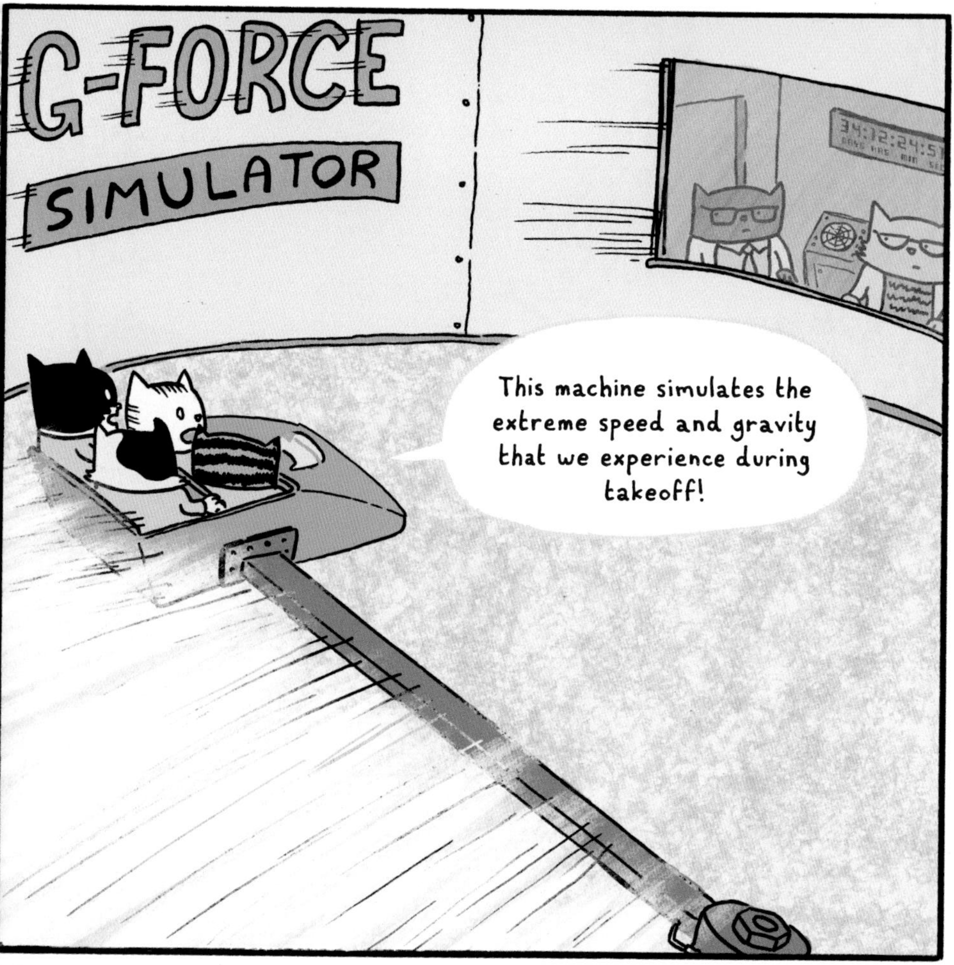
G-FORCE
SIMULATOR
This machine simulates the extreme speed and gravity that we experience during takeoff!

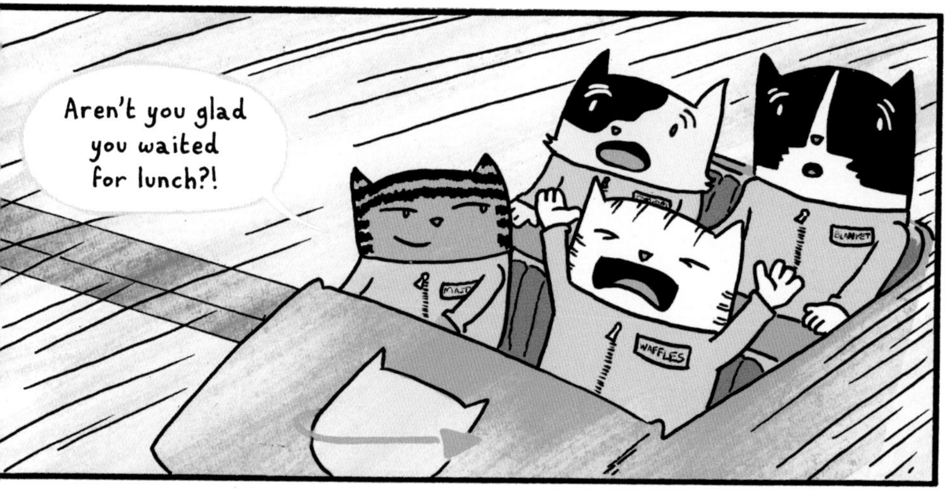
Aren't you glad you waited for lunch?!
BLANKET
WAFFLES

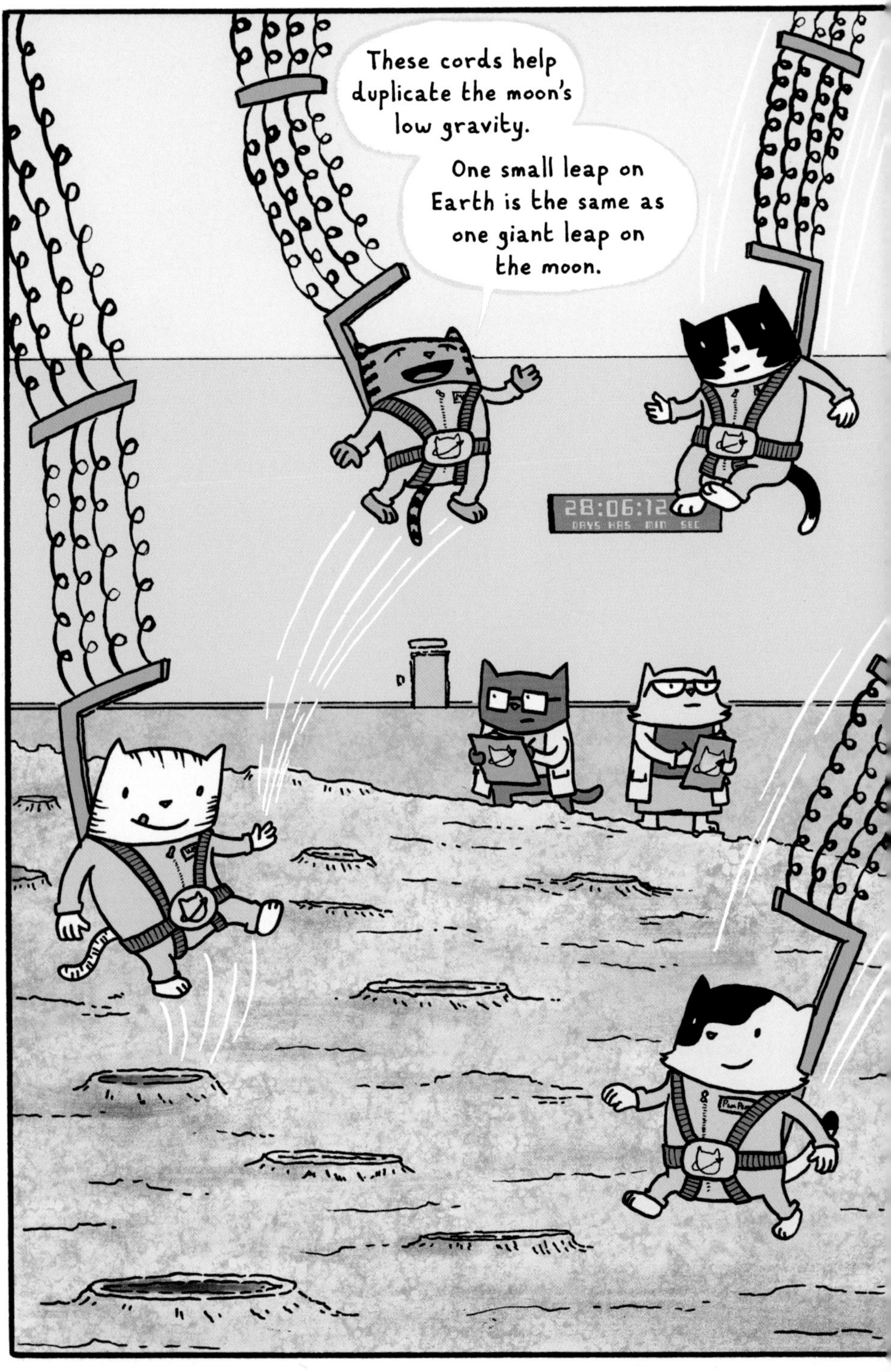
These cords help duplicate the moon's low gravity.
One small leap on Earth is the same as one giant leap on the moon.
28:06:12
DAYS HRS MIN SEC

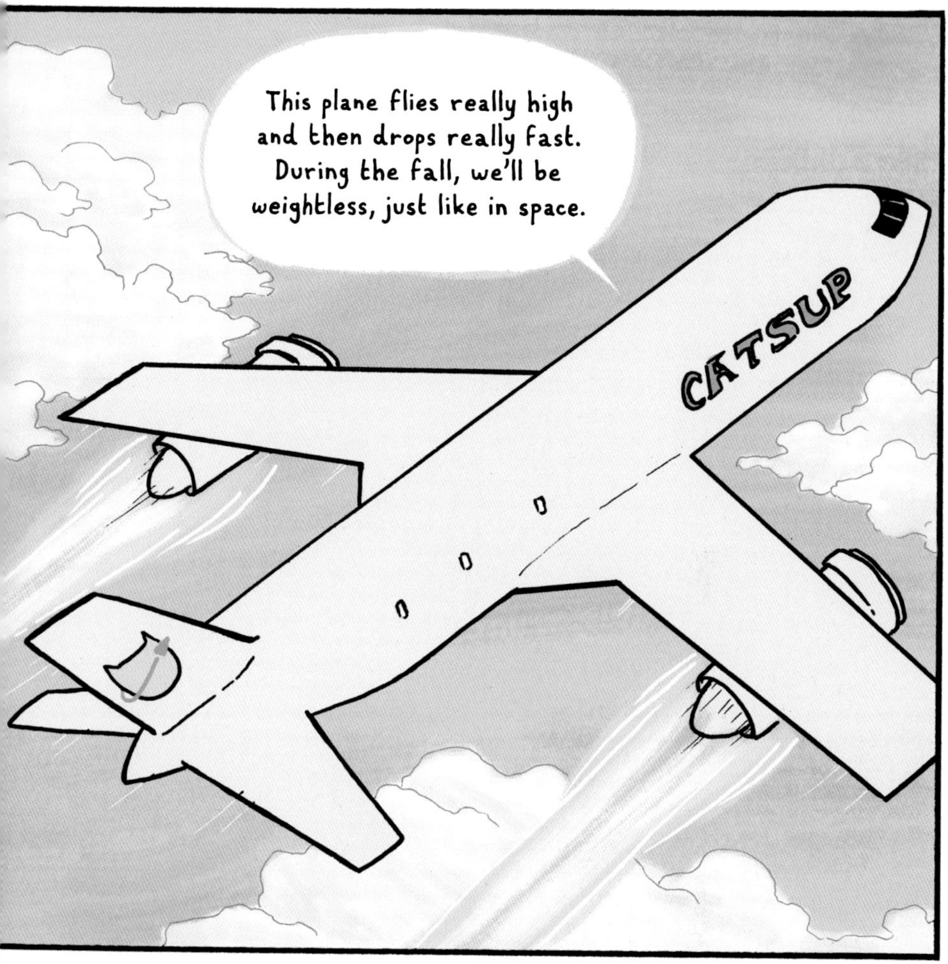
This plane flies really high and then drops really fast. During the fall, we'll be weightless, just like in space.
CATSUP

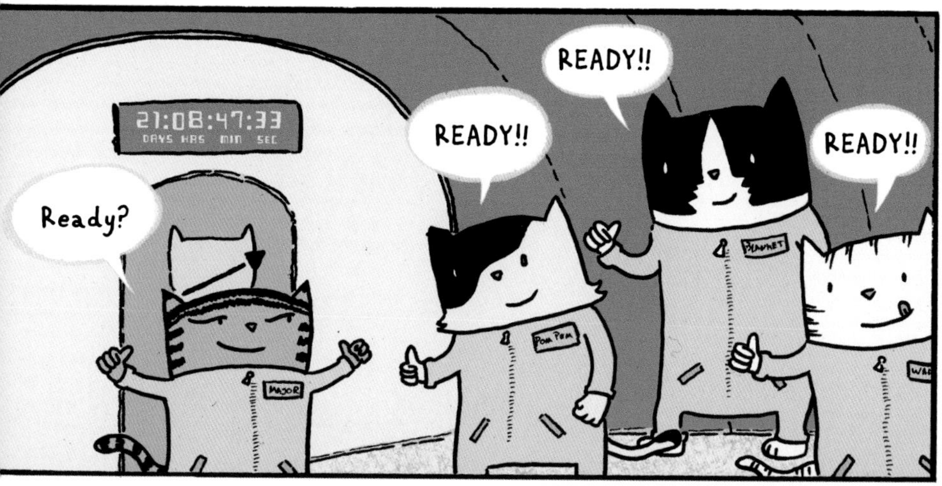
21:08:47:33
DAYS HRS MIN SEC
Ready?
READY!!
READY!!
READY!!
MAJOR
POM POM

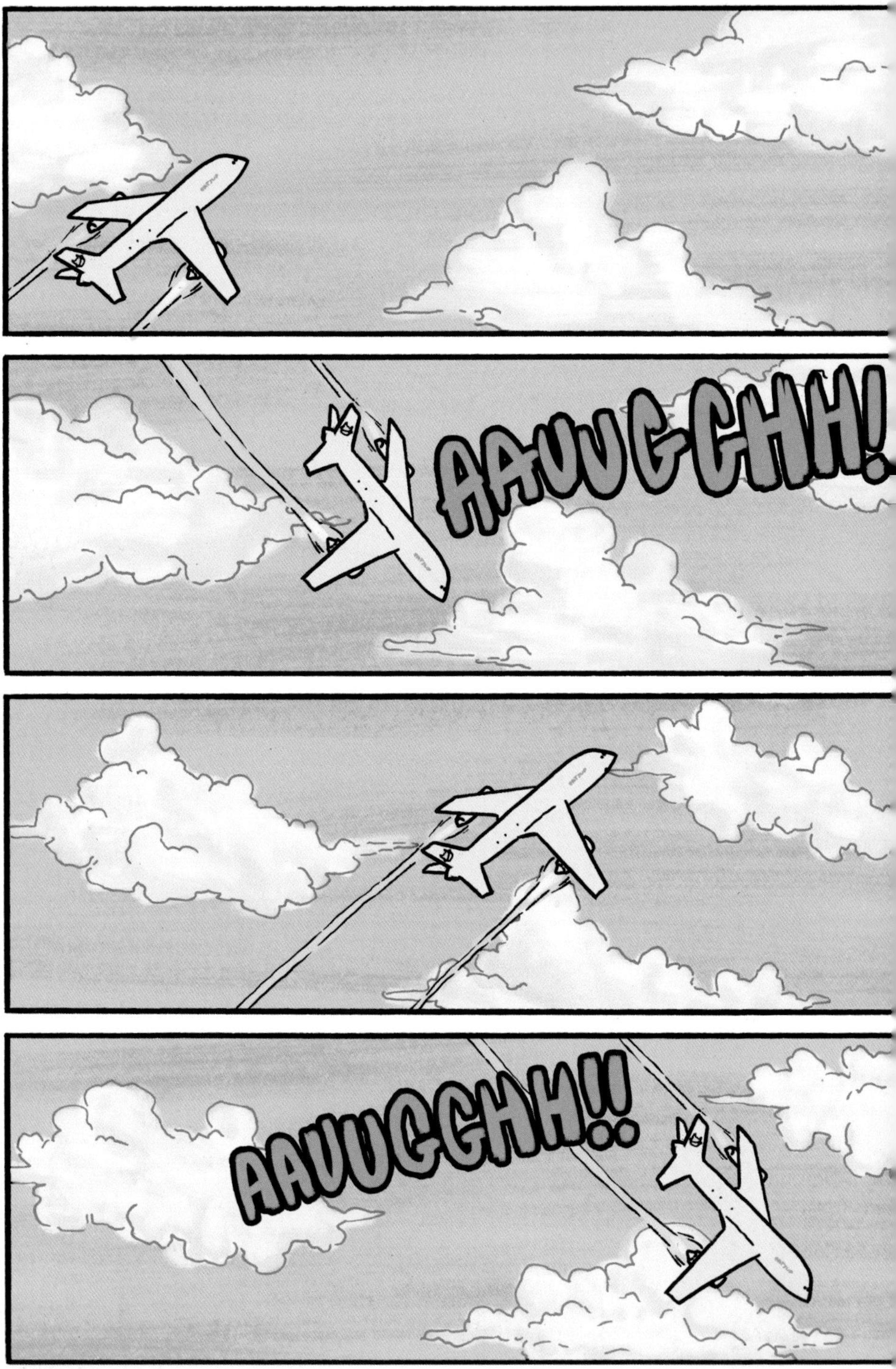
AAUUGCHH!
AAUUGGHH!!

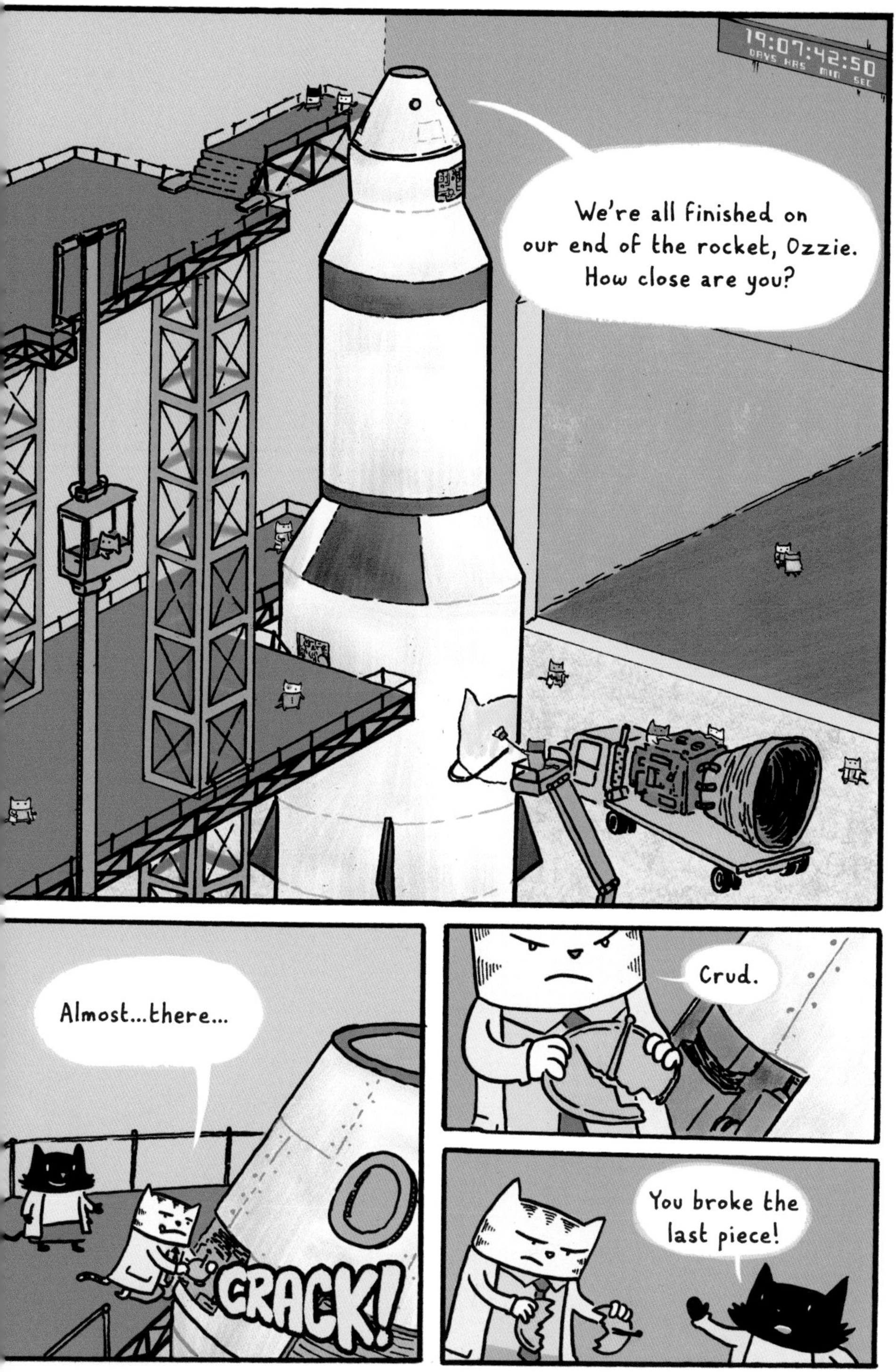
19:07:42:50
DAYS HRS MIN SEC
We're all finished on our end of the rocket, Ozzie. How close are you?
Almost...there...
CRACK!
Crud.
You broke the last piece!

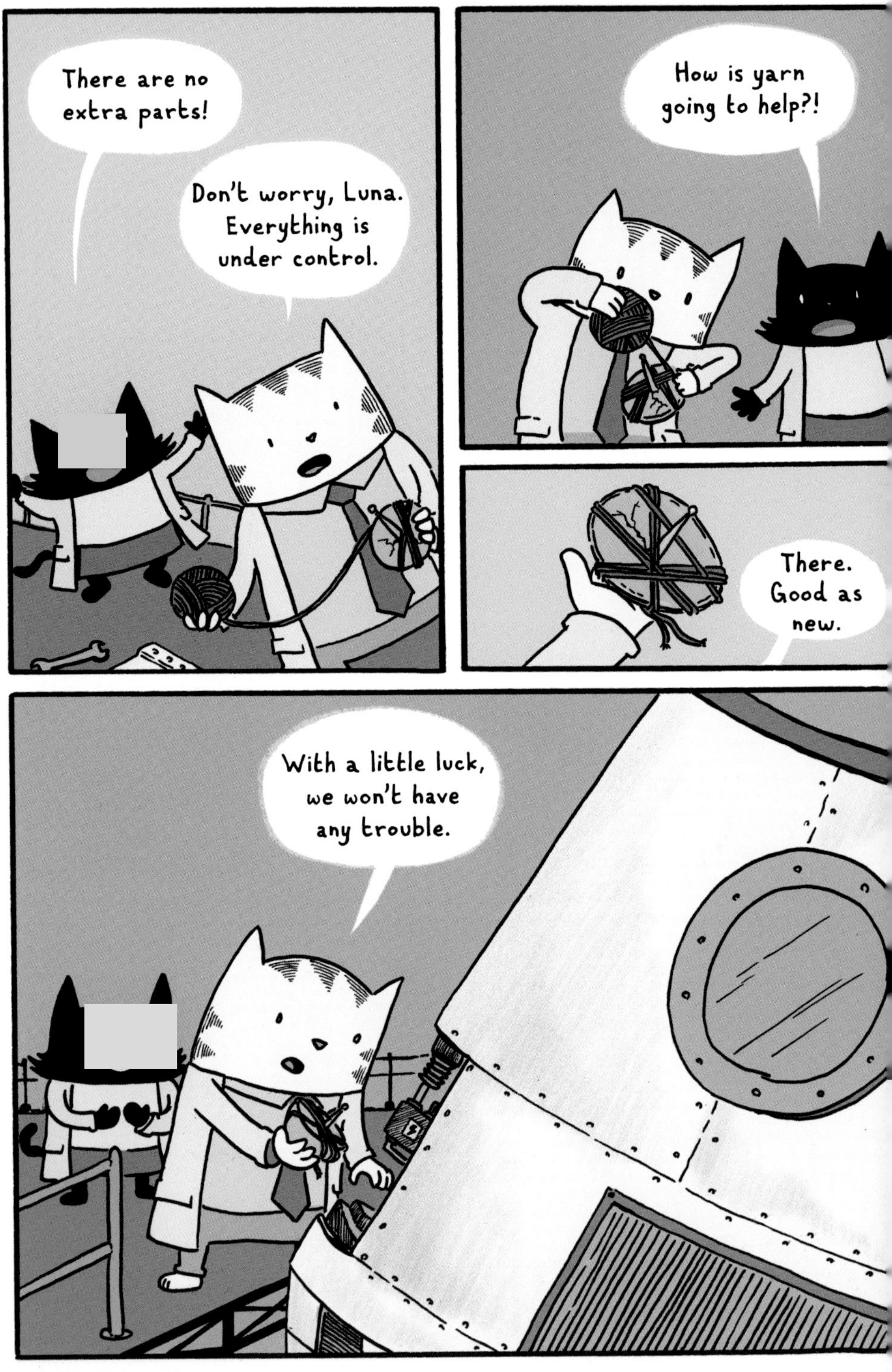
There are no extra parts!
Don't worry, Luna. Everything is under control.
How is yarn going to help?!
There. Good as new.
With a little luck, we won't have any trouble.

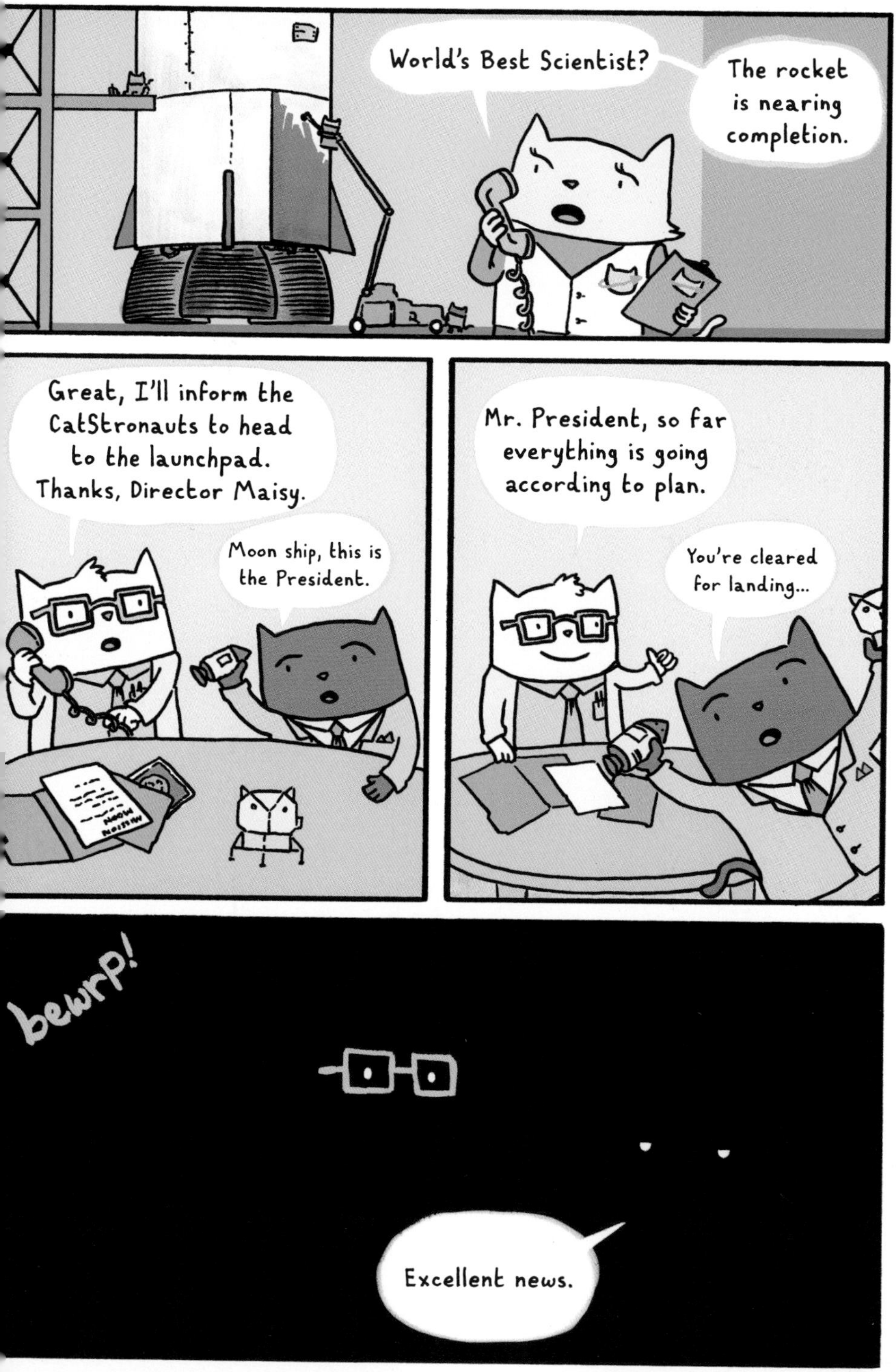
World's Best Scientist?
The rocket is nearing completion.
Great, I'll inform the CatStronauts to head to the launchpad. Thanks, Director Maisy.
Moon ship, this is the President.
Mr. President, so far everything is going according to plan.
You're cleared for landing...
bewrp!
Excellent news.

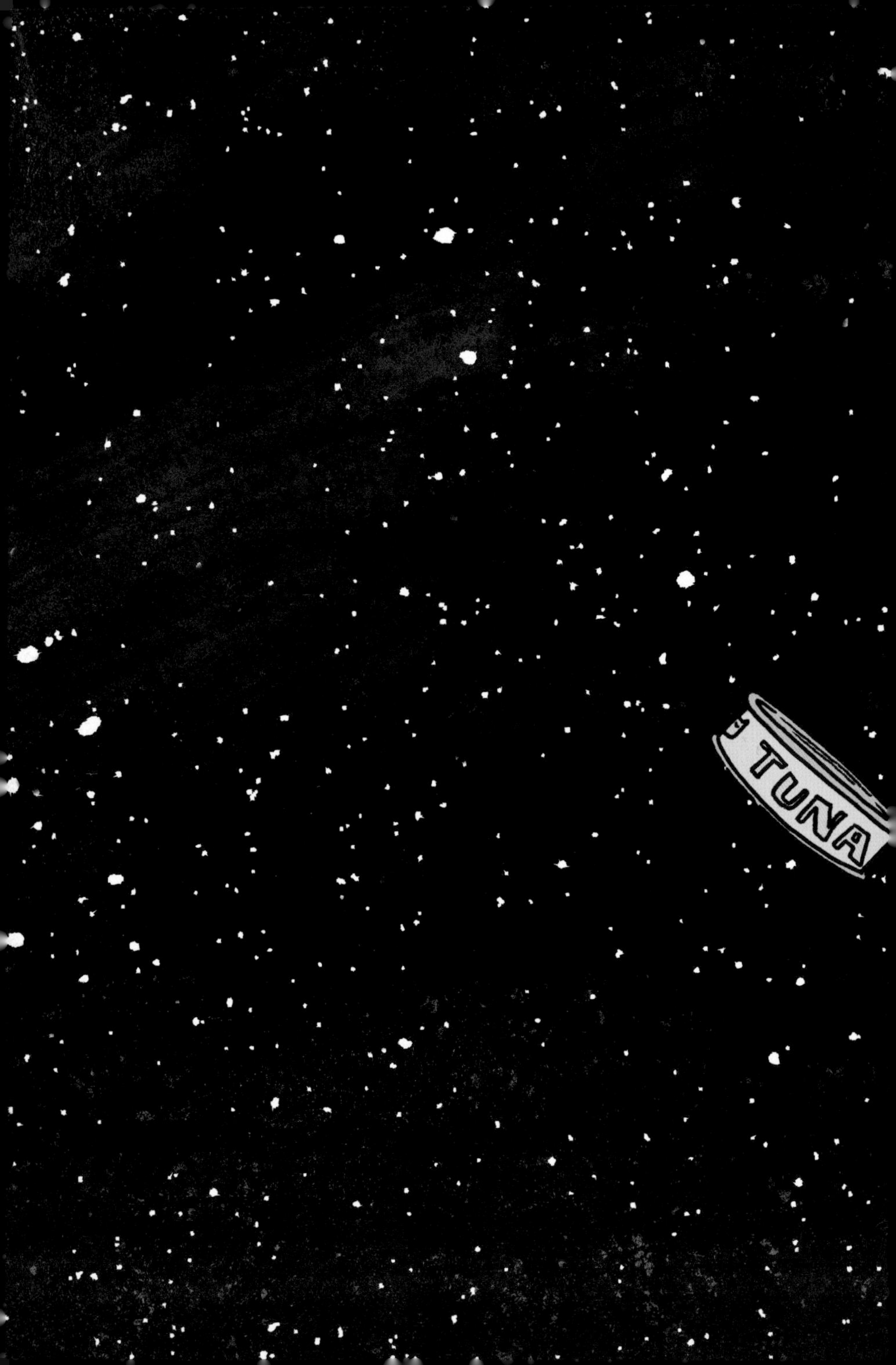
TUNA

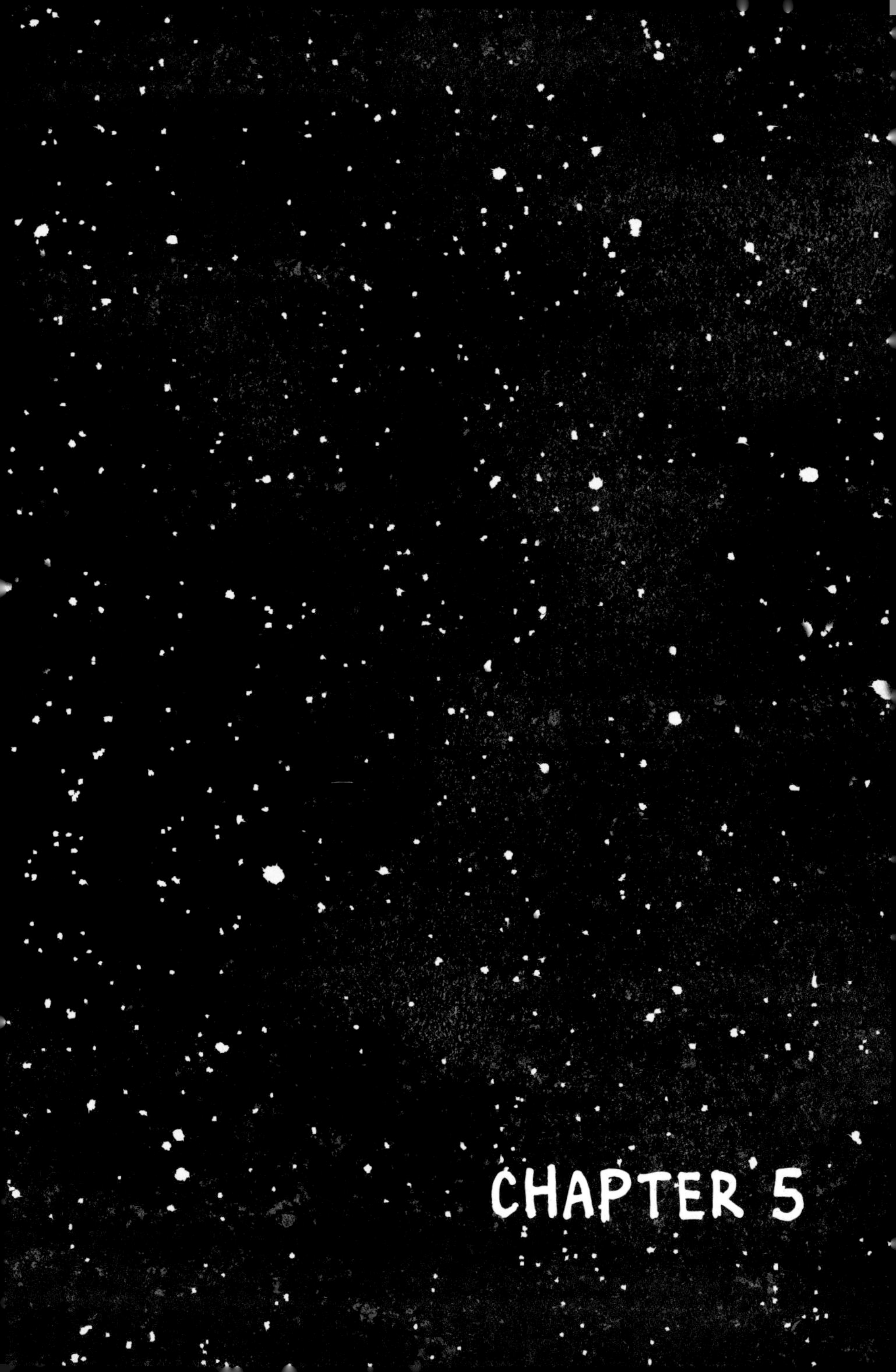

CHAPTER 5

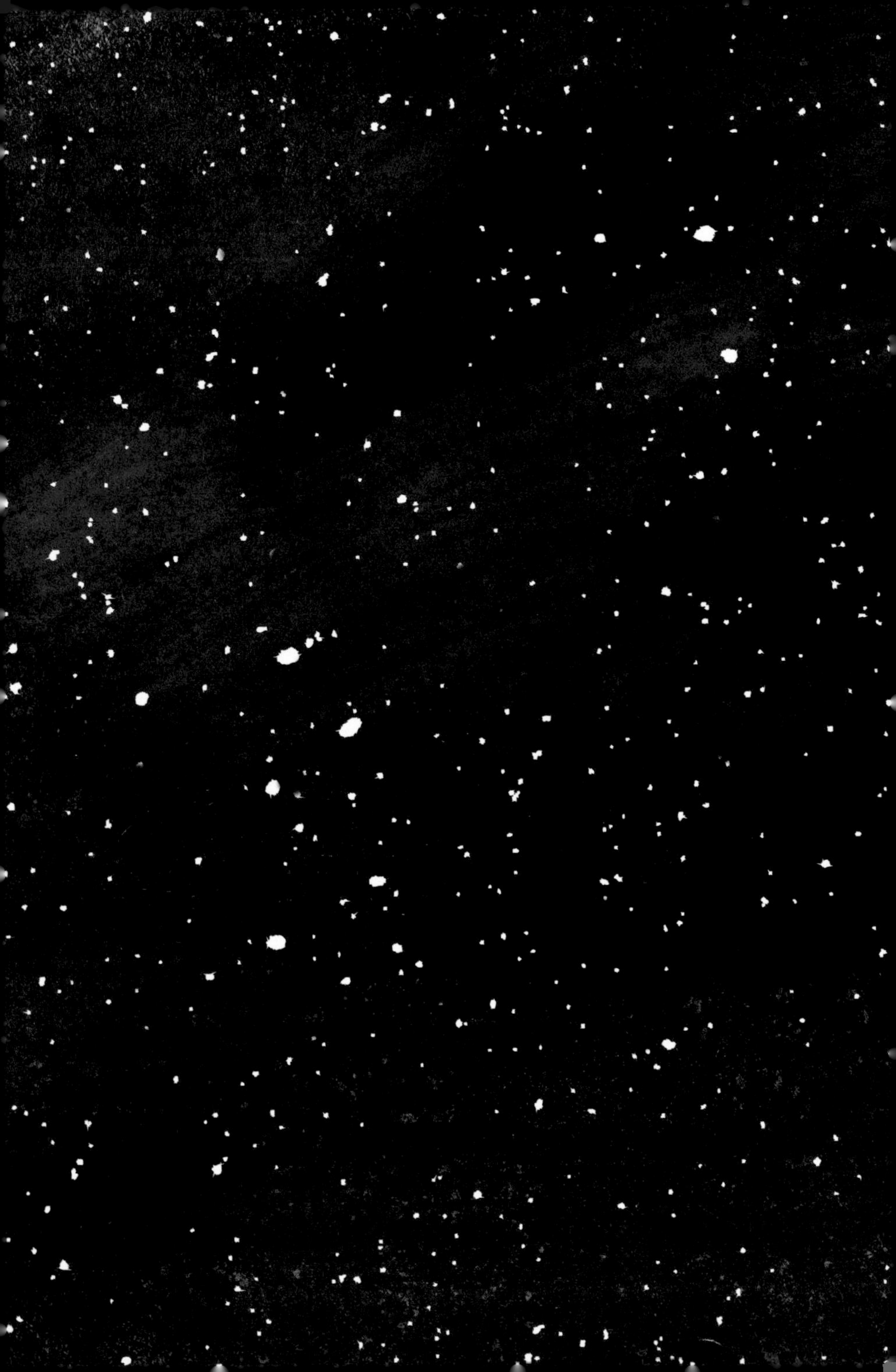

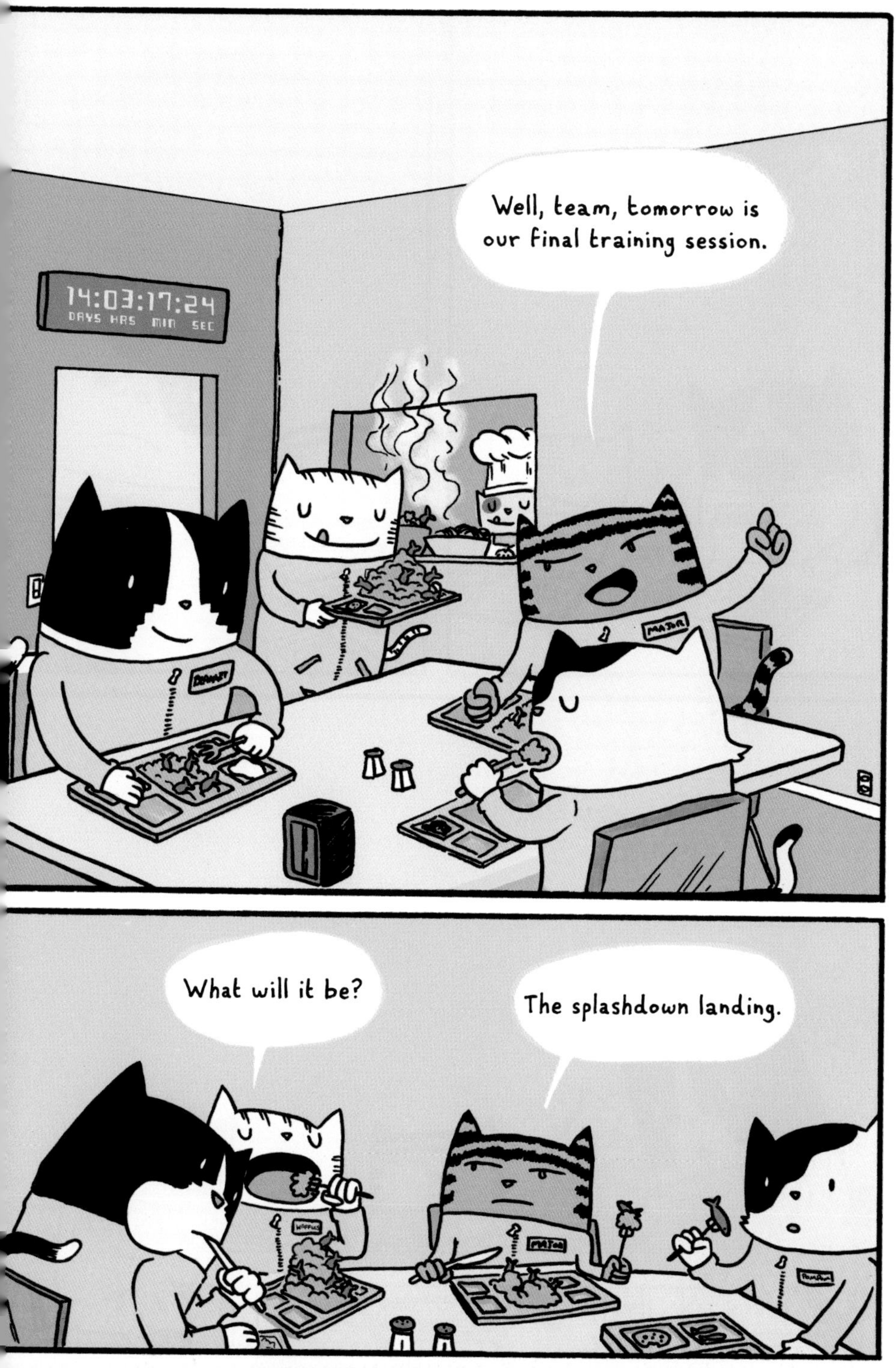
Well, team, tomorrow is our final training session.
14:03:17:24
DAYS HRS MIN SEC
What will it be?
The splashdown landing.

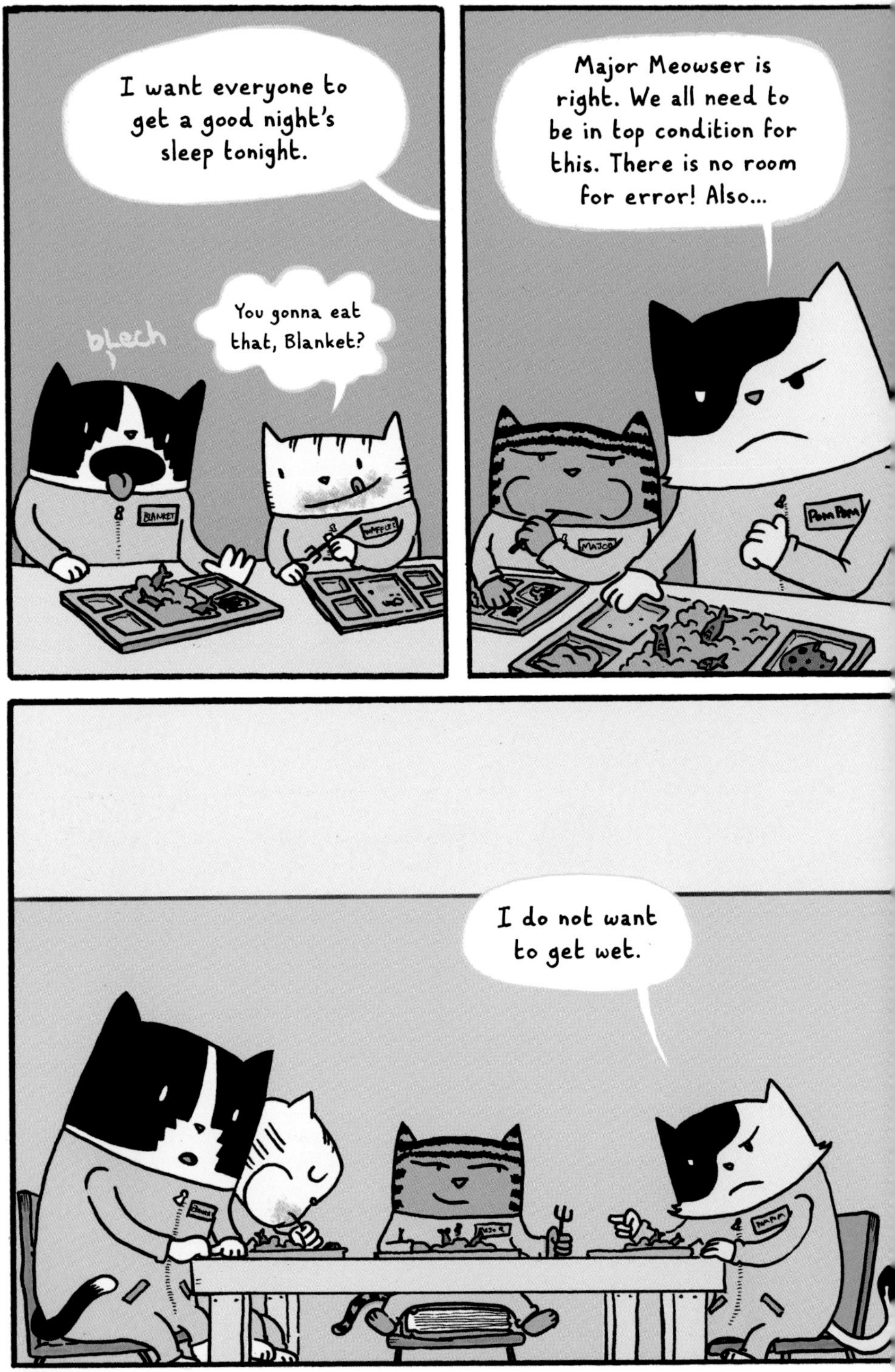
I want everyone to get a good night's sleep tonight.
blech
You gonna eat that, Blanket?
BLANKET
WAFFLES
Major Meowser is right. We all need to be in top condition for this. There is no room for error! Also...
MAJOR
POM POM
I do not want to get wet.

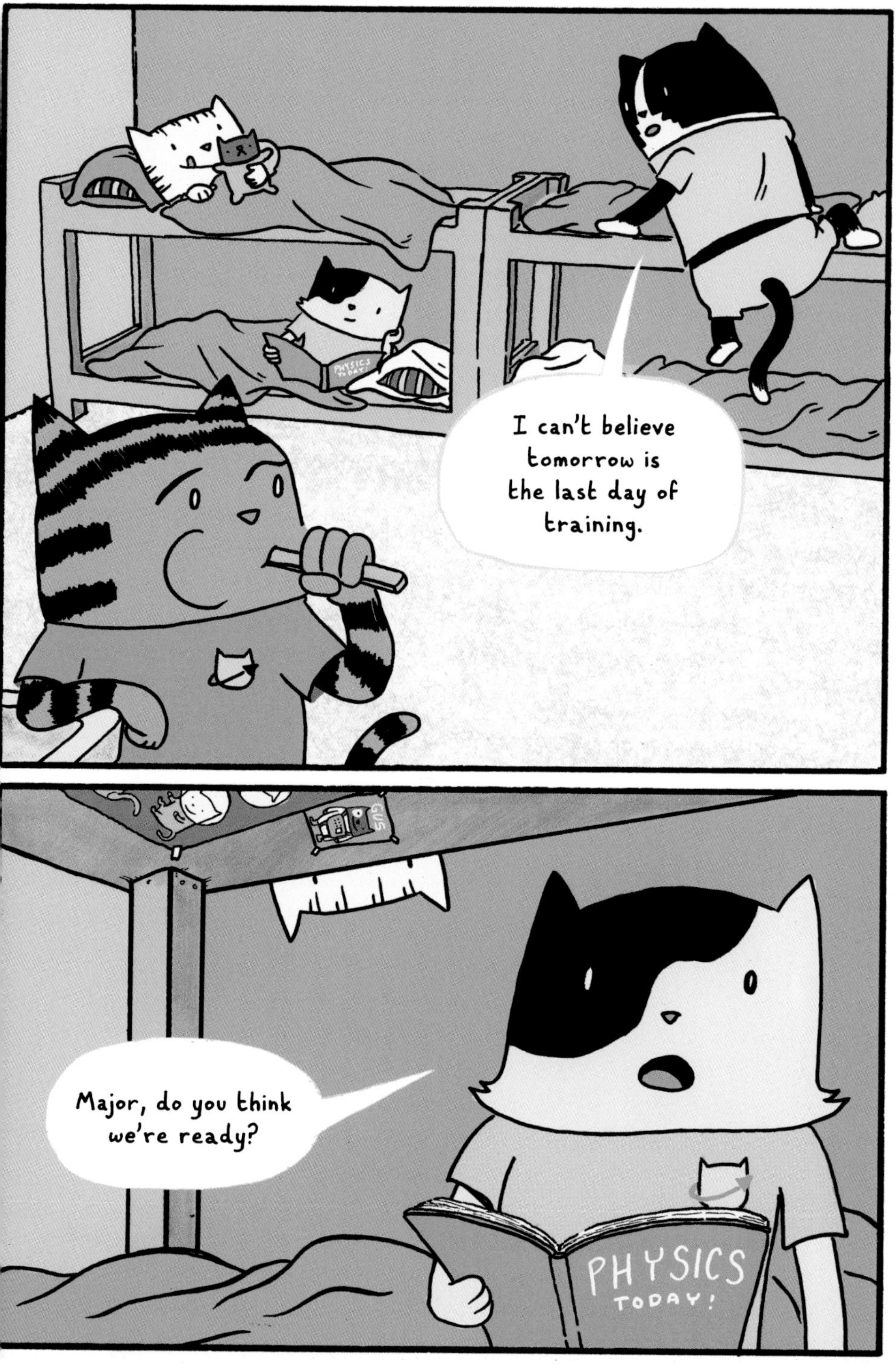
I can't believe tomorrow is the last day of training.
Major, do you think we're ready?
PHYSICS TODAY!

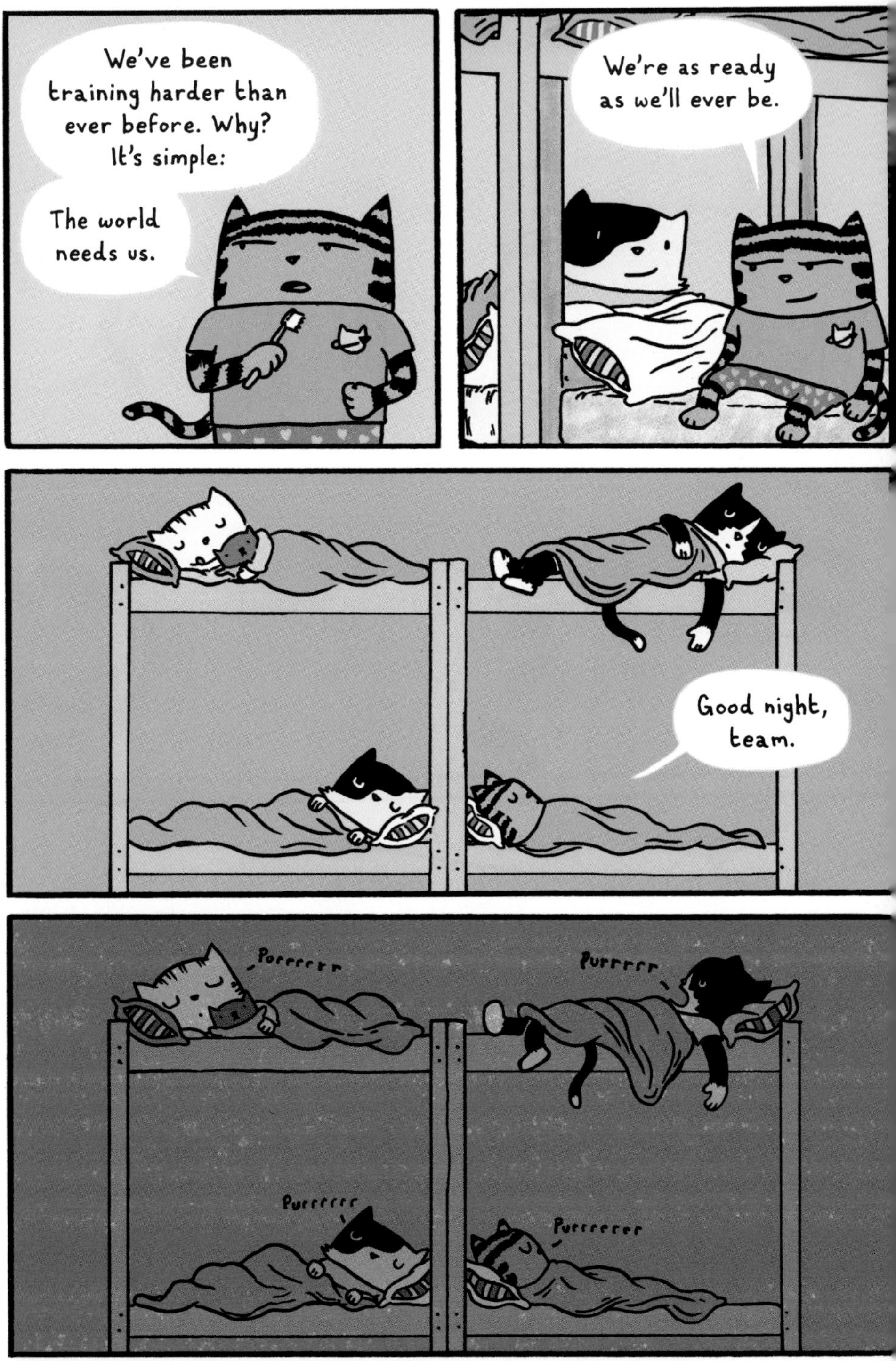
We've been training harder than ever before. Why? It's simple:
The world needs us.
We're as ready as we'll ever be.
Good night, team.
Purrrrrr
Purrrrr
Purrrrrr
Purrrrrrr

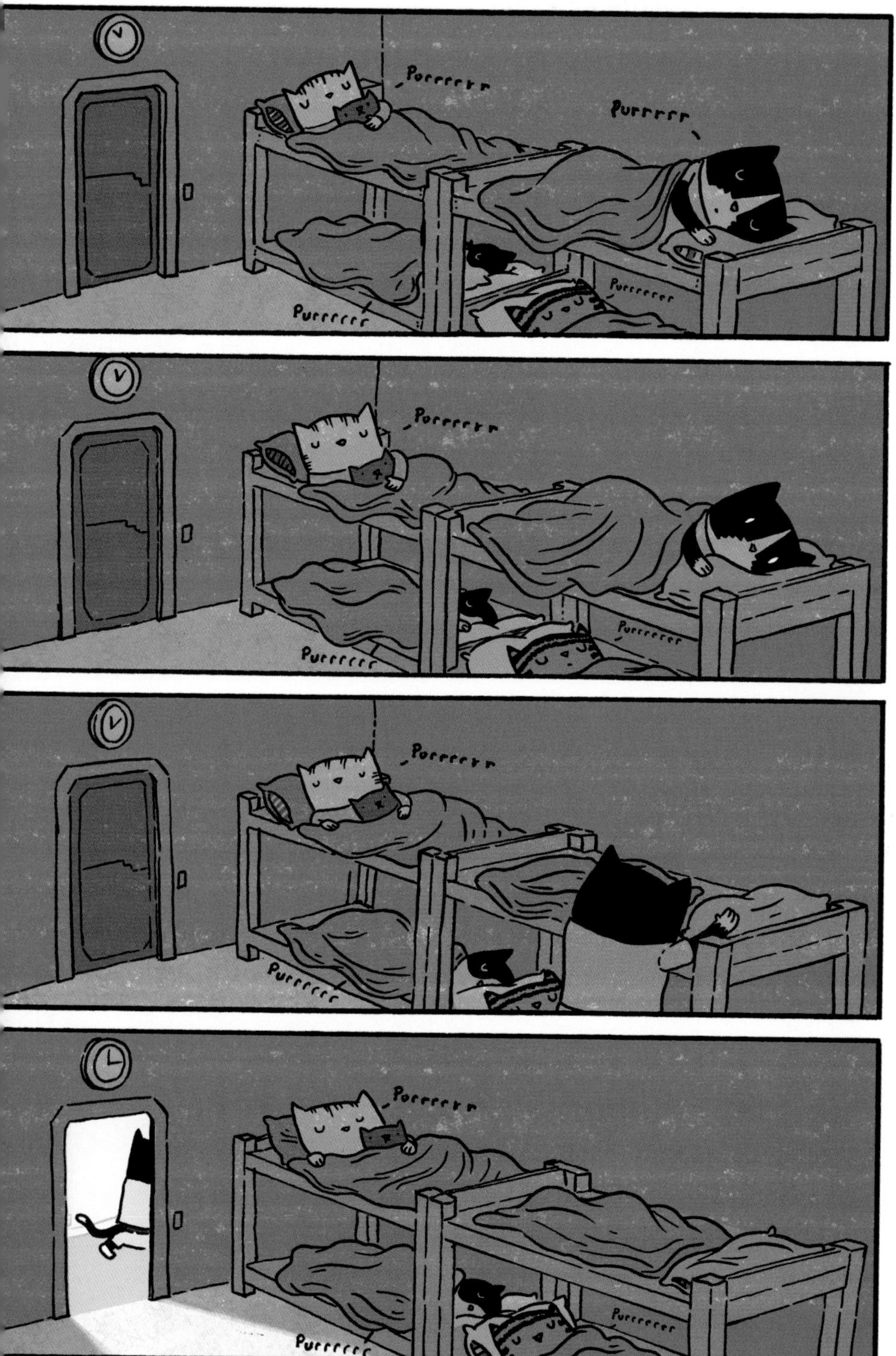
Porrrrrrr
Purrrrrr
Purrrrrrrr
Purrrrrrr
Porrrrrrr
Purrrrrrrr
Purrrrrrr
Porrrrrrr
Purrrrrrr
Porrrrrrr
Purrrrrrrr
Purrrrrrr

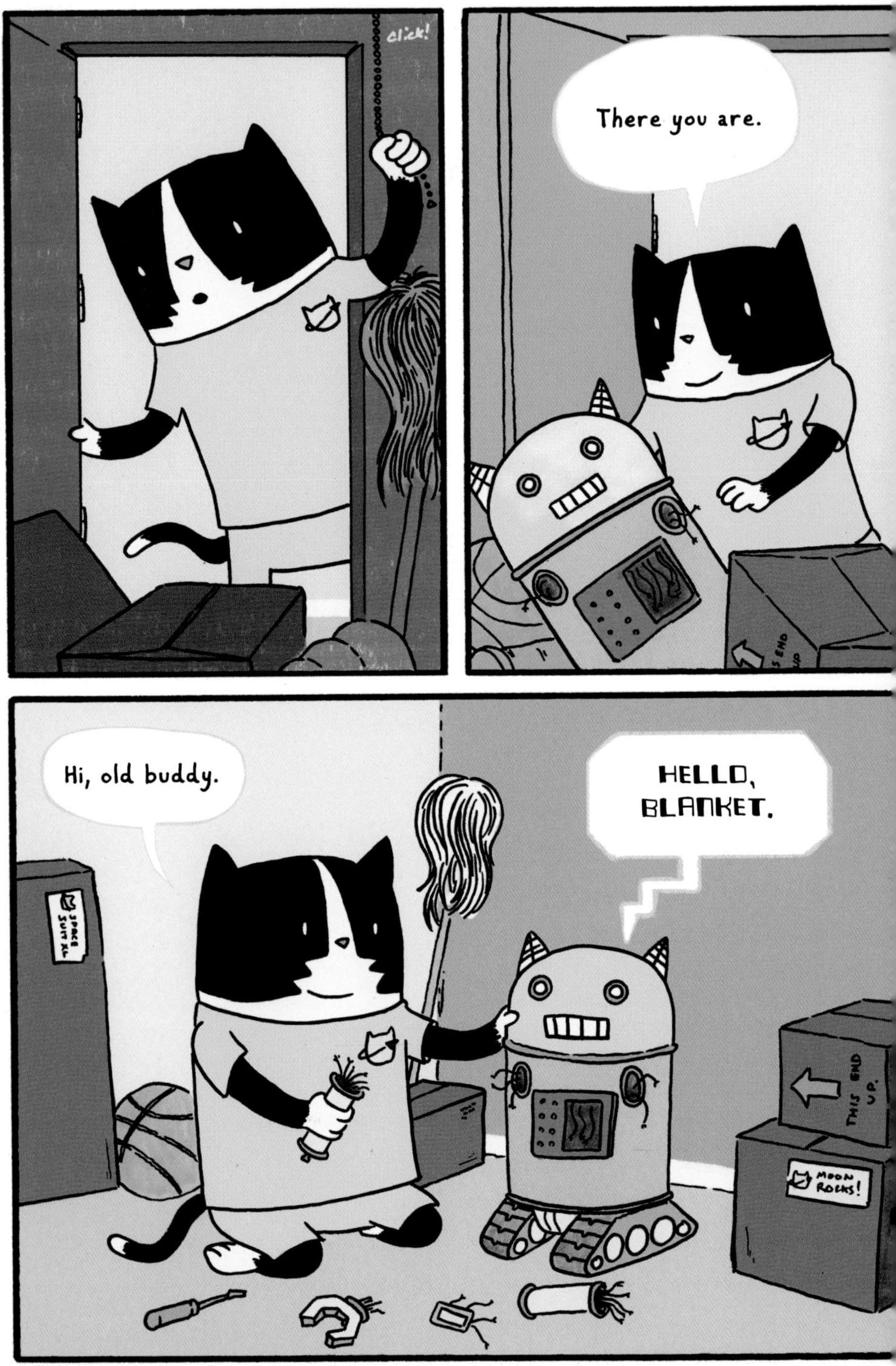
click!
There you are.
Hi, old buddy.
HELLO, BLANKET.
SPACE SUIT XL
THIS END UP.
MOON ROCKS!

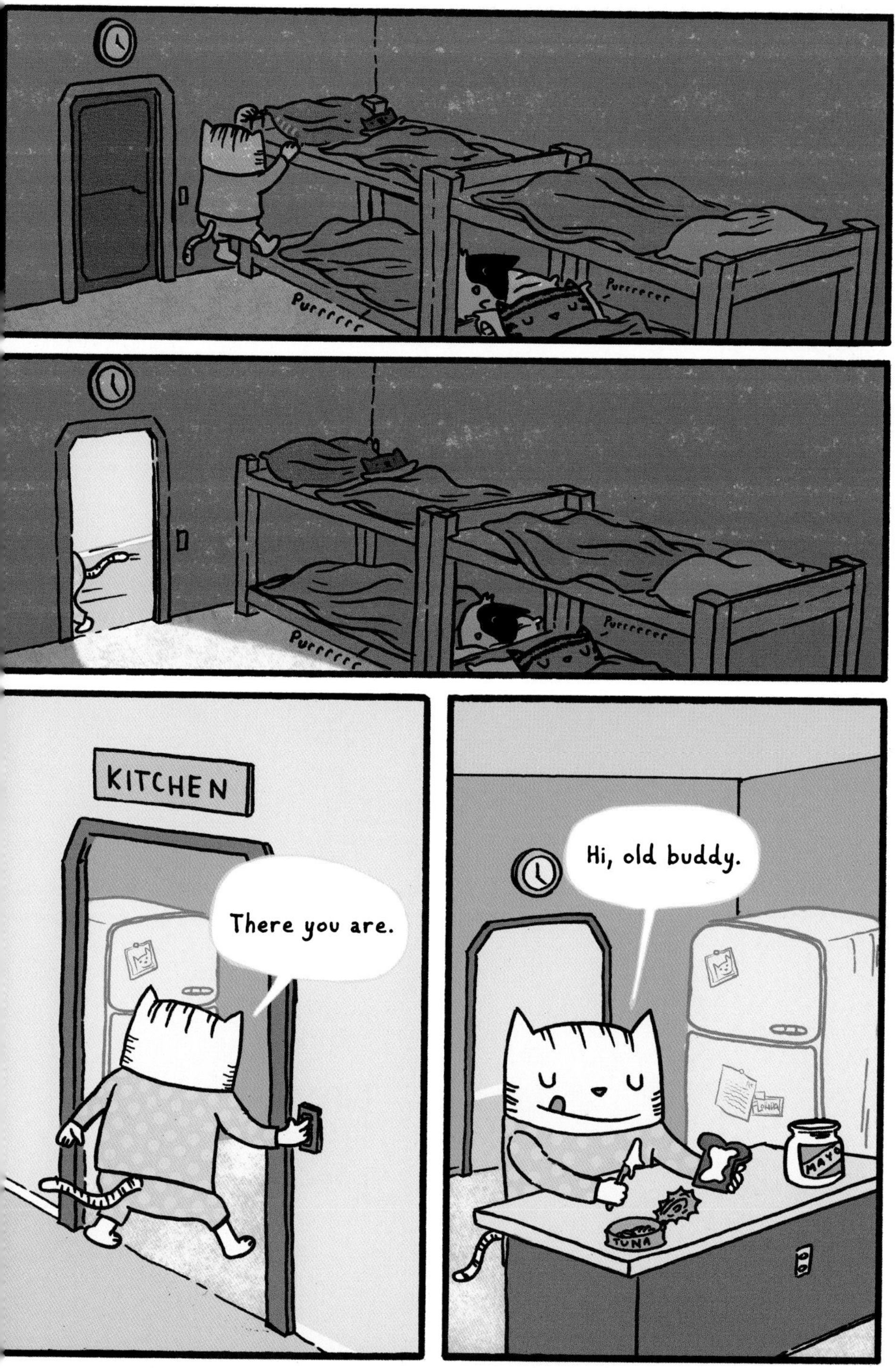

Purrrrrr
Purrrrrr
Purrrrrr
Purrrrrr
KITCHEN
There you are.
Hi, old buddy.
FLORIDA
MAYO
TUNA

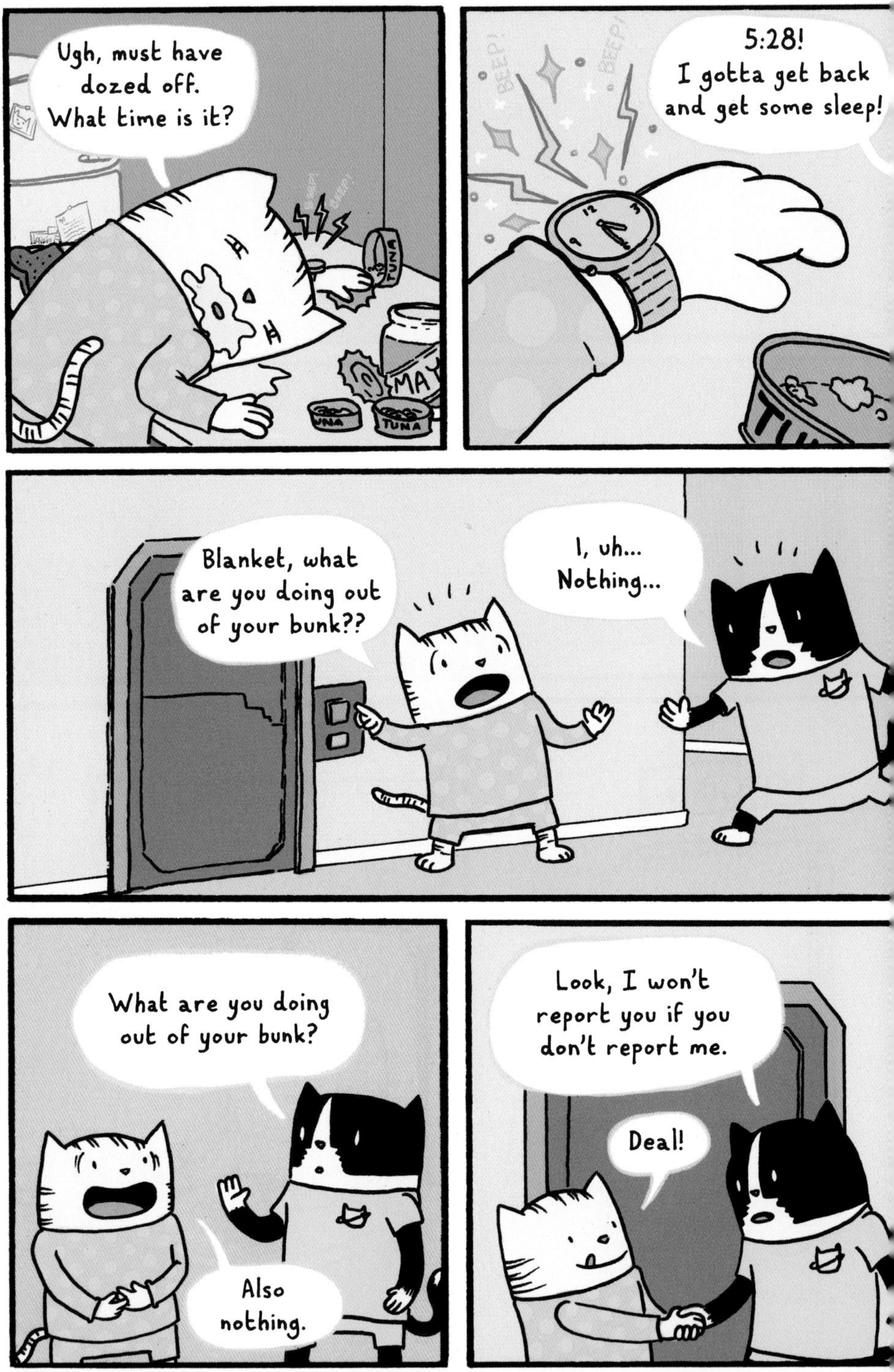
Ugh, must have dozed off. What time is it?
5:28! I gotta get back and get some sleep!
Blanket, what are you doing out of your bunk??
I, uh... Nothing...
What are you doing out of your bunk?
Also nothing.
Look, I won't report you if you don't report me.
Deal!

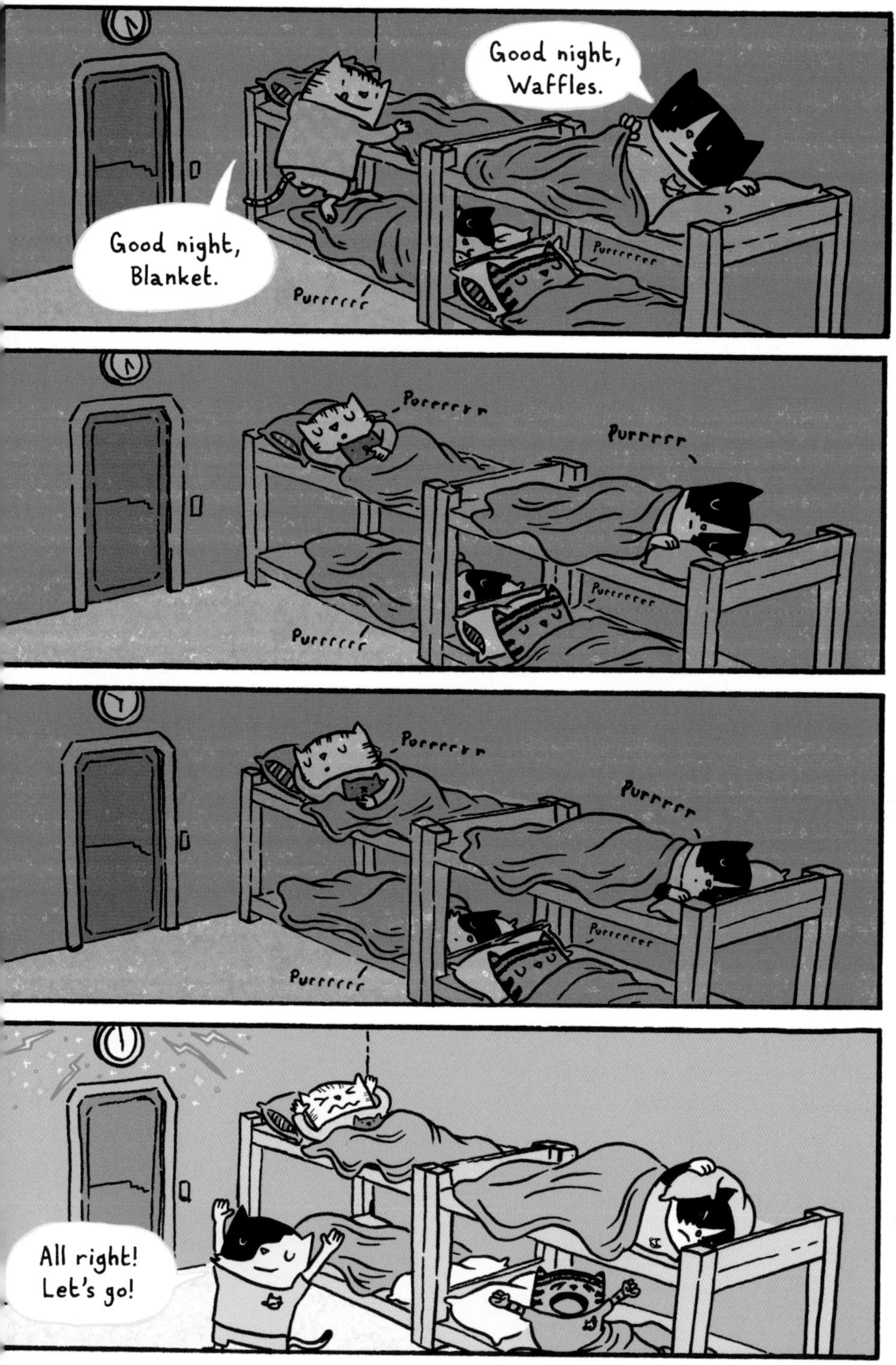
Good night, Waffles.
Good night, Blanket.
Purrrrrr
Purrrrrrr
Purrrrrr
Purrrrr
Purrrrrrr
Purrrrrr
Purrrrrr
Purrrrr
Purrrrrrr
Purrrrrr
All right! Let's go!

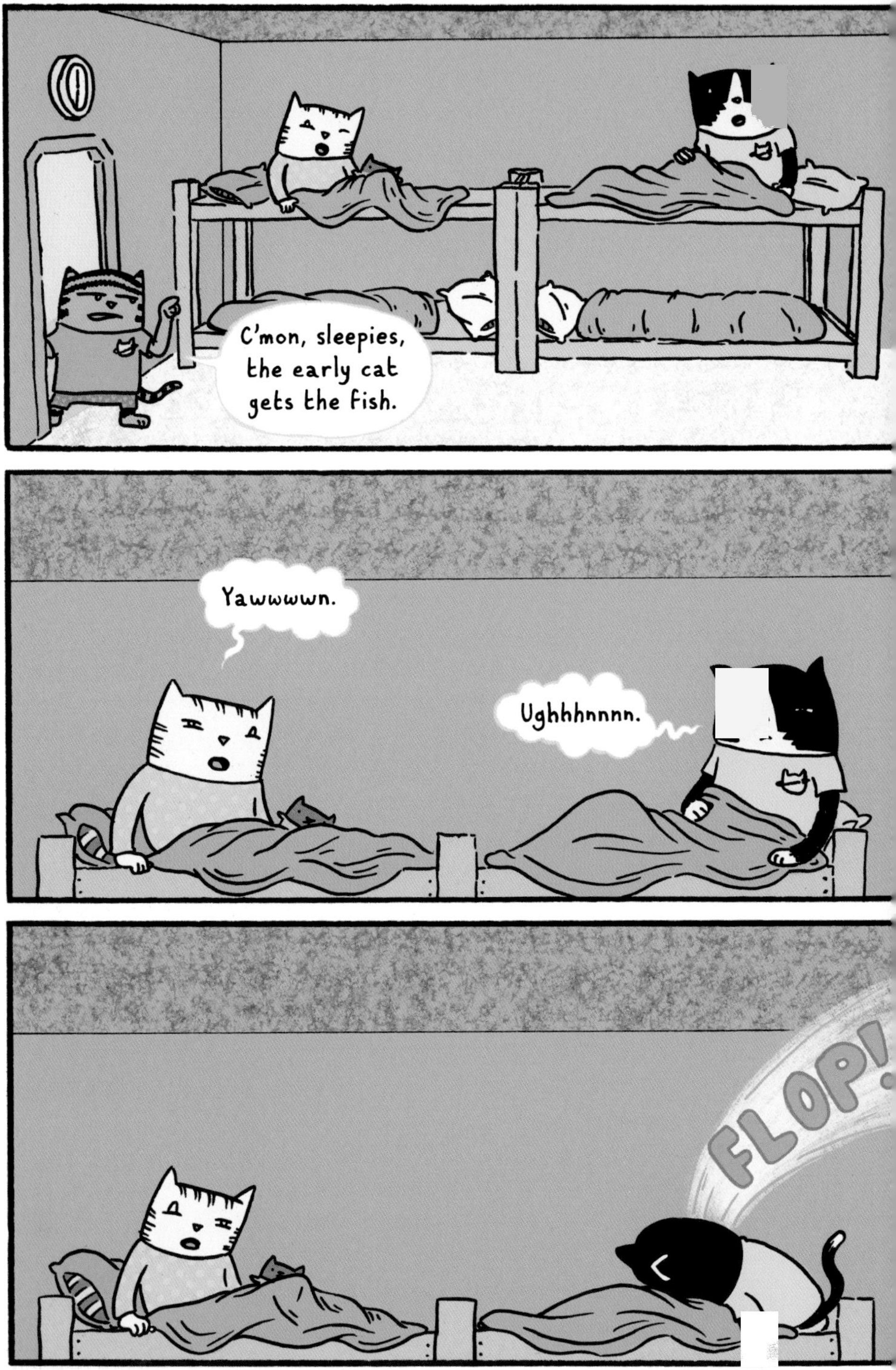
C'mon, sleepies, the early cat gets the fish.
Yawwwwn.
Ughhhnnnn.
FLOP!

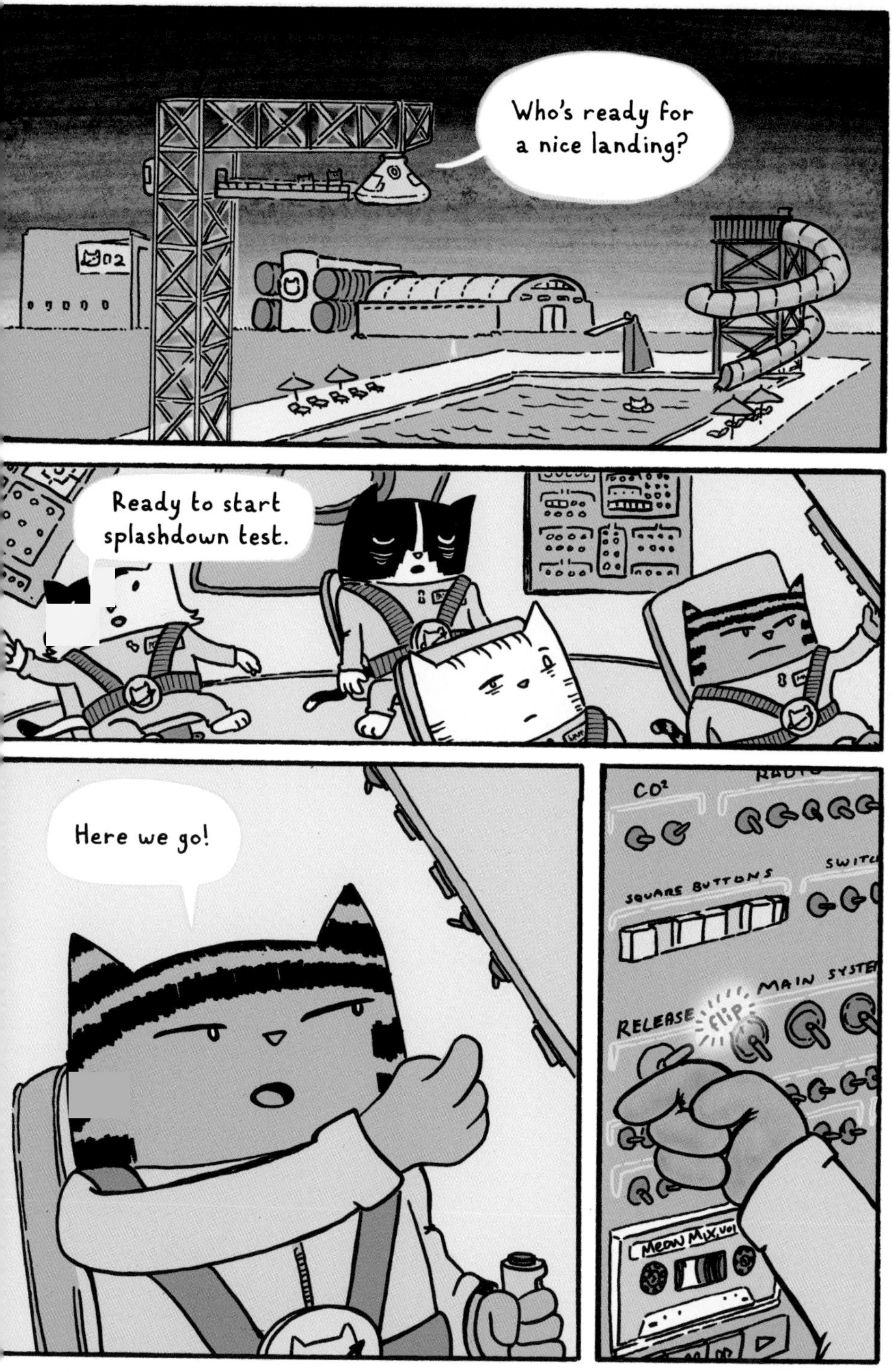
02
Who's ready for a nice landing?
Ready to start splashdown test.
Here we go!
CO²
SQUARE BUTTONS
RELEASE
flip
MAIN
MEOW MIX, VOL

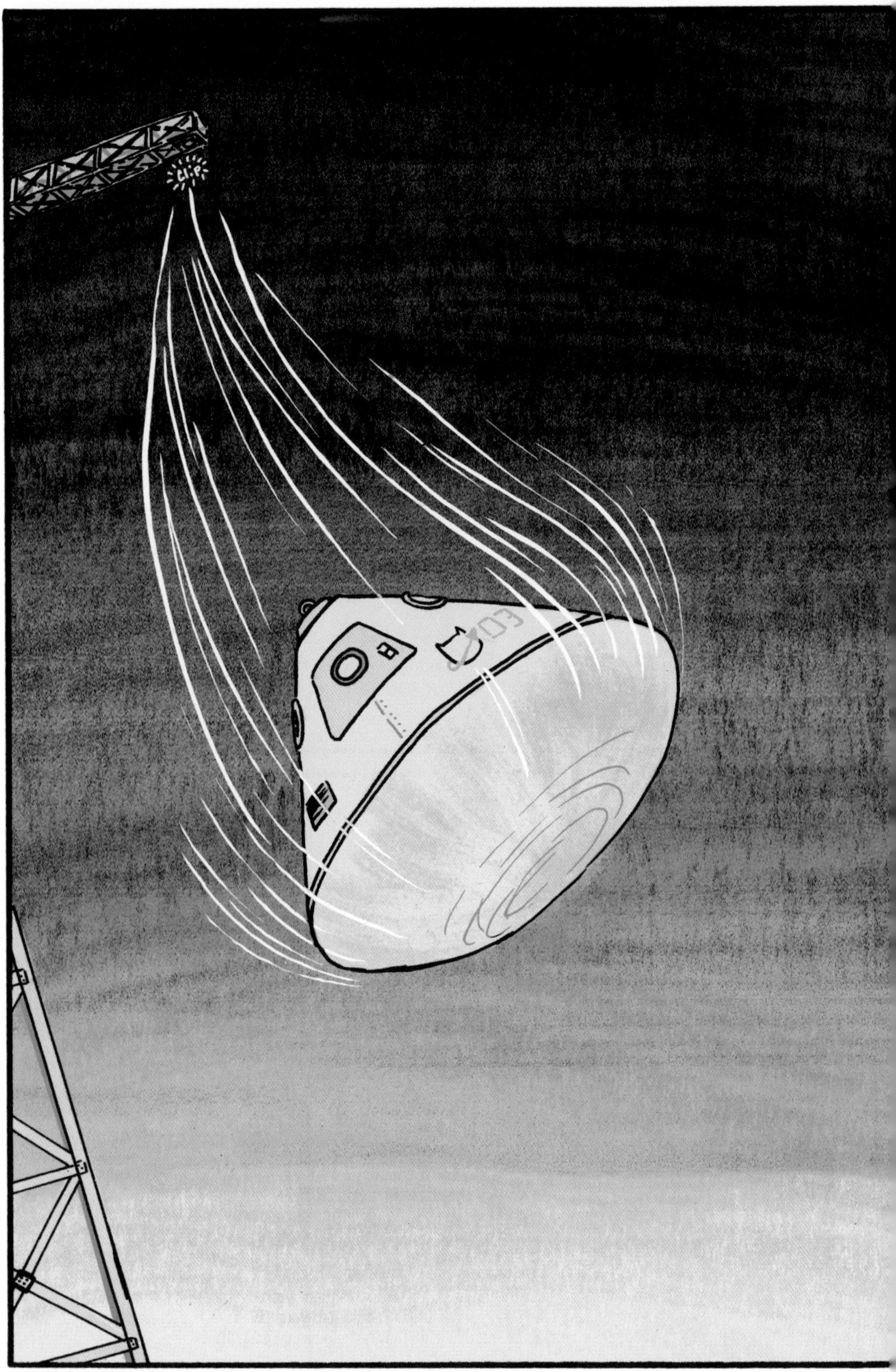
CLiP

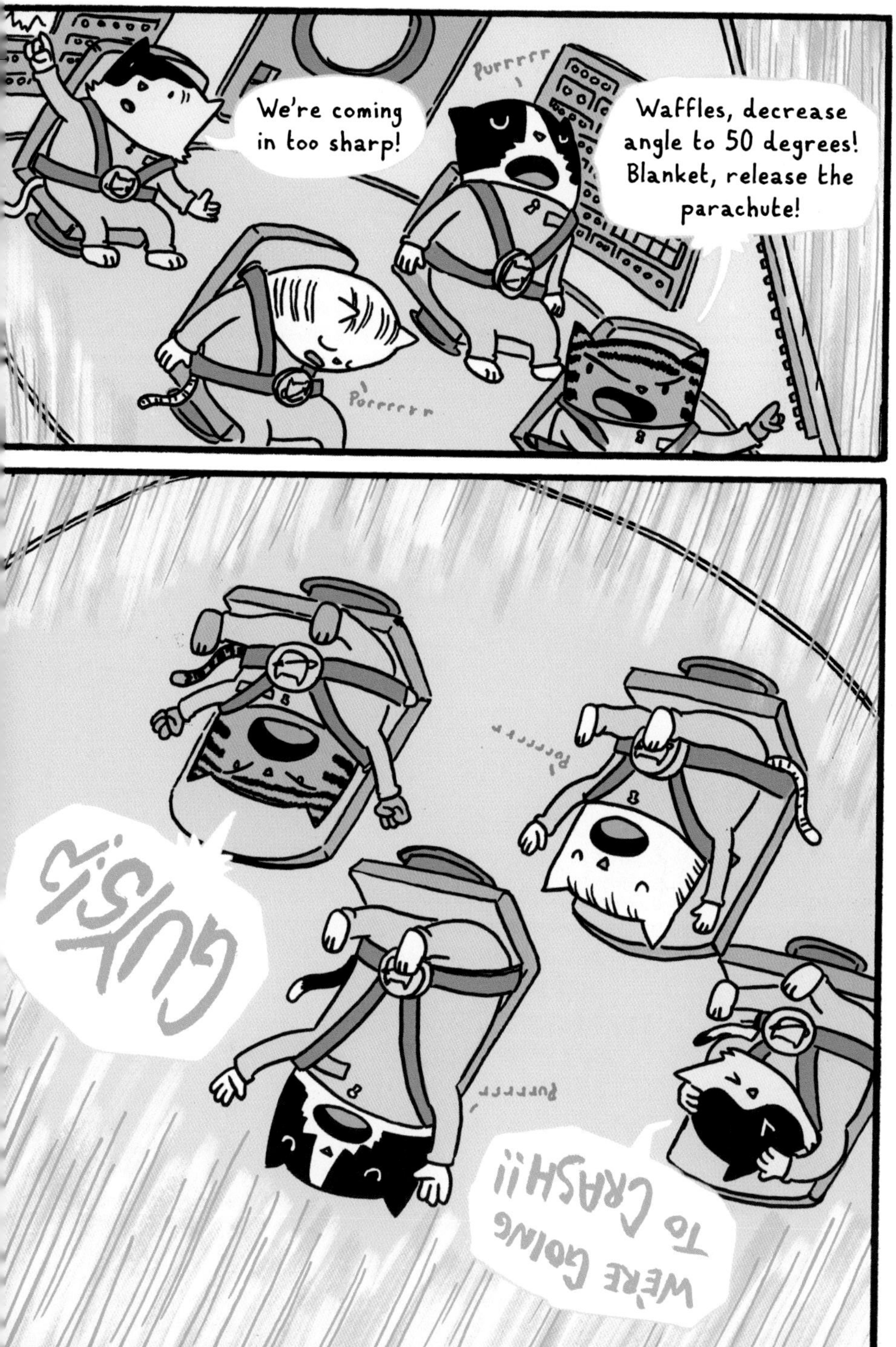
We're coming in too sharp!
Purrrrr
Waffles, decrease angle to 50 degrees! Blanket, release the parachute!
Purrrrrr
GUYS?!
Purrrrrr
Purrrrr
WE'RE GOING TO CRASH!!

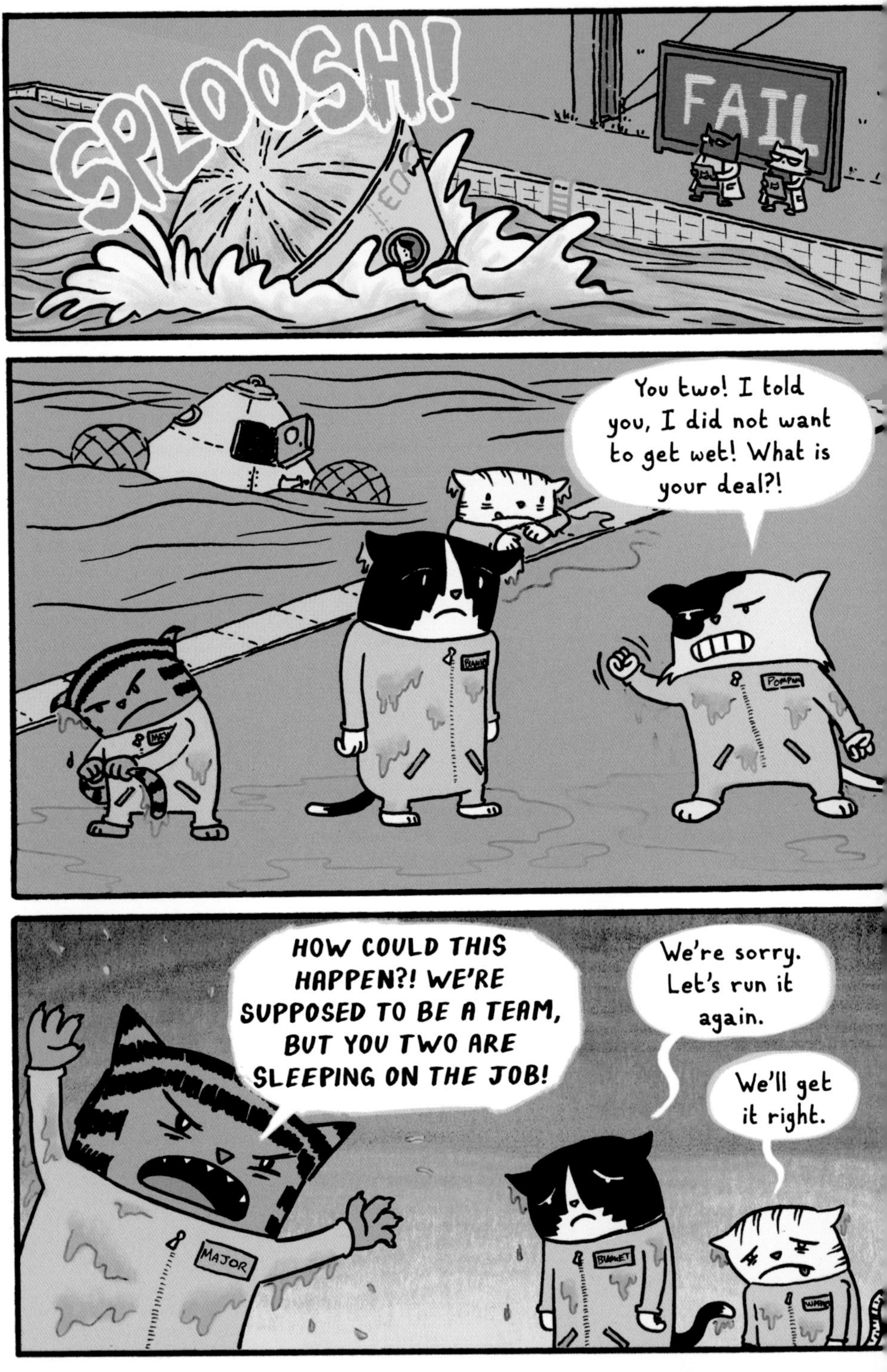
SPLOOSH!
FAIL
You two! I told you, I did not want to get wet! What is your deal?!
HOW COULD THIS HAPPEN?! WE'RE SUPPOSED TO BE A TEAM, BUT YOU TWO ARE SLEEPING ON THE JOB!
MAJOR
We're sorry. Let's run it again.
We'll get it right.

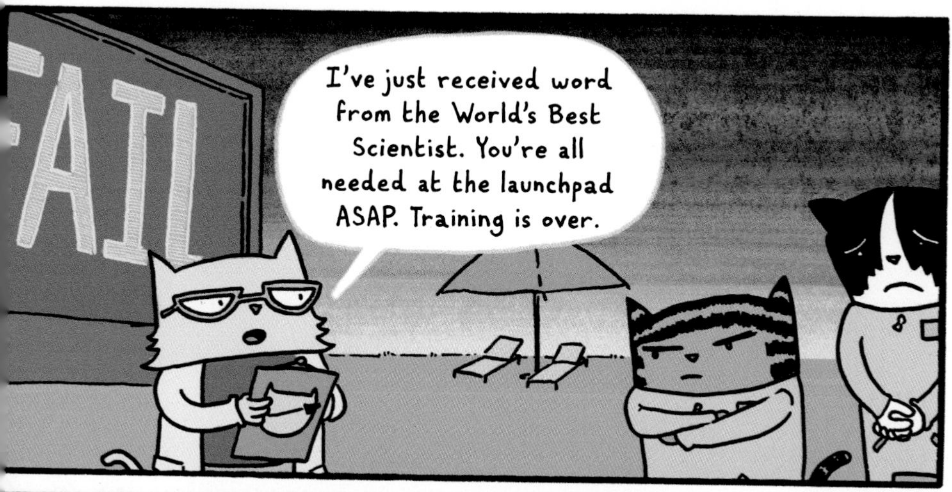
FAIL
I've just received word from the World's Best Scientist. You're all needed at the launchpad ASAP. Training is over.

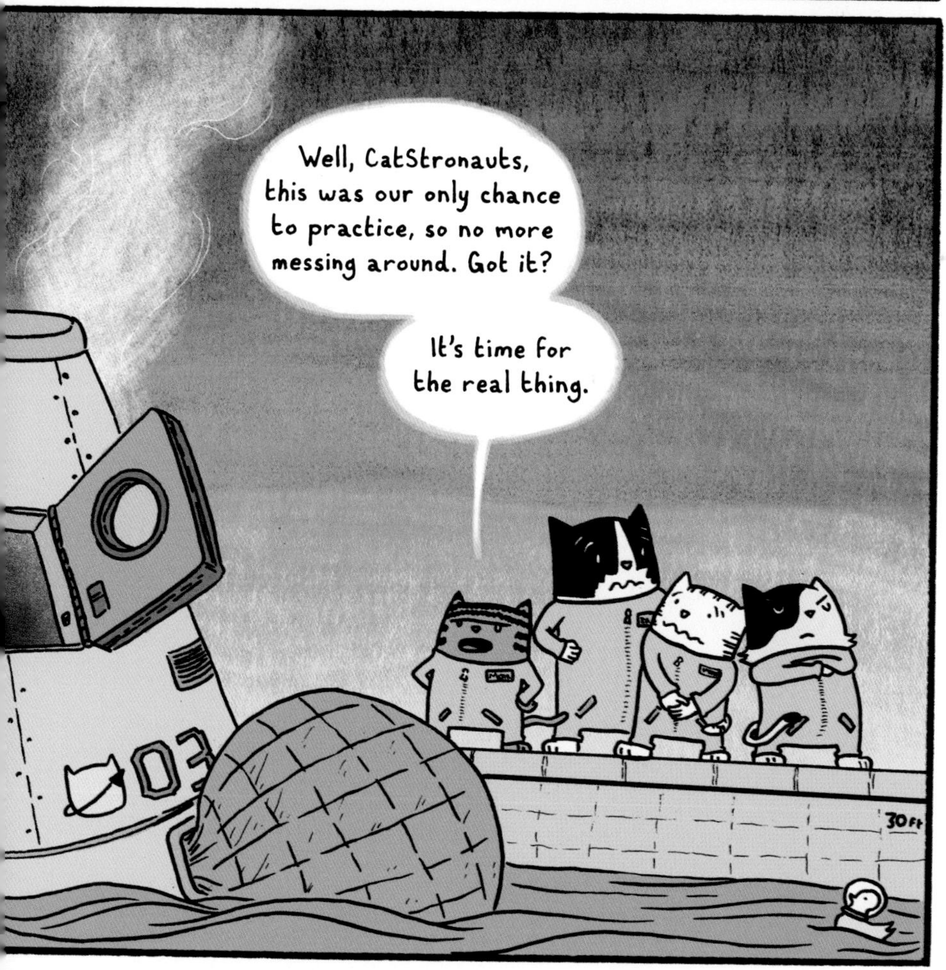
Well, CatStronauts, this was our only chance to practice, so no more messing around. Got it?
It's time for the real thing.
03
30 Ft

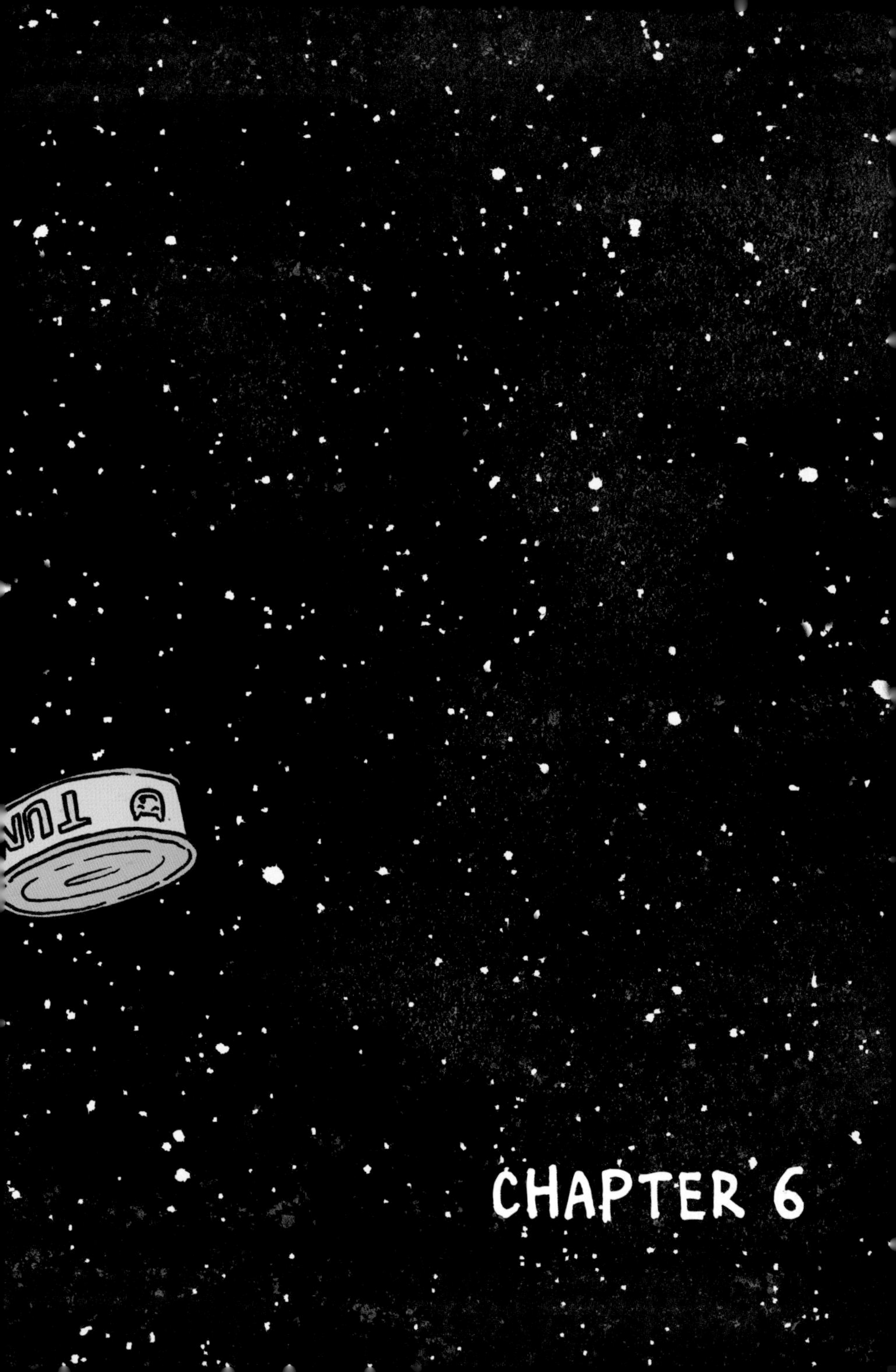

CHAPTER 6

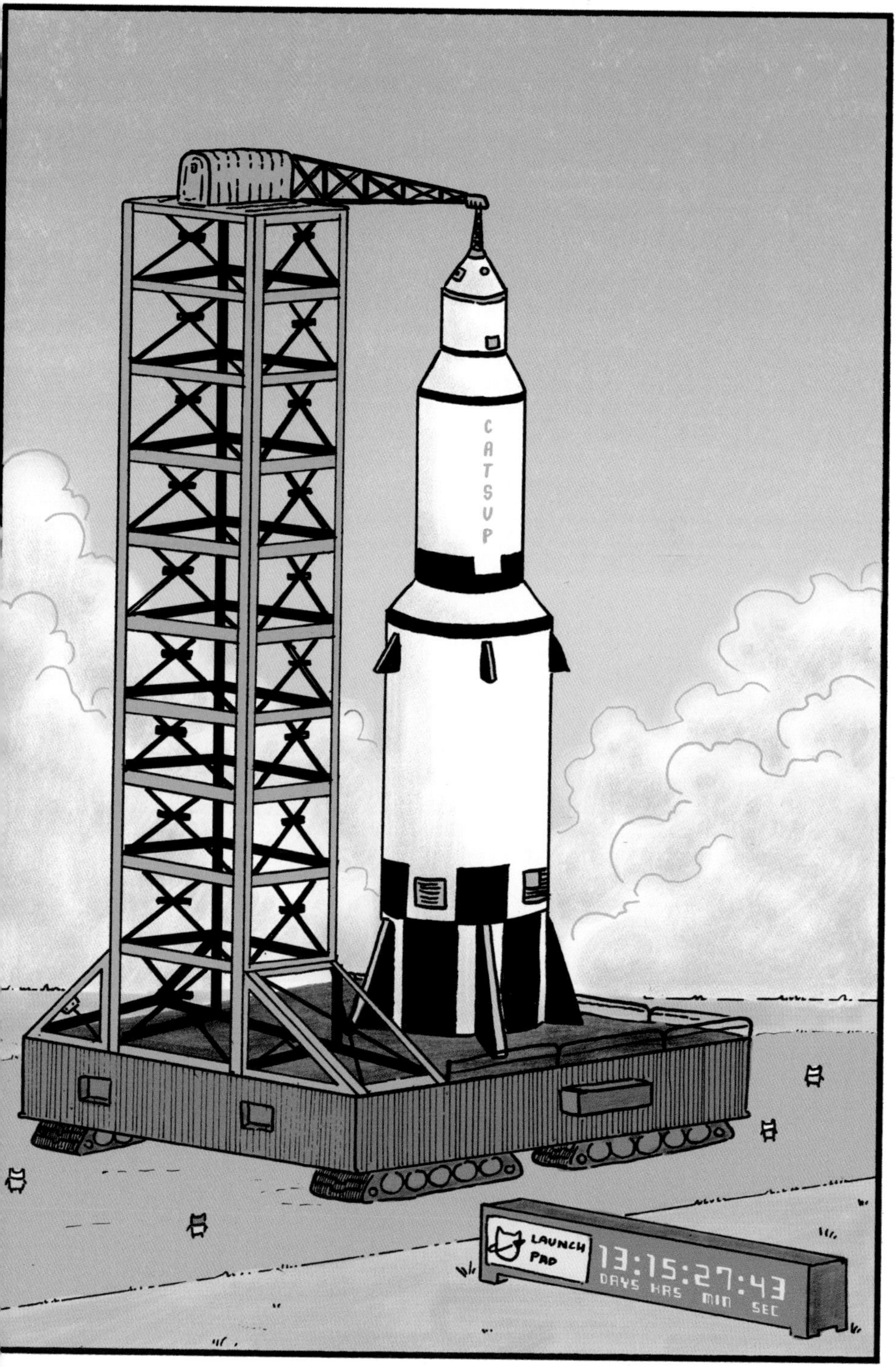
CATSUP
LAUNCH PAD
13:15:27:43
DAYS HRS MIN SEC

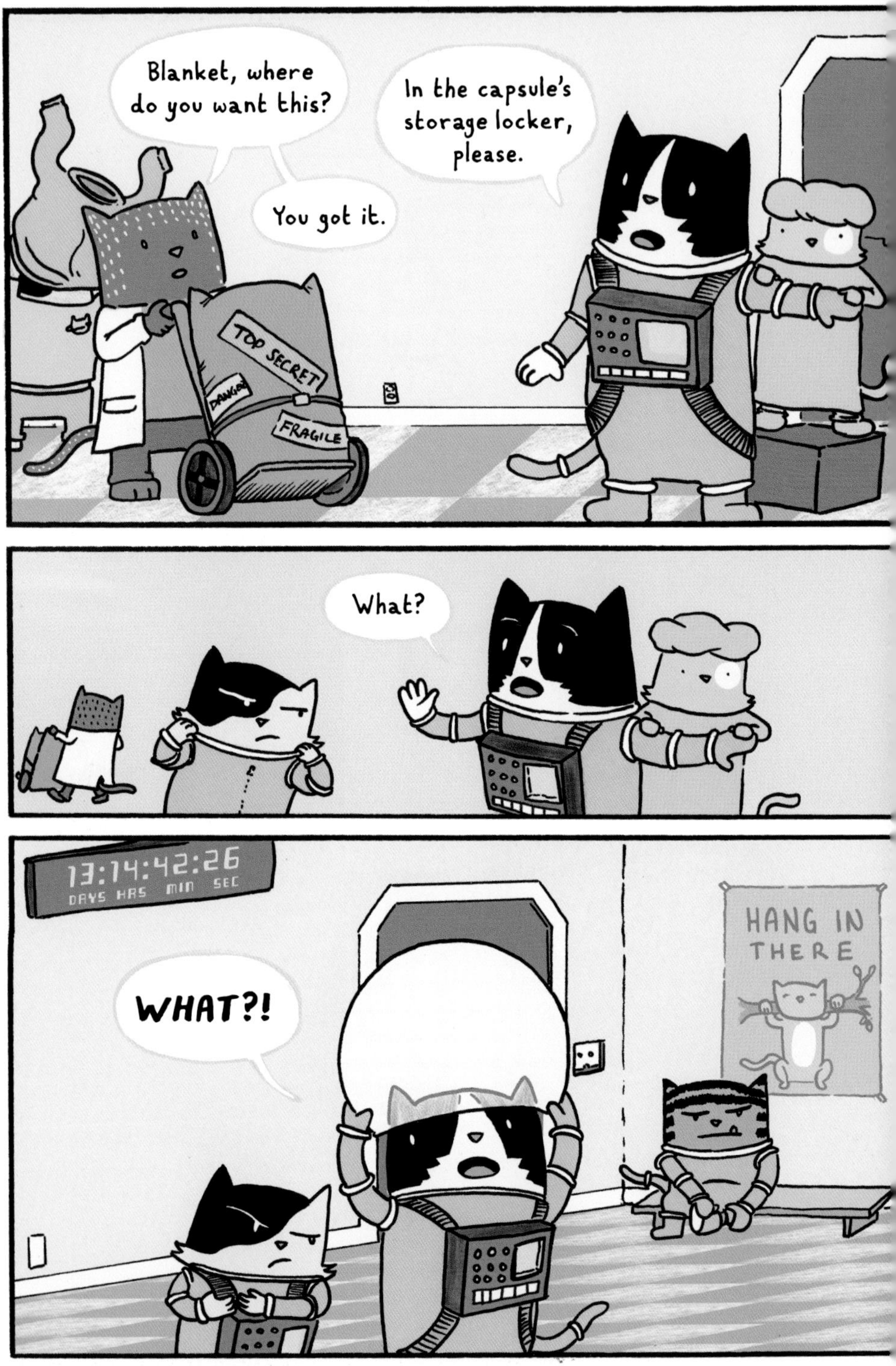
Blanket, where do you want this?
In the capsule's storage locker, please.
You got it.
TOP SECRET
DANGER
FRAGILE
What?
13:14:42:26
DAYS HRS MIN SEC
HANG IN THERE
WHAT?!

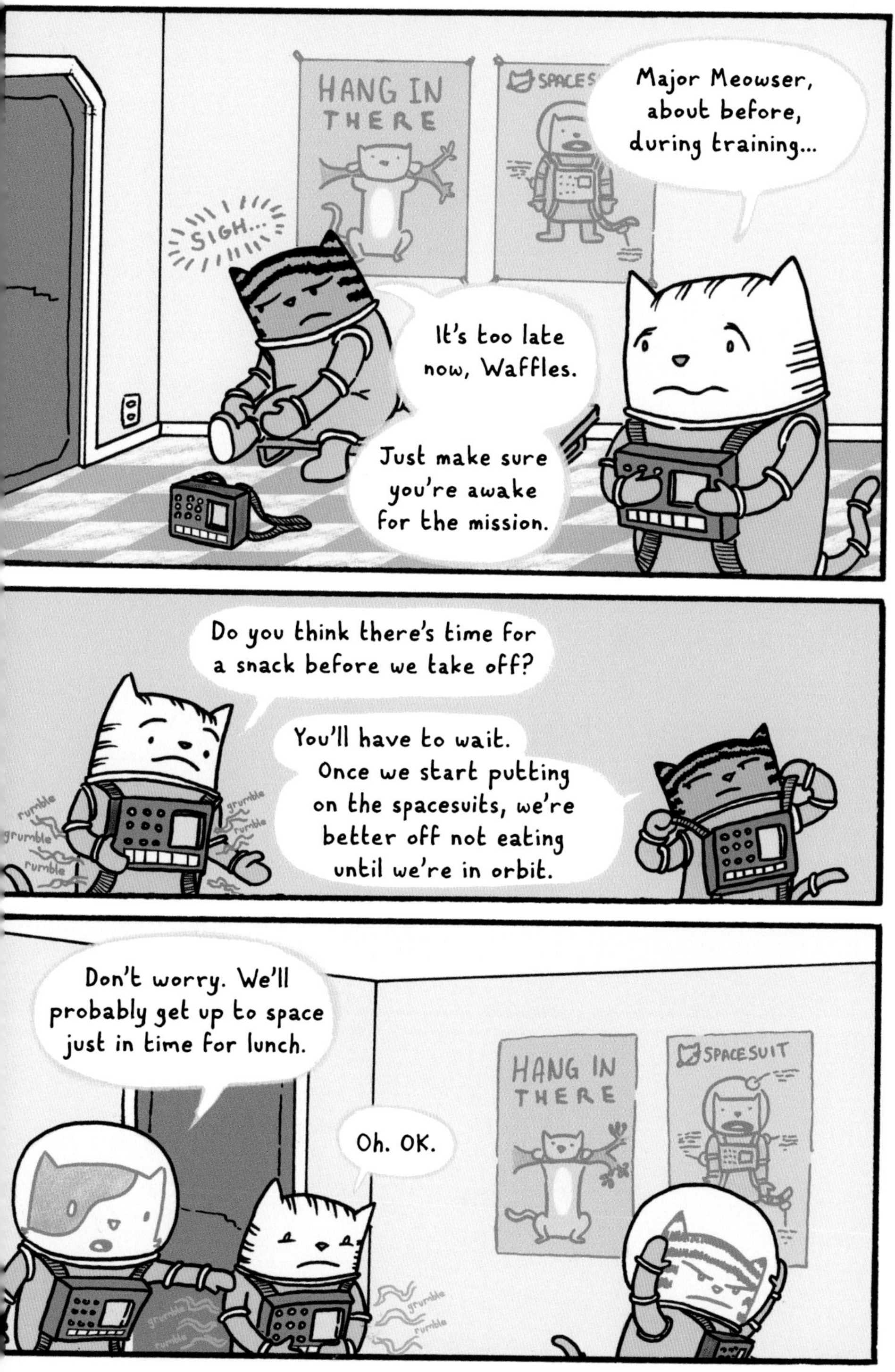
HANG IN THERE
Major Meowser, about before, during training...
SIGH...
It's too late now, Waffles.
Just make sure you're awake for the mission.
Do you think there's time for a snack before we take off?
rumble
grumble
rumble
grumble
rumble
You'll have to wait. Once we start putting on the spacesuits, we're better off not eating until we're in orbit.
Don't worry. We'll probably get up to space just in time for lunch.
Oh. OK.
grumble
rumble
grumble
rumble
HANG IN THERE
SPACESUIT

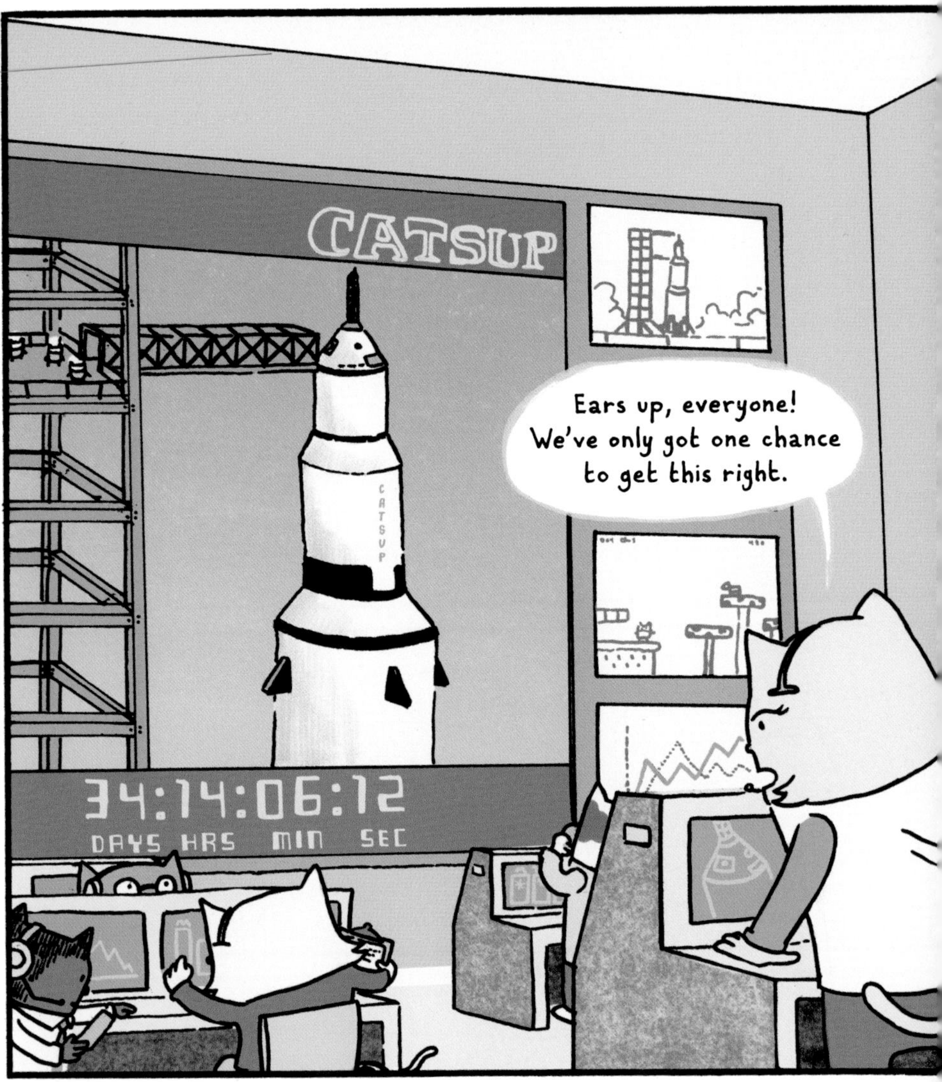
CATSUP
Ears up, everyone! We've only got one chance to get this right.
34:14:06:12
DAYS HRS MIN SEC

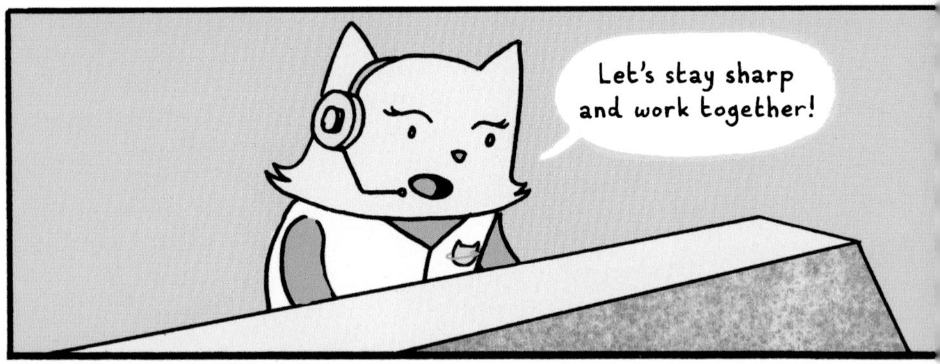
Let's stay sharp and work together!

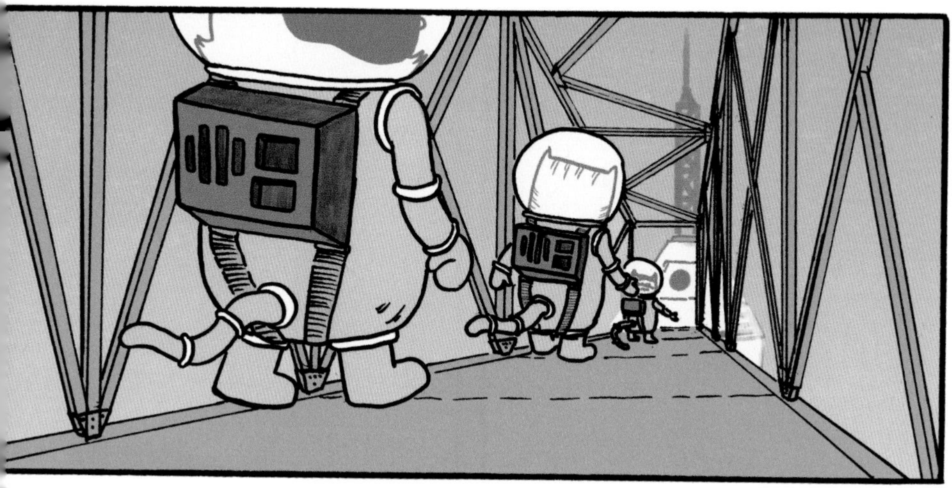

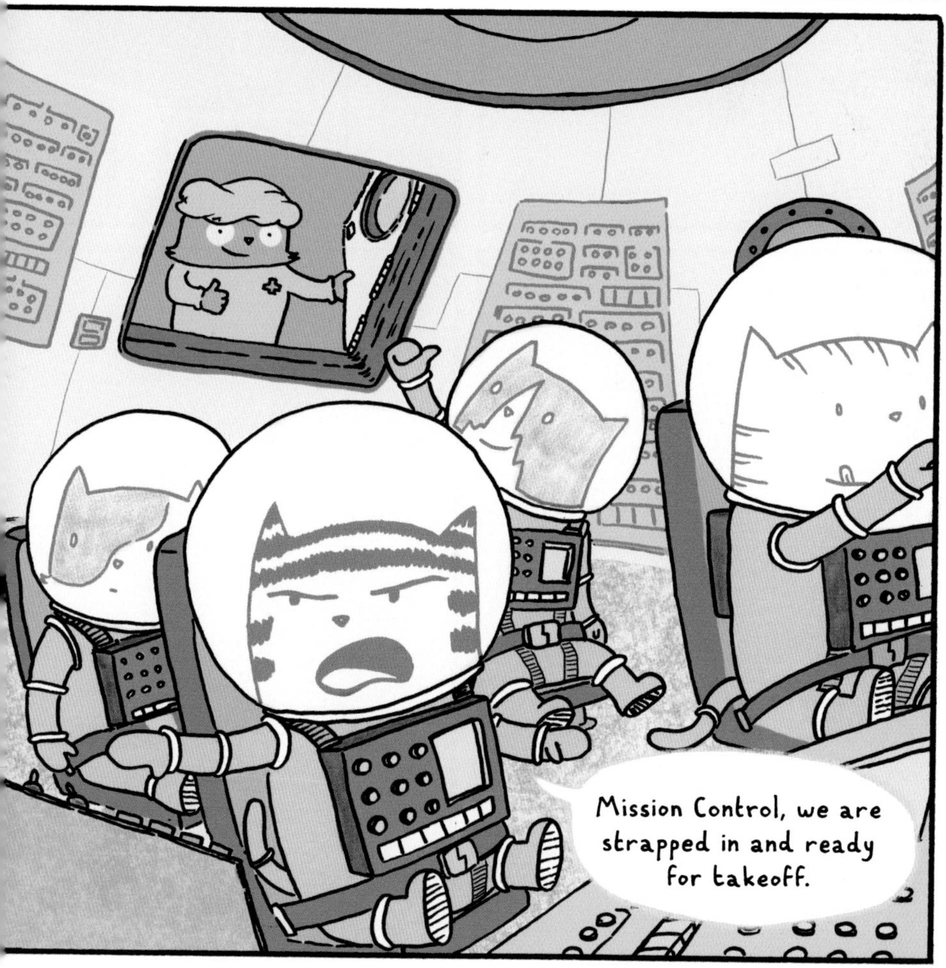
Mission Control, we are strapped in and ready for takeoff.

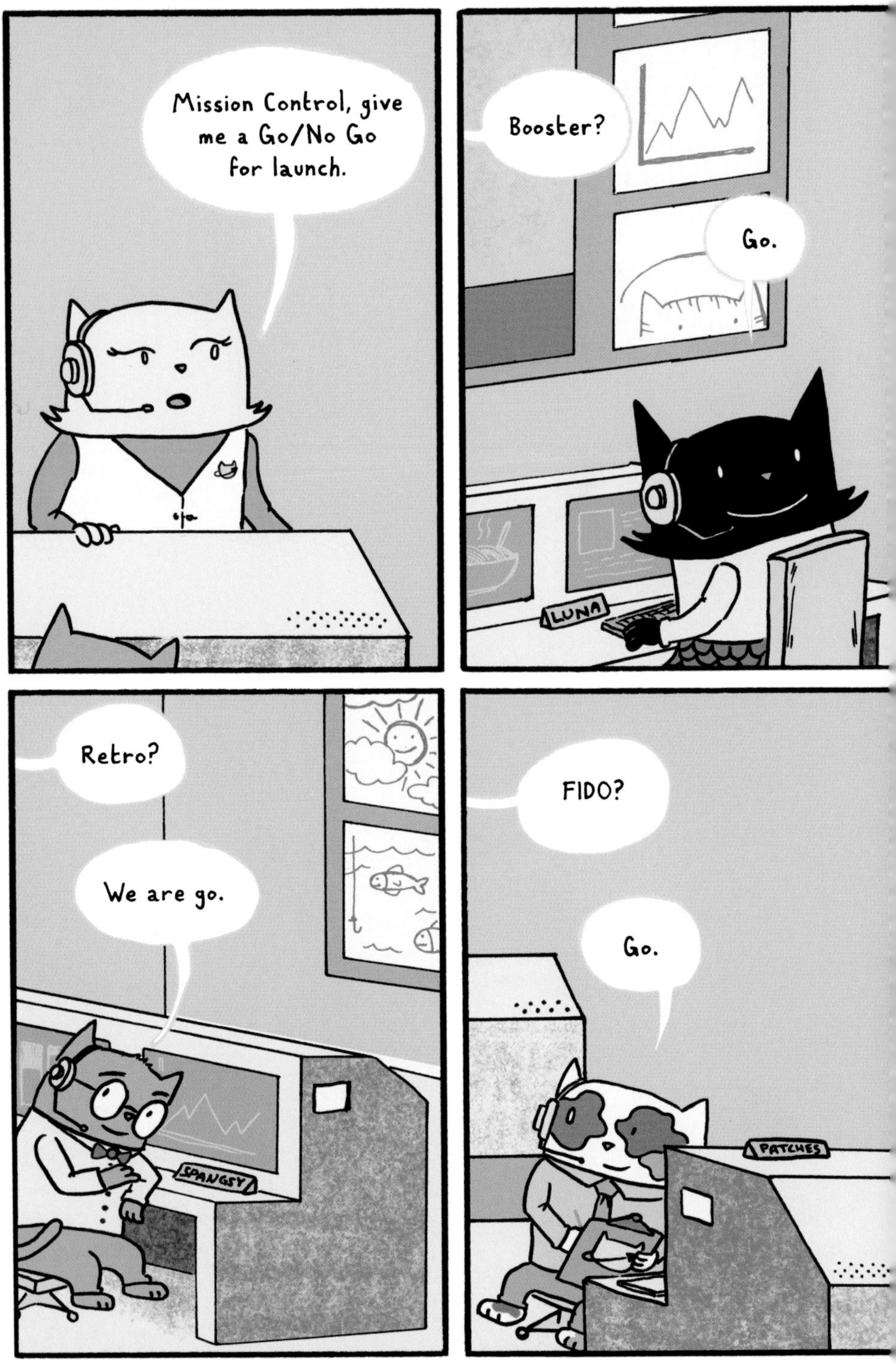
Mission Control, give me a Go/No Go for launch.
Booster?
Go.
LUNA
Retro?
We are go.
SPANGSY
FIDO?
Go.
PATCHES

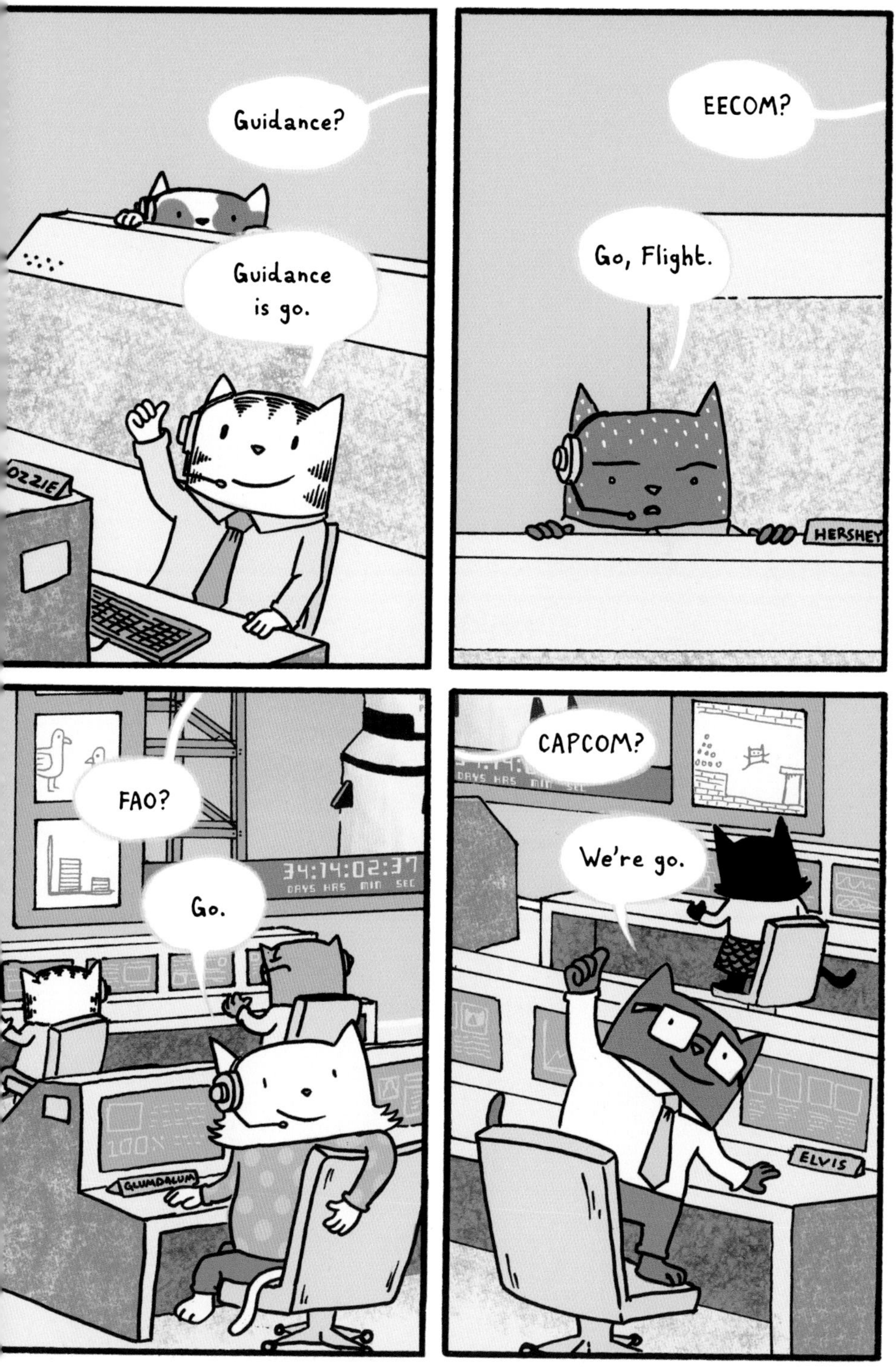
Guidance?
OZZIE
Guidance is go.
EECOM?
Go, Flight.
HERSHEY
FAO?
34:14:02:37
DAYS HRS MIN SEC
Go.
GLUMDALUM
CAPCOM?
We're go.
ELVIS

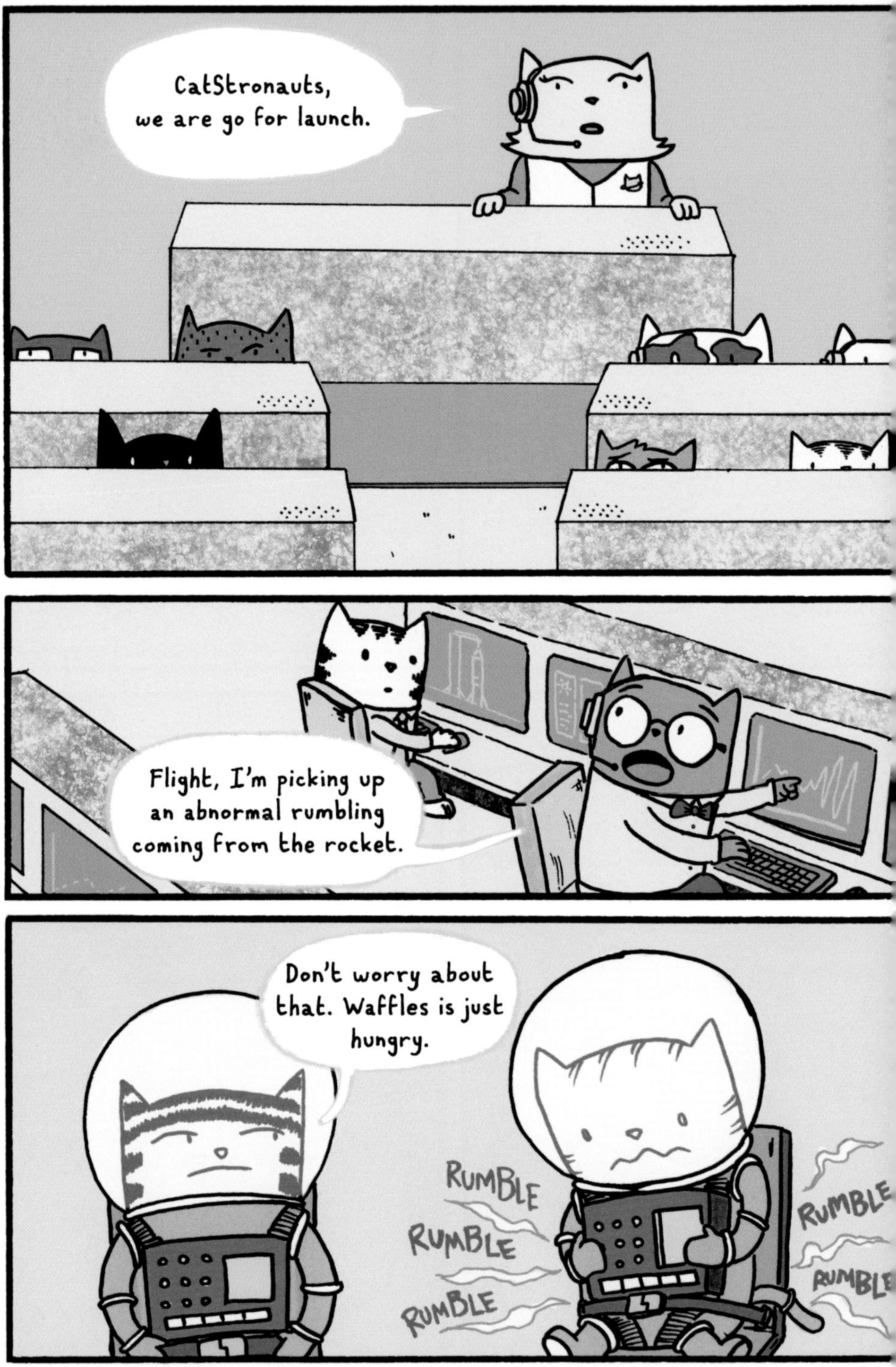
CatStronauts, we are go for launch.
Flight, I'm picking up an abnormal rumbling coming from the rocket.
Don't worry about that. Waffles is just hungry.
RUMBLE
RUMBLE
RUMBLE
RUMBLE
RUMBLE

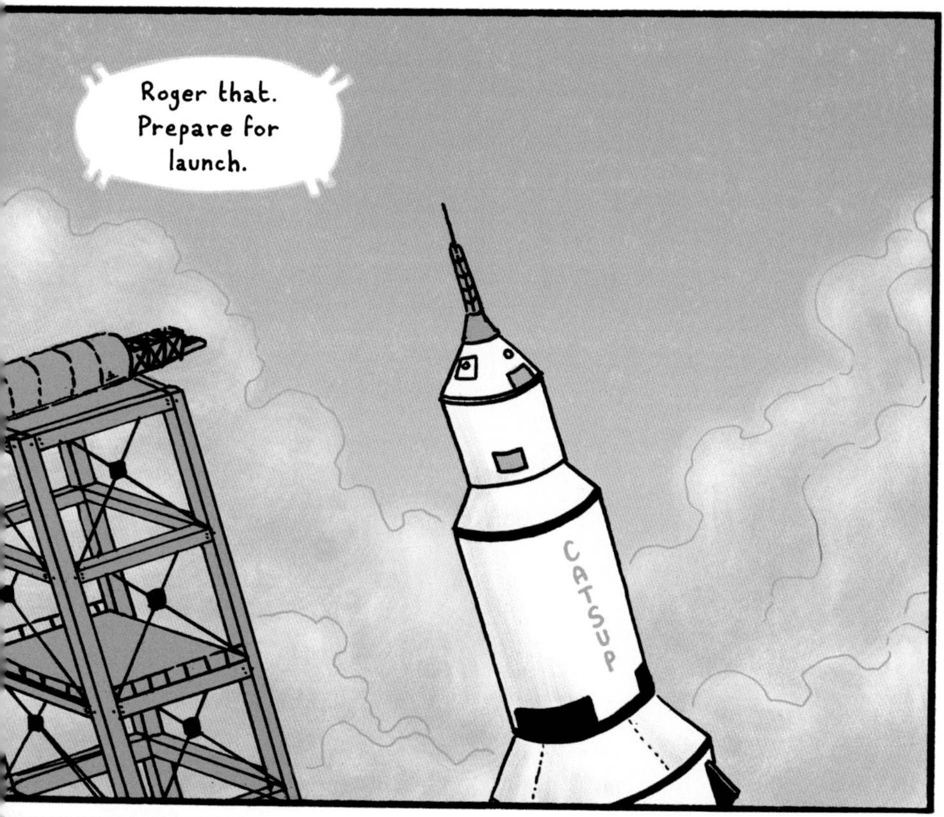
Roger that. Prepare for launch.
CATSUP

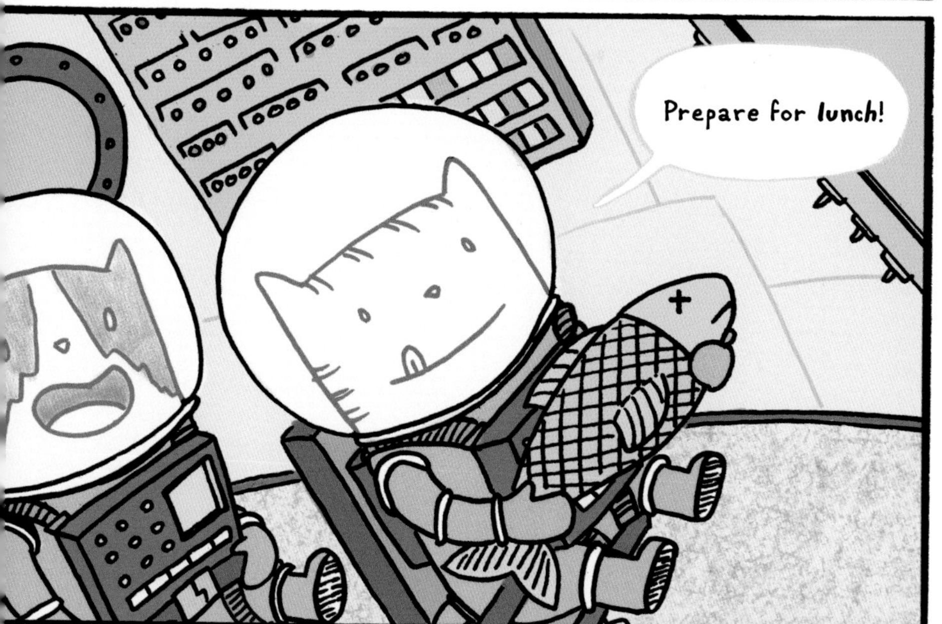
Prepare for **lunch**!

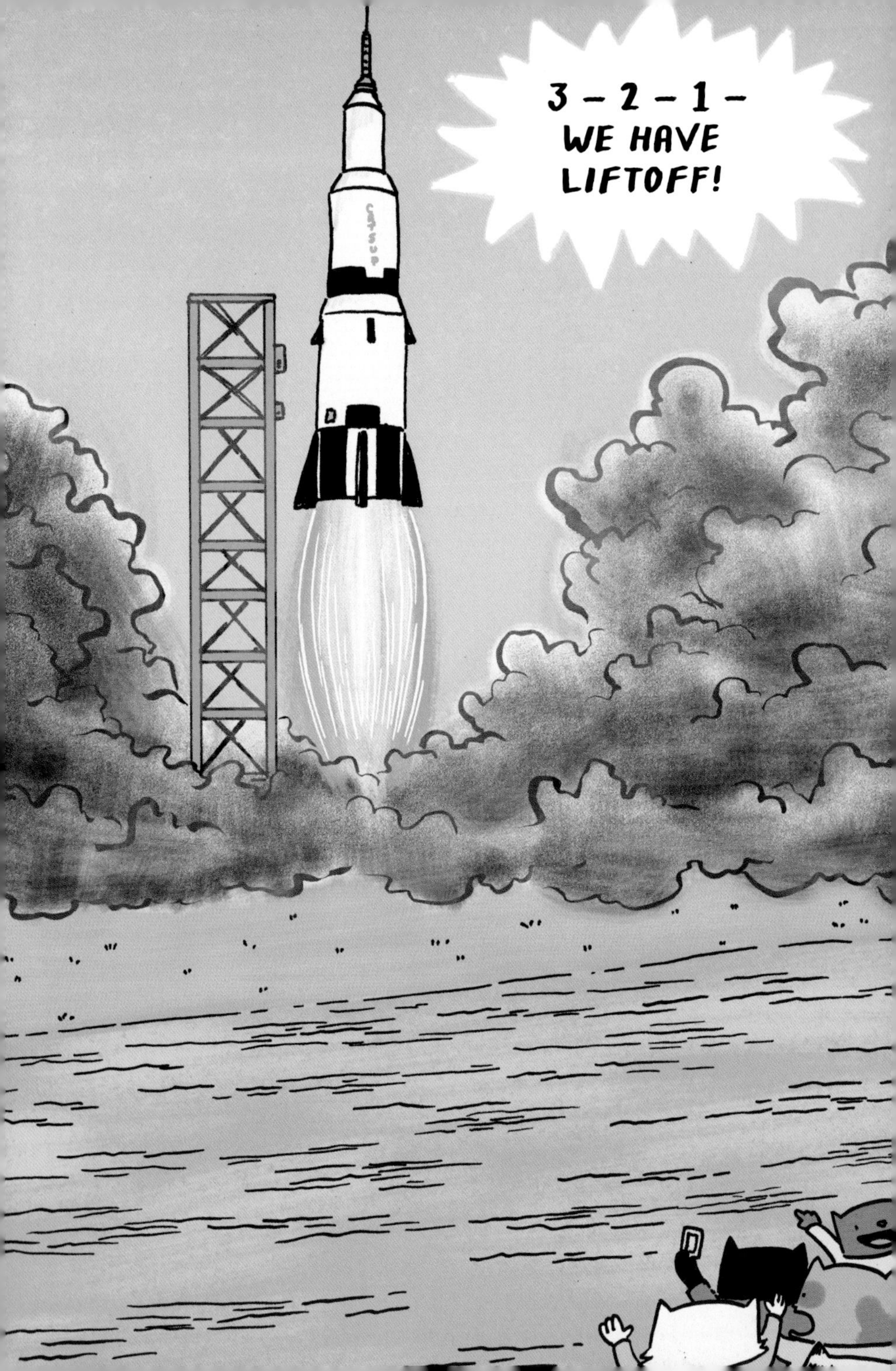
3 – 2 – 1 –
WE HAVE
LIFTOFF!

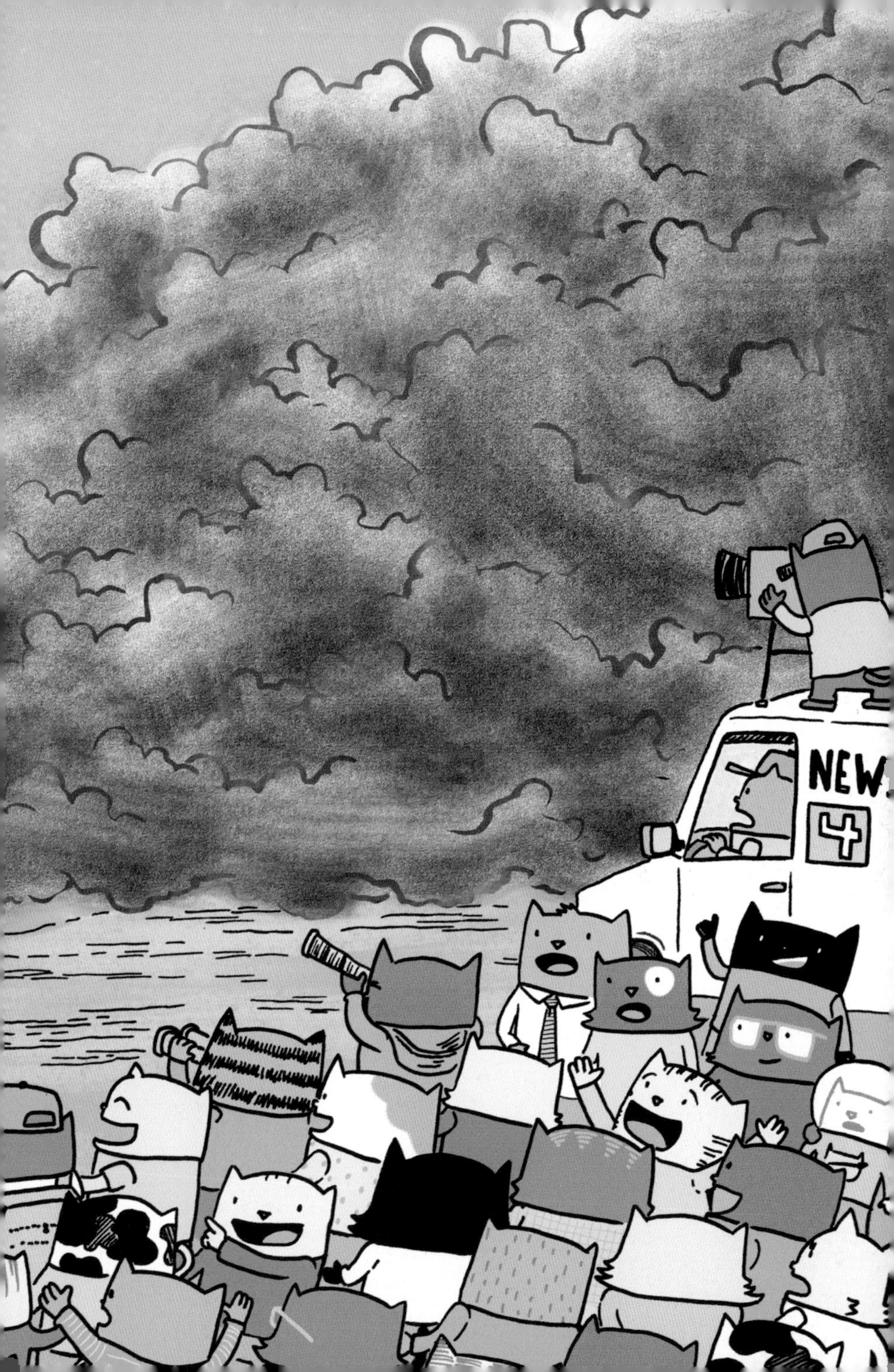
NEW
4

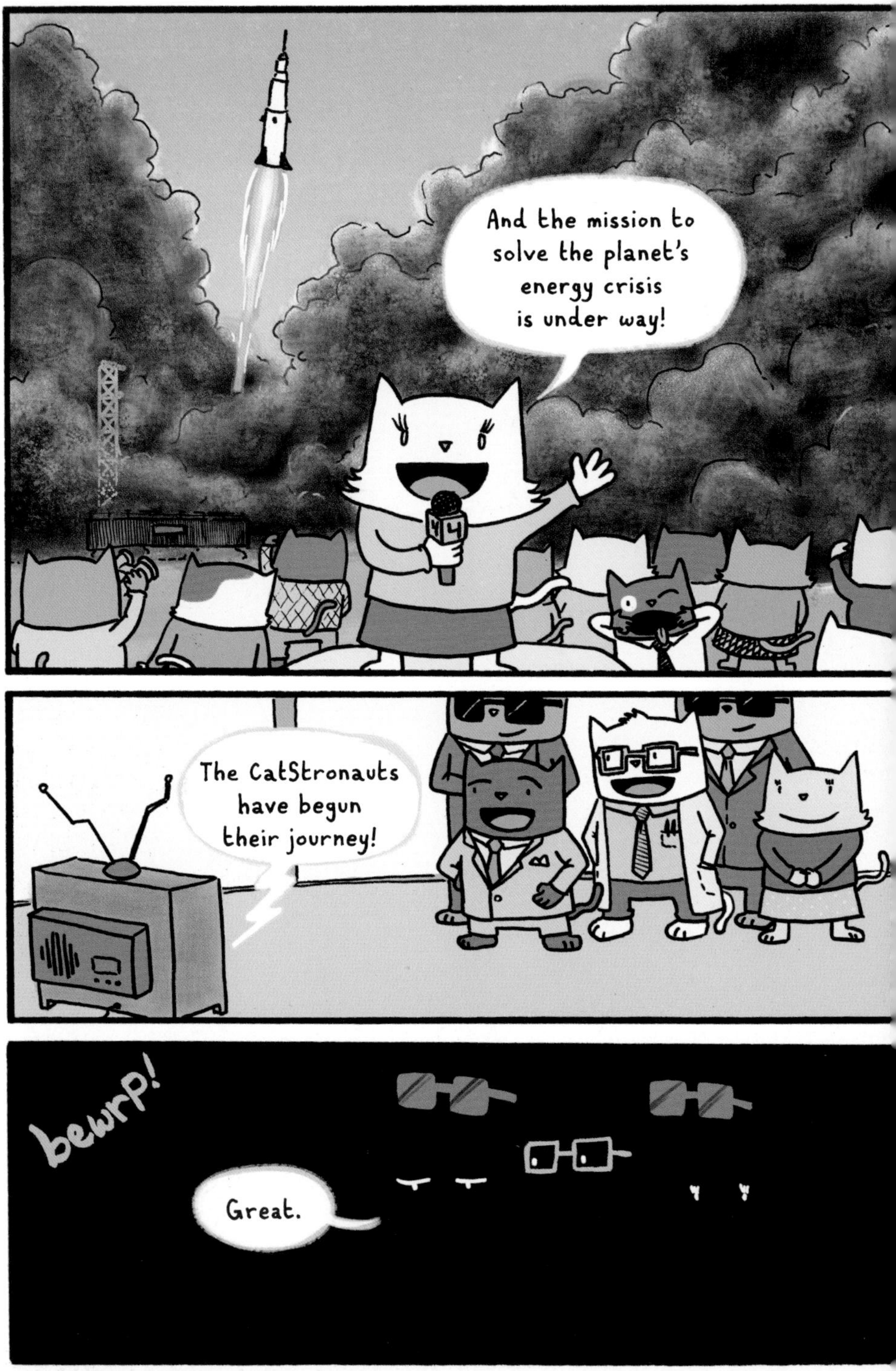
And the mission to solve the planet's energy crisis is under way!
The CatStronauts have begun their journey!
bewrp!
Great.

Well...Know any good jokes?

What is a cat's favorite type of show?

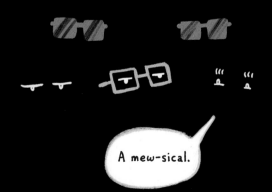

A mew-sical.

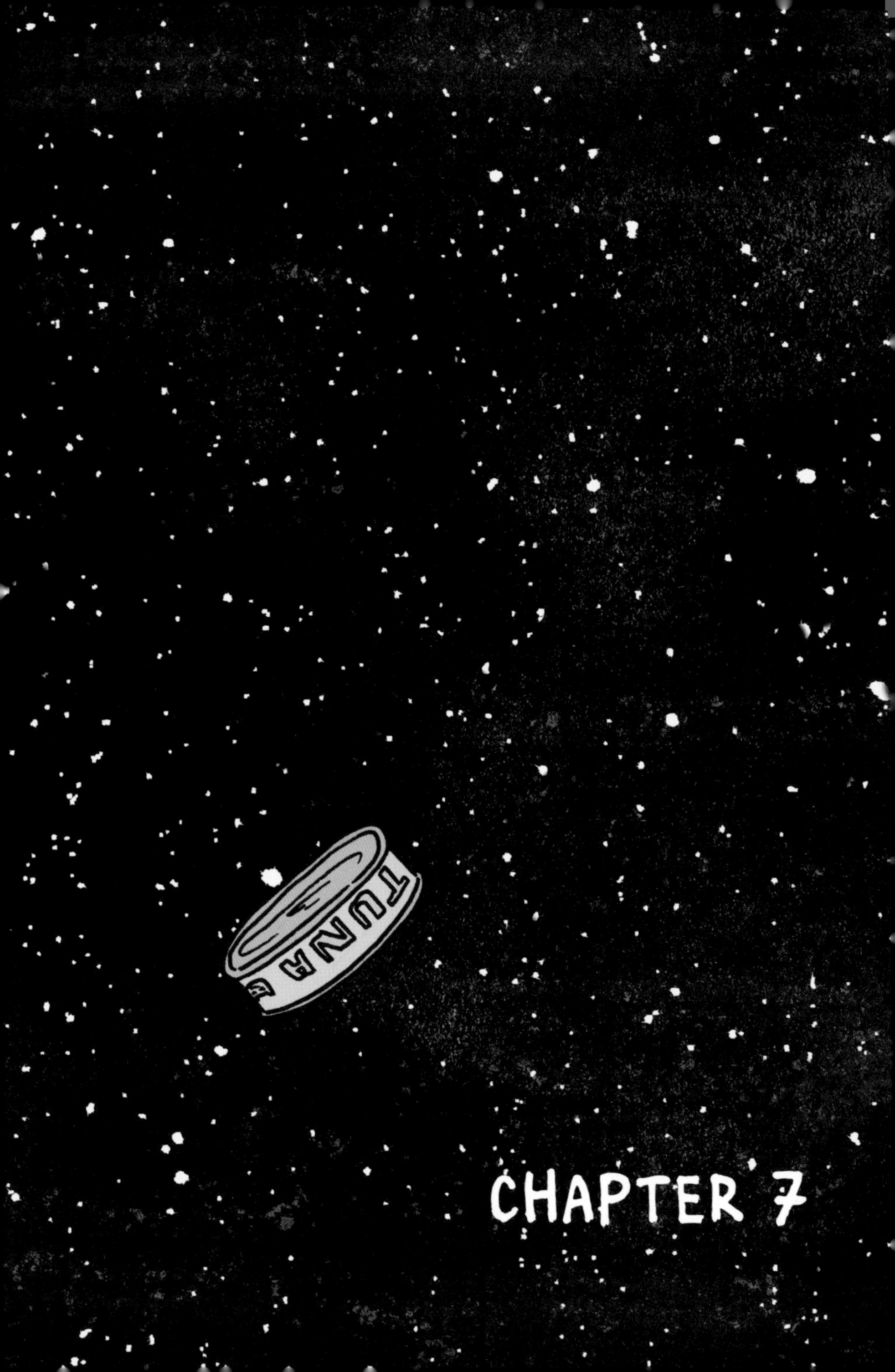
TUNA

CHAPTER 7

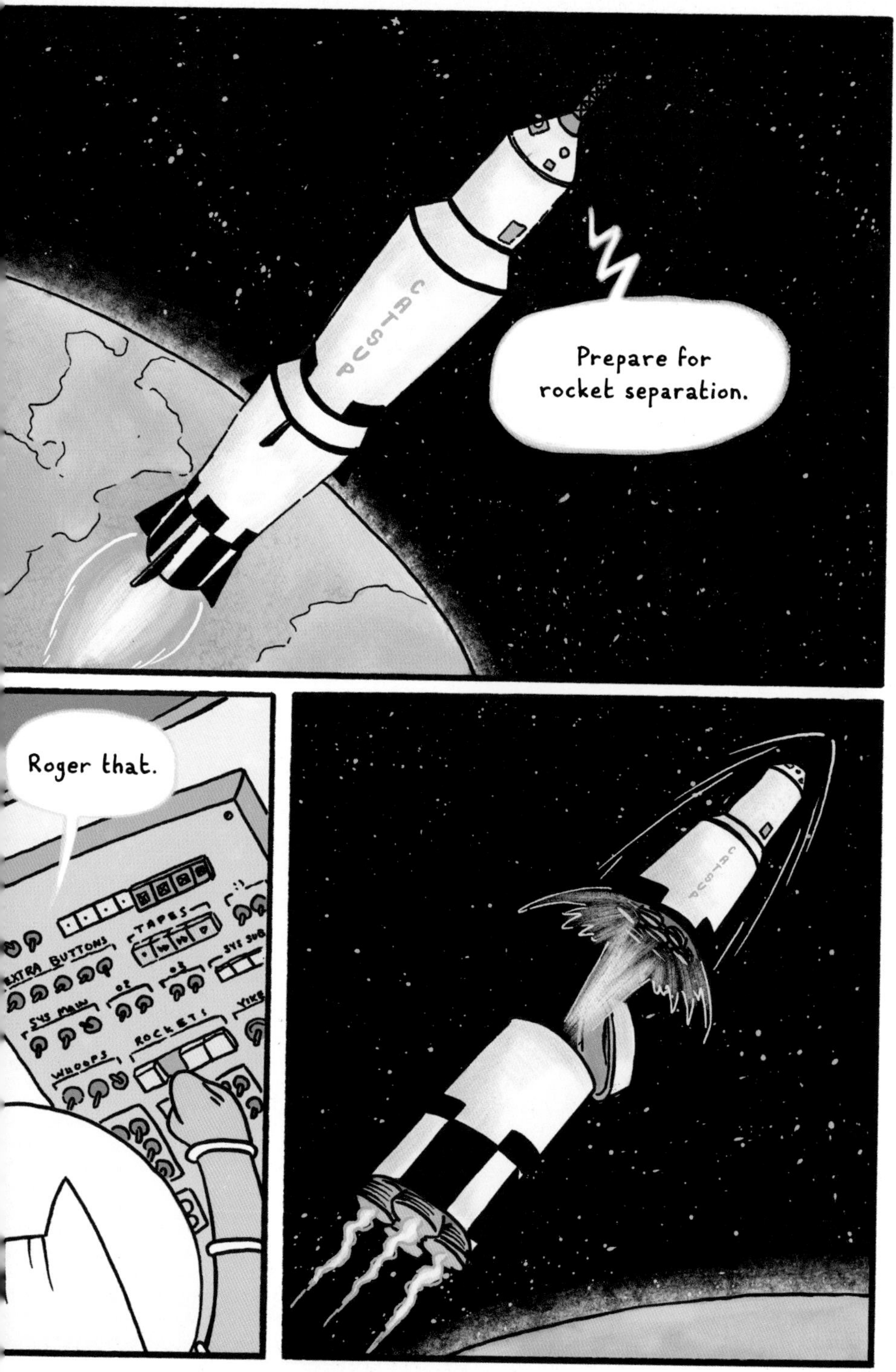
CATSUP
Prepare for rocket separation.
Roger that.
TAPES
EXTRA BUTTONS
SYS SUB
SYS MAN
O2
ROCKETS
WHOOPS
CATSUP

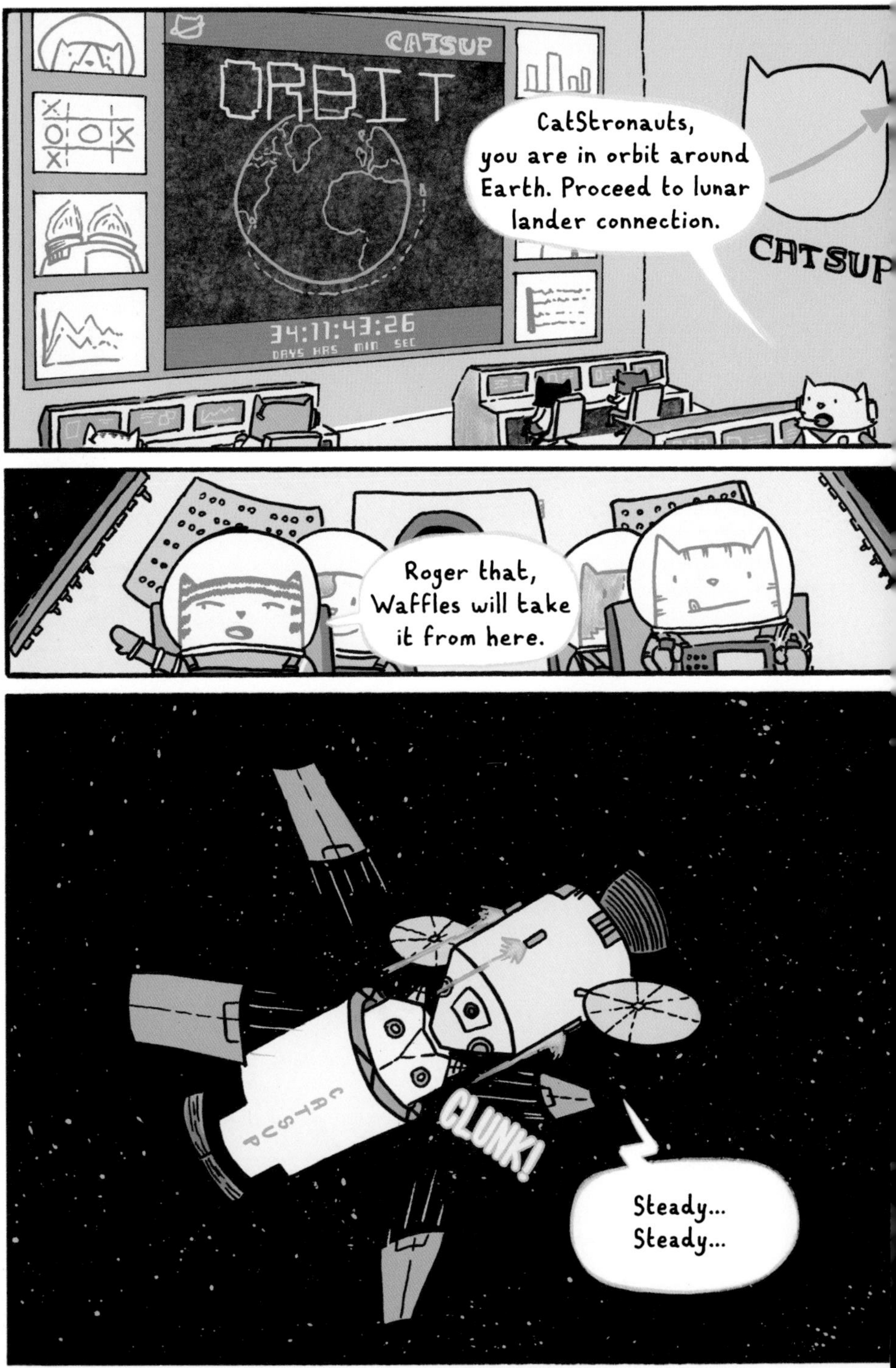
CATSUP
ORBIT
34:11:43:26
DAYS HRS MIN SEC
CatStronauts, you are in orbit around Earth. Proceed to lunar lander connection.
CATSUP
Roger that, Waffles will take it from here.
CATSUP
CLUNK!
Steady... Steady...

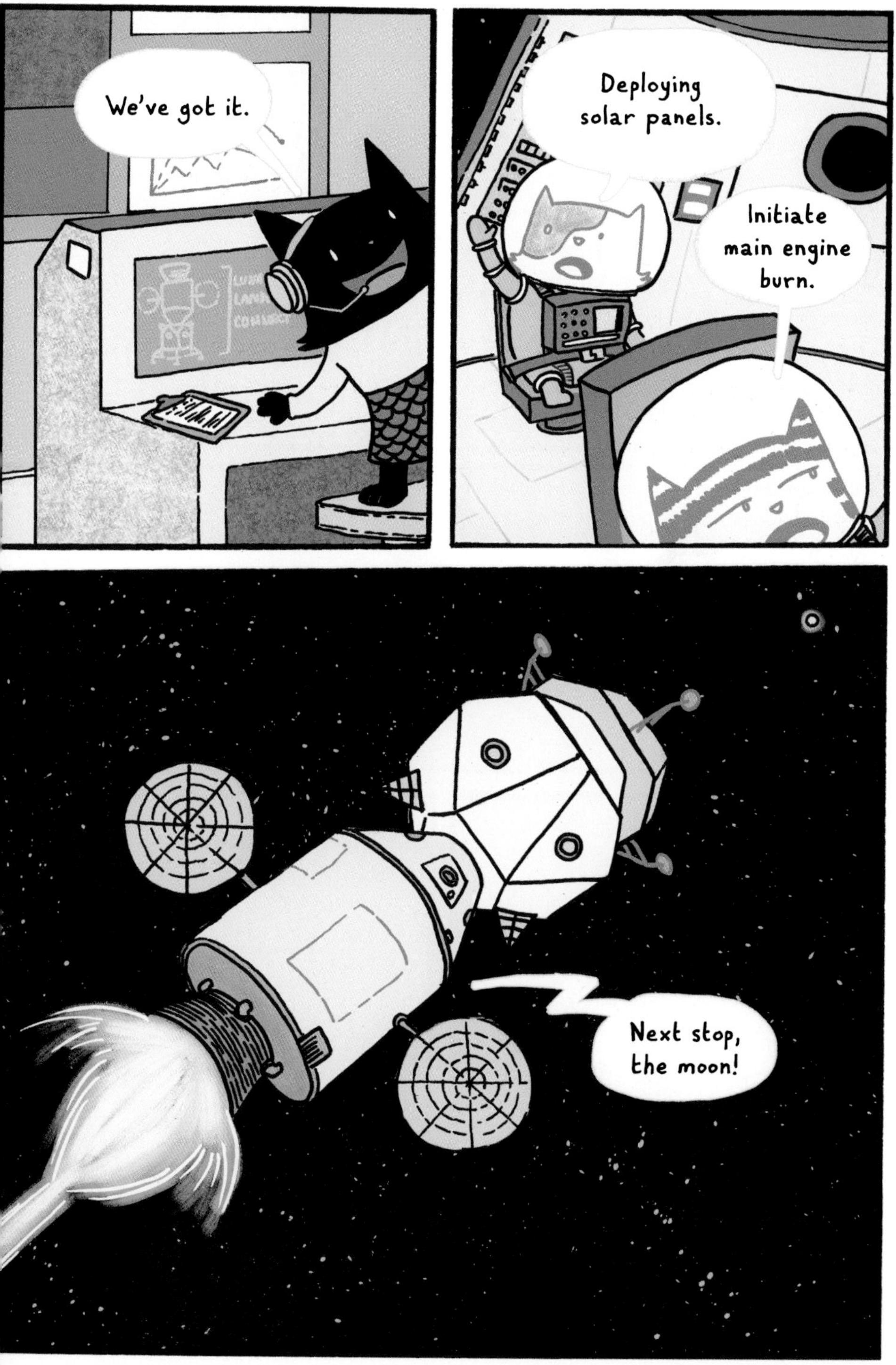
We've got it.
Deploying solar panels.
Initiate main engine burn.
Next stop, the moon!

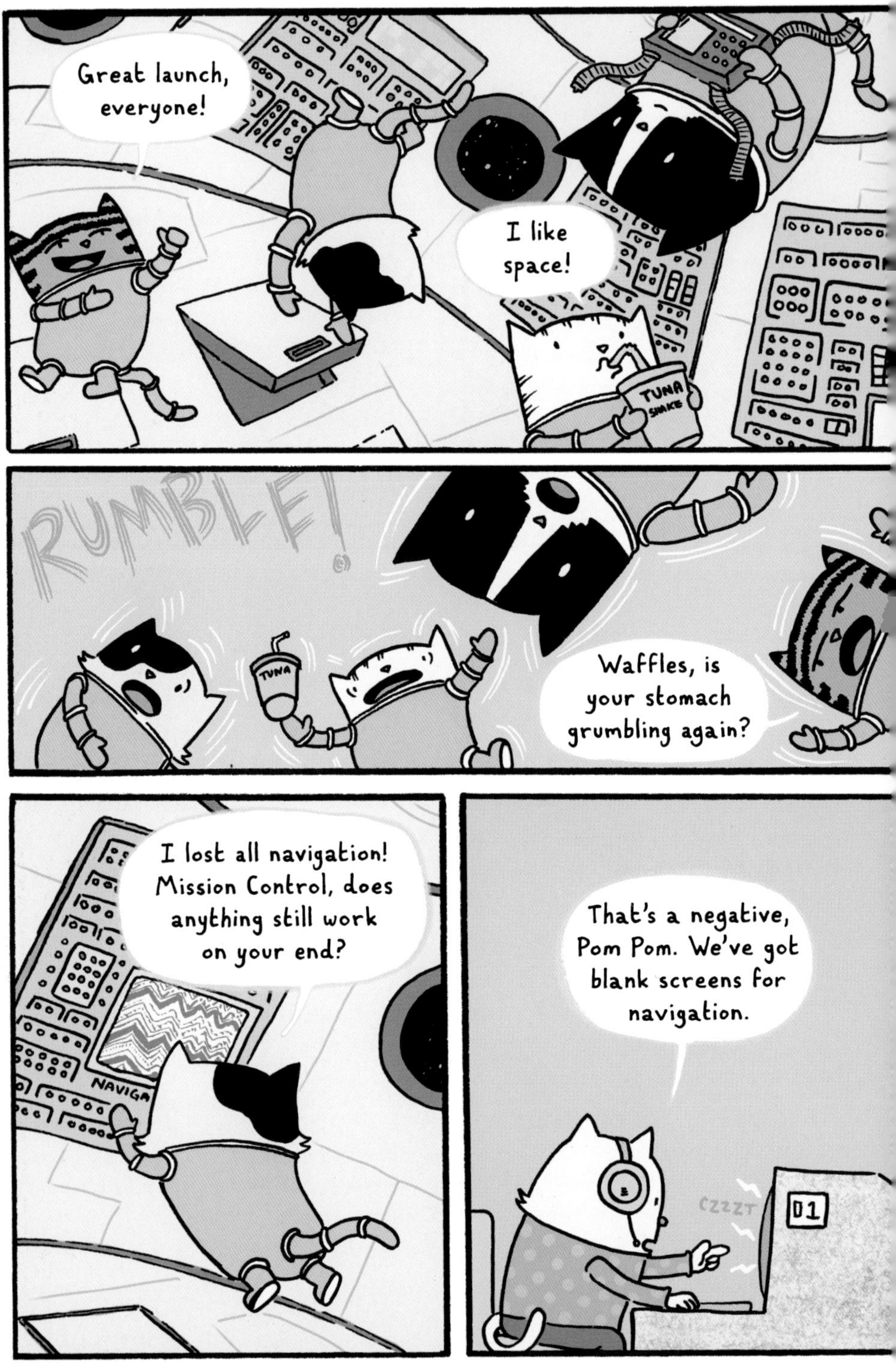
Great launch, everyone!
I like space!
TUNA SHAKE
RUMBLE!
TUNA
Waffles, is your stomach grumbling again?
I lost all navigation! Mission Control, does anything still work on your end?
NAVIGA
That's a negative, Pom Pom. We've got blank screens for navigation.
CZZZT
D1

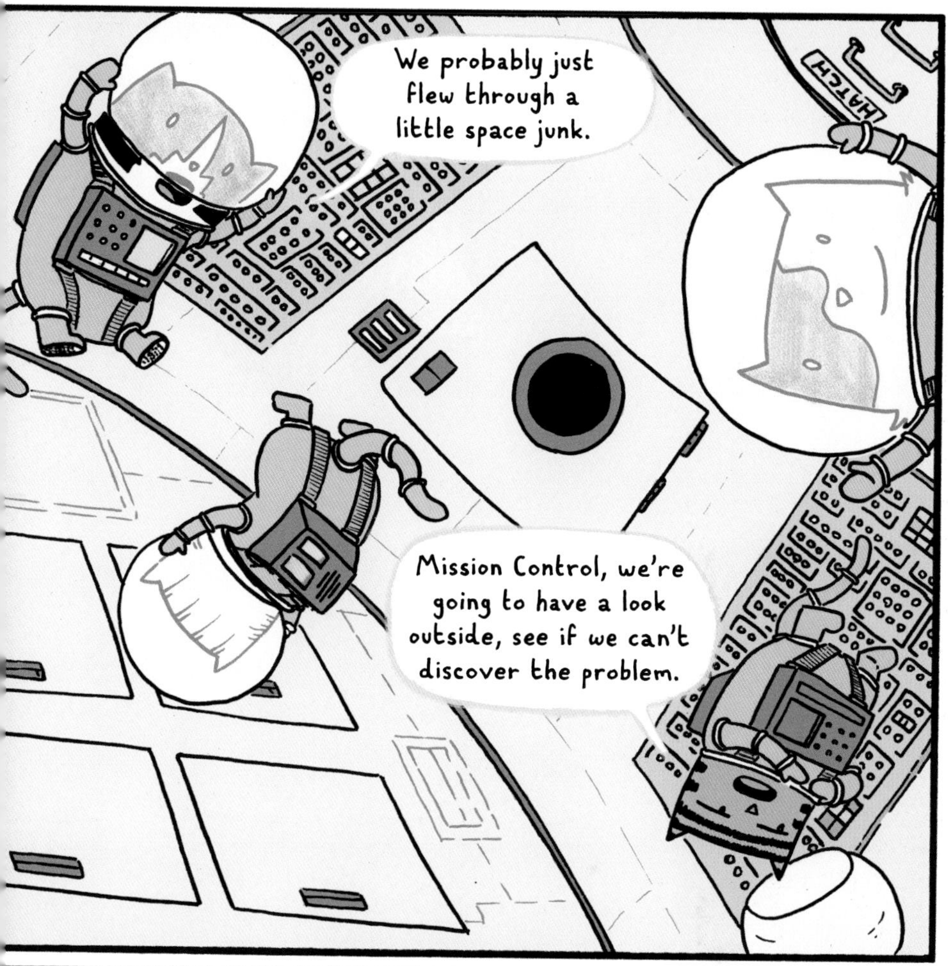
HATCH
We probably just flew through a little space junk.
Mission Control, we're going to have a look outside, see if we can't discover the problem.

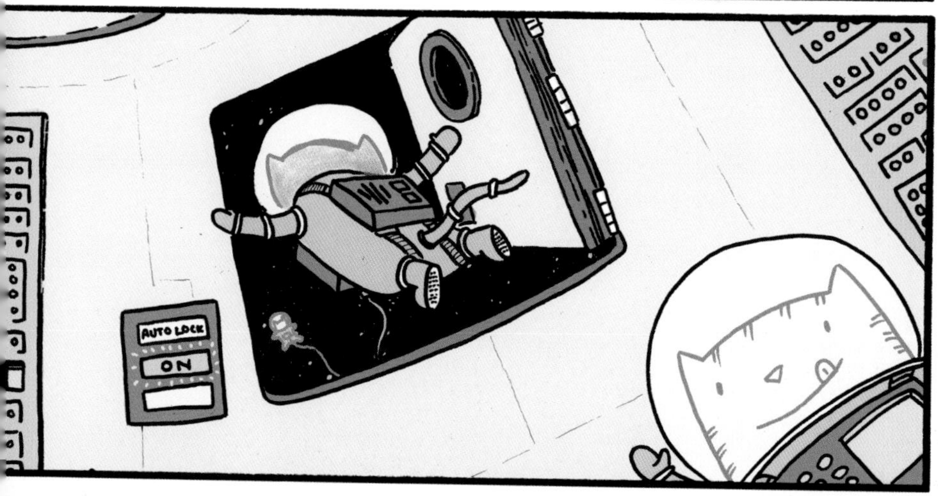
AUTO LOCK
ON

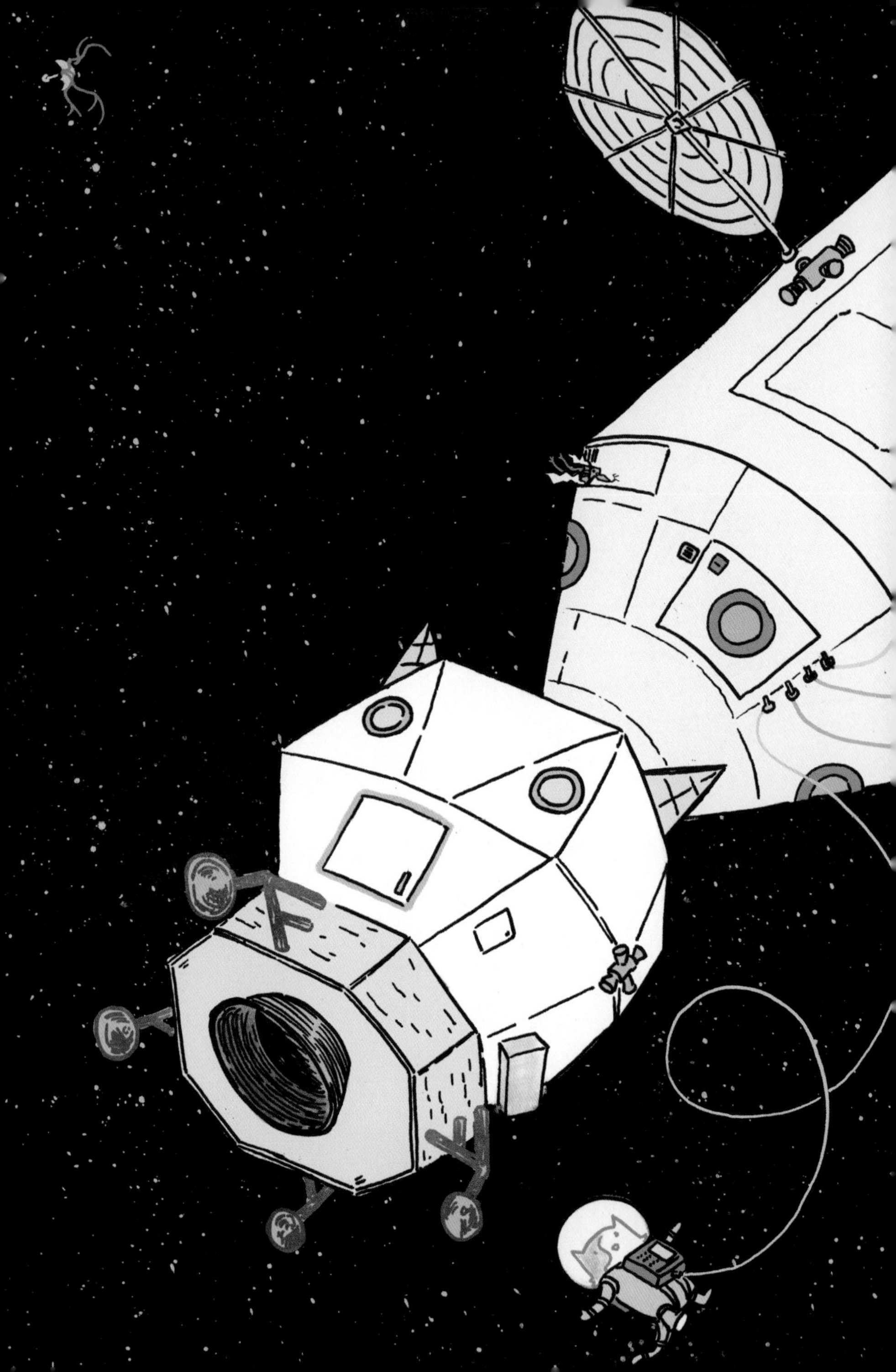

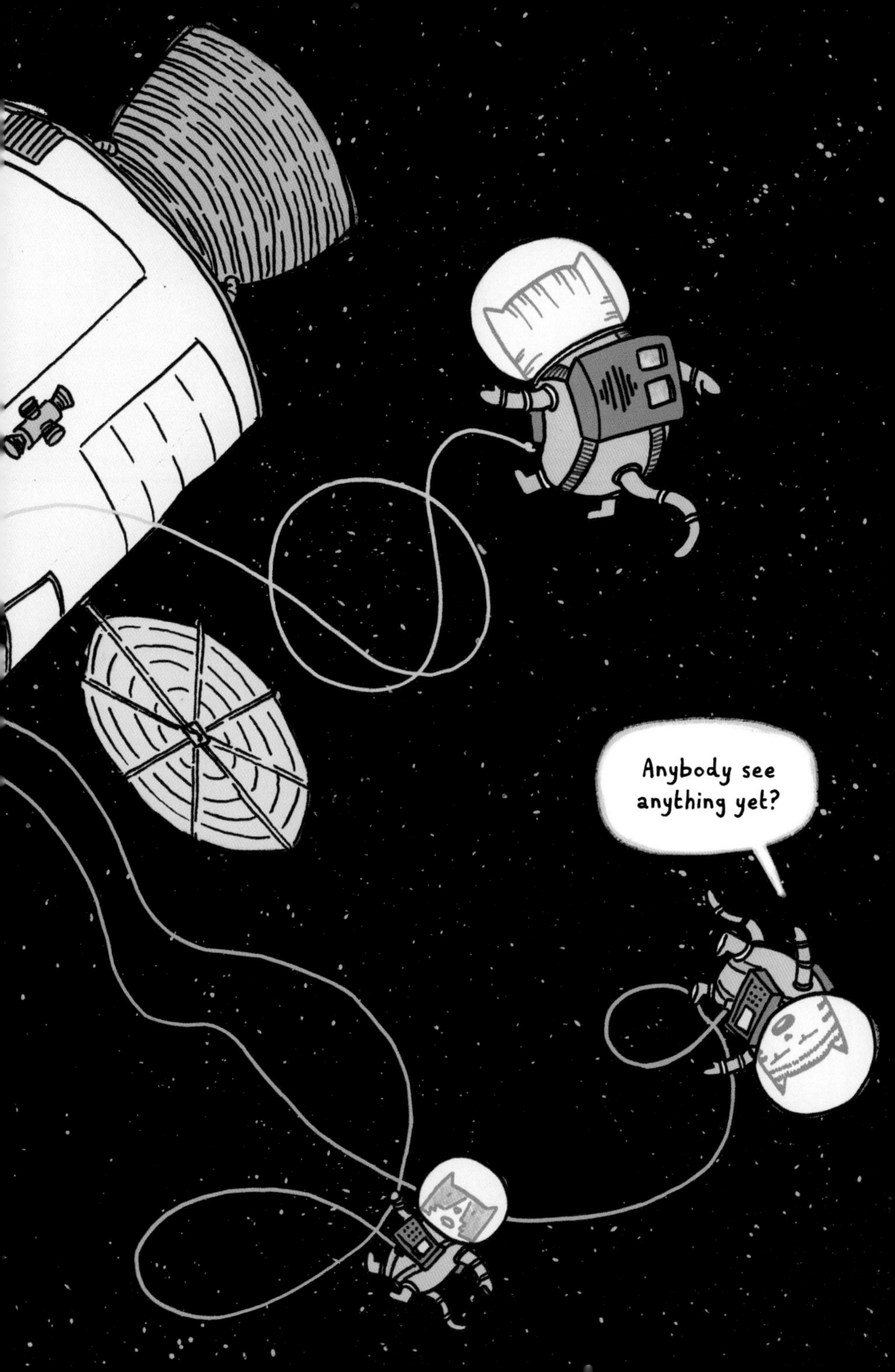
Anybody see anything yet?

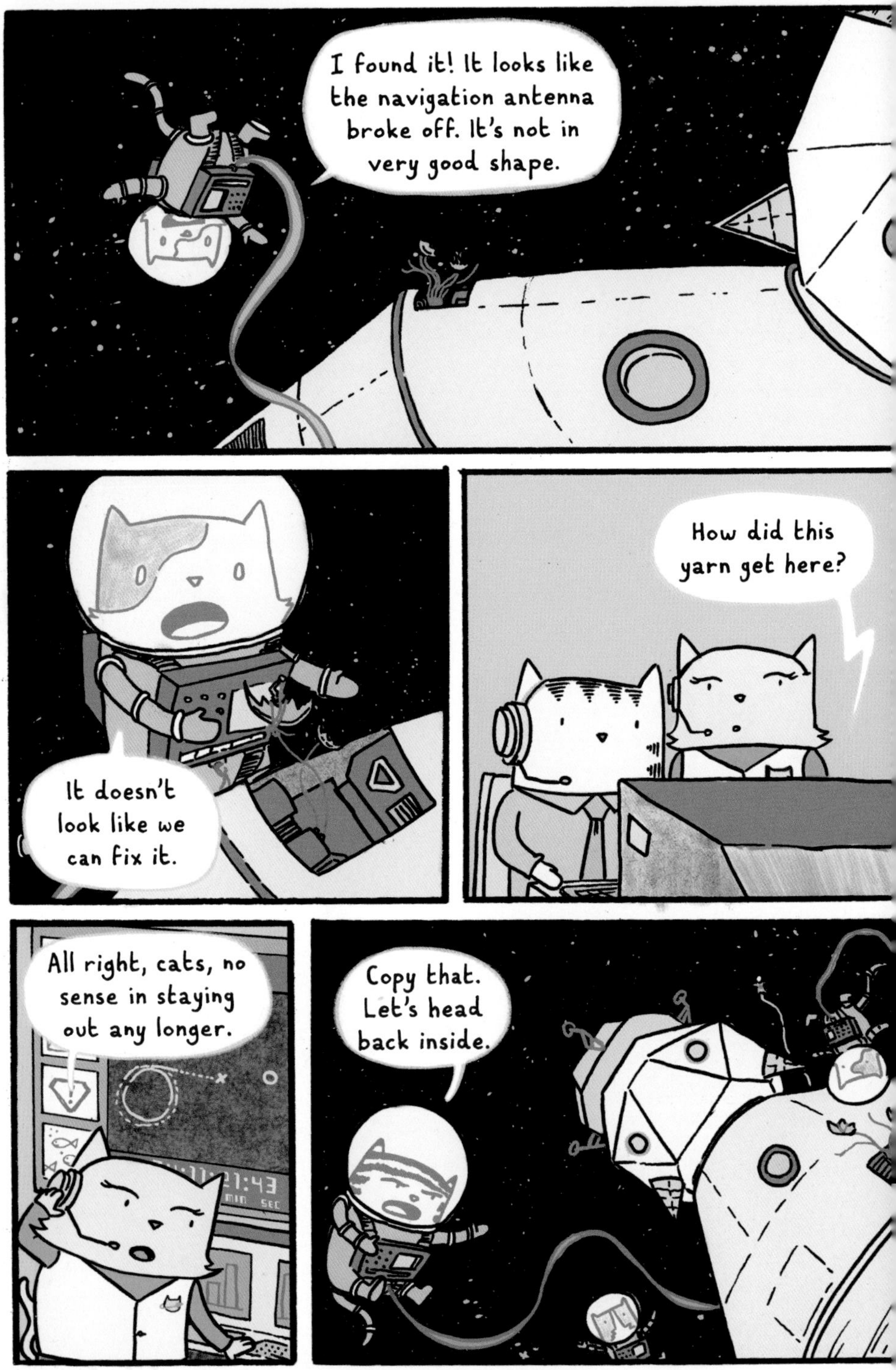
I found it! It looks like the navigation antenna broke off. It's not in very good shape.
It doesn't look like we can fix it.
How did this yarn get here?
All right, cats, no sense in staying out any longer.
Copy that. Let's head back inside.

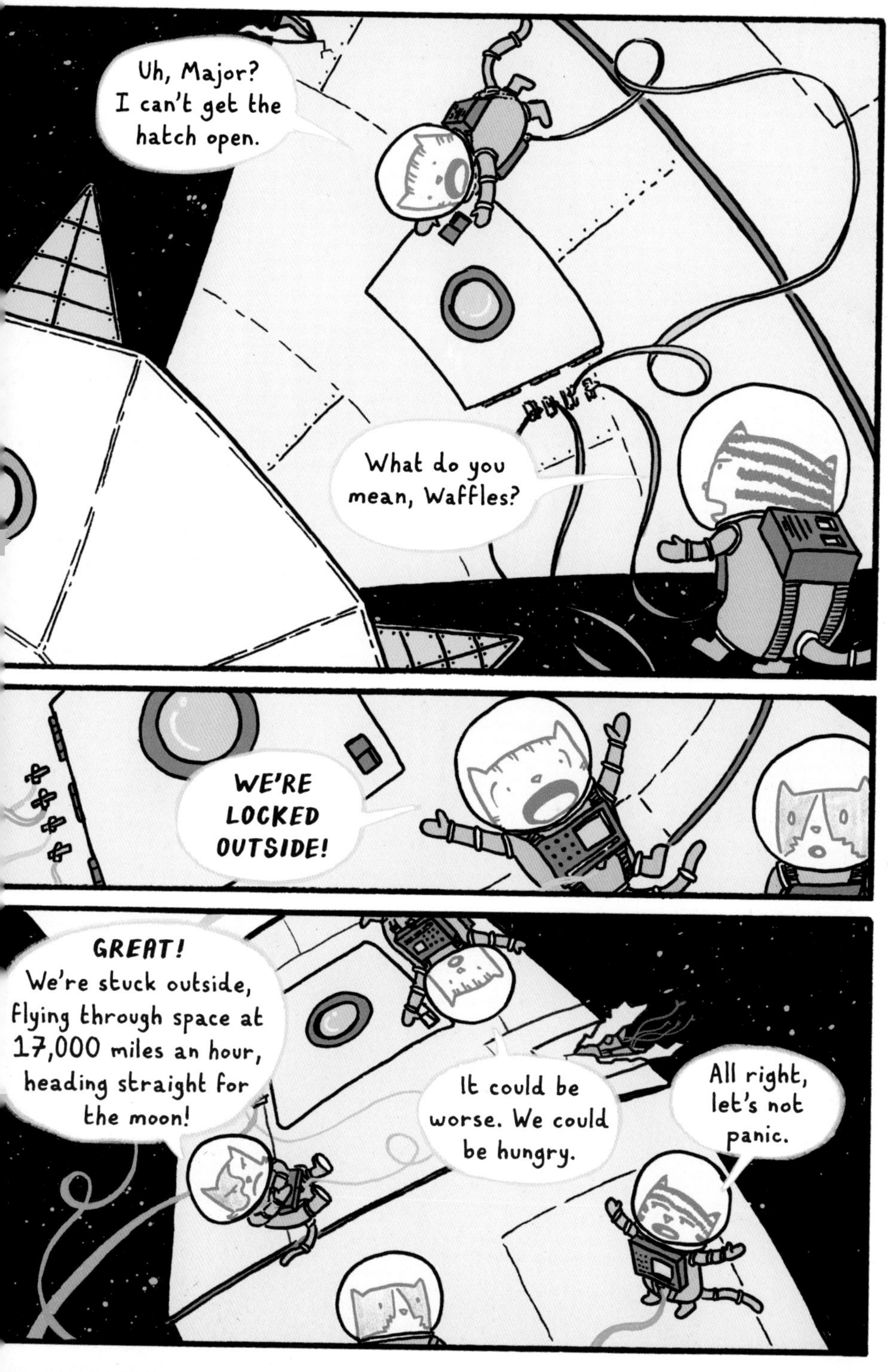
Uh, Major? I can't get the hatch open.
What do you mean, Waffles?
WE'RE LOCKED OUTSIDE!
GREAT! We're stuck outside, flying through space at 17,000 miles an hour, heading straight for the moon!
It could be worse. We could be hungry.
All right, let's not panic.

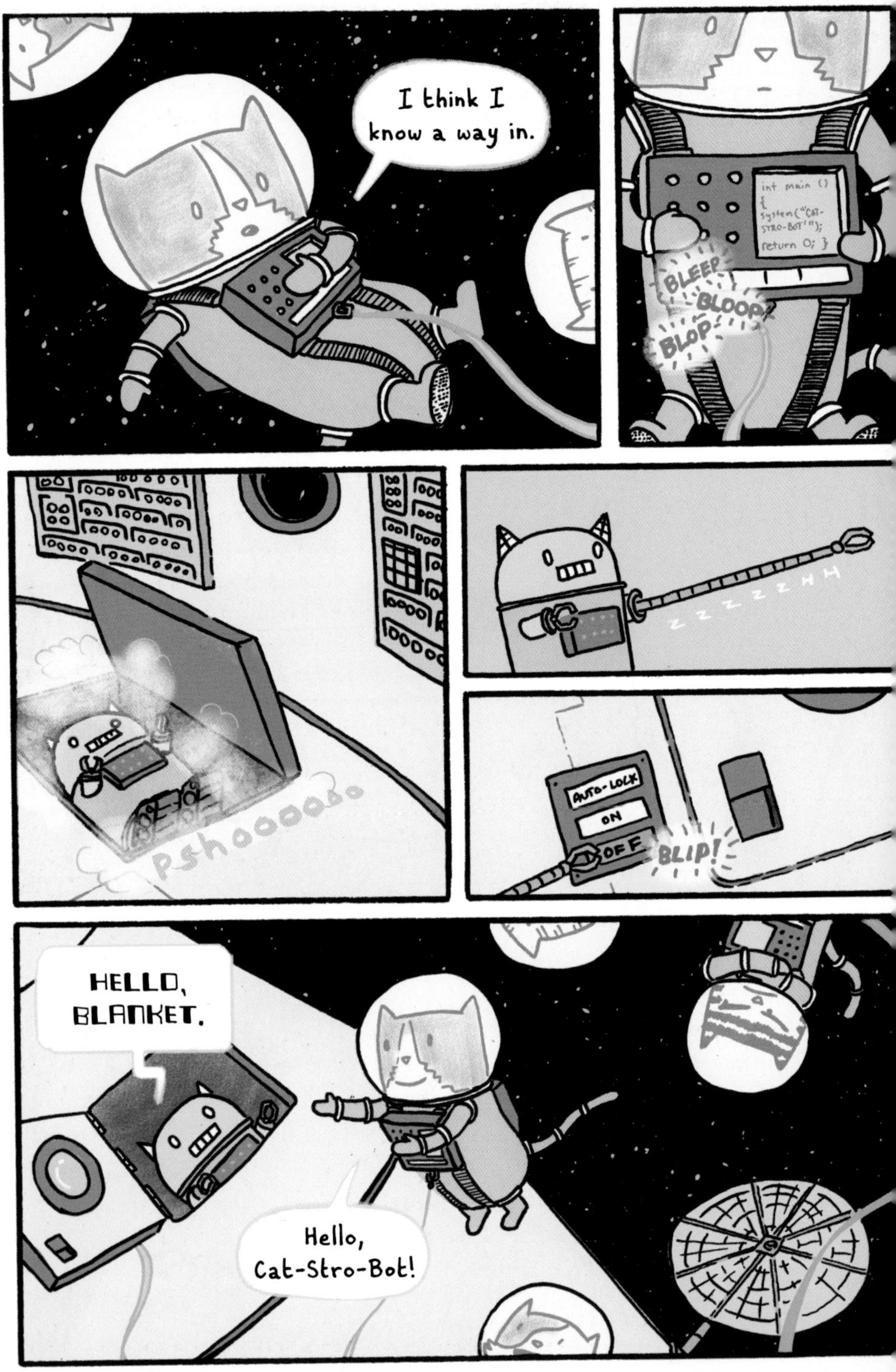
I think I know a way in.
int main ()
{
system("CAT-
STRO-BOT'");
return 0; }
BLEEP
BLOOP
BLOP
ZZZZZZHH
Pshoooooo
AUTO-LOCK
ON
OFF
BLIP!
HELLO, BLANKET.
Hello, Cat-Stro-Bot!

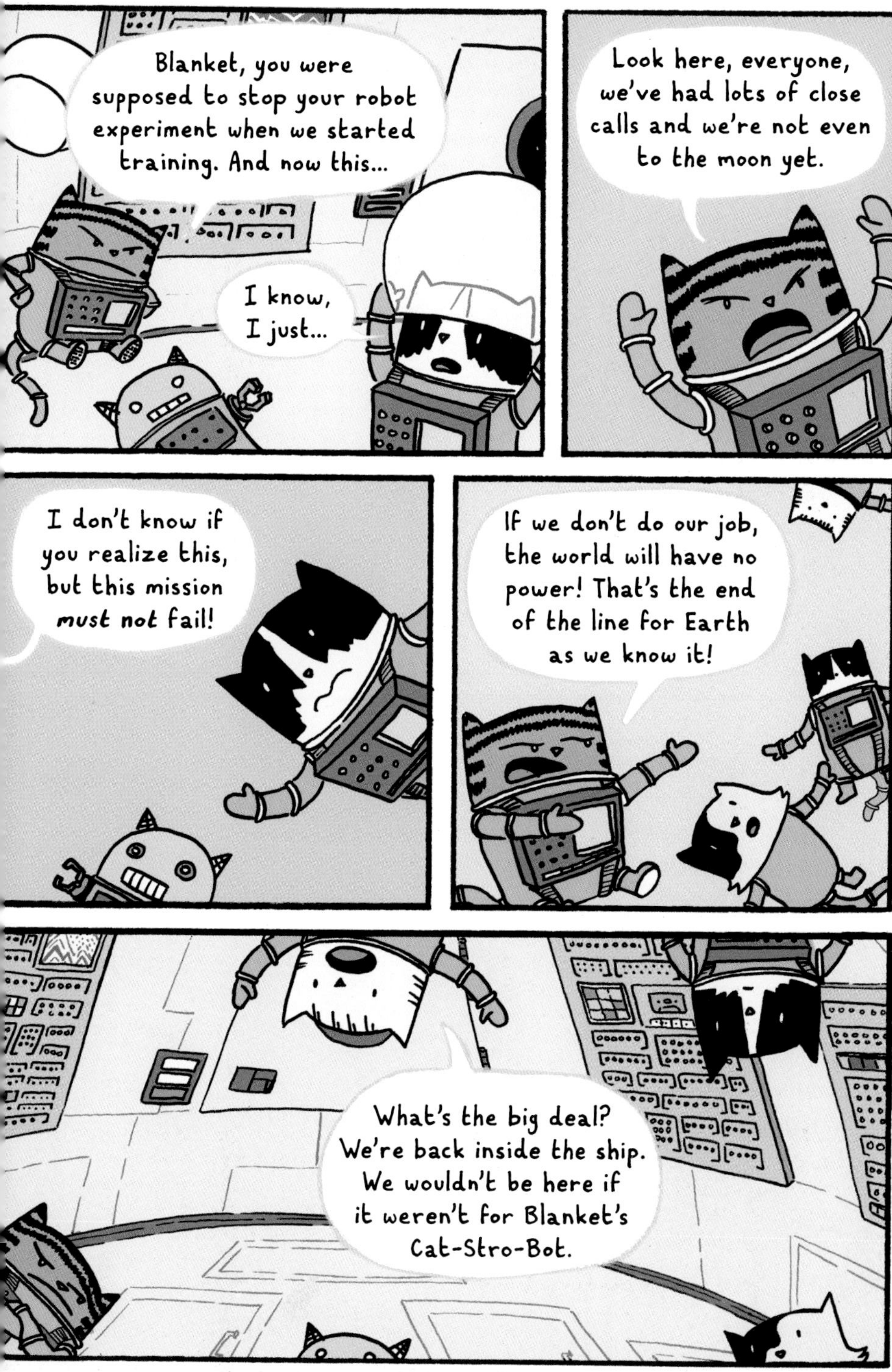
Blanket, you were supposed to stop your robot experiment when we started training. And now this...
I know, I just...
Look here, everyone, we've had lots of close calls and we're not even to the moon yet.
I don't know if you realize this, but this mission *must not* fail!
If we don't do our job, the world will have no power! That's the end of the line for Earth as we know it!
What's the big deal? We're back inside the ship. We wouldn't be here if it weren't for Blanket's Cat-Stro-Bot.

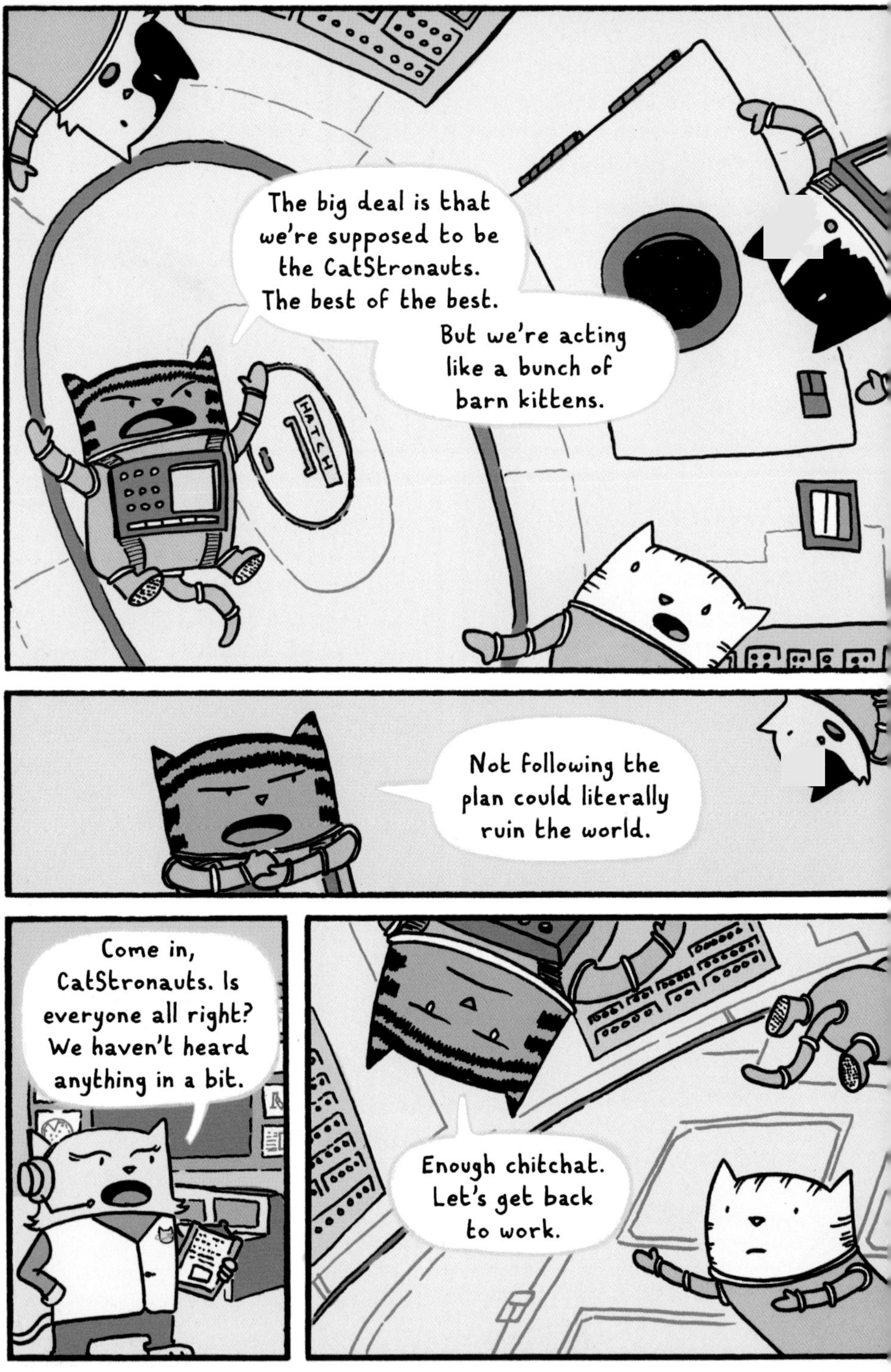
HATCH
The big deal is that we're supposed to be the CatStronauts. The best of the best.
But we're acting like a bunch of barn kittens.
Not following the plan could literally ruin the world.
Come in, CatStronauts. Is everyone all right? We haven't heard anything in a bit.
Enough chitchat. Let's get back to work.

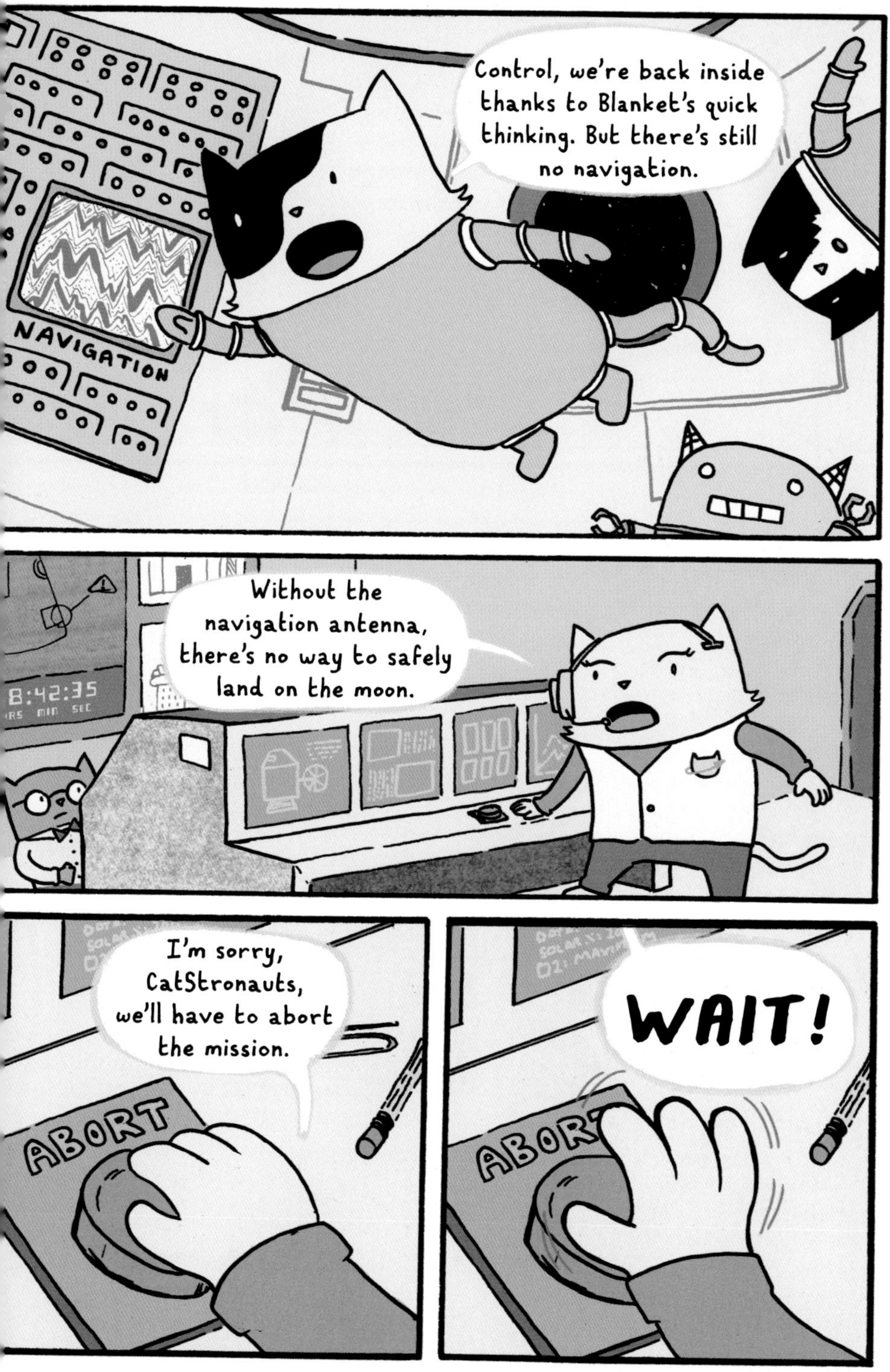
Control, we're back inside thanks to Blanket's quick thinking. But there's still no navigation.
NAVIGATION
8:42:35
HRS MIN SEC
Without the navigation antenna, there's no way to safely land on the moon.
I'm sorry, CatStronauts, we'll have to abort the mission.
ABORT
WAIT!
ABORT

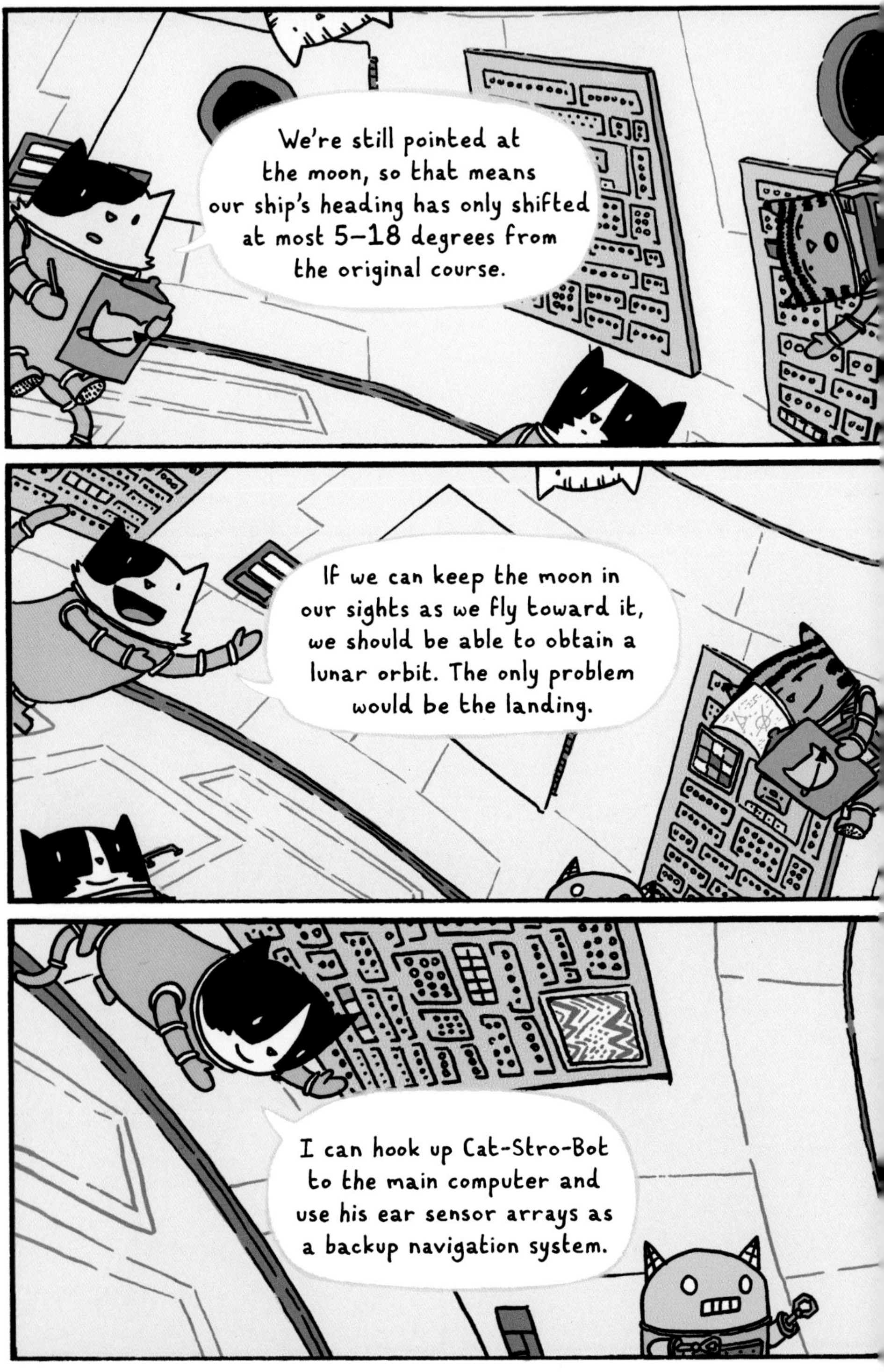
We're still pointed at the moon, so that means our ship's heading has only shifted at most 5–18 degrees from the original course.
If we can keep the moon in our sights as we fly toward it, we should be able to obtain a lunar orbit. The only problem would be the landing.
I can hook up Cat-Stro-Bot to the main computer and use his ear sensor arrays as a backup navigation system.

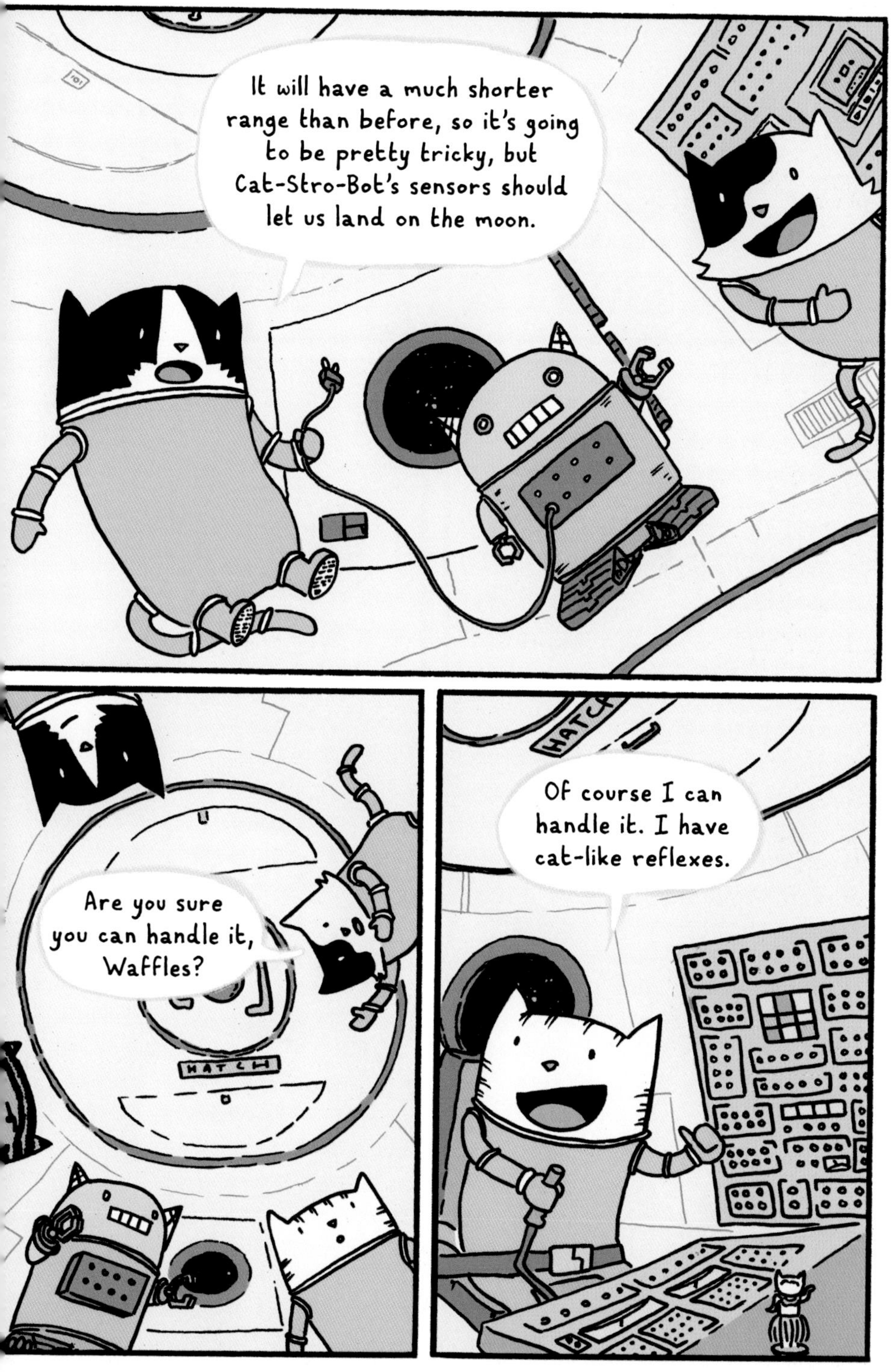
It will have a much shorter range than before, so it's going to be pretty tricky, but Cat-Stro-Bot's sensors should let us land on the moon.
Are you sure you can handle it, Waffles?
HATCH
Of course I can handle it. I have cat-like reflexes.

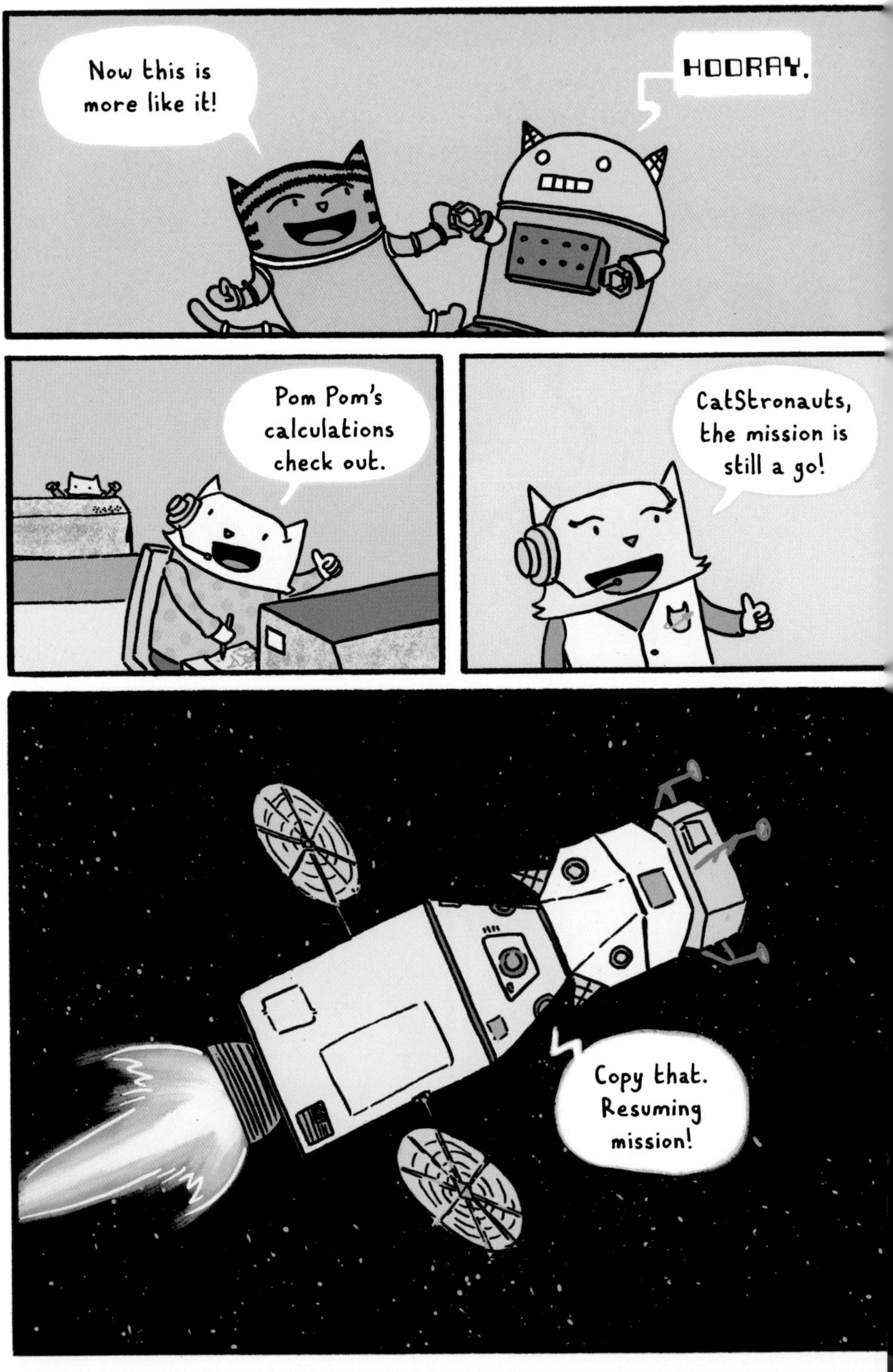
Now this is more like it!
HOORAY.
Pom Pom's calculations check out.
CatStronauts, the mission is still a go!
Copy that. Resuming mission!

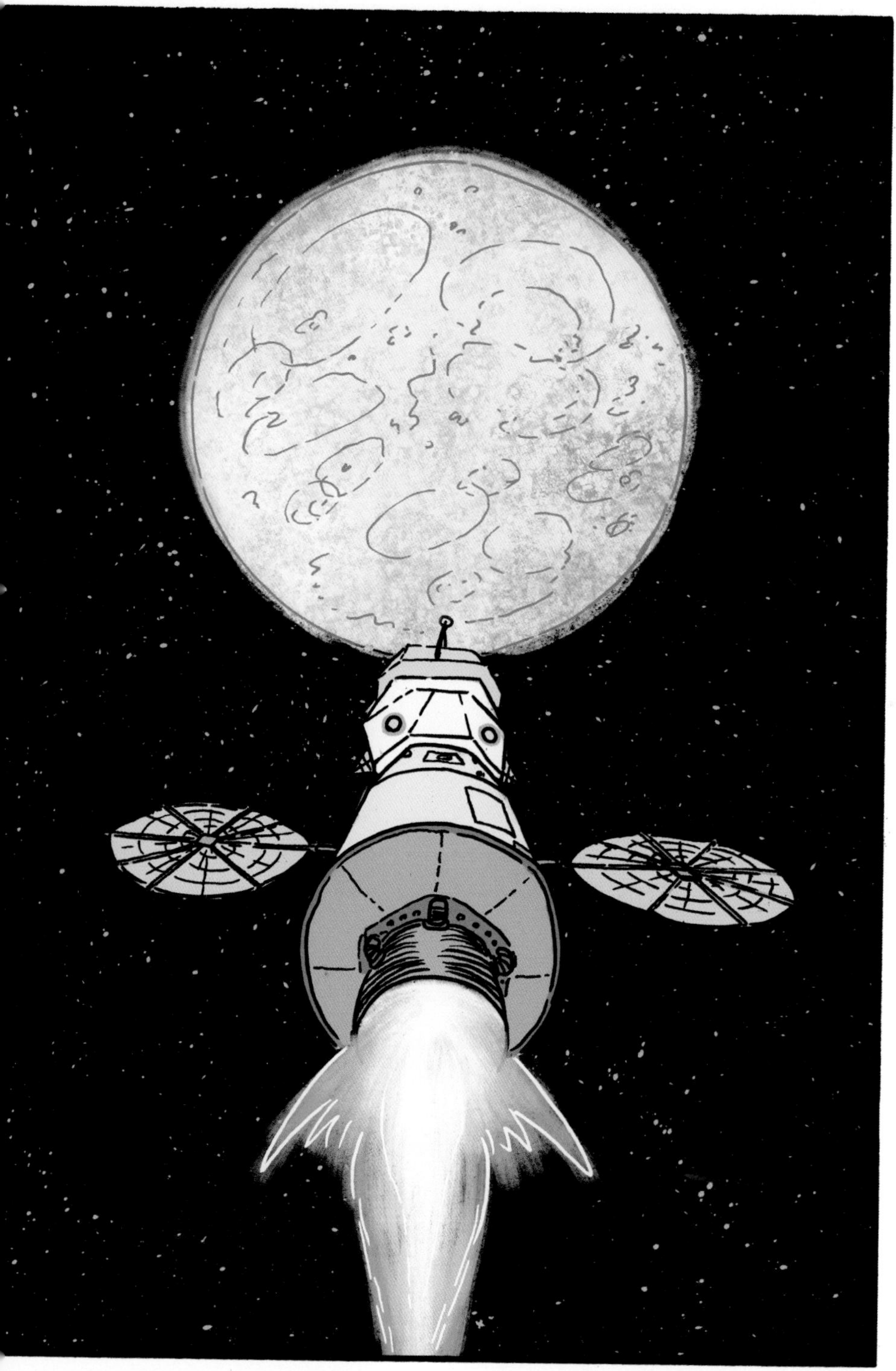

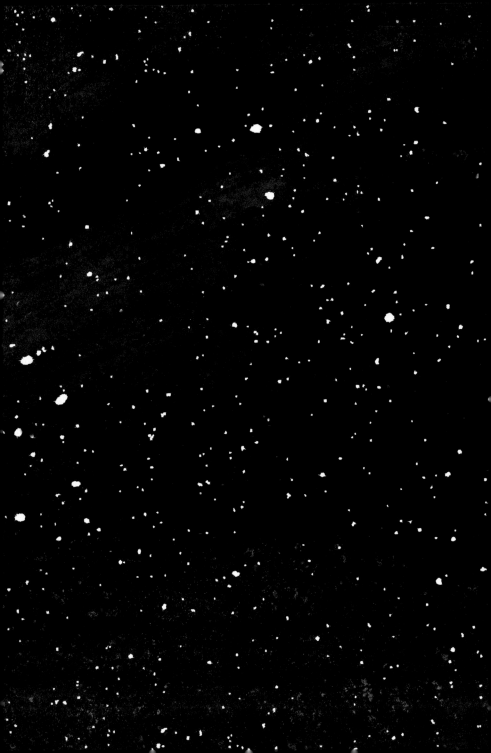

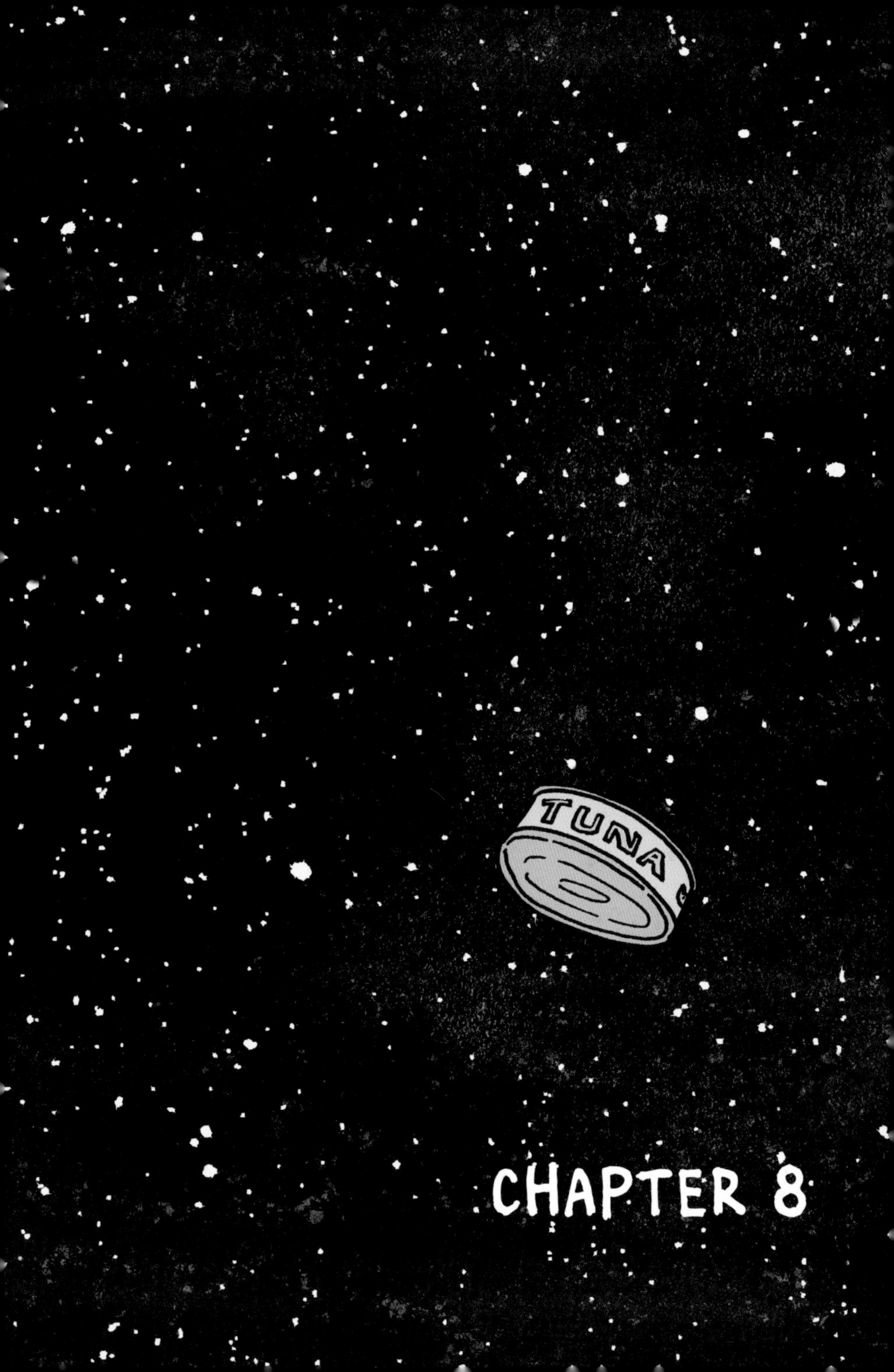
TUNA
CHAPTER 8

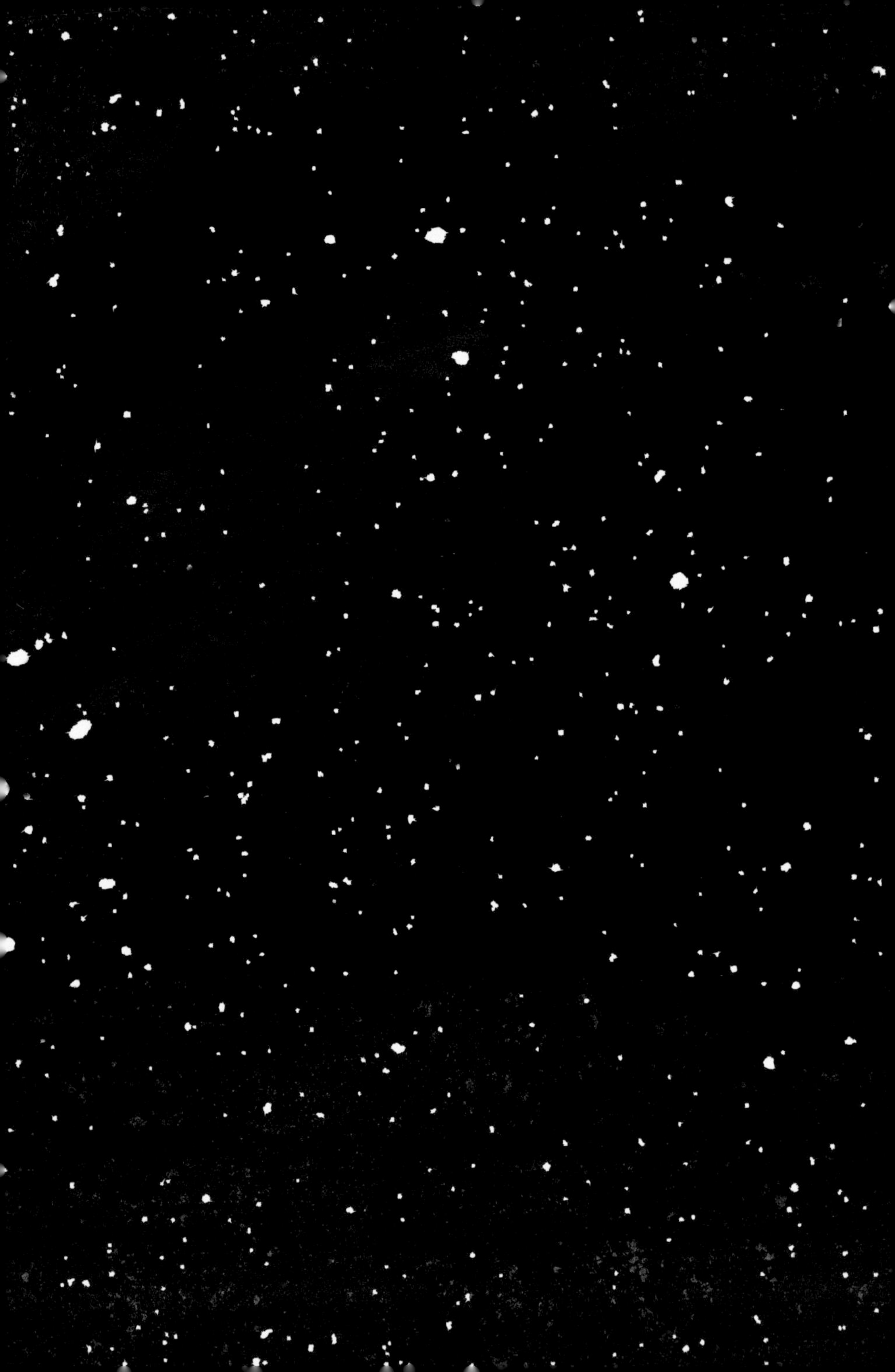

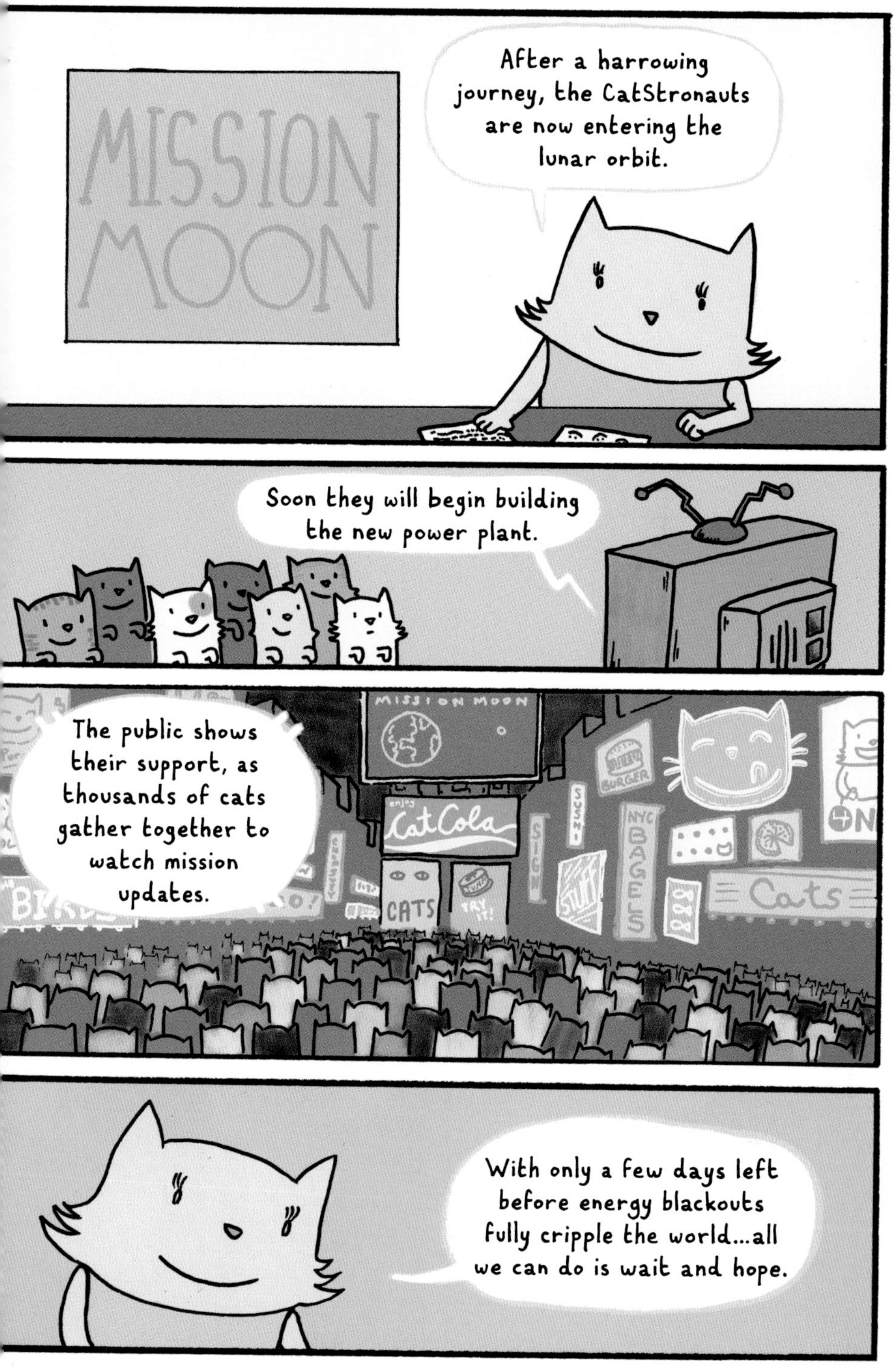
MISSION MOON
After a harrowing journey, the CatStronauts are now entering the lunar orbit.
Soon they will begin building the new power plant.
MISSION MOON
enjoy CatCola
SUSHI
SIGN
BURGER
NYC BAGELS
STUFF
CATS
TRY IT!
Cats
The public shows their support, as thousands of cats gather together to watch mission updates.
With only a few days left before energy blackouts fully cripple the world...all we can do is wait and hope.

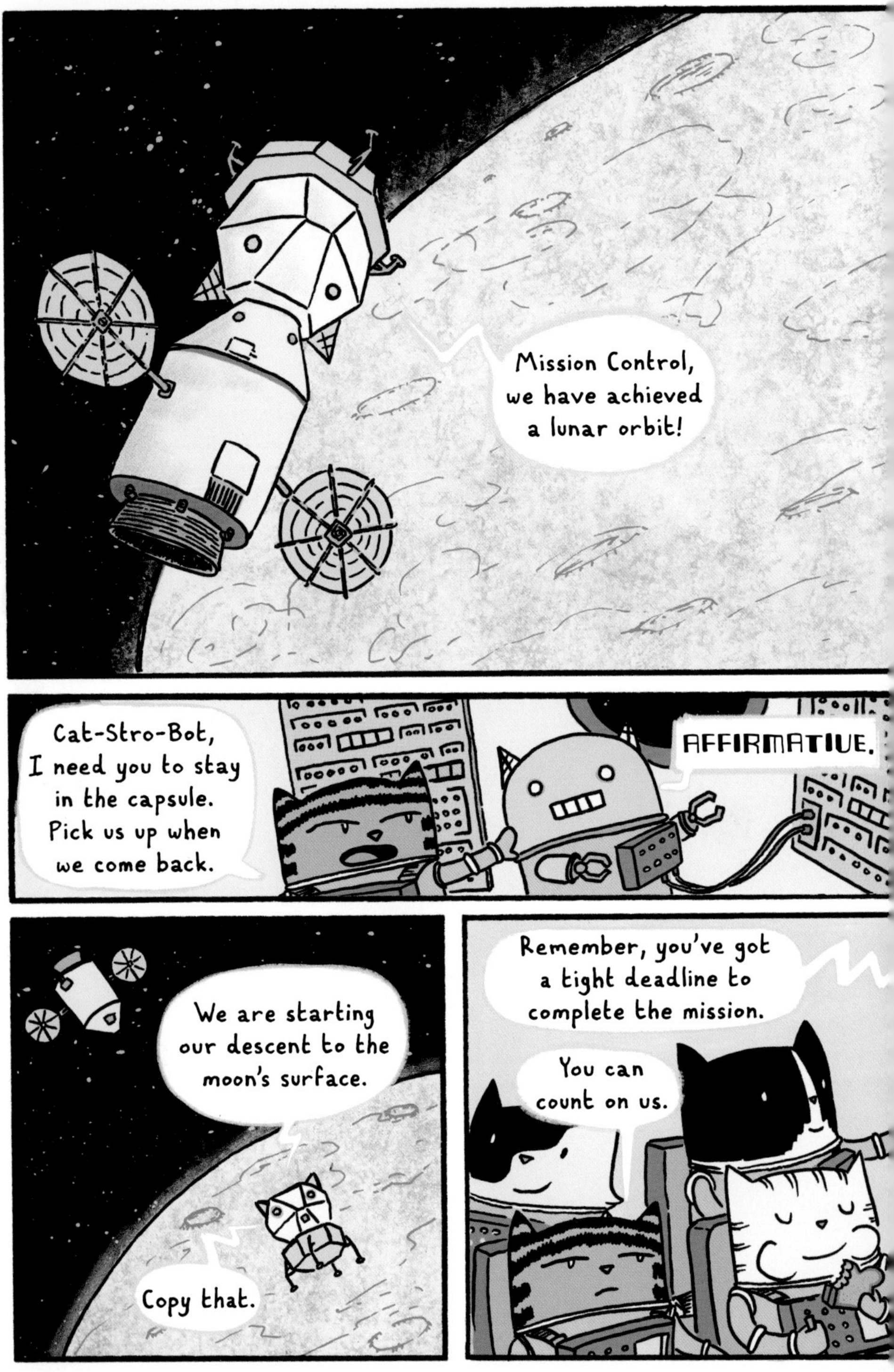
Mission Control, we have achieved a lunar orbit!
Cat-Stro-Bot, I need you to stay in the capsule. Pick us up when we come back.
AFFIRMATIVE.
We are starting our descent to the moon's surface.
Copy that.
Remember, you've got a tight deadline to complete the mission.
You can count on us.

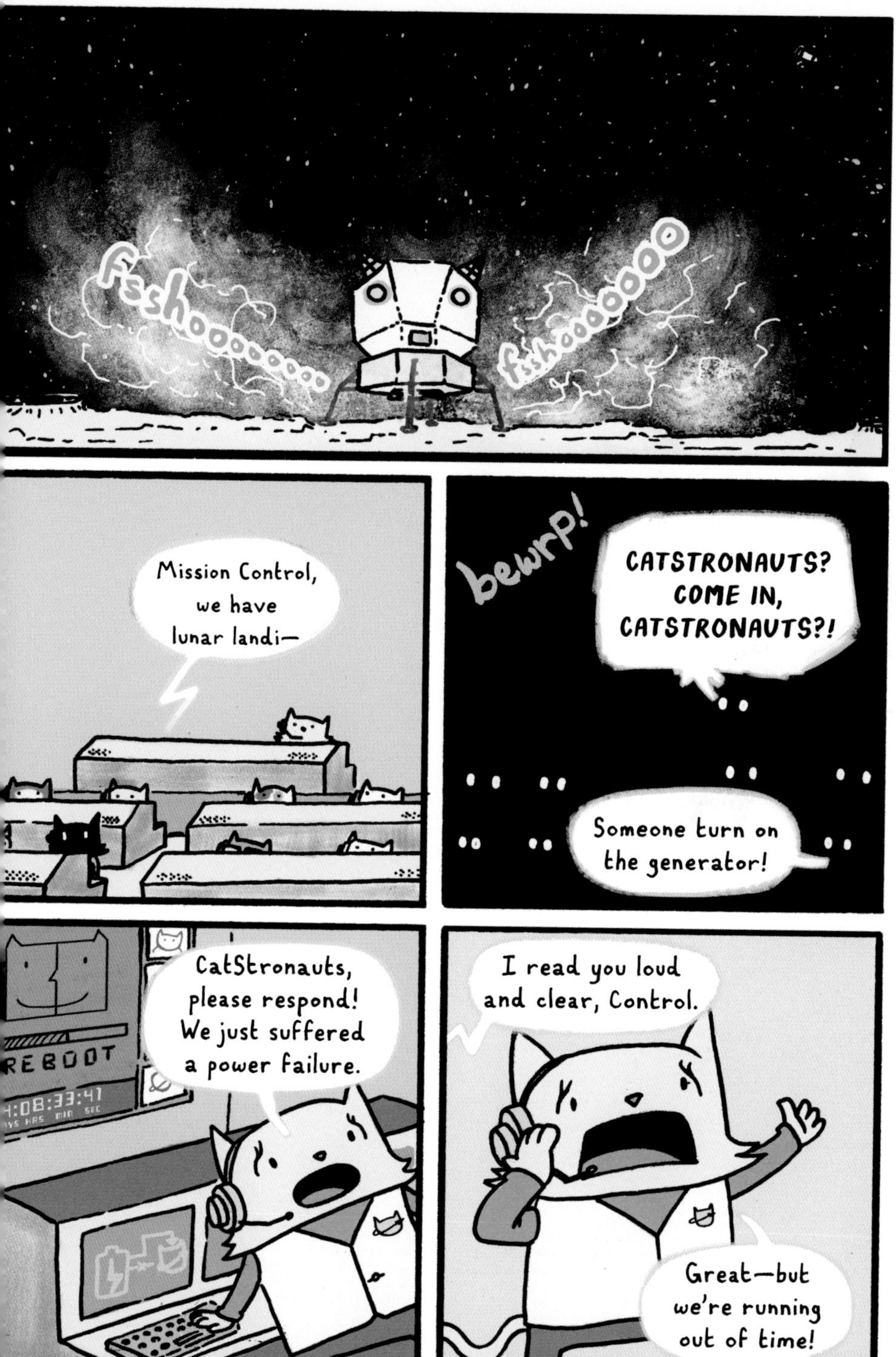

fsshoooooooo
fsshoooooooO
Mission Control, we have lunar landi—
bewrp!
CATSTRONAUTS? COME IN, CATSTRONAUTS?!
Someone turn on the generator!
REBOOT
CatStronauts, please respond! We just suffered a power failure.
I read you loud and clear, Control.
Great—but we're running out of time!

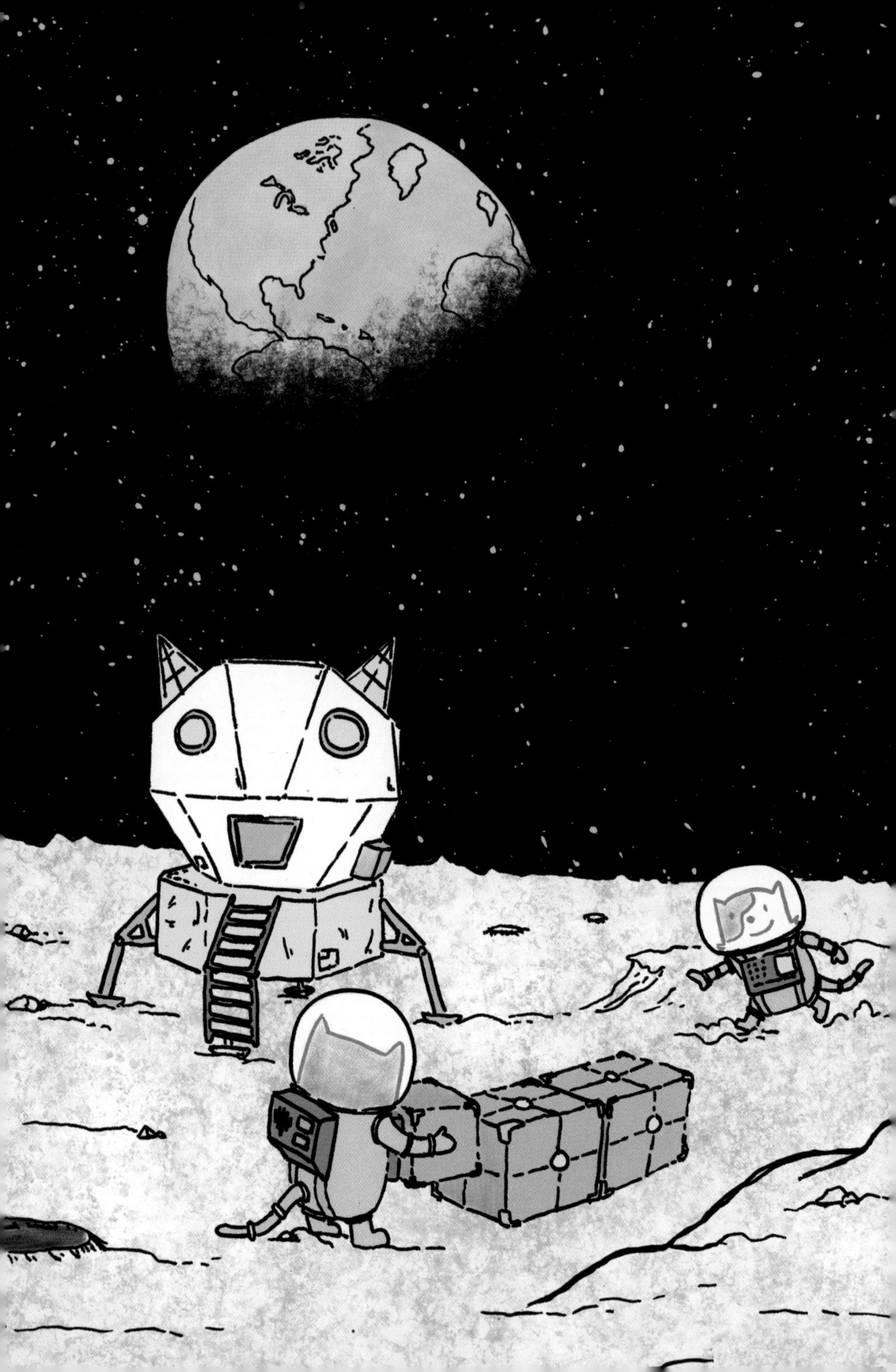

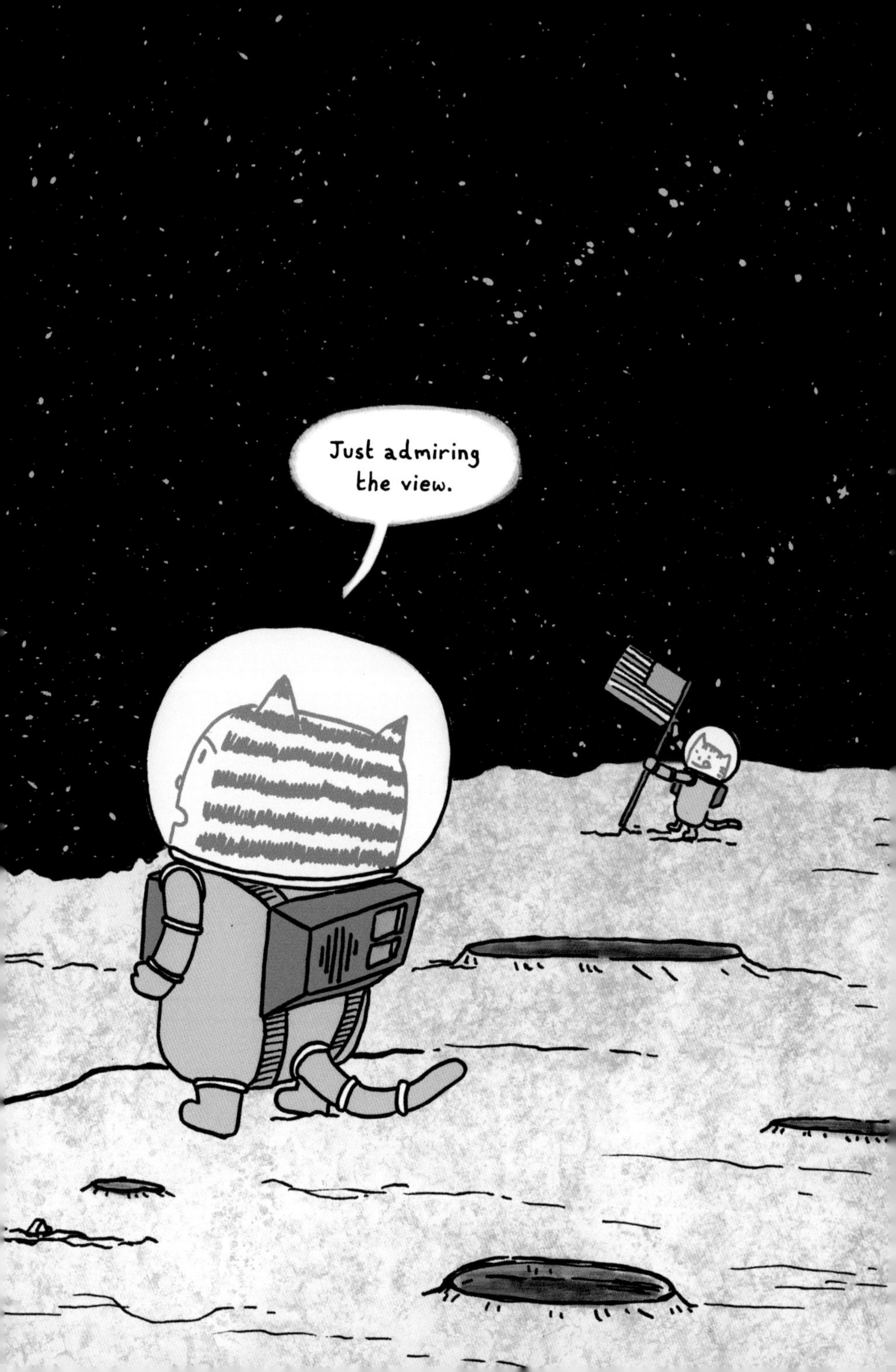
Just admiring the view.

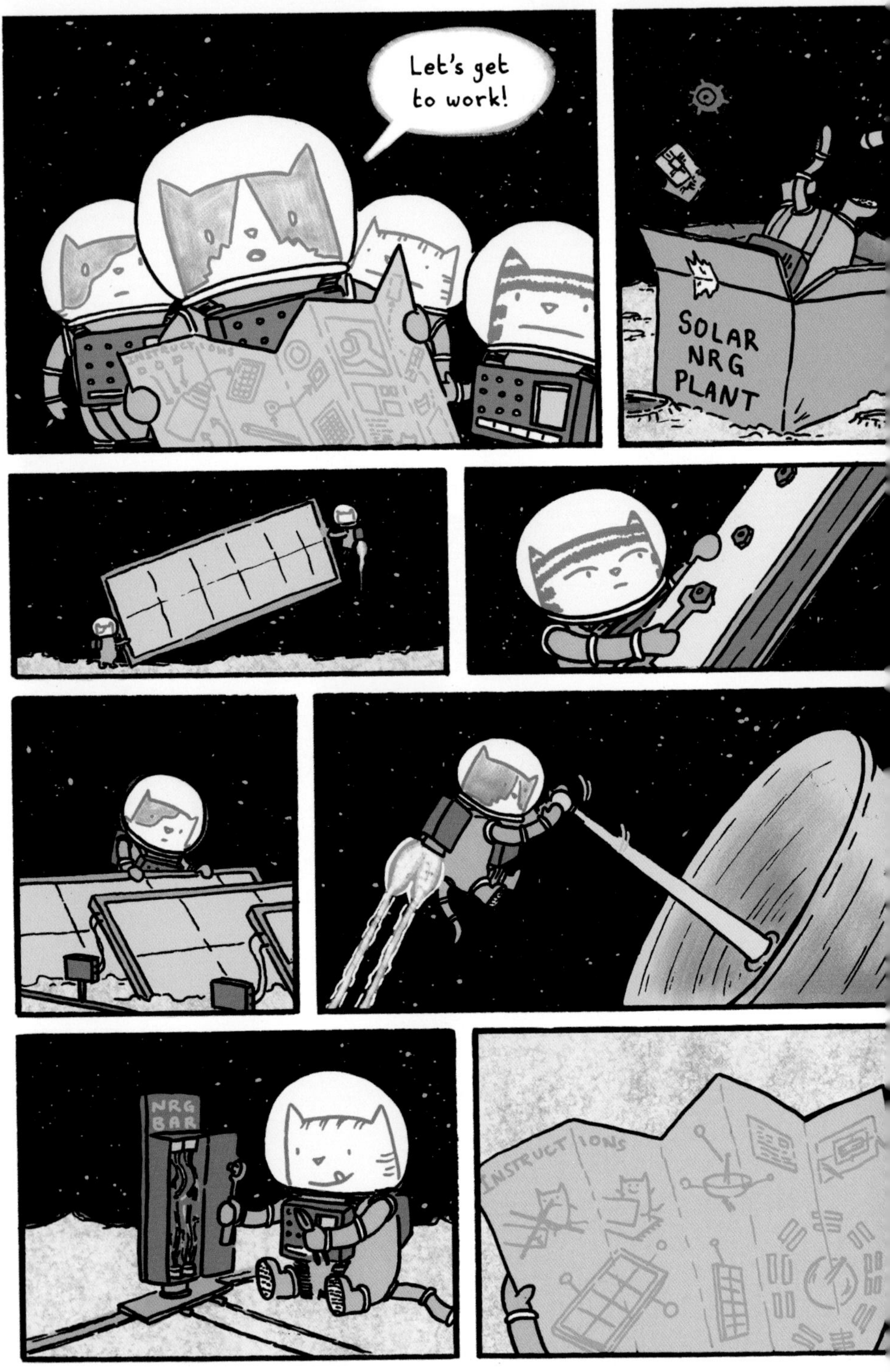
Let's get to work!
INSTRUCTIONS
SOLAR NRG PLANT
NRG BAR
INSTRUCTIONS

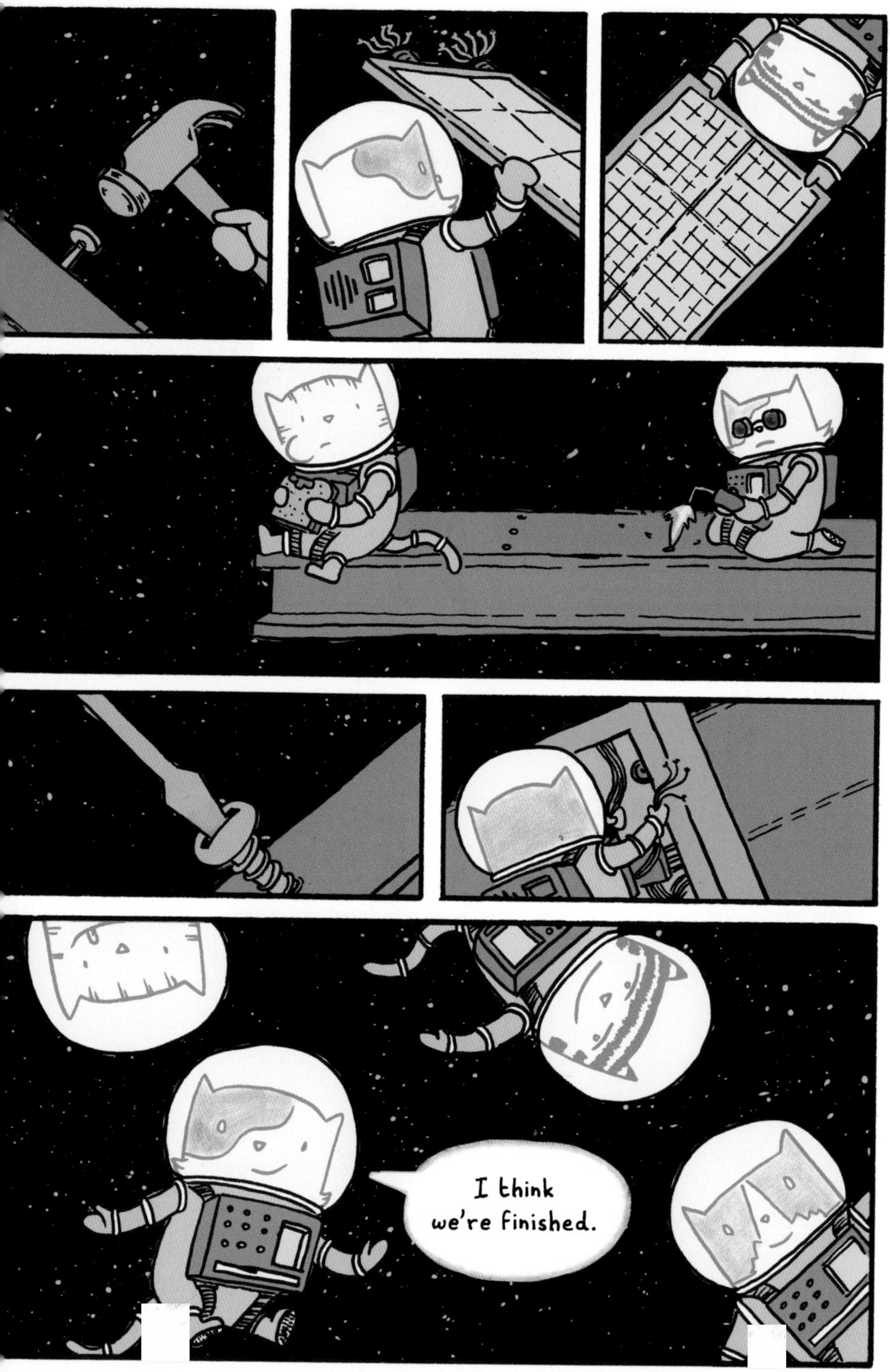
I think we're finished.

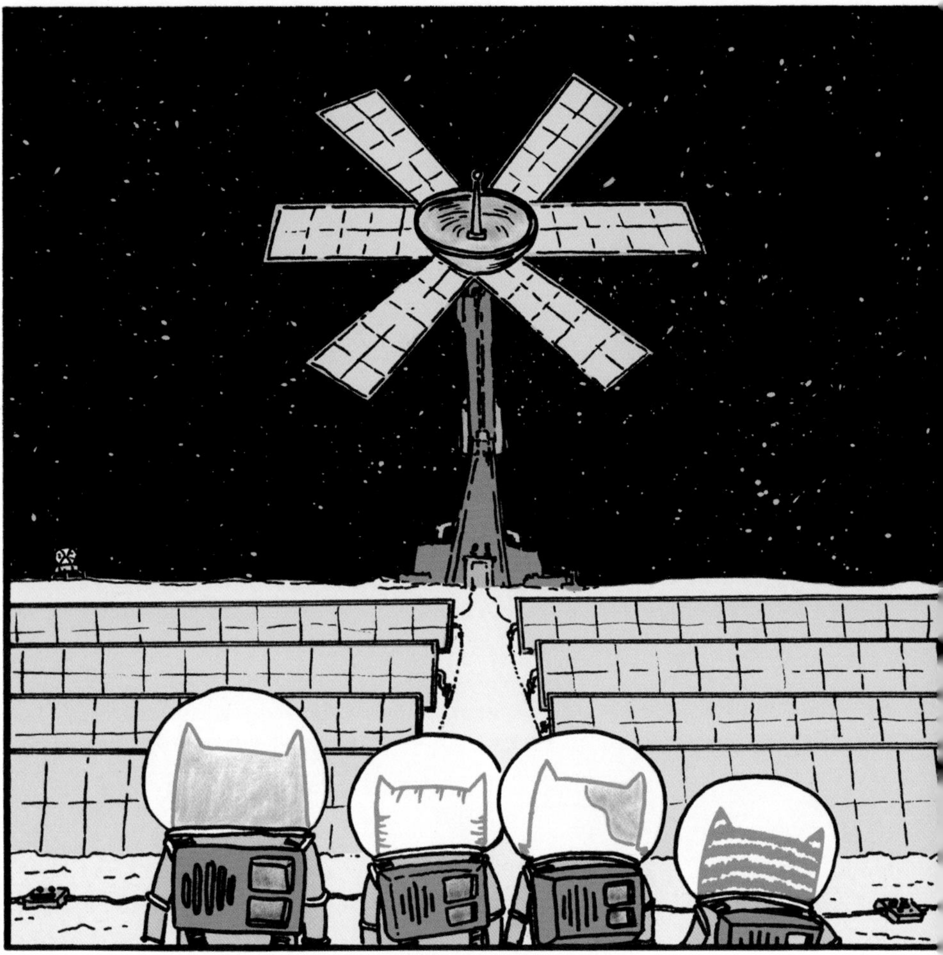

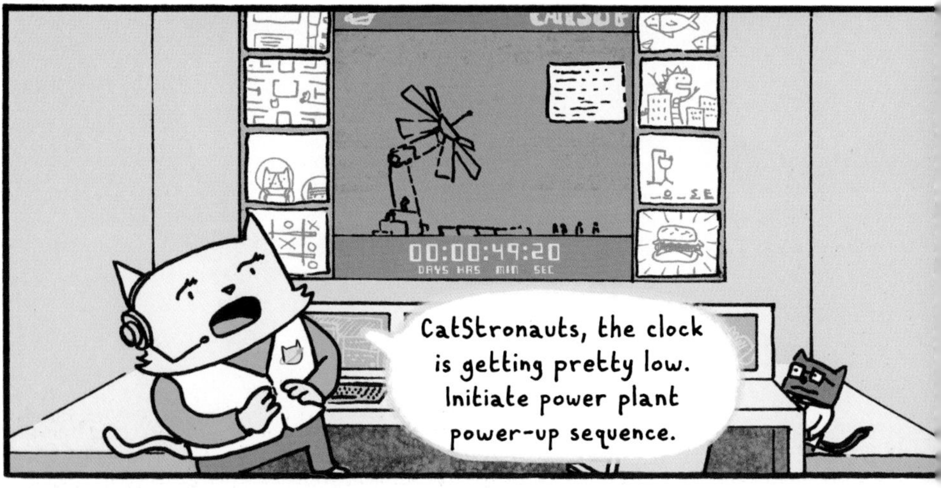
00:00:49:20
DAYS HRS MIN SEC
CatStronauts, the clock is getting pretty low. Initiate power plant power-up sequence.

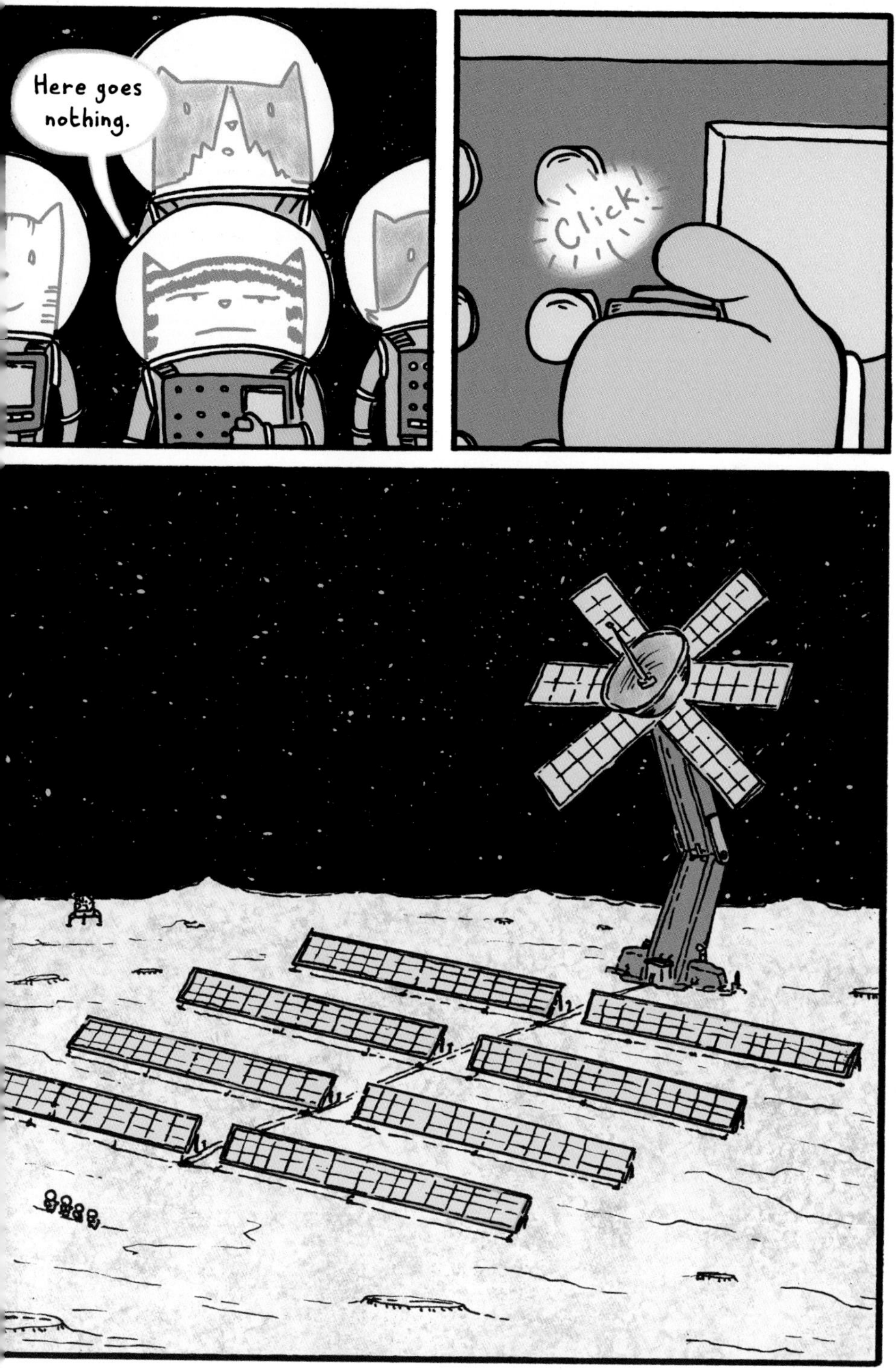
Here goes nothing.
Click!

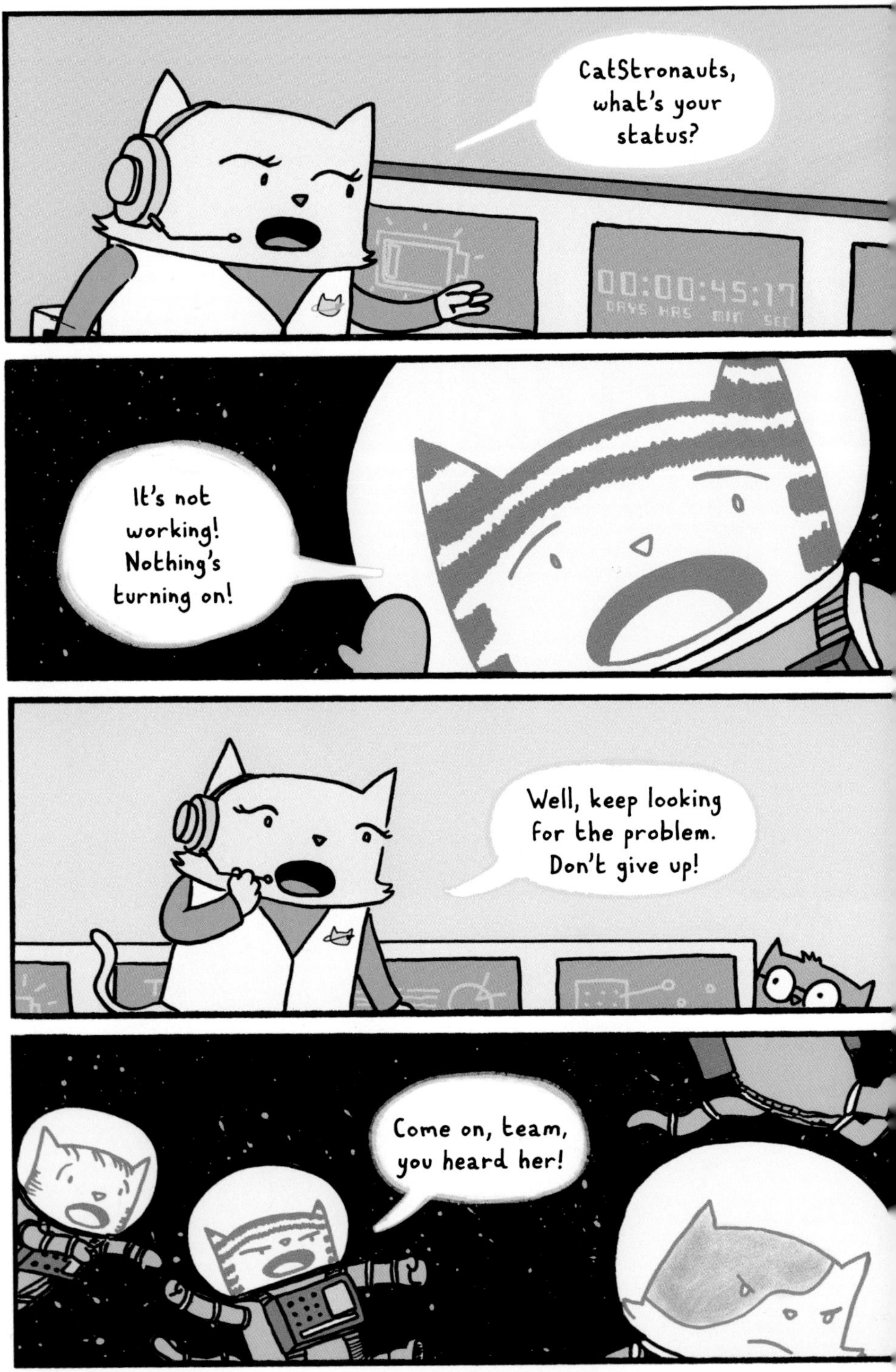
CatStronauts, what's your status?
00:00:45:17
DAYS HRS MIN SEC
It's not working! Nothing's turning on!
Well, keep looking for the problem. Don't give up!
Come on, team, you heard her!

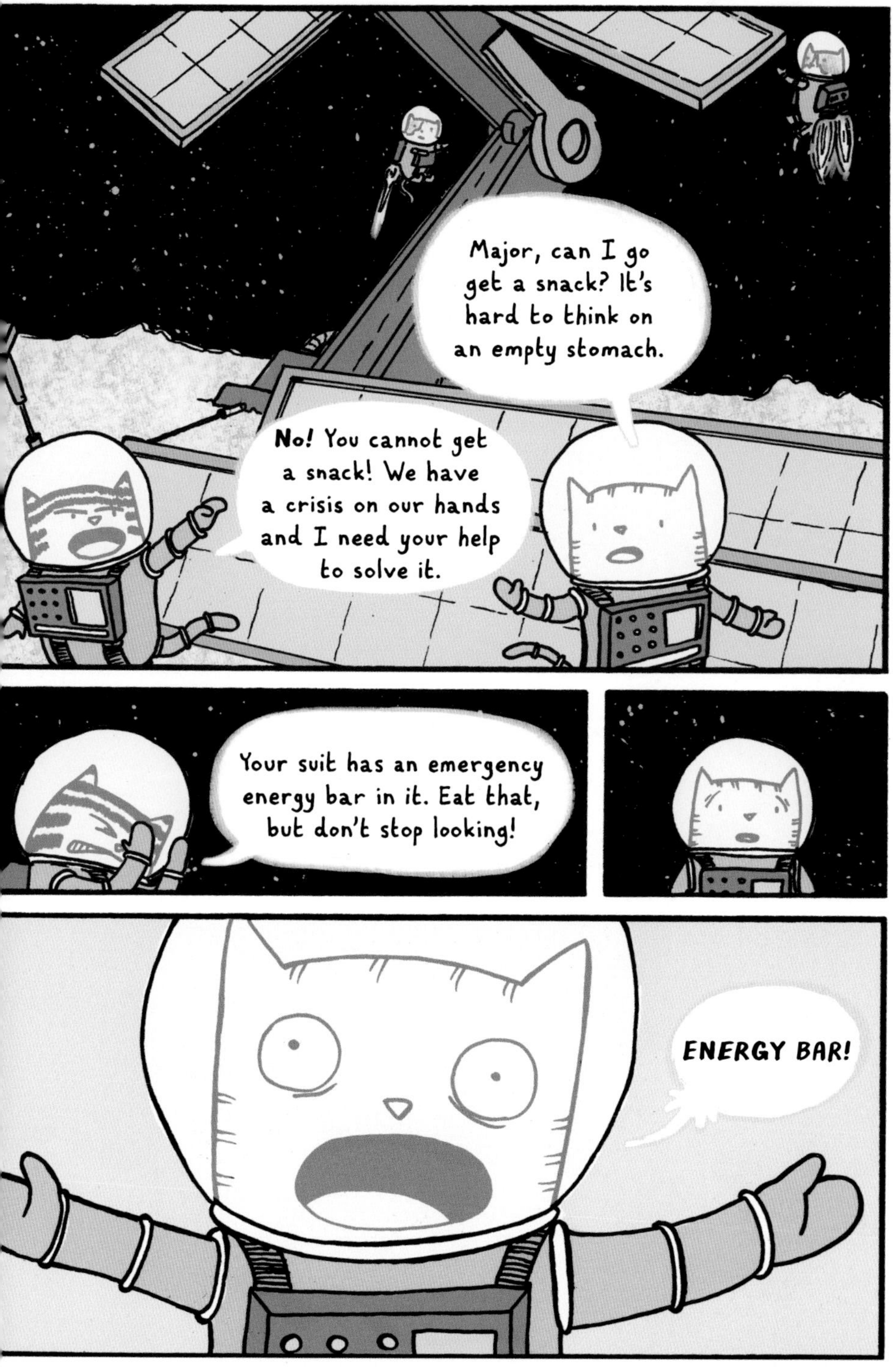

Major, can I go get a snack? It's hard to think on an empty stomach.
No! You cannot get a snack! We have a crisis on our hands and I need your help to solve it.
Your suit has an emergency energy bar in it. Eat that, but don't stop looking!
ENERGY BAR!

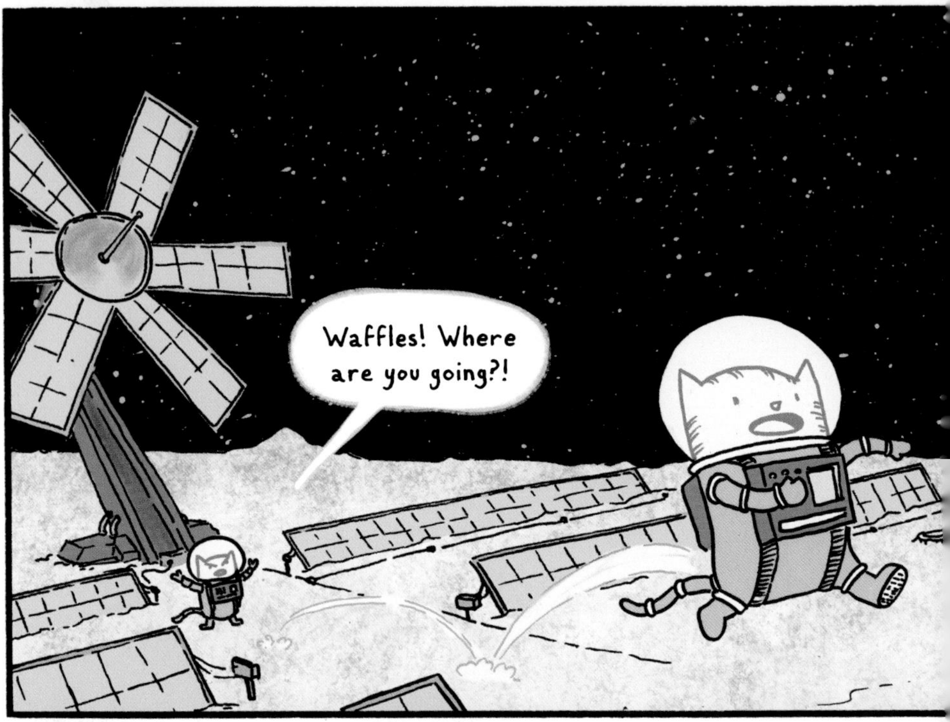
Waffles! Where are you going?!

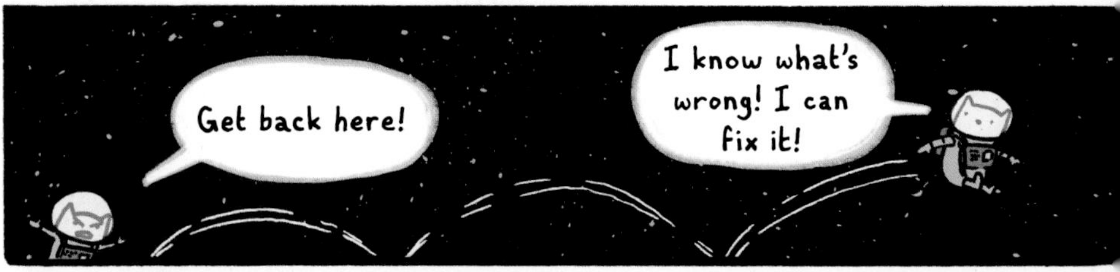
Get back here!
I know what's wrong! I can fix it!

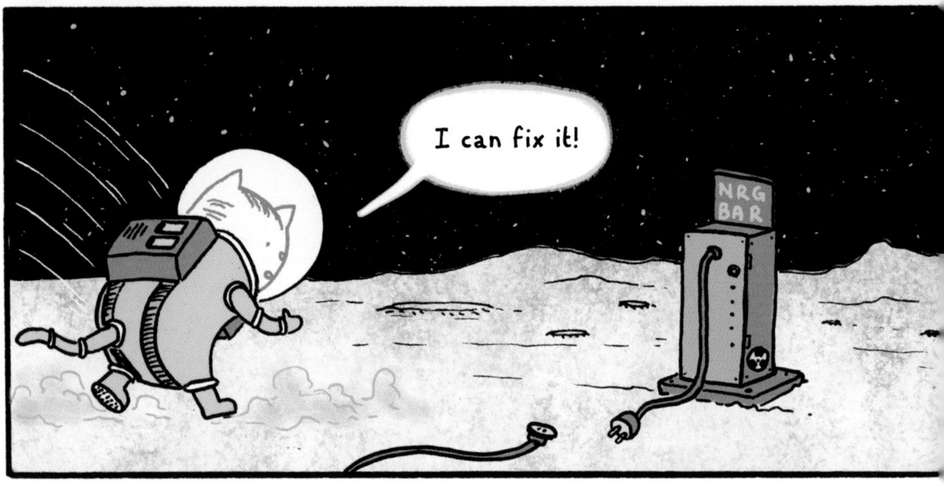
I can fix it!
NRG BAR

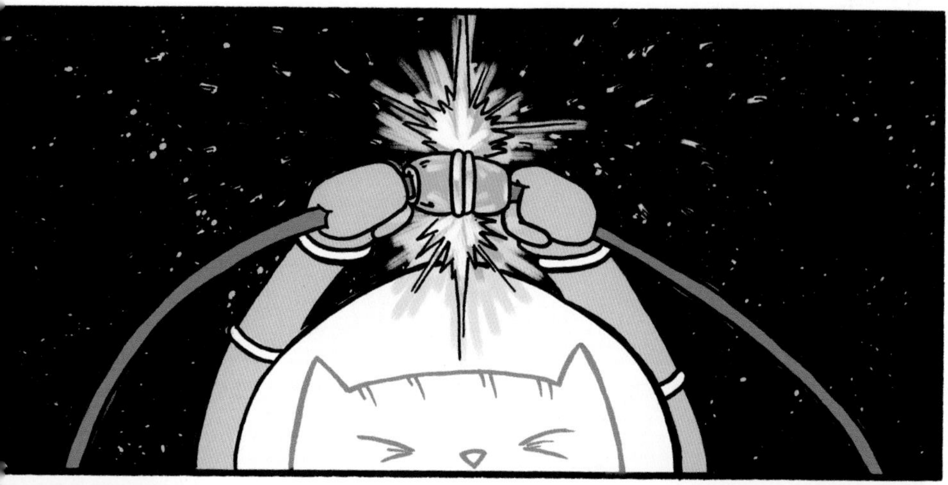

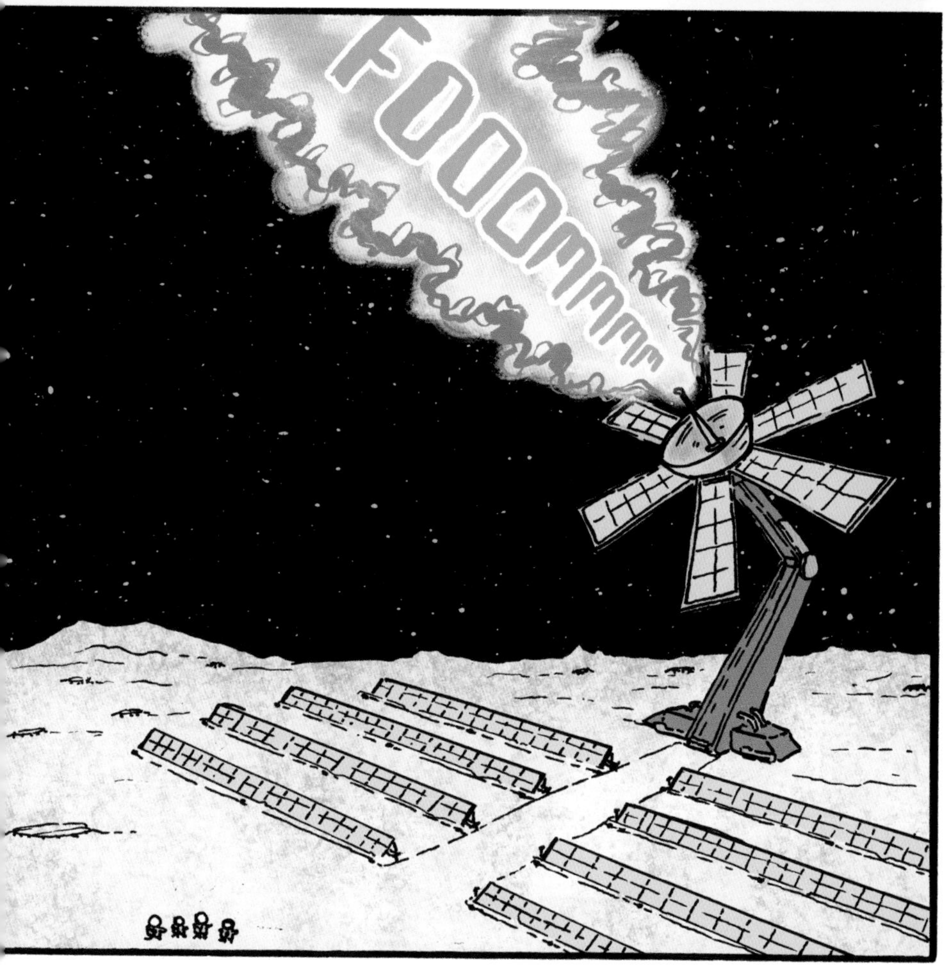
FOOOMMMMMM

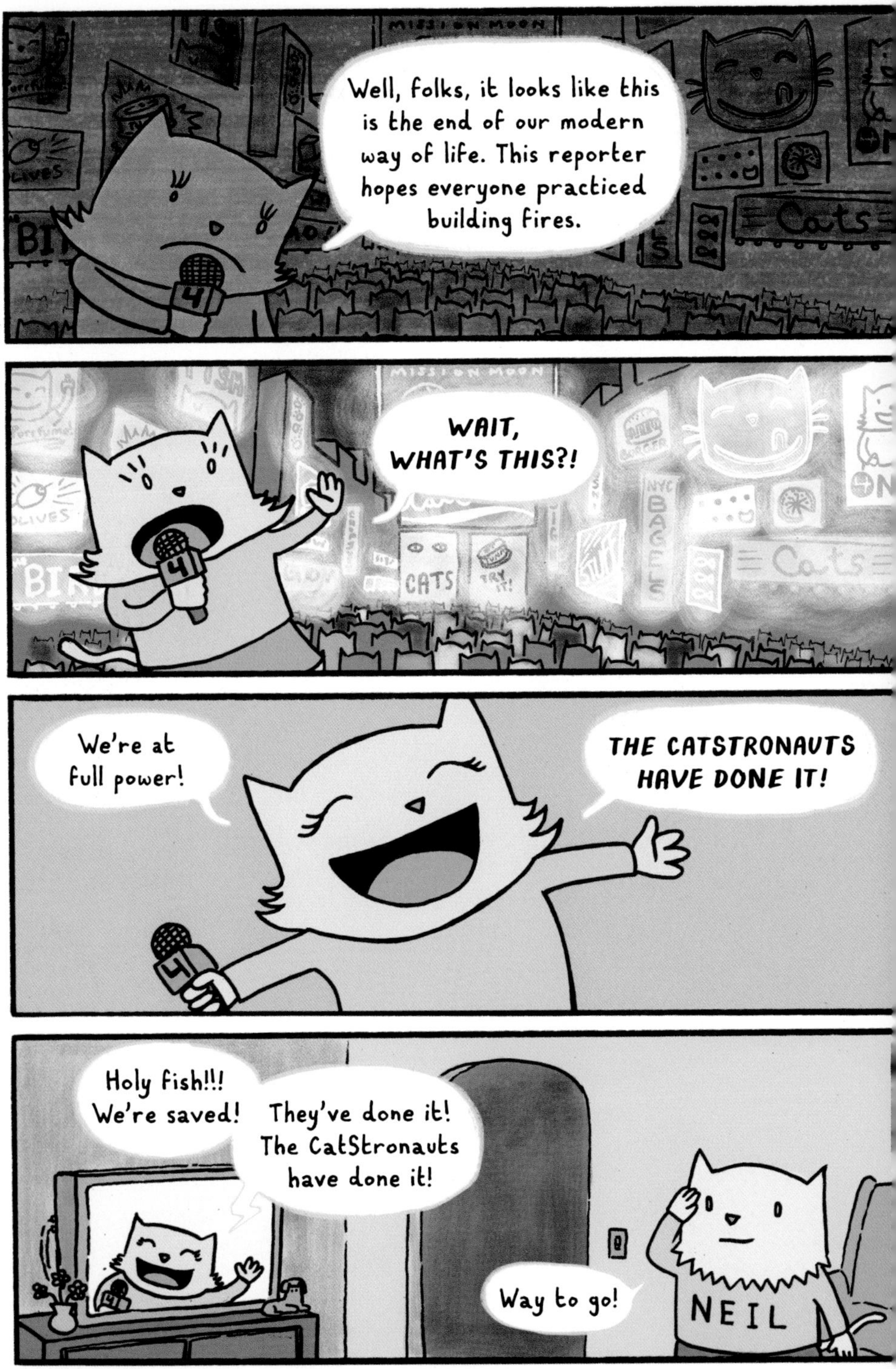

MISSION MOON
Well, folks, it looks like this is the end of our modern way of life. This reporter hopes everyone practiced building fires.
MISSION MOON
WAIT, WHAT'S THIS?!
CATS
TRY IT!
NYC BAGELS
Cats
We're at full power!
THE CATSTRONAUTS HAVE DONE IT!
Holy fish!!! We're saved!
They've done it! The CatStronauts have done it!
Way to go!
NEIL

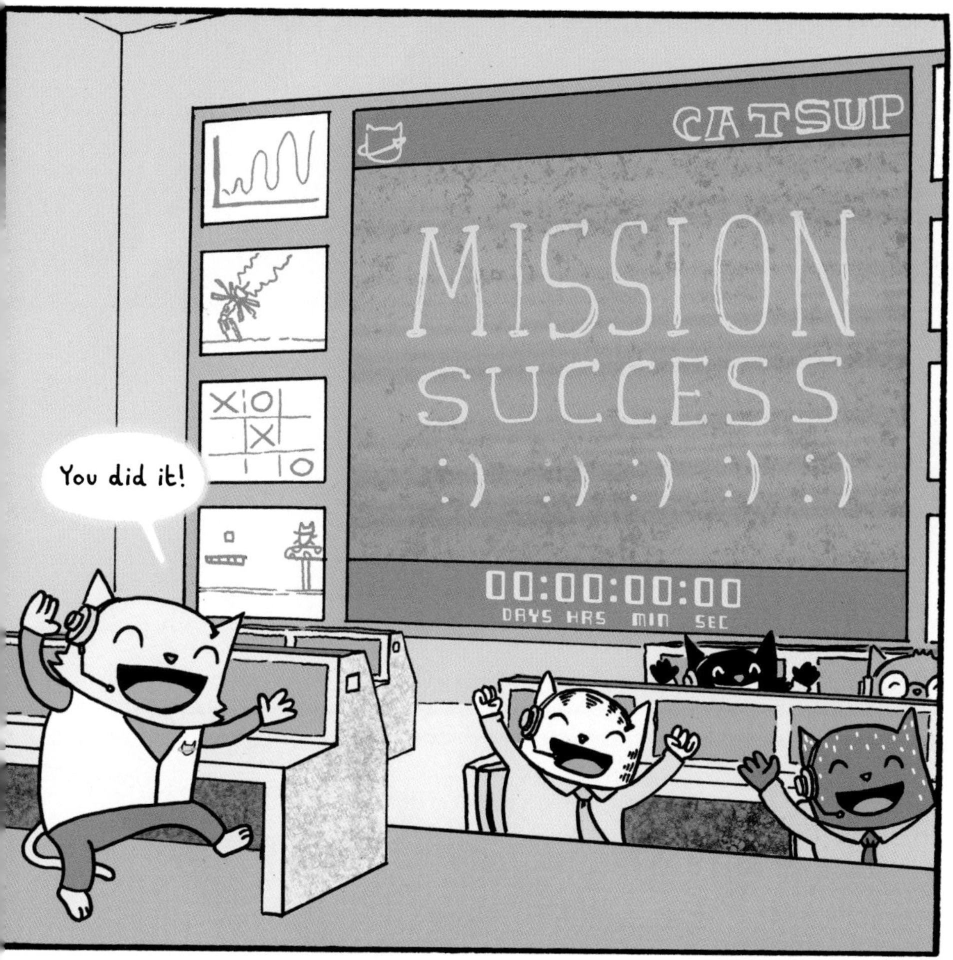
CATSUP
MISSION SUCCESS
:) :) :) :) :)
00:00:00:00
DAYS HRS MIN SEC
You did it!

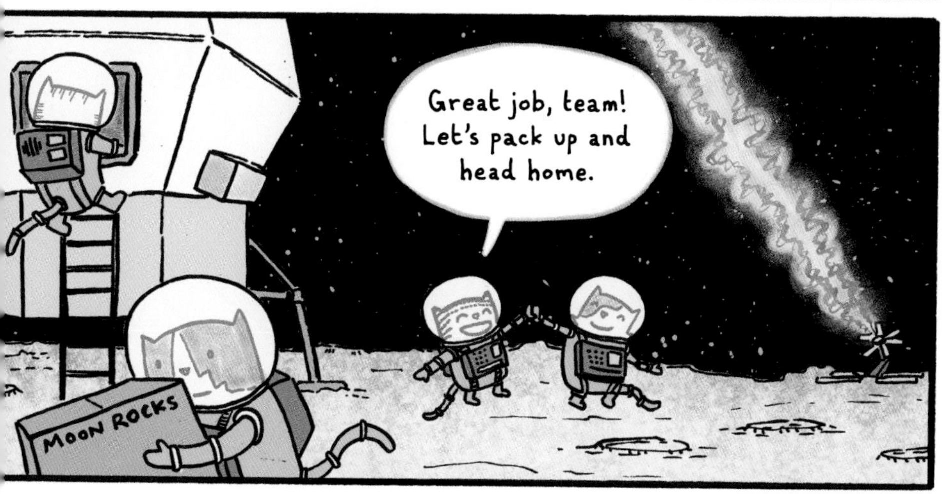
Great job, team! Let's pack up and head home.
MOON ROCKS

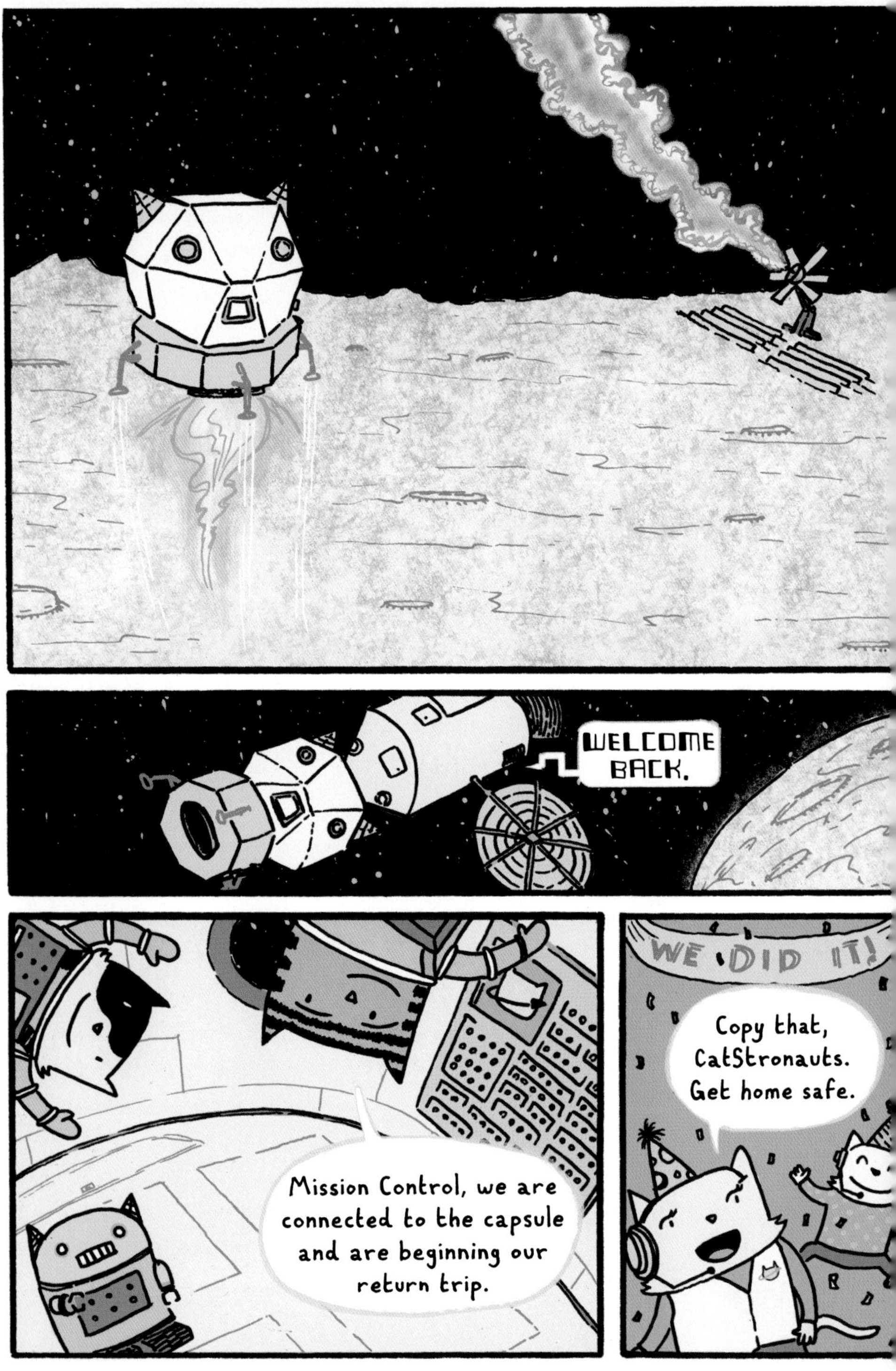
WELCOME BACK.
Mission Control, we are connected to the capsule and are beginning our return trip.
WE DID IT!
Copy that, CatStronauts. Get home safe.

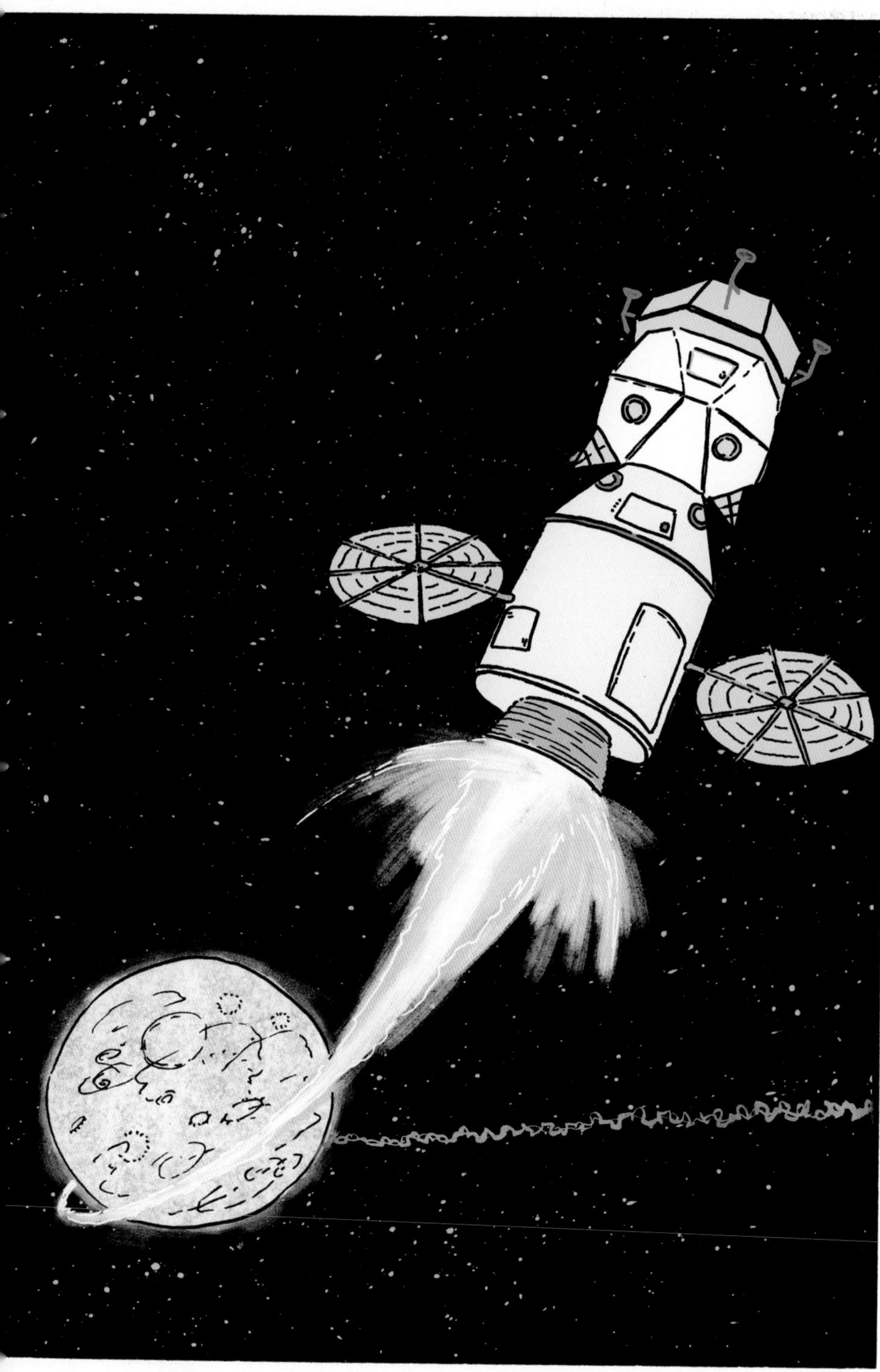

CHAPTER 9

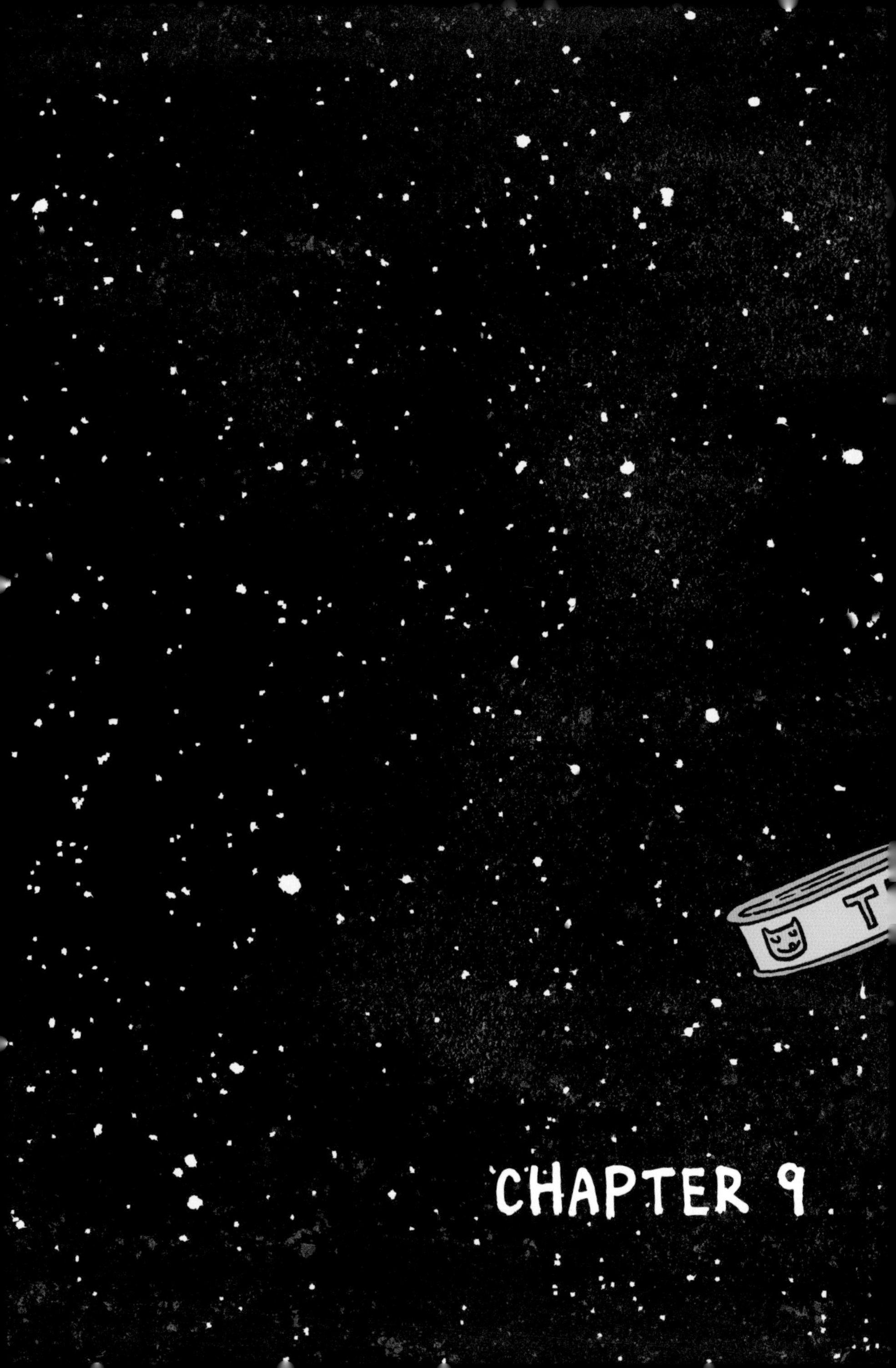

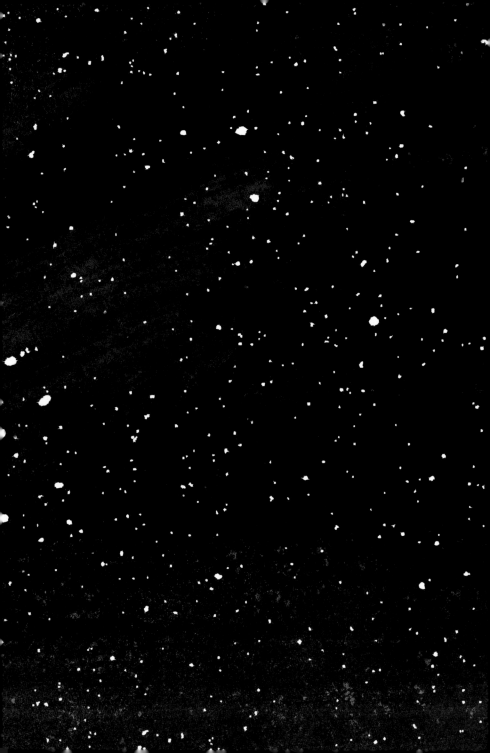

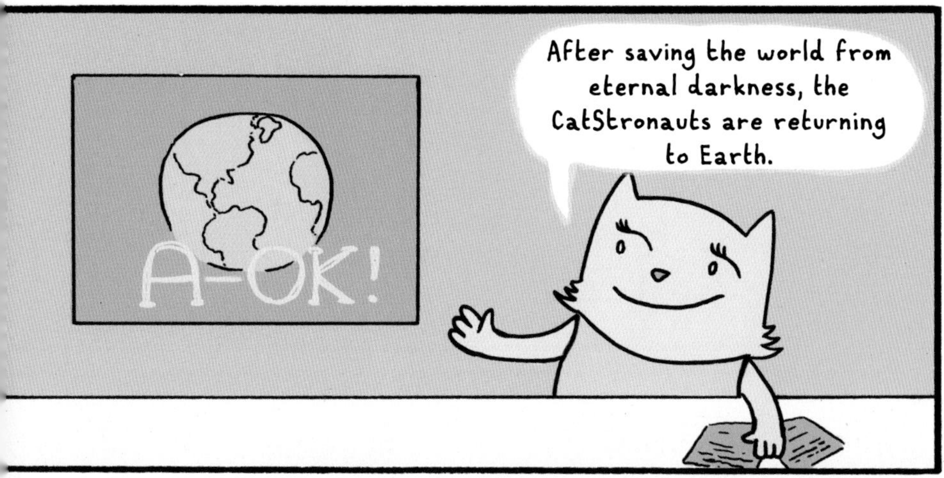
A-OK!
After saving the world from eternal darkness, the CatStronauts are returning to Earth.

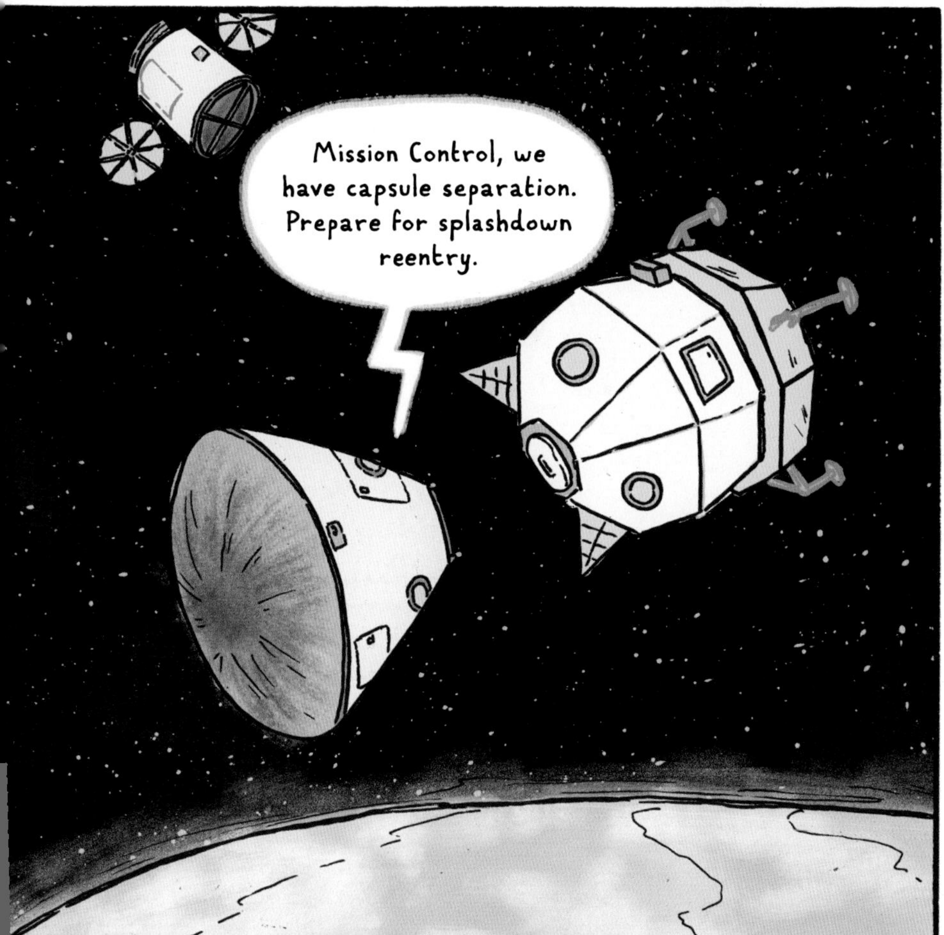
Mission Control, we have capsule separation. Prepare for splashdown reentry.

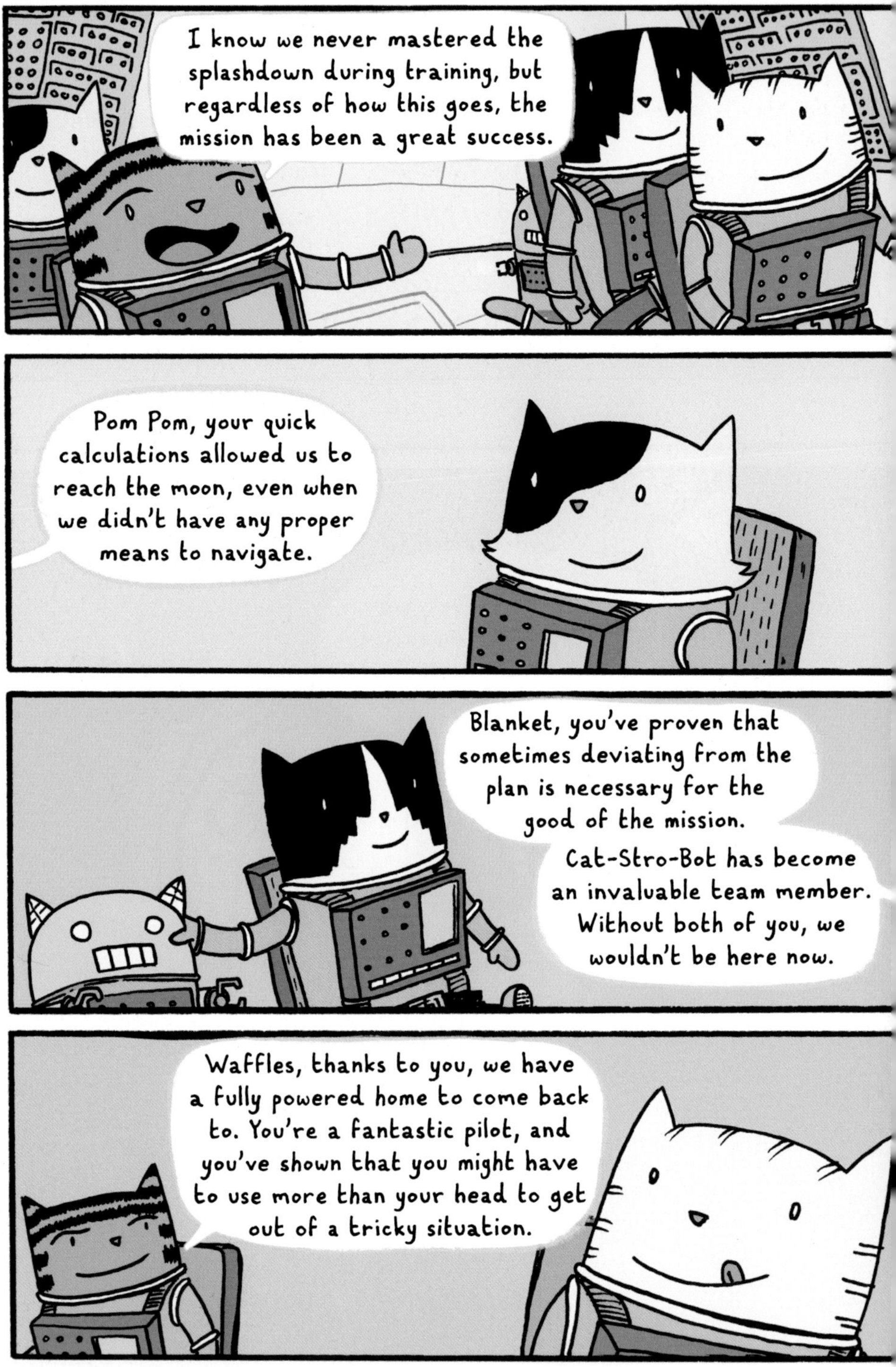
I know we never mastered the splashdown during training, but regardless of how this goes, the mission has been a great success.
Pom Pom, your quick calculations allowed us to reach the moon, even when we didn't have any proper means to navigate.
Blanket, you've proven that sometimes deviating from the plan is necessary for the good of the mission.
Cat-Stro-Bot has become an invaluable team member. Without both of you, we wouldn't be here now.
Waffles, thanks to you, we have a fully powered home to come back to. You're a fantastic pilot, and you've shown that you might have to use more than your head to get out of a tricky situation.

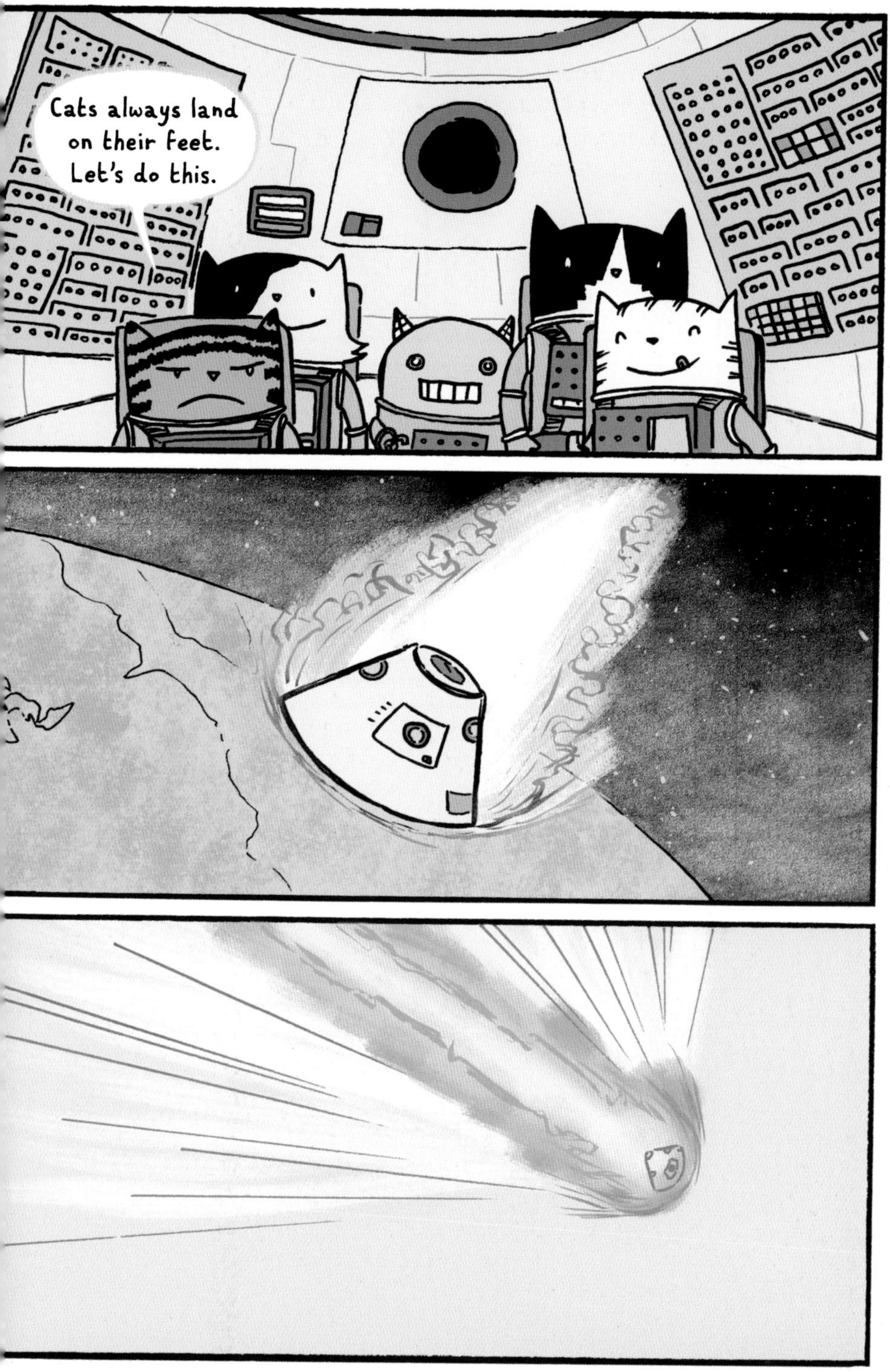
Cats always land on their feet. Let's do this.

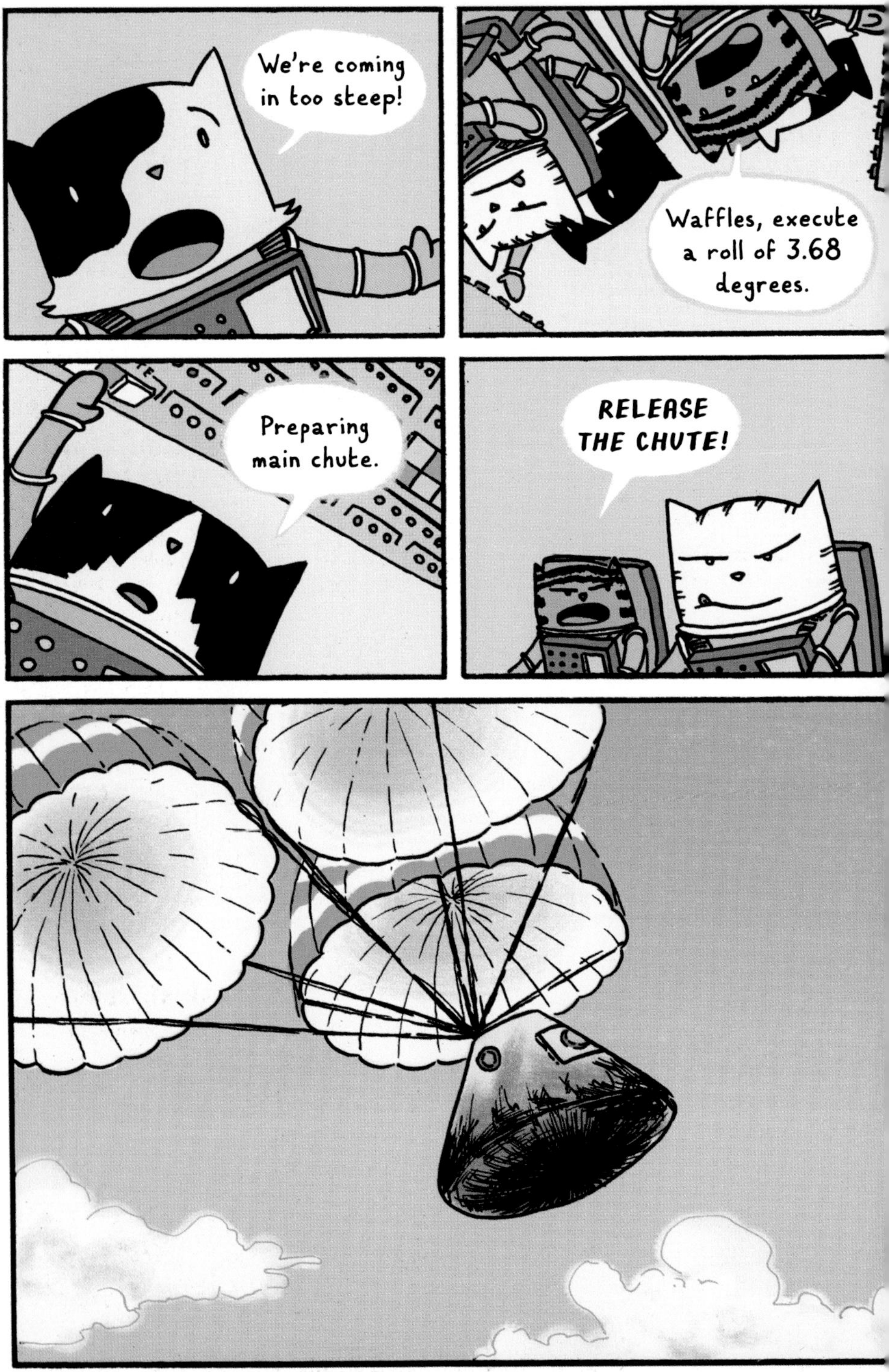
We're coming in too steep!
Waffles, execute a roll of 3.68 degrees.
Preparing main chute.
RELEASE THE CHUTE!

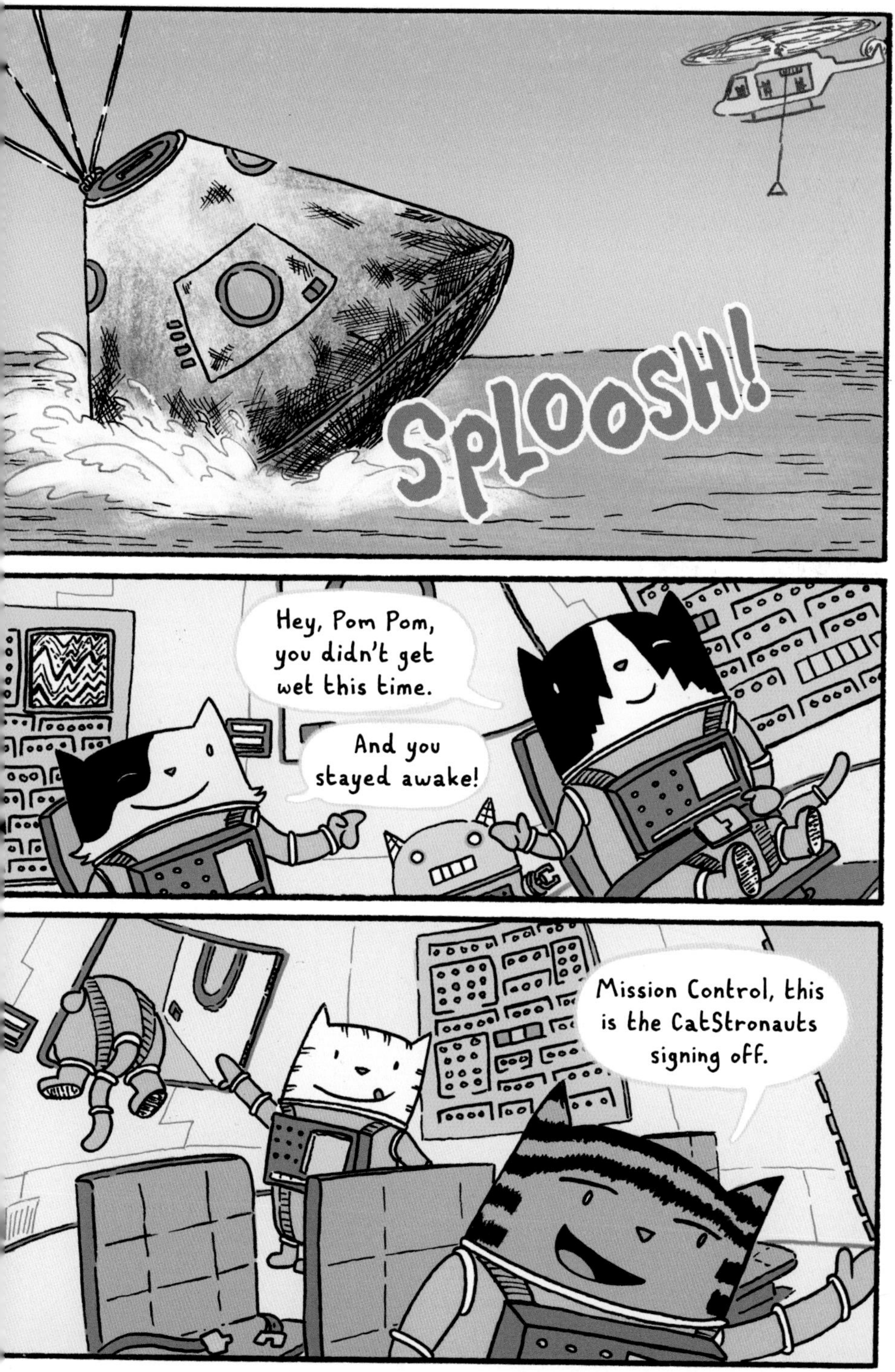
SPLOOSH!
Hey, Pom Pom, you didn't get wet this time.
And you stayed awake!
Mission Control, this is the CatStronauts signing off.

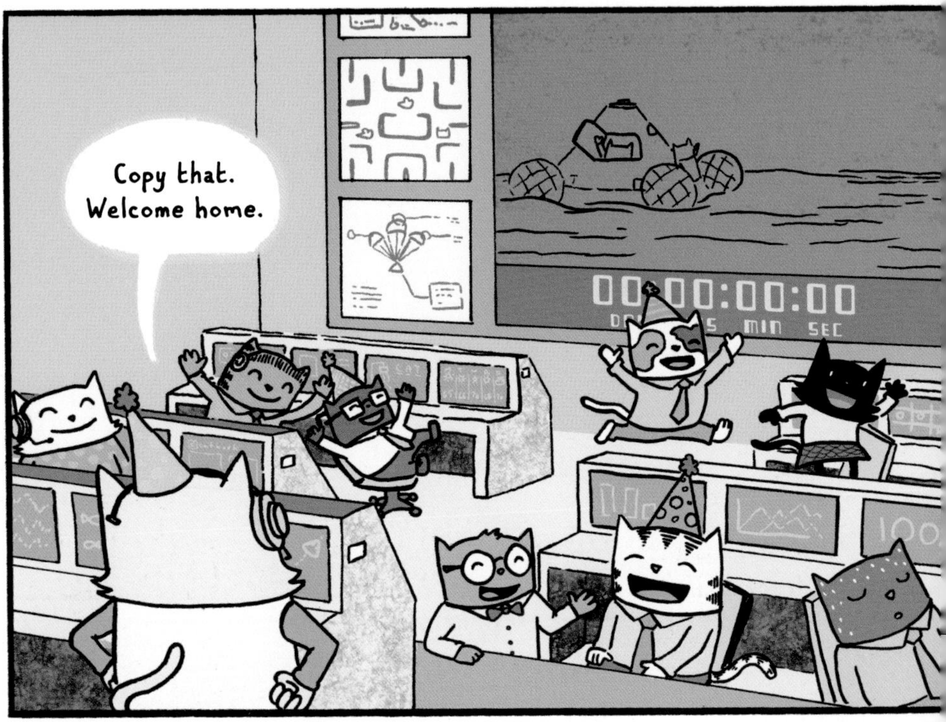
Copy that. Welcome home.
00:00:00:00
MIN SEC

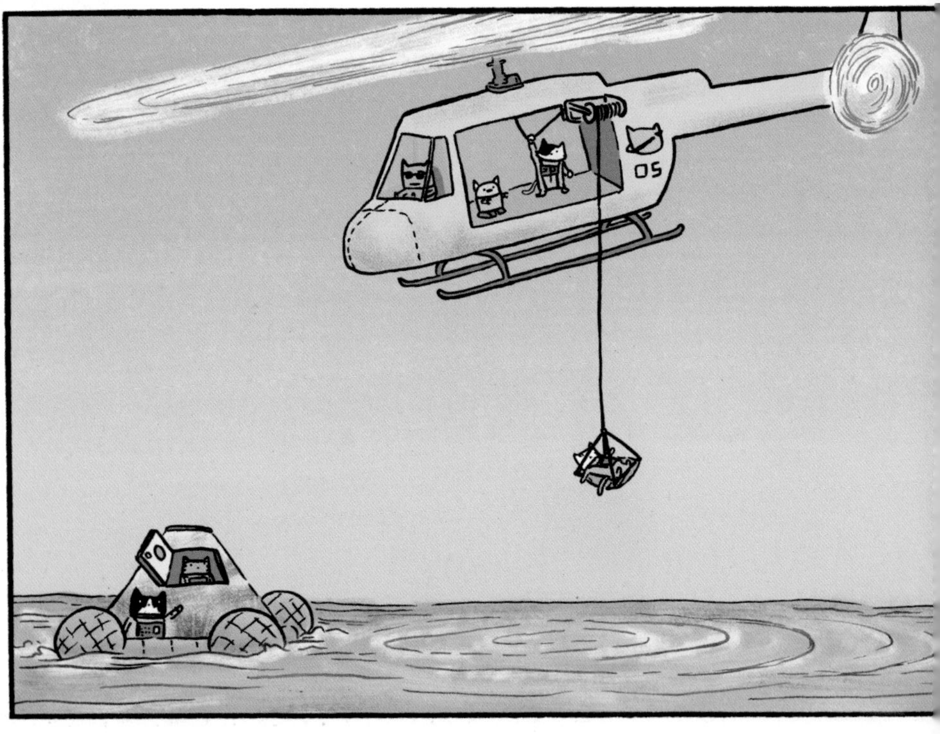
05

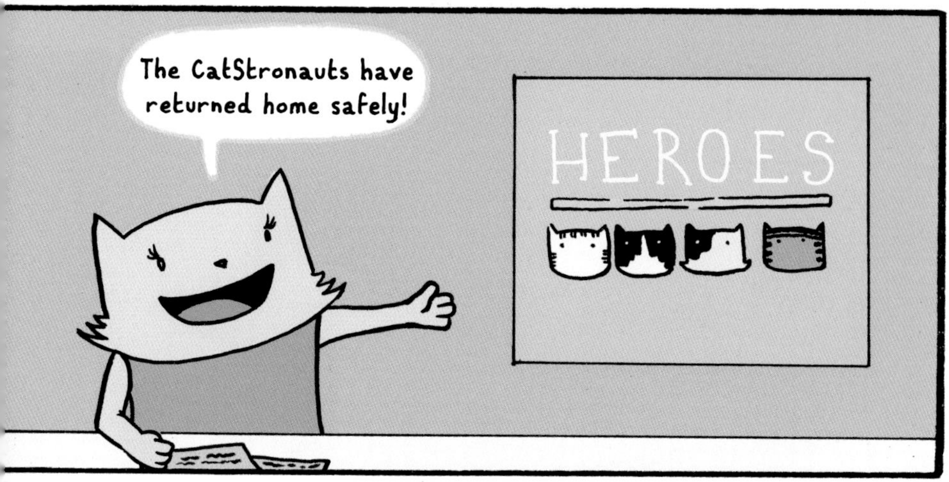
The CatStronauts have returned home safely!
HEROES

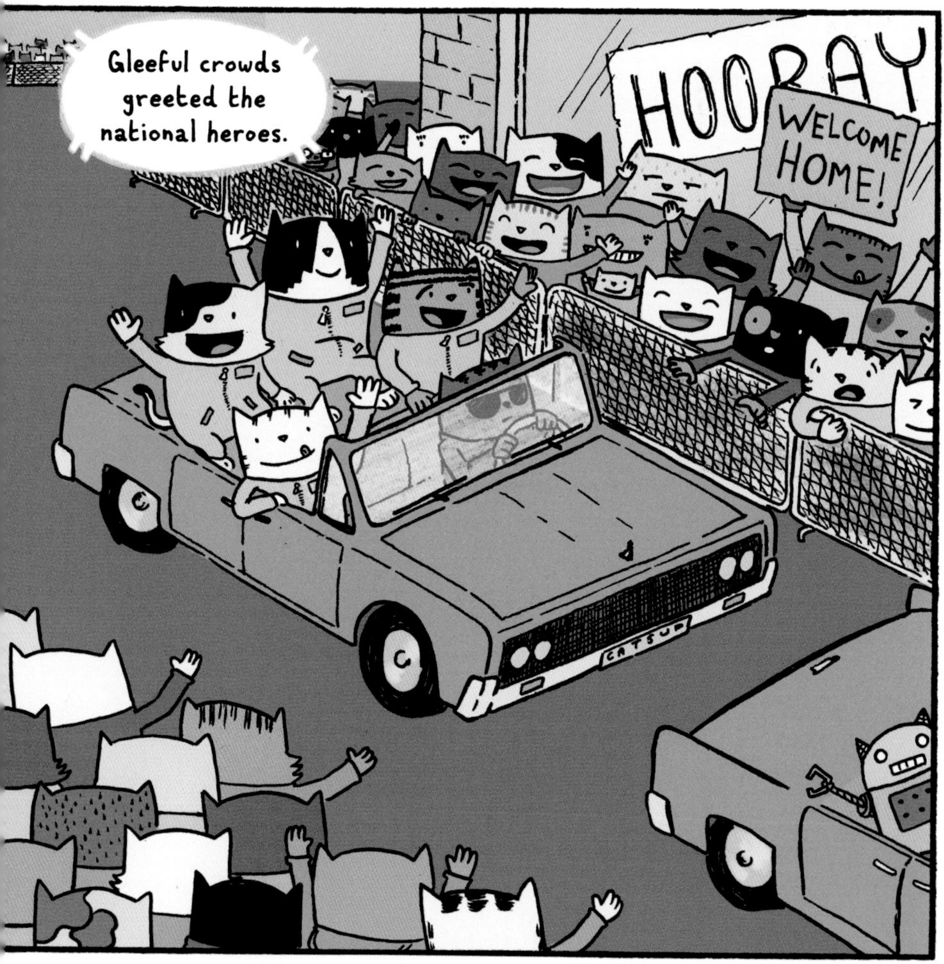
Gleeful crowds greeted the national heroes.
HOORAY
WELCOME HOME!
CATSUP

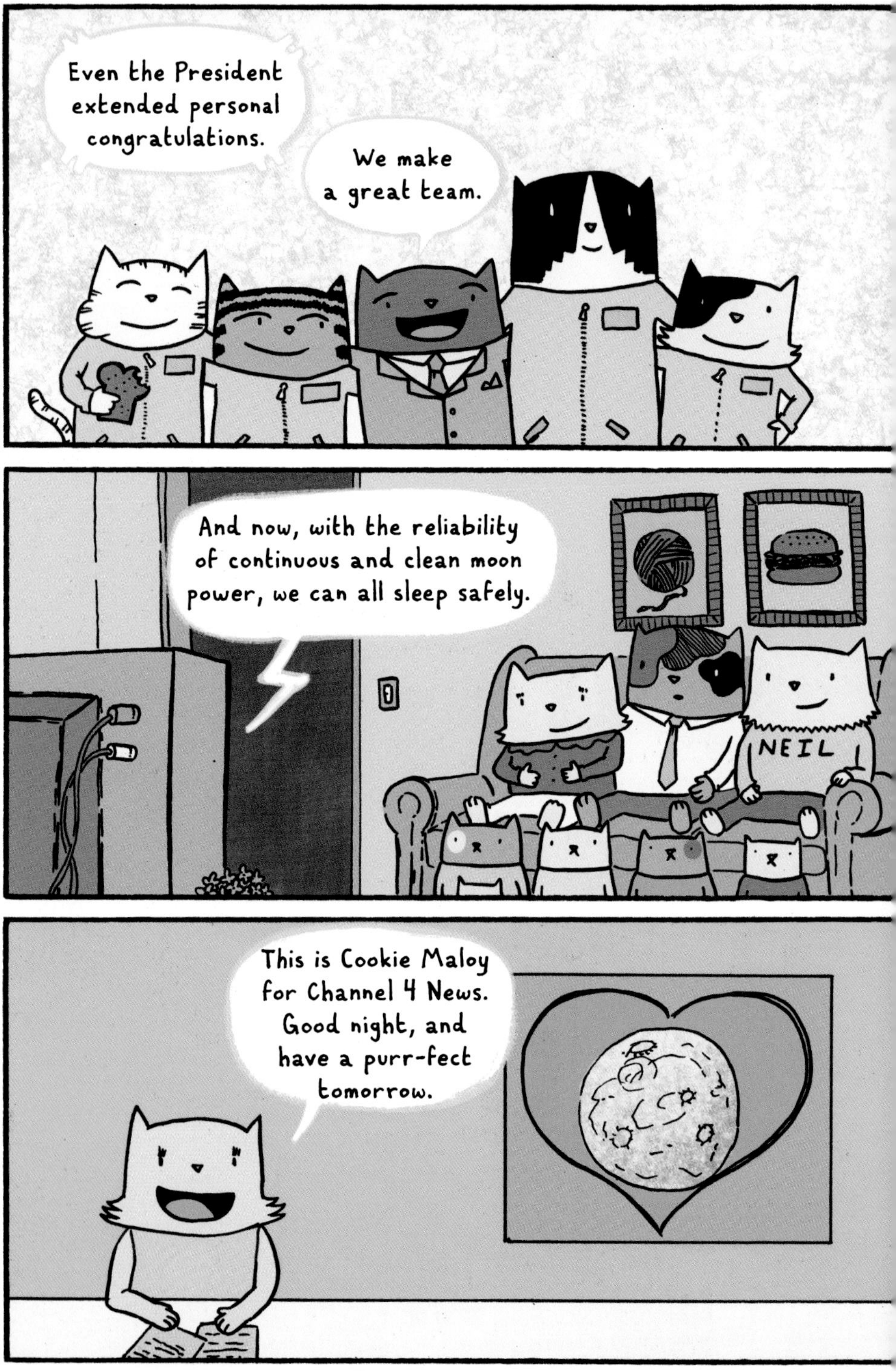
Even the President extended personal congratulations.
We make a great team.
And now, with the reliability of continuous and clean moon power, we can all sleep safely.
NEIL
This is Cookie Maloy for Channel 4 News. Good night, and have a purr-fect tomorrow.

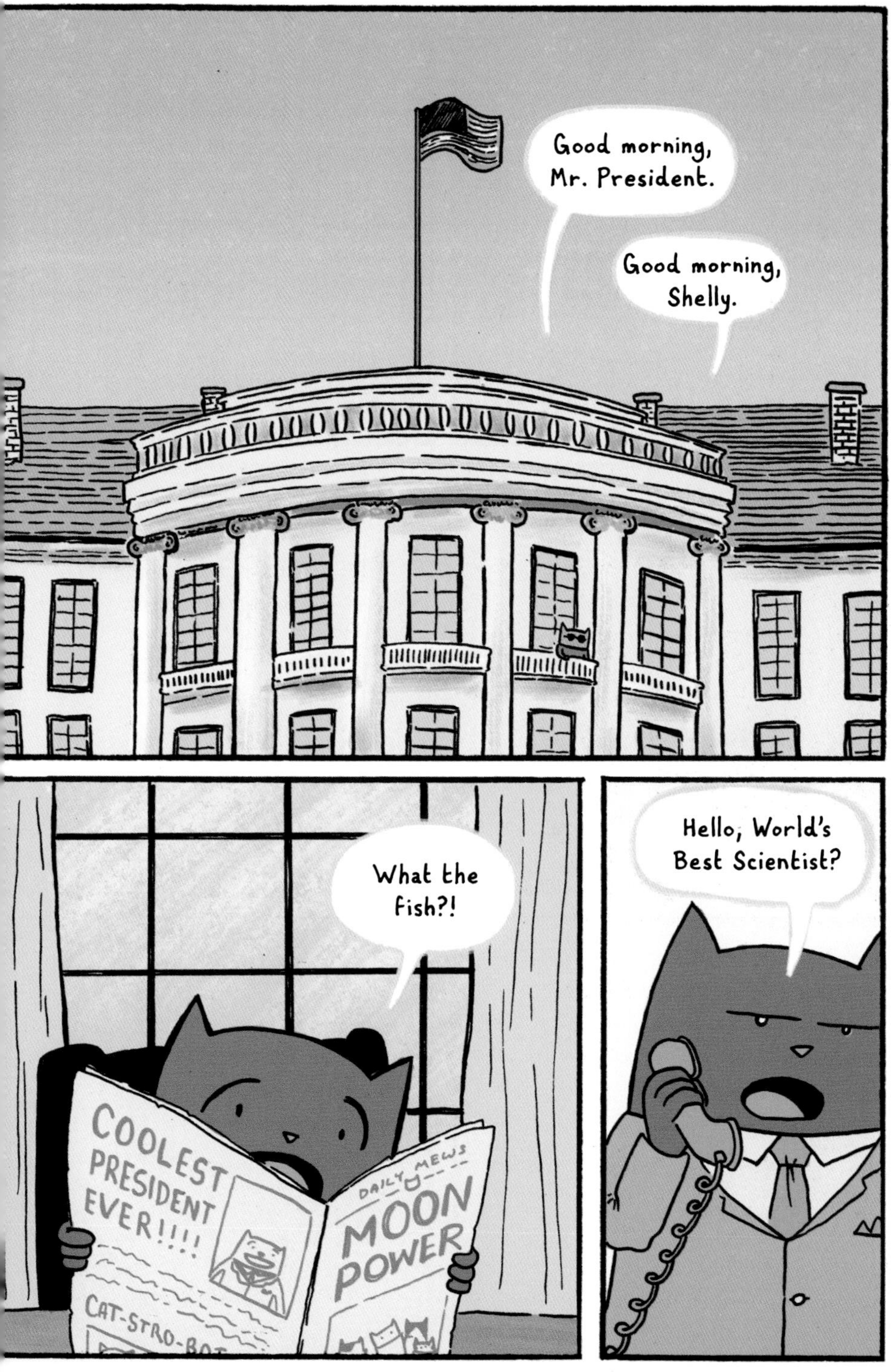
Good morning, Mr. President.
Good morning, Shelly.
What the fish?!
COOLEST PRESIDENT EVER!!!!
DAILY MEWS
MOON POWER
CAT-STRO-BOT
Hello, World's Best Scientist?

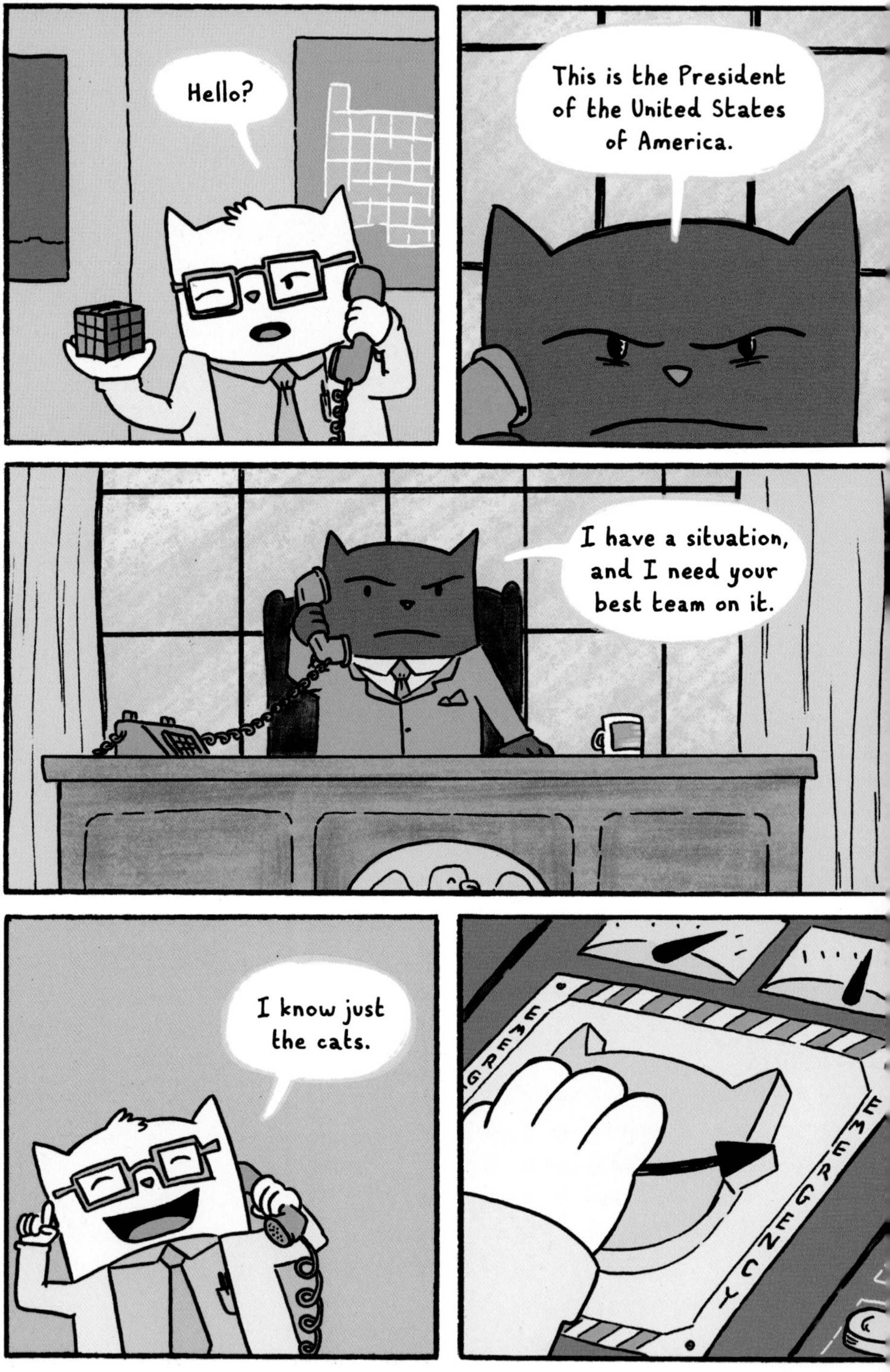
Hello?
This is the President of the United States of America.
I have a situation, and I need your best team on it.
I know just the cats.

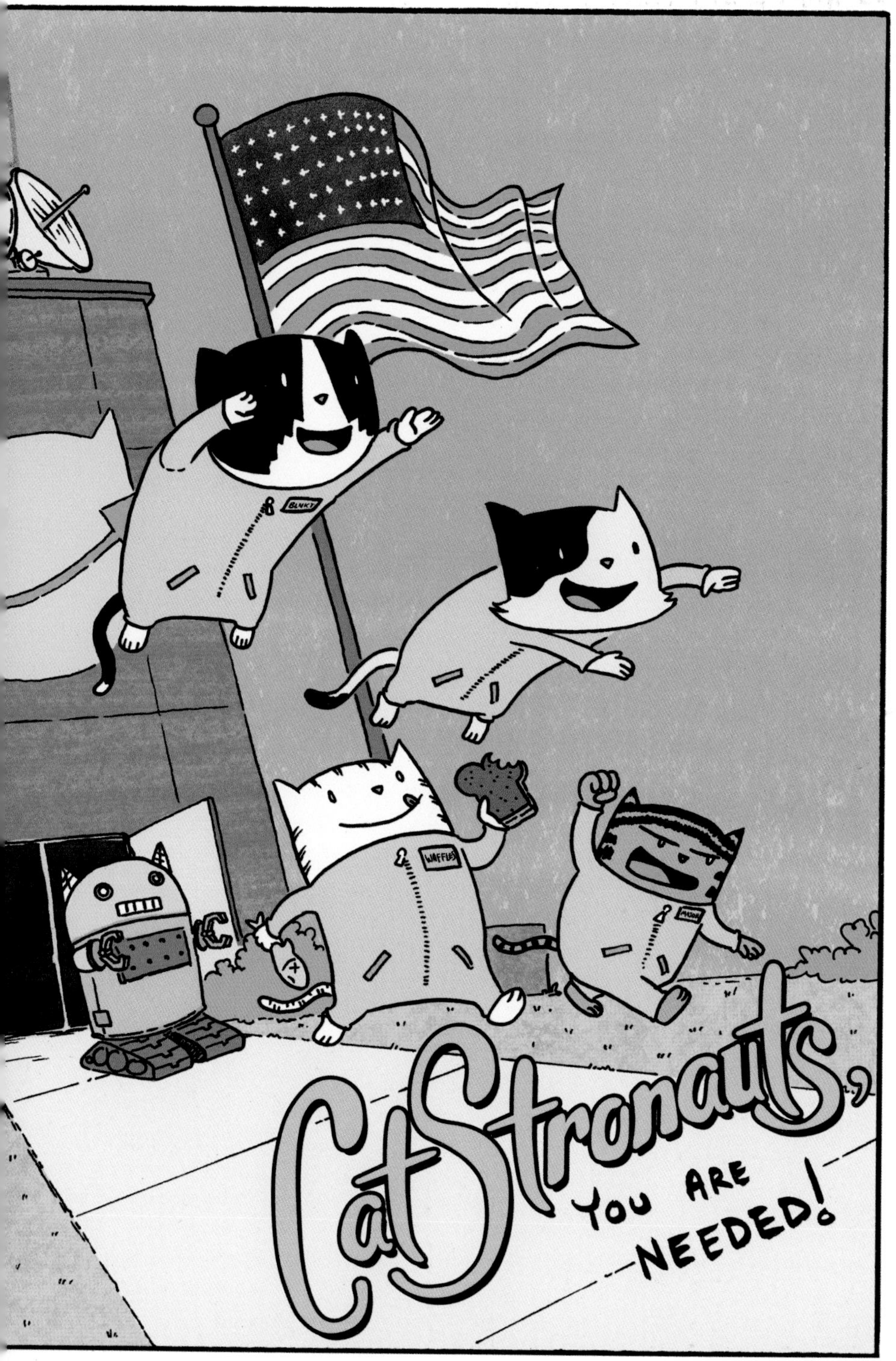
BLNKT
WAFFLES
MAJOR
CatStronauts,
YOU ARE NEEDED!

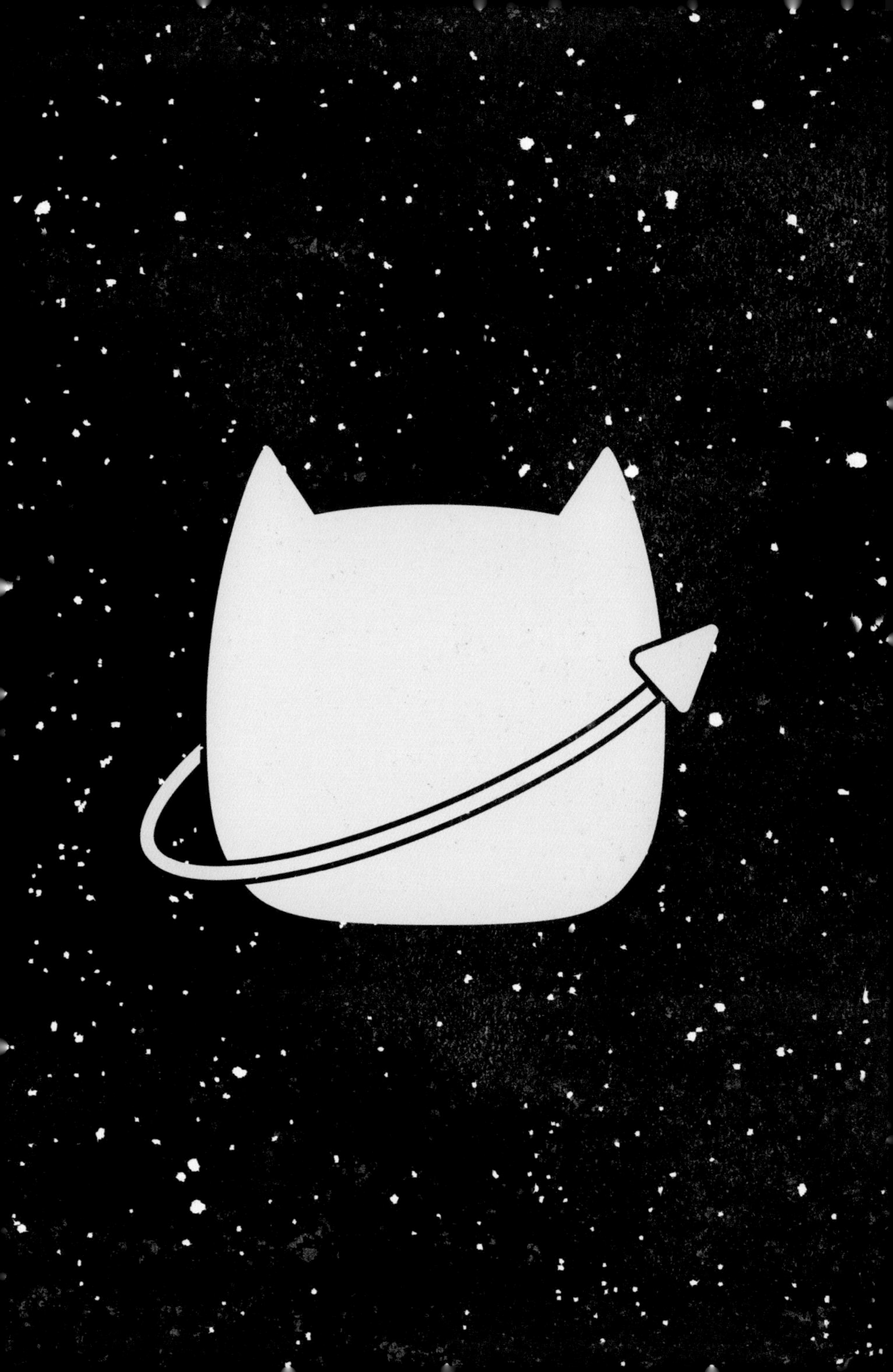

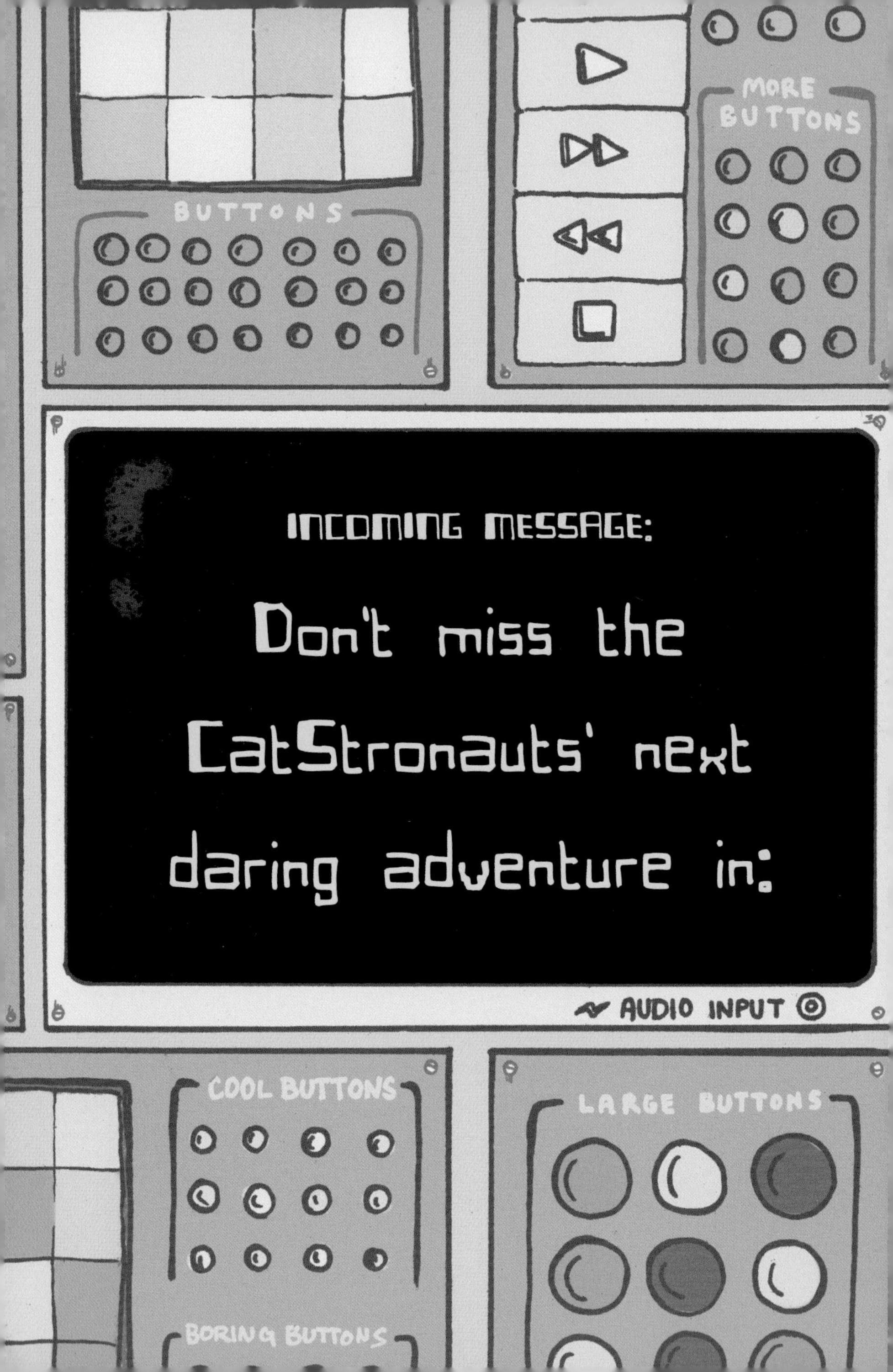
BUTTONS
MORE BUTTONS
INCOMING MESSAGE:
Don't miss the CatStronauts' next daring adventure in:
AUDIO INPUT
COOL BUTTONS
LARGE BUTTONS
BORING BUTTONS

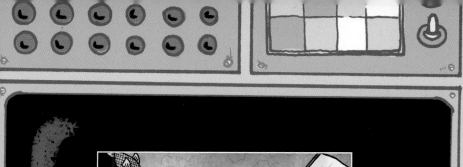

CatStronauts
RACE TO MARS

DREW BROCKINGTON

Available now!

COMM. MONITOR

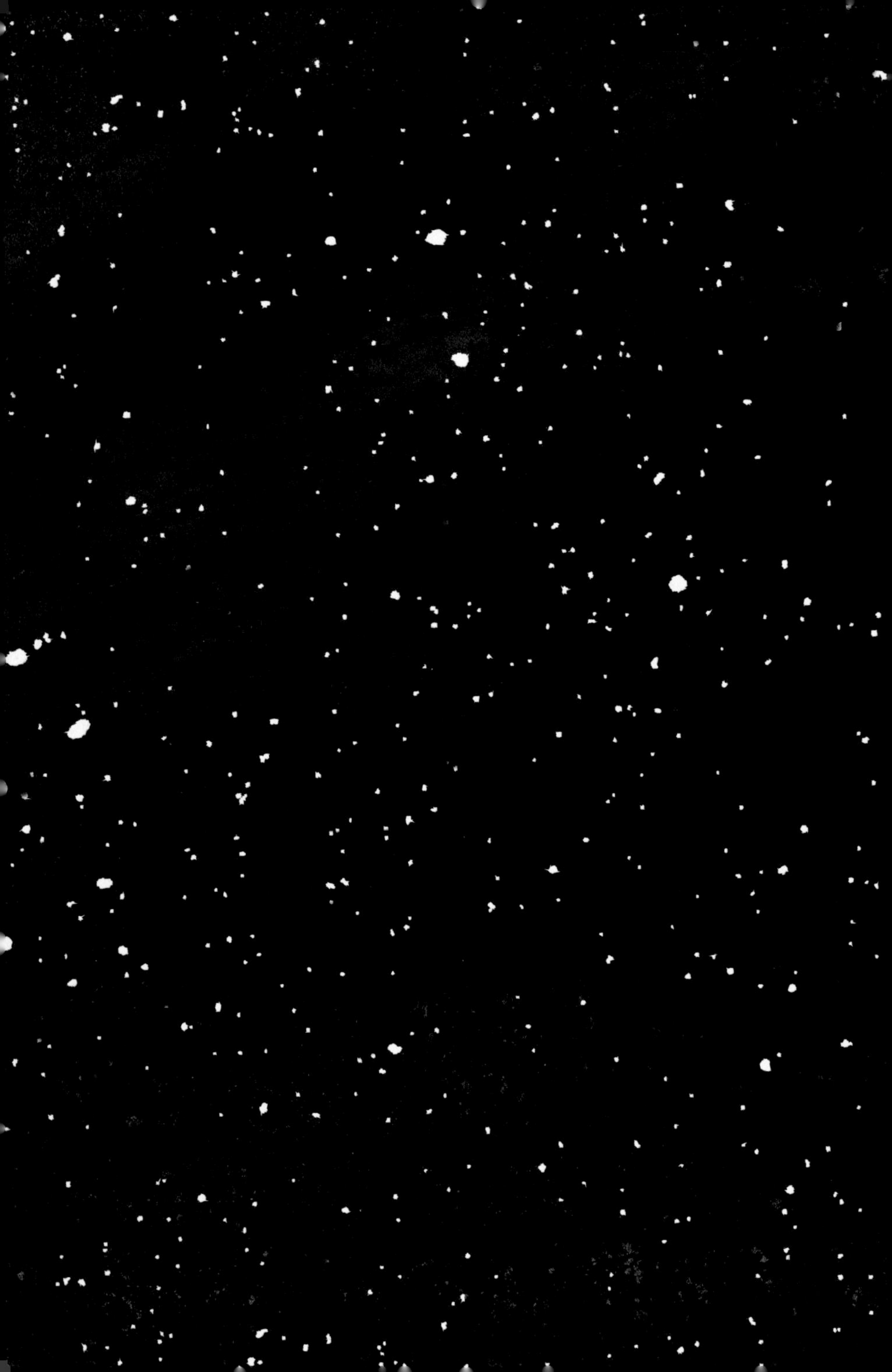

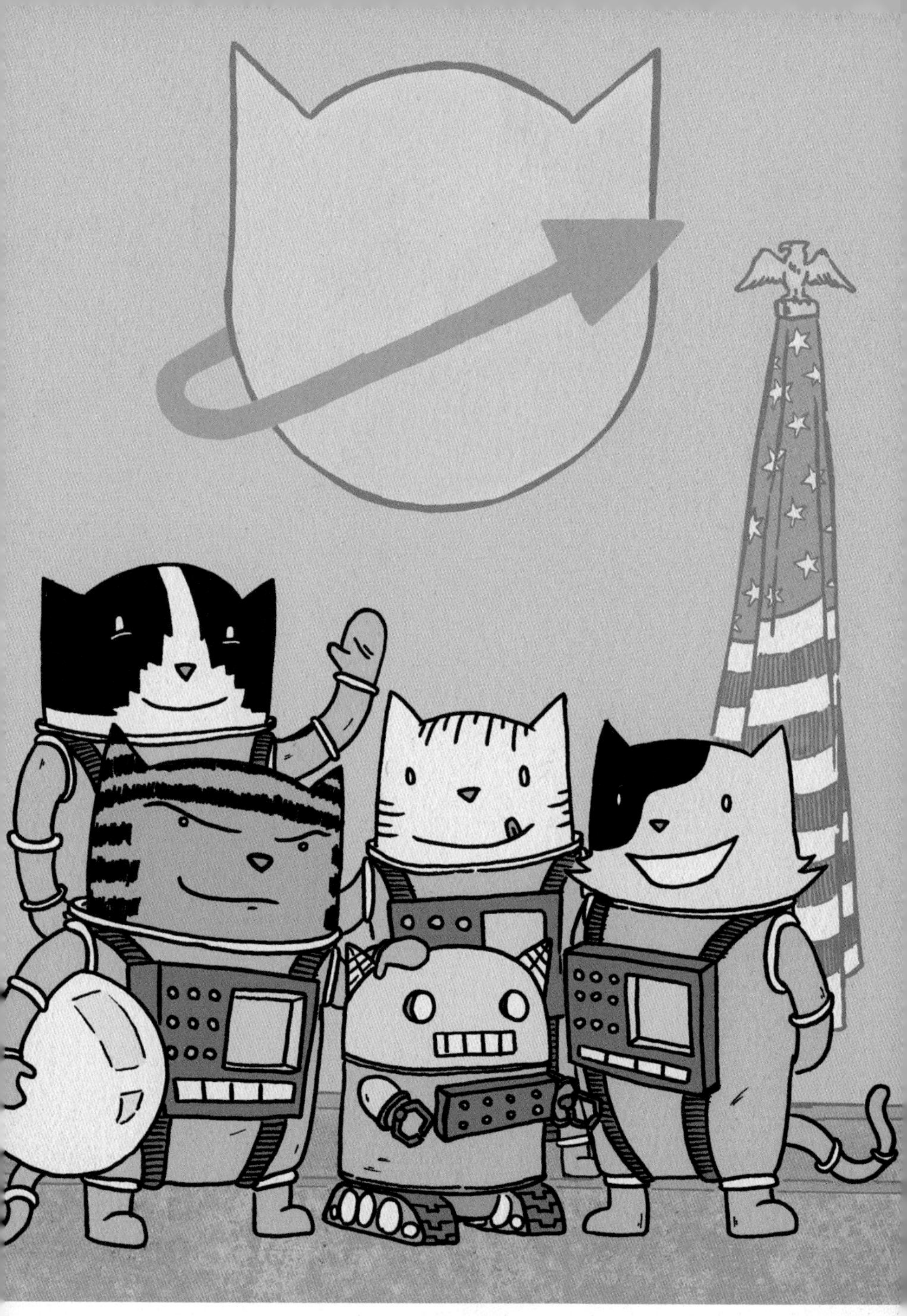

CatStronauts, Mission Moon

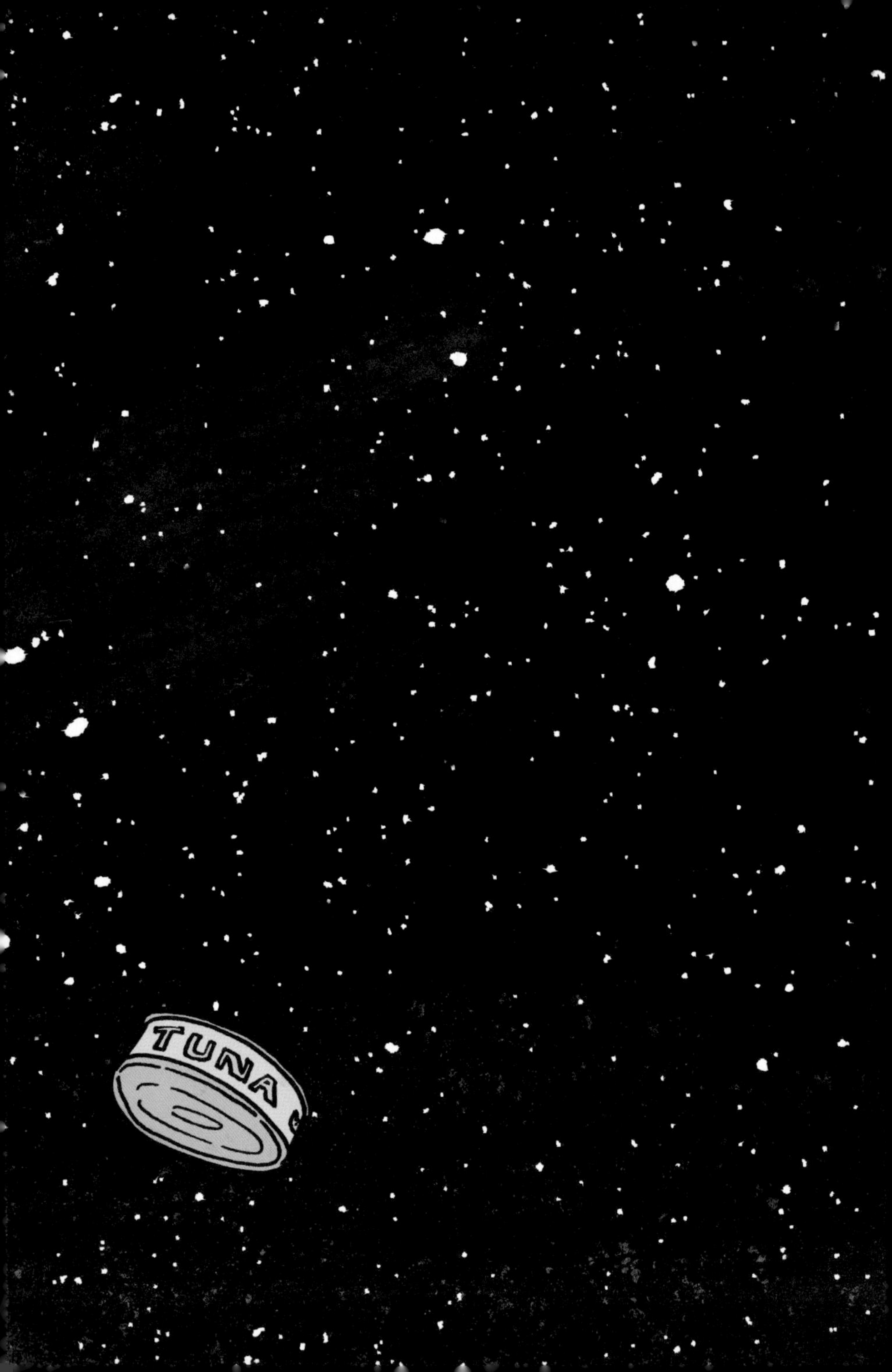
TUNA